Agilis Rising Under Sail

Richard Porter and Bjorn Amundson in the Age of Sail

Clifford Farris

Desert Coyote Press LLC
Littleton, Colorado USA

Dedication

For William Richard Donald Prowse "Don", a mariner, a
gentleman, and a friend.

*"To you, sir, a fair wind and following seas,
And long may your big jib draw."*

Roll on, thou deep dark ocean, roll!
Ten thousand fleets sweep over thee in vain;
Thy wrecks are all they deed, nor doth remain
A shadow of man's ravage, save his own,
When for a moment, like a drop of rain,
He sinks into thy depths with bubbling groan,
Without a grave, unknelled, uncoffined, and
unknown.

~Apostrophe to the Ocean, George Lord Byron

Agilis Rising Under Sail

Clifford Farris

Chapter 1—Beyond the Bay

Richard elbowed his way through excited crew members and passengers to the bow of *Agilis* and shouted, "Behold! The strait of the Golden Gate." Five white sails billowed overhead. "Good morning, California. How are we? When you know me, we'll be friends for life."

The tall young man with the curly chestnut hair erupted with joy to escape his indentureship as an orphan and just couldn't help himself.

He turned aft toward the stern and passengers, "We made it. What day is this?"

A young woman shouted from the open door to the cabin, "It's the Fourth of July 1849, and time to whoop it up."

Porter added, "And there's gold in the streets and hills." He waved his arms,

"We're here!"

The motley crowd of travelers and mariners roared back, "Yes! Thank God at last."

Porter said, "Our hopes and dreams outweigh the cargo we have dragged from Boston around Cape Horn. At least mine do."

A wave of agreement swept the deck from the excited but travel-weary passengers. "Our hopes and dreams do too."

The sunrise silhouetted his shadow against the fore-mainsail like a proud eagle.

Porter was the second mate and responsible to guide *Agilis* among the winds and waves. He knew from the charts that the fog, tidal currents, and hidden shoals made the Golden Gate hazardous. Other mariners had warned him the safe channel was not a mile wide and treacherous in the gusty winds.

Porter hollered to his riggers aloft as they fought the sails, "Watch sharp mates, I can't see everything from down here.

One of the riggers, Bjorn Amundson, shouted back, "Off to starboard." He pointed to the right as he stood on a foot rope hung under a yardarm. His long golden hair blew in the wind like a weather vane and his mighty shoulders showed his Viking ancestry.

Porter turned to the jumbled pile of timbers littering the shore. The fractured debris looked like the bones of a fish picked clean on a platter, but much larger. He said to the travelers, "Shipwreck on the rocks to starboard. That's the right side for you landlubbers."

The passengers crowded to the gunwale to view the shattered hulk. Many of them felt a sense of dread at the carnage.

Porter continued in his rich baritone voice. "The charts name that Fort Point Rock where that ship is wrecked." He shuddered as the waves crashed against the shoals and said aloud, "Look at that smashed lifeboat with the ditty box floating inside. I hope those fellows made it."

He looked up to Amundson and said, "Look familiar? That's like the wrecked brigantine off Cape Fear, North Carolina. I was sailing down to Charleston through the graveyard of the Atlantic. I pulled you out of the breakers hugging that plank for everything you were worth."

Amundson picked up the story, "I still can't swim. I signed on another ship out of Charleston headed to Honolulu. We lost ninety-eight sailors good men that day."

In a voice that carried a hundred and fifteen feet to the sailors atop the rigging, Porter said, "Danger to starboard. Mind your duties and the rocks." Amundson pointed for everyone to see.

A floating section of the wreckage bumped into *Agilis* and Porter read the name of the lost vessel, *Stag Hound.*

He saw his riggers were awkward in the vicious winds and burst into a sea chantey they'd sung for seventeen thousand miles.

> *And it's blow, boys, blow,*
> *For Californi-o!*
> *For there's plenty of gold,*
> *So I've been told,*
> *On the banks of the Sacramento*

With satisfaction, he watched his hands heave the sails in unison and felt *Agilis* respond like the first-rate ship she was.

Porter had sailed as an ordinary sailor on previous voyages and understood his crew well. They idolized his leadership.

He squinted into the sunrise as the passengers strained to see the famous Golden Gate. He said, "You've talked about nothing else since leaving Boston a hundred and twenty-eight days ago, and here it is."

The beauty of the channel awed everyone until Porter noticed an angry fog bank on his left. "To port, fog bank rolling in."

3

Chapter 2—Menace from the Fog

Porter's gut tensed as the dense fog bank rolled over Point Diablo on their left. "Fog off port side. Stay alert, boys."

He was astonished to see a black two-masted brig flying eleven gray sails emerge from the mist. Gleaming gold filigree accented her elegant hull as she knifed through the water. She was heading in the same direction as *Agilis*.

Porter shouted a warning, "Sails ahoy! Port side."

He yelled up to Amundson, a sailor high in the rigging on the mainmast, "You're the damn lookout? Where's your warning?"

Amundson cried, "Hell ship, *Zebra*, to port—,"

The *Zebra* sped through the waves as if she owned them and they were off-limits to lesser craft such as *Agilis*.

Amundson dropped to the deck with a thud and said, "The *Zebra* is commanded by Dirk Hornigold, that class A one bastard. He put me through hell until I deserted in Honolulu."

Porter was surprised. "I didn't know you shipped on the *Zebra*?"

"Once."

"I know of her reputation as Hornigold's hell ship, and where's her fog warning bell?"

The silence on the sea chilled Porter as the *Zebra* emerged from the fog like a black ghost. He said, "I'd hate to sail against her. That crew is reckless but good. Look at how her bow splits those swells."

The passengers lining the gunwales of *Agilis* stared at their counterparts on the *Zebra* and enjoyed the race unaware of the danger.

Porter faced the intruding ship and called out, "We have the right of way and you are cutting our path." He shouted to his helmsman, "Hard to starboard. Prepare for possible contact."

He fixed his eyes on the vessel that loomed so confident, so bold, so capable—hey, and so close. Woven into the front decorations, Porter could read her name. "She's the *Zebra*, all right."

Amundson said, "That Hornigold is one evil son of a bitch. I'd rather have the plague than serve under him again."

The vessels jockeyed for position through the passage and tried to steal each other's wind but they were too close to maneuver.

Porter knew a trick from the old pirates of the Caribbean. "Water the sails. Buckets aloft."

Several sailors hoisted buckets of water up the masts to the riggers standing on foot ropes. They emptied the buckets over the mainsails to seal the canvas and enhance the pull of the wind. *Agilis* pulled ahead, but the men on the *Zebra* knew the same trick and regained their lead.

Bowsprit to bowsprit, *Agilis* and *Zebra* sped full speed toward North Point which was the turning point south to San Francisco.

Amundson knew the behavior of the *Zebra's* hull and said, "Her helmsman can't control her with that spread of sails. Damn, she's twisting in the wind."

Out of the excited passengers on *Agilis'* deck, a squeaky, well-dressed little man raised an angry voice with wild gestures, "I demand you yield way," showing off his new naval lingo.

Porter faced him, "So now you appear, Mr. Otis. Stay out of our way and take your lady friend too."

Hornigold shouted back from the *Zebra*, "Ice from Sitka, Alaska, is melting in my hold. Get out of my way."

He squinted for a better look. "And who are you?"

Otis was insulted because he assumed everyone could see his importance, even though he was traveling incognito. "Don't you know who I am? My father owns the bank that built your boat, and he owns you."

Hornigold came back, "It's a ship you three-inch fool, not a boat."

"Pig farker on the foam."

"May your rats feast on your curdled fat."

Porter saw things were getting ugly and raised his hand, "Uh. Just a—"

Otis, hopping up and down in fury, pulled a loaded revolver from his boot and fired point blank at the *Zebra*. Then he aimed. The bullet creased the engraving on the *Zebra's* bell with a clang and passengers on both vessels dove under the nearest cover.

The sound of the pistol startled the lady emerging from the cabin. She waved the cloud of smoke away, coughed and screamed, "I cough, cough, huh, huh, huh, hate that noise. Bury that vile thing or you'll never see me again."

The little man kept flaunting his peashooter. "Back off, you polecat rustlers," confusing his stolen cowboy and naval lingo.

Porter leaped over the jumbled luggage at the would-be big man. "Drop that weapon!" but before he got one step, a serious gunshot answered from the deck of the *Zebra*.

Porter pivoted to the sound and saw the shooter surrounded by a white cloud of gun smoke. The man held a smoking dragoon revolver in his hand. Porter heard splinters fly when the bullet split the figurehead under the bow of *Agilis*.

The shooter glared over the parallel gunwales, "I know you, Porter, and your *Agilis* trash. One of your crew deserted me in Honolulu." He swung his gun back and forth to intimidate Otis's peashooter.

The hiss of the waves was the only sound as the vessels raced each other to North Point.

Porter's temper erupted as he plowed into the revolver-packing passenger. The momentum of Porter's one hundred and eighty pounds carried them to the deck. Porter grabbed the pistol on the way down and body slammed the skinny little man into the deck. From three inches away, he blasted Otis with his foghorn baritone voice, "No guns on deck!"

Otis shook his head to regain his hearing.

The lady companion sprang to his defense, "You're hurting my Holton." She snapped Porter's heavily muscled back with the first weapon at hand, her handkerchief. "Cough, cough. Stop that right now, you sweaty, filthy, stinking heathen. Phew, you smell." With a wrinkled nose, she tossed the contaminated handkerchief overboard.

Porter tucked the revolver down the back of his trousers and released the sputtering little man. The passenger jumped to his feet, panted a moment to regain his breath, and shrieked, "I am a paying passenger and have my rights on this ship—which I happen to own." He caught himself with a peculiar look on his face and hesitated for a moment.

He changed attitude, brushed his coat and grabbed for the pistol. "Give me that."

Porter twisted and said, "I don't care who you are, sir. You can hurt your fair lady or me."

They were joined by the master of *Agilis*, Alex MacIntyre, who said, "I know Hornigold, Mr. Otis. He smuggles slaves and opium, or tea as a last resort. That man has no known scruples."

Otis said, "I know him as well. His crew of Chinese pirates has robbed many of my ships. But what are you going to do about this attack on my person?" He pointed at Porter.

MacIntyre said in a deep commanding voice, "Mr. Porter, return this man's property immediately. I do not abuse passengers on my ship."

"But sir—"

"Now, if you please!"

Porter flashed his eyes back and forth between the two.

MacIntyre said to his ruffled passenger, "I am sorry for your inconvenience, my good sir. This hand will be severely disciplined."

Porter said, "This lunatic was endangering—"

"Now!" as he pointed to the handle of the pistol.

Porter reluctantly pulled the firearm from his trousers. Before handing it over, he tipped the cylinder but the balls were well tamped and would not budge. Instead, he popped off the primer caps, rotated the cylinder to the empty chamber, and let down the hammer. The revolver was as inert as he could make it. He slowly held the grip out to Otis, careful to point the muzzle toward open water.

The man grabbed his pistol with a smirk and rotated the cylinder back to an active chamber. He inserted new primer caps from a little pouch and slipped it into his boot, loaded and dangerous.

The arrogant little man strutted around the deck with raised eyebrows, his nose in the air, and a supercilious smile. He pointed to Porter,

"Lock that scoundrel in the brig. We'll *keel haul* him later."

Porter said, "You don't even know what keel haul is."

"You'll still get it, note that, MacIntyre? Make it a double haul keel."

Porter said, "Ha," as he flipped his head.

Otis said to MacIntyre, "You'll lock him in irons post haste, I am certain."

MacIntyre said, "I need all my hands at the moment. Punishment will come later."

Erratic winds swirled around the brigs as they left the passage between Fort Point Rock and Point Diablo and headed to North Point.

Porter could hear the helmsman of the greedy *Zebra* complain, " Too much sail. I can't hold her against this current."

Hornigold yelled, "Starboard to the wharf, you worthless bent shitcan."

"I'm doing my best, sir."

The *Zebra* careened to the near shore, out to the far shore, and straight at *Agilis*. *Zebra's* bowsprit punched through the shroud lines and rat lines until her filigreed bow crunched against the hull of *Agilis*. The bowsprit crossed over the deck of *Agilis* athwartships, fully side to side.

Hornigold yelled to his helmsman, "Now see what you've done, you ripped ditty bag."

Porter shouted, "Knives, mates." He stabbed the 'a' in the filigreed name, *Zebra,* on the carved bow jammed against the port gunwale, "Got you."

Agilis" crew hacked through the lines on the *Zebra's* bowsprit. With a whoosh and a zing the lines parted and whipped through the air. The *Zebra's* foremast collapsed backward into the mainmast.

Hornigold stormed the bow where he shouted at the faces on *Agilis* that he could almost touch. "You're destroying my ship." He pounded the gunwale. "I'll get you for this."

Porter said, "You rammed us. Chop at will, men. We'll never get closer to this damned hulk."

He looked at the passengers and said, "You're welcome to join us." Four passengers pulled their knives.

One of them growled, "You beat me for no reason, you son of a bitch," and he carved a skull and crossbones into the *Zebra's* bowsprit.

"I'd cut your heart out if I could reach it," said another as he cut two stretched lines and carved a heart with an X over it.

"Payback time," said Amundson, as he attacked the *Zebra's* bowsprit and carved a quick "BA" into the spar for a final insult.

The sails hanging from *Zebra's* foremast dropped their wind, of course, and her hull lost it's momentum. The bowsprit slipped out of *Agilis* and the incident was over. The *Zebra* ended up much the worse for the encounter.

Porter hollered, "Don't think it wasn't fun. It was."

Agilis turned south around North Point, followed by the wobbling *Zebra.*

Even Porter's crew was hard put to control the intact *Agilis.* The canvas sails fought every gust, and the chaotic waves challenged both helmsmen to prevent a second collision. The competing crews were too busy to look, but they could still hurl insults from the masts.

"Most notable coward."

"Away, you dried bull's-pizzle."

"Your face curdles milk and sours beer."

Otis added to the confusion by stumbling back and forth. He had been months at sea and was more irritated than ever. He molested MacIntyre while keeping a wary eye on Porter. "What is the name of that mountain?" pointing to starboard.

"That summit is two hundred and seventy-five feet high and known as Loma Alta," said Porter before MacIntyre could answer.

"That is a stupid name."

"So is Otis."

Porter turned to the bow to help the crew belay some lines.

Someone had left a little guitar on the windlass at the bow. Porter picked it up and strummed a chord that soared high into the morning air. In his rich baritone voice, he sang some words of inspiration.

> *Red clouds and yellow bars*
> *Soar halfway to the stars.*
> *San Francisco,*
> *Your sun will shine for me.*

For the rest of the day, the people on deck hummed the tune and sang the words.

Porter called out, "Somebody forgot their guitar when they used the head. Come and get it."

A sheepish passenger took his instrument and scurried out of sight.

Porter looked as the first mate, Alfonso Ferreri, stormed up to him. Porter mentally measured himself against the mate.

He is the same height as me, but a hell of a lot leaner. He never smiles like a real Italian does.

Ferreri shoved his way to Porter's front. "Heed your duties, Mr. Porter. No time for singing."

Porter said, "The boys like it, sir. You could afford to loosen up yourself, sometimes."

Ferreri shifted to his native Italian accent that he had tried so hard to overcome and accentuated his words with hand gestures,

"Watcha close, thisa channel hides hazards in the water. Alcatraz Island is the shadow on port."

He gestured with his left arm over the port gunwale at the following fog bank,

"Doesa hills behind be Point Diablo."

He pointed with his right arm to starboard,

"Doesa ruins be Castillo de San Joaquin on Fort Point Rock. Wreck a ship on rocks. Watch and no song!"

Porter's excitement flipped to irritation and he said, "Dammit Ferreri, talk English. Who the hell understands your Italian gibberish?"

Ferreri's Latin temper erupted, "My English is better than your Italiano, fanciullo. You got no room to talk."

Porter did not know what a *fanciullo* was but it sounded derogatory.

"Fanci-, huh?" and he swung his own arms into Ferreri's waving arms.

Master MacIntyre pushed them apart, "Stop that infernal bickering, you two, and land my ship. I am weary of your arguments."

He was splendid in his blue uniform with gold braid that he had brushed to meet the dignitaries on shore. MacIntyre was forty-eight years old and had been Master of *Agilis,* since the conversion from a slaver to merchantman in 1845.

Unlike Porter, MacIntyre knew the hazards of the Golden Gate first hand. He motioned to the rocky promontory behind them on the right,

"Just mentioned by Ferreri, Colonel Frémont captured those ruins on Fort Point Rock three years ago. 'Twas a good thing since they guard the harbor well."

Porter looked at the tumbled pile of adobe blocks that had been the fort. "Looks peaceful enough now."

MacIntyre said, "Watch ahead Porter. See the buoy on that bastard Blossom Rock. It is only five feet down at low tide and will sink you."

Porter's eyes followed Macintyre's arthritic finger over the bowsprit. He could vaguely see through the glare of the sunrise where the jagged teeth of Blossom Rock lurked as they glided by Alcatraz island.

Macintyre's jubilant mood overcame his usual stoic manner, and he said to the mates, "Porter greets the sunrise as I, a wee lad o'twenty-four, did in 1809 when I sailed up the river Clyde to me Glasgow, Scotland. I have traversed many blue oceans since, and I ween Porter will as well."

Porter was admiring the view for a moment at the bow when he felt a little tug on his trousers. He thought it was the ship's cat,

Morgan, and pushed it away, but the tugs continued and he looked down. Two shining faces on little boys about eight or nine looked up at him. They were insistent to get his attention.

"Mr. sailorman,," tug, tug.

"Mr. sailorman."

Porter said, "Hello little men. How are you?"

The boy holding the right leg said, "Good."

The left boy announced with great seriousness, "My brother is dumb."

The right boy said, "Am not."

"Am too."

"Am not dumb."

Porter said, "Nobody is dumb. What's the problem?"

The first boy said, "My brother calls that thing in front a ram."

"It is a ram. I saw a Roman ship with one."

"It is not!"

Porter said, "Wait a moment. The Romans did have a battering ram on the front of their ships."

"I told you."

"But we call ours a bowsprit, not a ram. Can you say that, 'bow and sprit'?"

Each boy said, "Bow . . . .sprit, bow . . . sprit."

"Good. The bowsprit is the pointy pole at the front of a ship. Now see that rope, we sailors call it a line." He pointed to the stayline at the front of the bowsprit.

"That line at the end of the bowsprit goes waaaaay up to the top of the foremast." He pointed to the top of the foremast.

"Oooooooh," as they looked up in wonder at the unimaginable height.

"Remember this, the bowsprit holds the line that holds the foremast."

Both boys repeated as Porter waved in rhythm, "The bowsprit holds the line that holds the foremast.

"Got that?"

"Yes sir, Mr. sailorman. The bowsprit holds the line that holds the foremast." They grinned at their new sea knowledge, and said to a nearby man, "The bowsprit holds the line that holds the foremast."

"The bowsprit holds,"

Boom! uum, uumm into distant echos.

A blast from Fort Point Rock shook the ship and the boys broke off their slogan to scream in panic and run to their mother. The passengers ran for cover or scattered like rats.

Porter turned to starboard and saw a second cloud of white smoke at the summit. A spectacular flame the length of three men shot through the smoke and the cloud hid two cannons as the concussion shook *Agilis*.

"Only a little cannon fire," Porter said with a grin. "They are welcoming us with an early Fourth-of-July celebration."

"Welcome hell. It is like my bombardment with real firepower from thieving ladrones off Singapore," said MacIntyre.

Porter said, "Sir, cannon fire is common around Boston during reenactments of the revolutionary war. I played the gunner since I didn't have a handgun. Don't you love the noise, the smoke, and the excitement?"

"Christ all mighty!" said MacIntyre.

Porter's love was sharpened by the third spear of flame that was longer than the first two. The concussion shook the leaves on the bushes and the gun emplacement disappeared completely behind a growing smoke screen. *Agilis* trembled from stem to stern from the concussion.

Porter's sharp eyes saw it burst out of the cloud and cried, "Heads up! Incoming cannonball!"

Porter watched the black ball fly over the gunwale. It was too fast to see as it grazed his scalp, but he heard it crack the mainmast and roll over the deck to a stop against a satchel. Screams filled the deck as people fought for deeper cover, but no more explosions broke the tense silence.

Porter scooped up the warm twelve-pound ball with his callused hands and presented it to MacIntyre with a bow; "This may be of interest, sir."

MacIntyre exploded with a cloud of nautical profanity bluer than the cloud hiding the hill. "The warning bell," he said to Porter pointing at the foremast.

Porter stumbled over cluttered belongings to the bell and jerked the clapper like there was no tomorrow, which was almost true for him. He knew the artillerymen on the hill heard his warning because the ring carried a mile and the fort was only a quarter-mile away.

Porter screamed at Fort Point Rock, "Hold your fire. We are unarmed." He shook his fist thinking the gunners were more likely infantry than naval.

There was a deadly silence from the hillside gun emplacement. Only the sounds of faint pops drifted over the hills, but a display of colored rockets that rivaled the sunrise crowned the hilltops. The woman at the door of the cabin said, "I love the Fourth of July celebrations. Don't all of you?"

MacIntyre handed the cannonball back to Porter, "I do not want this."

Porter stashed the ball in his ditty box and rejoined the chatter on deck. Calm returned as Porter directed the helmsman around North Point and toward the village of San Francisco.

Porter took several deep breaths and gripped the gunwale to steady himself. His good friend, Bjorn Amundson, that he'd sailed to Gibraltar with stood alongside. Porter could sense the concern in his face.

Amundson said, "Did that ball knock some sense into your thick head?"

Porter felt of his scalp and pulled his hand away dripping blood. "Only a scratch," as he shook his head and collected his thoughts. He wiped the blood off on the newly painted gunwale, since he was wearing his clean white duck trousers to go ashore. He stared at the passing ocean.

"Hey, Amundson," said Porter.

"Yeah?"

"You know mining?"

"A little."

"Just thinking."

"You can think?"

"I think we've talked about nothing but gold since we left Boston."

"Guess so."

Porter said, "I want a gold mine."

"You?"

"Yeah, me."

" If you say so."

"I've heard rumors of gold up river."

"That's all over Boston."

"Let's get a gold mine, you and me."

17

Speaking carefully Amundson said, "My father and I mined gemstones in the Otra river in Norway."

"How'd that go?"

"I can find gems, but not much gold."

Porter was emphatic, "I want a gold mine!"

He waved his fictitious air sword and said, "With my mine, I'll be that man of distinction on a horse with a sword in the Boston victory parade."

"OK. Put 'er there," said Amundson and he held out his hand.

They shook hands as *Agilis* rounded North Point and headed south to San Francisco.

Porter said, "I count about seventy-seven ships anchored in front of us. And look at that armada of boats, rafts, boards, and even a few swimmers surrounding them." The fleet of craft trailed *Agilis* too as Porter looked for an open berth, but MacIntyre took charge from the mates and pointed to a spot of water near the bottom of Clay Street.

He said to the helmsman, "Over there."

The helmsman aimed *Agilis* to a tolerably safe mooring in Yerba Buena Cove. Before they had even set anchor, they were besieged by floating odds and ends that filled the cove like a pub packed with drunks. Each one contained a shouting occupant offering goods, a service, news, or woman, and all had their hands out for money.

Porter spotted a sinister gang of ex-harpooners rowing their stolen whaleboat through the melange and matching the speed of *Agilis*. He suspected they wanted to steal his crew as they waved and yelled in a chorus, "Sailors! Join us! You've suffered enough." They came alongside and climbed up the gunwales to steal any cargo they could seize.

Porter said, "Avast you thieves. Men of *Agilis*, stay with me." He pushed the first harpooner backwards off the gunwale. A Hawaiian sailor named Kawai and his companion Kanakas took care of the rest and repelled the boarding attempt.

A whaler said as they rode away, "We'll take the next one."

Chapter3—I'll Bet

Ferreri strode amidships and pushed Porter aside, "I will moor us properly. Stand down from the deck, Mr. Porter, and learn."

He ordered the riggers to stop the ship.

"No! No!"

"Brace back the topgallant sails, fore and main."

"Put those sails opposite."

"A little more; brace back the mainsails."

The tars aloft struggled to douse the sails in the force of the wind, and furl the loose canvases above their respective yardarms.

"You four—put your hands on the capstan and turn the damn thing."

"Let go the anchor."

Willing hands rotated the capstan to drop the howling anchor chain. The anchor set the hook in two fathoms of water and *Agilis* jolted to a stop against the taut chain. She faced the Clay Street wharf between a vacant schooner to port and an abandoned clipper to starboard.

Porter thought to himself, What a mess. Ferreri can't command a slug, let alone my men.

Porter walked to the bow of *Agilis* like a master of the sea and said, "We're here!"

He looked over the bay to the *Zebra* and heard Hornigold also say, "Let go the anchor." While his black brig matched

Agilis in displacement, her anchor set in twelve fathoms of water as he said to his crew, "We'll have no desertions on my command. None of you can swim."

Only their grumbles reached the beach and he ignored them.

Porter scanned a row of hastily-constructed warehouses along the waterfront and noted a thousand colored tents blanketing the hills. His instinct told him the village of San Francisco would become a city someday. A few lonesome dockworkers groaned under heavy loads being moved from warehouses to customers.

He gazed up Clay Street for several blocks to the base of California Hill, A myriad of glass windows reflected the sunrise like drops of dew on a lawn. People filled the streets to celebrate the holiday, even at this early hour.

MacIntyre and Ferreri crowded next to Porter in the narrow deck at the bow. MacIntyre said to the mates, "Never have I seen such a gathering of vessels, but they appear to be abandoned. There is not a soul in sight."

Ferreri said, "It's disgraceful. I cannot see a single solitary lookout."

MacIntyre continued, "The crews jump ship and traipse into the Sierra foothills. Rumormongers assert that gold litters the ground. Humph."

Ferreri said in a knowing tone, "They'll discover their folly soon enough. We'll get them back penniless."

Porter thought, My gold mine is somewhere in those hills. I'll find it as soon as I can.

Now that the sails were tightly furled to the yardarms, MacIntyre announced to the crew, "We will stay on board until tomorrow morning. No one will unload a ship for a reasonable wage on the Fourth of July."

In a low voice, he said to Porter and Ferreri, "I expect the crew to disappear when they hit the beach. We must get unloaded first."

"What? I do not think so!" came a startled exclamation. Otis confronted MacIntyre in a rage. He recoiled at touching the wooden railing with its slash of fresh blood, and wrinkled Macintyre's coat sleeve instead, as he gripped it for stability.

"I demand to go ashore this instant. Bring my luggage."

Porter was ecstatic but Macintyre's feelings were a mix of irritation at his demand and genuine relief to get him gone. MacIntyre knew he could not keep the other passengers confined either and motioned Porter and Amundson to lower the dinghy.

Porter and Amundson helped the banker and his lady down the ladder to the boat with their luggage. Before Amundson could climb back aboard, Otis stabbed his finger at the wharf. "Go!"

They reached the rickety wharf in a moment, but a man stopped them and said, "That will be one dollar, if you please."

Otis looked at him in amazement and said, "What do you mean?"

"I mean its one dollar to step onto my wharf."

"I won't pay it."

"Fine. The next wharf is a dollar and a half. You are welcome to walk in the mud instead."

Otis turned to Porter, "Pay the man. It's your boat."

Porter said, "No money."

Amundson said, "Me neither."

Grumbling, Otis pulled a dollar from his pocket and handed it to the wharf attendant. "Highway robbery, I say."

Porter and Amundson helped Otis and his lady friend out and tipped their luggage after them. As they turned back to the dinghy, Otis made a new demand. "Take us to the City Hotel."

"Where's the City Hotel?" said Porter.

"You ignorant tars," Otis said, showing off his naval jargon again. "It's that tall building up the hill." He pointed seven blocks up the hill.

"Surely you know of its owner, William Leidesdorff, the most successful Negro in this region."

"No, sir."

"Just go."

After tugging the heavy luggage up the steep hill and maneuvering around the mud, dirt, debris, and manure in the street, Porter and Amundson, panting, deposited the luggage in the lobby. Ready to explode from the complaints, they nudged each other and became instantly deaf.

The lady barely managed to slip a note into Amundson's hand as they ran out the front door.

Porter and Amundson sprinted down the hill and rowed back to *Agilis* faster than a speeding bullet. They were so giddy with relief that desertion never entered their minds.

MacIntyre was packed when the rowers returned to *Agilis*. He said to Ferreri, "I have business on shore. Take command until I return. Keep the crew aboard for the night."

Ferreri was crestfallen as he had expected to go ashore immediately. "Aye, sir."

MacIntyre turned to Porter, "Drop me ashore with my luggage, and keep those white trousers clean."

The three rowed to the same wharf they had just left, and MacIntyre paid another dollar.

"Come with me," he said to Porter, "and return the dinghy," to Amundson.

Amundson rowed back to *Agilis*, weighing whether to jump ship or not. Back on deck, he crouched in a private corner to read the note from the City Hotel. He could barely make out the name since he didn't really read,

Maria Juana Castañeda Rojas, Hacienda of Tio (uncle) General Vallejo, Sonoma.

He hid the note in his ditty box with a big grin.

At the same moment Porter and MacIntyre paid their dollar under protest and stepped onto the Clay Street wharf, a dinghy bumped into the larger Central wharf. The tall Russian, Gurii Chernov and Master Dirk Hornigold from the *Zebra* raised their knees to step out.

"That will be a dollar and a half."

"What do you mean a dollar and a half?" Hornigold said to the attendant.

That's the cost to use my wharf."

"Pay the man," he said to Chernov.

"Son of a bitch," he mumbled.

Chernov paid with a grimace. They started up Commercial Street to the business district but were cut off by a gregarious man. "Welcome to San Francisco, my friends."

He grabbed the arm of Hornigold and pulled him to the equally reluctant arm of MacIntyre.

"Glorious Fourth of July, wouldn't you say gents?"

MacIntyre grunted, "Humph."

Hornigold said, "Not bloody likely."

"Now gentlemen, let's be civil for the day. I am Thaddeus Leavenworth, the next mayor of San Francisco."

"Who?" said Hornigold. "I've never heard of you."

"Yes you have. I distribute your ice from Sitka to the restaurants."

"I remember. What do you want?"

"The luminaries of this town are celebrating today and both of you are invited.

MacIntyre was skeptical, "What luminaries?"

Hornigold said, "I'm no damn luminary. What are you talking about?"

"It's a rare day to find us all together. The civilian, military, and commercial leaders are joining hands for the future. Unfortunately, the Bishop is detained in Monterrey."

"Future hell, I just arrived," said Hornigold.

Leavenworth continued, "The good people of California are desperate for food. It's a wide open market for ships like your *Agilis* and *Zebra*, and you will reap a good profit. You have an opportunity that is not to be missed, if I say so myself."

MacIntyre thought, I do need a freight of cargo after I unload. Possibly Leavenworth can oblige.

Hornigold thought differently, but still to himself, They're in trouble. This is my kind of juicy pigeon.

Leavenworth beamed, "Please join us for dinner in the new Niantic. A fine restaurant has just opened in the cabin on that converted whaling ship."

He pointed to a bowsprit protruding over Montgomery Street between the Burr Gray General Store and the Eagle Saloon, "The abandoned whaler *Niantic* is being converted into a hotel. You can see the workers dumping sand around the hull and hear the carpenters.

"I apologize for the short notice, but this afternoon is the only chance we have to all gather."

MacIntyre said, "A meal on terra firma is a welcome change from eating at sea. The naval atmosphere of the Niantic's cabin sounds comfortable."

Leavenworth added, "The hotel completed five new sleeping rooms just this morning. You mariners of the world would be most comfortable there." He neglected to say that he was an investor in the *Niantic*.

Hornigold said, "I won't stay in a hotel with him," pointing to MacIntyre. "I'll sleep in the City hotel, if you please, but I will join you for dinner."

Leavenworth said, "I'll see you early this afternoon, ahead of the parade and fireworks."

Porter followed his master in a blue uniform through a door on the *Niantic's* hull as two workmen hung a sign over the door that read,

Niantic Dining Emporium

MacIntyre said, "Some of the best scallops in the world come from the village of Niantic back in Connecticut. I hope these measure up." Crossing the deck to the dining room he said to Porter, "Do not touch anything and keep your mouth shut- especially your mouth."

Porter said, "Aye aye, sir." His trousers were still white, even after rowing the dinghy back and forth because he sat on a folded sail.

Intricate rosewood carvings on the walls of the restaurant told nautical stories and a deep carpet softened the floor. Wall sconces highlighted the damask linen tablecloth draped over the center table. A classical guitarist completed the elegant mood by strumming Spanish ballads in a corner.

Five other important guests seated themselves around the table next to the mariners from *Agilis*. MacIntyre and Hornigold glared at each other from opposite ends, while Porter and Chernov sat behind their masters in straight-back chairs. Each mate was as tense as a crouching tiger and poised to attack. The waiter served a before-dinner cordial to the guests around the table. He ignored the occupants of the straight chairs.

Leavenworth stood up, "Let's introduce ourselves, shall we. I am Thad Leavenworth, the next mayor of our fair city." On his left, the redheaded man said, "I am Lieutenant William T. Sherman, Adjutant to the military governor of the territory of California." Next came a sullen, "Dirk Hornigold." Across the table, a heavy man raised his glass and intoned, "Julian Skinner here. A merchant at your service." MacIntyre completed the introductions, "Alex MacIntyre of *Agilis*."

The men shook hands and settled into the luxurious leather chairs freshly polished with neat's-foot oil. The aroma of the oil enhanced the luxurious atmosphere.

The maître d'hôtel said, "Welcome to my humble establishment, gentlemen. Might I point out our silver flatware? This set was engraved with our crest by Bernard and Sons Limited of London at great expense. I hope you enjoy your dinner."

Porter was awestruck at the elegance and took it all in. Chernov was accustomed to fine living and only grunted.

Lieutenant Sherman addressed MacIntyre. "Before we get started, I wish to formally apologize for my gunner who fired on your ship. Please submit any damage reports to my office and I will reimburse them."

MacIntyre said, "Apology accepted but unnecessary. There was no damage and accidents do happen. I doubt your difficulties with training on land are greater than mine on the water."

Sherman continued, "Nonetheless, my procedures were insufficient. I can assure you that problem has been resolved."

Porter felt the gash on the side of his head, which was still oozing a little blood and thought, No damage, my ass. Speak for yourself.

He sneaked a white napkin off a side buffet to wipe his scalp, and hid the red cloth under his chair hoping no one would notice. The waiter quietly removed it without comment.

He was a gun fighter and bouncer in his other job, and used to blood.

Courses followed delectable courses until the company was stuffed. The occupants of the straight chairs received plates of leftovers from the waiter.

The after-dinner brandy and *Principe de Gales* cigars from Havana loosened every tongue. Tales of bravery, joy, tragedy, and disaster spread camaraderie through clouds of fragrant cigar smoke, and mellowed the company, even the masters.

Porter had never experienced such an august setting and studied every gesture. He noted which piece of silverware was used for what food.

The Russian came from the House of Romanov, and was accustomed to a higher standard of etiquette; but a lower standard of manners.

Loud debate raged on every topic imaginable.

"I say, that horse Esclavo was clearly ahead of Goldfinder II—at least by a nose," said Julian.

"There's no better fishing spot than the confluence of the San Joaquin and Sacramento rivers," asserted Lieutenant Sherman.

Leavenworth was clearly excited when he said, "You sporting men make your points well, but I personally favor the señoritas at the weekly fandangos. Our guitarist, who entertains us so delightfully for dinner, leads the musicians in the latest dances from Spain and Mexico.

"How about that four-way bare knuckle wrestling match in the square last night," said Hornigold. "I didn't expect anyone to walk away with all the blood on the ground."

Serious arguments erupted on the merits of this ship over that. But the conversation soon hardened into boasts about personal vessels.

Hornigold said, "The *Zebra* has a guaranteed full crew while I predict *Agilis* will lose hers tomorrow by desertion." He raised his chin to MacIntyre, and Chernov backed him up with a punch of his fist.

MacIntyre said, "*Agilis* mounts more sail than your *Zebra*. I daresay she can beat any black hull to Honolulu." He blew a smoke ring toward the ceiling and made a small tent with his fingers on the table. Porter held his thumb up in triumph.

Hornigold grunted, "Harrumph. You misplace your confidence amongst the present company, my dear MacIntyre. The *Zebra* outclasses your *Agilis* three ways to Sunday. My crew is best at anchor, our hull the cleanest, and we are simply faster-"

MacIntyre interrupted, "That black tub with the houghmagandy (fornicating) gold trim skulking in the harbor will be lucky to limp to the Pacific."

Hornigold came back with a vengeance, "That effete hulk with the jury-rigged mast and discombobulated (ass up) spar can't find a rock to wreck on."

The Masters stomped to their feet, capsized their chairs, and threw their brandy snifters at each other. The glasses collided in mid-air and spewed glass shards everywhere. It was fortunate that the sconces burning on the wall were too high to ignite the extravagant alcohol vapors flooding the carpet.

MacIntyre coughed and his face turned red.

Porter leaped to his feet and grabbed a knife from the table. Chernov did the same and charged around the table toward Porter, but stumbled over a side chair. The waiter put his hand on his gun under his white apron.

Hornigold choked and turned blue.

Leavenworth saw the melee brewing and held up his hands to quell it. "I say, calm down everyone. Both of your commands look dashing in the harbor. He stared down the two Masters and their mates, and motioned at the waiter to restore order.

The waiter thought to himself, I'd expect a fight in a bar, but not a fine restaurant. The dope I get from these men is not worth this shit. What's wrong with these people?

The Masters righted their chairs and sat back down, glaring like wild animals. The waiter cleared away the broken glass and daubed up the brandy with a towel. He, as a gun fighter for hire, was familiar with bloody broken glass and was ready to assert his armed authority when called for.

Only after calm was restored did Porter and Chernov sit down. They were men of action, not diplomacy.

Leavenworth spoke in a silky soothing voice, "Allow me to propose a modest wager between these two beauties."

"And what is that?" said Hornigold.

"I lay before you, for your consideration, a challenge between *Agilis* and *Zebra*. I suggest a trip to the Hawaiian Islands to bring food to the immigrants flooding California."

MacIntyre said, "That sounds eminently sensible to me."

Leavenworth said, "I saw two ravenous souls fighting over a scrap of garbage yesterday, not to mention those hungry soldiers in fisticuffs. Would you not agree, Lieutenant Sherman?"

"That's right," said the redheaded Sherman, who was aghast at the temper tantrums thrown by two grown men.

Porter was ashamed of MacIntyre. He had a temper but never directed it against others, usually. The second mate expected his superiors to always maintain their self-control. Gurii Chernov was proud of Hornigold.

Leavenworth described his proposal, "I suggest that each of us pledge five thousand dollars for a pot of twenty-five thousand. The winner takes all." He looked each man in the eye with a raised eyebrow.

Sherman commented first. "I assure you the biggest thieves in San Francisco are the suppliers to the United States Army. You've heard that expression, 'eat like a horse'? That's beast and man alike. Count me in."

To himself he thought, My entire regiment doesn't spend five thousand dollars a month. I can pull strings for that money, but I'll be court-marshaled if my wager leaves this room.

The party chewed on their cigars and muttered among themselves.

"By Jove, I think so."

"I do not see why not."

"Not a contest."

"I need a cargo."

"Cannot happen."

"How much profit in that food?"

"But of course."

Porter's mouth gaped open in astonishment. He had never imagined such a huge sum of money in his entire life.

MacIntyre said, "I accept your wager, my good man. My crew may desert, whether for better or worse I cannot say. But I will point out that my officer core is intact, and my steward is raising a crew as we speak."

He glared at Hornigold, who studied a low swinging chandelier that would be deadly at sea.

Hornigold said, "I accept, although it pains me to steal your money. My crew is ready to load and lead. You'll never get a crew, MacIntyre, especially on the Fourth of July."

Porter stopped his mouth just short of blurting out loud,

What the hell are you agreeing to, MacIntyre? We can't beat a *Zebra*.

"Julian?" said Leavenworth.

"I'm in. I need those goods to fill my stores."

"Capital. The pot will be twenty-five thousand dollars. I'll deposit our pledges in the Banco de California tomorrow morning."

MacIntyre and Hornigold folded their arms and scowled at each other. Over their shoulders, Porter challenged Chernov with all demeanor of a soldier headed into battle.

Leavenworth defused the tension with a diversionary rule. "This contest is for seamanship, not dock activities. The race will begin when your ships are loaded and ready to embark," said Leavenworth.

The men around the table nodded in agreement.

"Lieutenant Sherman, have your Quartermaster place an order for your requirements with each Master. If you would, prepare your cannons to start the contest. I suggest loading them with blanks, and please to face the open water. We'll commence from the wharf at Clay Street."

Porter and Chernov stood up ready to start the contest right there.

The pot shall be awarded to the first vessel who returns this silver to the wharf where they commenced." Leavenworth handed an elegant silver fork to MacIntyre and a companion knife to Hornigold. Good luck to both of you.

Each master slipped his silver piece into a secure pocket. The guests, except the Masters, shook hands and retired to their vessels.

The maître d'hôtel grumbled, "Who is going to pay for those silver pieces?"

Without a word, Porter and MacIntyre left through the kitchen, while Chernov and Hornigold left through the entrance door.

Porter muttered to himself, You'll do anything for that extra dollar, Hornigold, but not this time. I'll bring *Agilis* home for MacIntyre, if it takes everything I've got.

Chapter 4—SF Doesn't Want You

With the master and Porter away and with nothing else to do, Ferreri complained to Steward Jackson back on *Agilis*, "That banker harassed the entire crew. Who is he again?"

Jackson looked around for privacy and whispered, "Holton Gray Otis."

"Nothing to me."

"His father is Harrison Gray Otis who owns the East Boston Savings Bank. He has more money than God."

Ferreri said, "You mean the banker who built *Agilis*?"

"That's him."

Ferreri said, "Where did that squeaky son-of-a-bitch come from?."

Jackson said, "How the hell did I know he owned the *Agilis*? He picked us in Panama.

"Hell's bells and buckets of blood, we're so lucky."

Jackson said, "Here came the American consul in the mail boat waving his arms. 'May I come aboard?' MacIntyre welcomed him with a brandy. I overheard the consul moan, 'I need your help.'"

Ferreri spit and stomped back and forth a couple of times. Jackson counted unused provisions.

Jackson continued, "The consul's very words were, 'We are drowning in gold seekers traveling to San Francisco, but the northbound ships are full. Would you take some passengers to

California?' MacIntyre agrees, "I can take ten on the open deck. They will bring their own food, but Cook Silva will prepare it."

Ferreri kicked the bulkhead in frustration, while Jackson continued, " 'Splendid. You have my gratitude, Master Macintyre'. "

Jackson said, "Gratitude, I'll bet. Otis has Porter in irons, MacIntyre evicted from his bed, and luggage stored in Babbitt's bunk. He demanded Bosun Babbitt hang a privacy curtain, but there's more."

Ferreri said, "What?"

Jackson whispered, "Otis is incognito to scout out investments in the gold rush. Only we know his identity, and are sworn to secrecy.

The sound of the dinghy scrapped the hull with MacIntyre and Porter returning from dinner.

"Come aboard, sir," said Ferreri. All's well."

MacIntyre said, "I am sure it is, but I have to follow up on this morning. Porter will spend the night in irons for his assault on my passenger."

Porter was stunned. He had avoided Otis and his lady ever since Panama. It was the attack on the *Zebra* that triggered his temper.

MacIntyre motioned to several idle crew members,

"Lock Porter in irons for the night, and let this be a lesson on how to treat passengers."

Several sailors seized Porter in a pantomime of force, and he reciprocated with a charade of resistance. They forced him down the hatch to the brig, where iron rings were attached to the hull. They only used the room for storage.

The men grinned in friendship as they rattled Porter's chains and didn't lock the shackles. The rusty chains made streaks like

Chinese characters on his clean white trousers, but he was unfettered.

He heard Ferreri and Jackson finish their conversation through the bulkhead. The whispers were magnified in the corner of the store room where Porter sat still as a church mouse, or church rat. He was not obligated to keep Otis' secret, and thought, Mr. Otis, I hope your high-class manners are better than what you've shown so far. Incognito is not an excuse.

Porter recoiled at the dark, foul hold. He found the bucket for his waste since MacIntyre always said, "A clean ship is a healthy ship." Unaccustomed to idleness, his thoughts began to ramble, Trouble stalks me right or wrong, but I couldn't let that shooter kill someone, could I?

Porter carefully leaned his chestnut hair against the bulkhead. His head was still sore from the crease of the cannonball and he rested his hand on the floor to keep his balance.

I'd forgotten the smell of harbors. We're surrounded by floating waste from the tents on the hill, buildings, and animals. We've dumped ours too. There's brandy, manure, guano, lumber, spices, oils, and pine tar from the oakum and the planks. None of this is me, is it?

He took a sniff,

"Nah, thanks to Cook Silva's Bay Rum lotion."

He stroked the old planks that were worn down by many feet over the years, but was surprised when his fingers felt a groove.

"What's this?"

He traced out the grooves that made a pattern of three nested V's carved into the floor. In a flash, Porter remembered the black sailor on his Atlantic voyage. Garong Wek had the same scars on his forehead as the carvings in the floor.

Porter said out loud as he rattled the loose chains, "Save chains! These very links were clamped on Wek's legs."

Porter talked out loud, "The East Boston Savings Bank built *Agilis* as a slaver in 1840 and converted her to a merchantman on the collapse of the slave trade. 'We had some good times, didn't we, Wek. It was better than slave mongers kidnapping you on the Congo River.'"

Porter felt relieved all over again at escaping the Boston landowner and sympathized with Wek.

You were the master carver of the Bor Dinka tribe and cut your mark in these boards when they carried you in chains to Jamaica. You wanted somebody to know.

Porter laughed at the image of Wek impersonating a turncoat guard and escaping on a pirate vessel. Porter carved an 'RP' next the V's and stabbed his knife at the floor to sit up. The tip of his blade slipped into the oakum-filled seam and hit something hard with a metallic clunk. He pried out a coin hidden at the tip of the V's.

"You old son of a gun," said Porter aloud, holding the heavy coin in his fingers. "I wondered where you hid that piece of eight from Gibraltar." He scraped away the tar and held the coin up to the dim light. He could barely see the words on the front and back, *Hispaniarvm Rex 1687, Carolvs II*

Porter tossed the coin in his palm. It had to be gold since it was too heavy for silver. He smiled, It's that gold escudo Wek found in the sand. The money changer said they're sometimes called doubloons.

Porter waved good luck to Wek in the dark and said, "Good thing you left Gibraltar with John Petherick's expedition up the Nile to Khartoum and home. But you forgot your doubloon."

Porter put the coin in his shoe.

He drifted to sleep on waves of pleasure. The fragrance of the pine from the oakum and swaying tall masts reminded him of the New England forests of his youth.

Becky Revere and Porter walked hand in hand through the forest to escape the hot sun. He could hear her gleeful words,

"Hide and seek, you're it. Count to twenty and catch me if you can."

"One, two, three,. . .,fourteen, twenty! Ready or not, here I come," as he searched the forest. "Gotcha."

He never figured out that Becky always left a little clue to her location. A corner of a dress, a little scratch in the dirt, or perhaps the tip of a shoe. She always hid in a deep bed of leaves.

Porter always jumped in.

Becky said one day, "I'm indentured for seven years like you, but mistress Podwinkle is so cruel."

"What? I'll fix her. Where is she this afternoon?" Porter jumped up ready to fight.

"No, no, I didn't mean that. It's all right."

Porter sat back down, and they rejoined each other's company.

He glowed to remember the romantic Sunday afternoons alone with Becky in the bushes.

"Creak, thud."

A sound from the hatch ladder shattered his dream. He wasn't with Becky in the sunny woods, but in the foul hold of a stinking ship with rusty chains across his legs. He looked up to see Cook Silva descending with something in his hands.

"It's dim, but maybe you can see to write." He handed a journal and a cup of grog to Porter.

"Much obliged, my friend."

Porter sighed, and turned to the little journal which he could read in a rare shaft of sunlight that lasted for only a few minutes. The title page read, "Journal of a Distinguished Man, Richard Porter, His Book."

He brought his notes up to date;

> We rounded a point and beheld the glorious
> Golden Gate. A brilliant sunrise heralded us as
> we moored in a collection of masts as thick as the
> Maine forest. I'm hidden in this prison, but such
> is my California adventure.

Richard leaned back as the floor swayed to and fro. The pungent odor of the white oak planks blended with growing aromas from the galley. He listened to the random grumbling about Macintyre's order to remain aboard that night, and his thoughts drifted. Harbor still stinks, but Silva's galley stove hides it. Damn, that smells good. An extra night lets me enjoy the bread and water."

The wizard of the galley, Cook Marco José Tavares Silva, had an idea; "I'll make a gone-away dinner to celebrate Otis's leaving."

Otis had browbeaten Silva along with everyone else during the passage north from Panama. As a further insult, Silva had to prepare his meals, as well as those for the other passengers and the crew. Silva withheld his culinary talents from Otis much as he could, and spit in every dish he carried to the banker.

The gone-away dinner grew into a special feast for the entire crew to mark their last night aboard. They would remember it for a long time.

The thrifty Silva had saved the best tidbits from the Chilean provisions, and planed to bring them to culinary perfection. He hummed a tune as he dumped in great quantities of the famously hot scotch bonnet peppers from Central America. The rising aroma made every stomach growl, and most of all Porter's as his bread and water diet didn't cut it.

No one noticed Silva when he sneaked a plate of food down to Porter. "Your Caribbean feast, my friend."

Porter dug in voraciously, but with a forced grin as the Jamaican spices assaulted his taste. "Excellent eating, huh, huh, hand me the grog if you would."

"De nada, el señor mi amigo. (It is nothing for my friend, sir.)"

What a table Cook Silva set for the other officers that night.

"I present to you Jamaican patty pastries filled with spiced beef, jerked chicken with scotch bonnet peppers, rice and peas, black cake with rum, and dried fruits from Valparaiso."

Cook Silva was proud to show off his skills when he had the chance.

"Straight from Kingston," as he served MacIntyre and the officers. My food dances on your tongue."

The diners around the table agreed, as they downed copious glasses of wine and anything else wet. They broke out in a sweat from the heat of the Caribbean cuisine, and panted for more.

Silva tamed down the dinner for the crew with less of the spices and milder heat, since they were accustomed to bland fare. It wasn't enough.

Bjorn Amundson's response in the forecastle was the opposite of that in the cabin. "What the hell is this stuff? My God, it's eating my mouth. I'm gonna die." He gulped down his ration of grog to wash away the first small bite. "Ah, ah, ooooh, got to have a drink."

Cook Silva jumped down the hatchway, "My food you no like? I throw out."

He threw Amundson's cup out the hatch. It flew overboard. The other men were afraid to say anything. They kept on the good side of Cook Silva by force of habit, even during the last night aboard.

The wise old salt, Levi Pembroke with his peg leg crossed over his good leg said, "I'm here to tell you, Silva gives you a snack in the night and a warm place to hide if he likes you. There's a cup of coffee-but only if he likes you. If he don't, you'll freeze in hell or the rigging. Best stay on the cook's good side," as he glanced sideways at Silva glaring at the company.

Amundson borrowed a spare cup and forced another serving of raging spicy dinner down with a violent cough. His second double ration of grog was gone well before the food, and he sweated in silence under the watchful eye of Cook Marco José Tavares Silva.

After the fiery meal had settled, the loud grumbling began.

"Who does that old fart think he is?"

"No leave on the Fourth of July."

"Hell, we've suffered down here for months."

"I can't wait to get off."

The complaints penetrated the bulkhead to Porter. He said loudly through the wall, "Stifle that talk, you ungrateful bastards. You should thank Silva for a fine dinner and the food you stuffed down your gullet. One more night won't matter."

A sailor changed the subject with enthusiasm, "Grab the dice and let's go, mates, it's Ship Captain and Crew."

Kawai, an able-bodied Kanaka from the Hawaiian Islands interrupted, "I know dice, but what is Ship Captain and Crew?"

Amundson looked at him in disgust but Levi Pembroke, the colorful 40-year old seaman with a peg leg and a standard green parrot on his shoulder, held up five ivory dice with black dots on the sides. "We throw these down and read the dots. Six dots make a ship, five a captain, and the rest your crew.

The parrot screeched, "Squawk, squawk, ship crew," and flapped his wings.

"You make a bet to throw a ship, a captain, and crew in three tries. Hold if you do and pass if you don't. The next player the same. Biggest crew breaks a tie and I keep track of the rounds."

Amundson said, "We're paid tomorrow but Pembroke, I mean Broken Pen, can write so he'll track our bets and winners. We're watching you close, old man, even if we can't read."

Pembroke had cut the left leg of his grungy bell-bottom pants short and tied it off just above a hook in his carved wooden limb.

The parrot piped up, "Squawk, Rudy like a winner, Rudy like dice. Squawk."

"Shut up you damn bird," Pembroke said as he pulled a small tablet from his ditty box to keep score.

Amundson laid down the rules. "Everybody ante up one dollar," as he put down a dollar. Four sailors joined and brought the pot up to five dollars. Pembroke wrote down one for the first round, one for the ante, and a five for the pot.

Amundson shook his cupped hands with five dice and was about to throw down when he heard a wild pounding on the bulkhead.

Porter shouted, "I want in too. Roll for me after yourself." Amundson put in another dollar and Pembroke changed the pot to six.

Amundson made the first throw. "I get a six for my ship and a miserable crew. Can't sail without a Captain." He threw again. "Five sorry ass crew ain't worth nothing." This is it. "here's a Captain and four crew but no ship. This game is worthless."

A seamen called out, "You'll never make a sailor, Mr. Amundson." They all laughed.

Amundson blew on the dice, shook them, looked up and down, and said, "Rolling for Porter in the irons." He threw.

"He is worse than I was. Porter log's a crew of five. No ship and no Captain. You don't sail no better in the forecastle than on deck." They all cheered in high spirits.

The game of Ship Captain and Crew continued through the night. At dawn, Amundson was up ten dollars, Porter down four, and the rest of the crew divided into winners and losers. The forecastle allowed it was a rip roaring good time.

On the other side of the bulkhead, Porter woke up, stretched, and yelled through the bulkhead, "Time to hit San Francisco, mates. Are you ready?"

They were ready to storm San Francisco, but San Francisco did not want them.

Early the next morning of July fifth. while Porter roused the hands, Steward Jackson and bosun Babbitt prowled the stinking deserted waterfront. Jackson said, "I don't see a stevedore anywhere."

Babbitt said, "Not between their hangovers and the lure of gold upriver, sir.

Jackson and Babbitt scoured the alleyways, hunted behind the bars, groped the scrawny trees in the park, and glanced into secret hideouts. They finally snagged a sorry crew of hung-over stevedores at the obscene rate of fourteen dollars a day.

Jackson said to Babbitt, "Get these men to work. They're costing a fortune."

Bosun Benjamin Babbitt packed twenty-four years of experience into his thirty-four years of age. His dark brown hair set off his five-foot six frame that packed a hundred and fifty-two pounds. He came from a refined family in Charleston, but was tough enough when necessary even when he was wrong. He over-painted everything to maintain appearances.

He drove the reluctant hands relentlessly.

"It's not my fault your head hurts, move it."

"Get that barrel out of the hold."

"You—help with the crate."

"Don't scratch the paint!"

"I said 'Don't drop it', how often do I have to warn you?"

Somehow, they got the trade goods off by the end of the day and each sweaty man got his fourteen dollars from Jackson. He paid it grudgingly with a foul humor. "Damn shirkers, should have been done by noon."

Master Alex MacIntyre stepped from his cabin door and said to Ferreri who passed the command on to Babbitt, "Call the crew."

Babbitt barked, "All hands on deck, including Porter. Now!"

Porter climbed the ladder from the irons corner and blinked in the bright sunlight. His trouser whites looked like a Chinese manuscript from the marks made by the rusty chains.

Steward Jackson sat at a small table. "Line up."

Porter fell in line by seniority with the rest of the crew to get his wages. The line stretched across the deck like a dragon with its mouth ready to devour the table, or at least the money on it.

Jackson checked the payroll account one last time. "We have

MacIntyre at $1500,

Six officers for $1200,

Six able-bodied seamen for $600,

Six ordinary seamen for $450,

And those five vagrants today for $70, damn thieves."

He thought to himself in dollars rather than words, 'Even after deductions, our payroll is under four thousand and that leaves a nice profit when we sell the cargo. Those passengers from Panama were a bonus at two hundred dollars each, but I should have charged Holton Otis double for his trouble.

Jackson cleared his throat and gave his standard speech to the line; "Don't spend this all in one place, but put a little aside in the Sailor's Bank. You'll be glad someday."

The crew responded with their standard, "Yes, sir." They fully planned to invest their money in the debauchery that beckoned on shore.

He barked the name of the first man and handed him his wages, less accumulated charges. The hand grumbled at the deductions, but grabbed his money.

"Next," and down the line with two exceptions, who were the rowers.

The rapture of the passengers in their hopes and dreams showed as the tars rowed them and their belongings, boat by boat, to the beach of San Francisco, at the center of California, at the center of their destiny.

Chapter 5—Irish Huckster's Gold

Six crewmen with the highest seniority leaped into the dinghy. "Here I comes ladies, gimme a drink," the steward's advice long forgotten. A seventh hand rowed the men to shore in anticipation of his ten-dollar bonus on top of his pay when he returned.

That is, he tried to row to shore, but the dinghy plunged into a fleet of floating craft like they had never seen. A screaming barker stood in every one and offered inducements to the lonely sailors with hot money in their hands.

"Best entertainment in Fris'co."

"Wet your whistle at the Blue Crane Saloon."

Most obvious was a hag of a strip dancer who poked a leg through a split red dress and gyrated on a flatboat,

"See Tia Juana Tease at the Red Iguana."

The oarsman bumped and pushed the hawkers away until he finally scraped the beach. The whooping sailors jumped out and the rower returned to *Agilis*. They ignored the nearby Clay Street Wharf.

Ferreri pointed to Porter and said, "You, take the rest of the crew over."

He watched Porter throw his ditty box into the dinghy and leap in alongside the excited crew. He said to MacIntyre, "Porter is taking his ditty box like the rest of them. It is this damned gold fever. Vagabonds, every last jack-tar."

MacIntyre watched the kaleidoscope of humanity from around the world on the shore. Behind him the ugly steamship, *SS Oregon,* was marooned for lack of coal, and looked out of place amid the beautiful tall ships. He sighed with resignation and reminded Ferreri, "These men are free when we pay them, but I am sorry to lose Porter."

Porter churned the water to a froth in his eagerness to join the gold rush. He called back as he was leaving, "Goodbye *Agilis,* it's been a whale of a run."

Porter with his back toward the bow of the dinghy barged through the riff-raff. The front-facing sailors could see a jaunty fellow on the beach who was wearing a green vest that matched his muddy shoes. They could barely hear him talking over the splash of the oars, while Porter facing backward couldn't hear anything.

The crew picked up bits of an Irish brogue as the fellow approached a drifter walking along.

"Cheers, and a good day, my lad. How are ya?"

"Who are you? I don't want any," said the grubby drifter.

"How are things in the gold mines?

"Aint no business of your'n."

"Whoa there my friend. I have a friendly proposal for an honest confidence man."

The drifter looked at him, "With money?"

"Want an easy twenty dollars?"

"I'll take your money."

"All you have to do is show this jar of gold dust, and I'll do the talking." The huckster pulled a yellow bottle the size of his thumb from his pocket. "Can you pan a little color?"

"I can when they's gold dust around, and sometimes when they ain't."

"There is dust around," said the huckster, as he poured a small amount into the dirt. He shuffled it in and drew an X with his toe.

"Pan color right here when I tell you. Got that?"

"Yeah, I ain't dumb."

"Keep the gold you get and here's twenty dollars for your help."

He pulled a gold piece from his pocket and showed the conspirator who grabbed for it but the huckster pulled it back, "Afterwards."

The huckster and the drifter welcomed the rowdy *Agilis* sailors like lambs to the slaughter. They watched as Porter beached the boat and the eager sailors jump out with their ditty boxes. Porter jumped out last and called to their companions up the hill, "Wait for us!" as he threw the oars back into the boat.

With a whoop, they headed for the famous Barbary Coast district of bars and bawdy houses. Their goal was to fritter away their money in debauchery as fast as seafaringly possible.

Porter forgot his dream of a gold mine in his rush to join his seafaring companions.

"GOLD!"

The shouted word stopped them dead in their tracks. Visions flashed before their eyes of maps to buccaneer treasure hidden on a remote island. Every tar had heard the rousing tales of piracy in the Caribbean sea. Some might have participated recently, but that was their secret.

The jaunty Irish huckster walked up to the tallest, biggest, and toughest ringleader, Richard Porter. A big Irish smile displayed a gold tooth that contrasted with his green vest. His flat hat concealed a pair of dark shifty eyes. He was only a little drunk and looked able to hold his own in a bar fight.

"Welcome to San Francisco, mates. This is the right place. You come for the gold rush! Right?"

Richard Porter glanced at Bjorn Amundson, nodded to the huckster, and said "Just what I need." Richard was re-obsessed with his gold mine and wanted it now.

The Kanaka sailors from the Hawaiian Islands continued uphill hollering,"We don't need no gold, got hundred dollar. We needs rum, tobacco, and ladies." They headed to the William Whippy Kanaka House to drop off their ditty boxes.

This boarding house had been founded by William Whippy in Nantucket, with a second house in the Hawaiian Islands. His recently opened third establishment here was as popular with the Kanaka seamen as the other two.

One Kanaka, Kawai, rejoined Richard Porter and Bjorn Amundson. He said, "I come back Mr. Porter, my friend."

Porter said, "Call me Richard on land, Porter is for the ship."

Kawai said, "I remember Richard, Mr. Porter."

"Richard, and this is Bjorn."

"I remember Mr. Richard—you see."

Richard said to the Irishman, "Don't mind those Kanaka, we're listening. By the way, do you have a twin brother in Boston? Like the one who cheated me out of twenty dollars?"

The huckster never missed a beat, "I passed through on the way from the old country. Didn't stop, no brother and all Irish men look the same."

He went to the second biggest sailor, Bjorn Amundson, and said, "Gather 'round." He held up a ring made from a nugget the size of his thumb. The ring stayed on his bent finger as he tugged on another nugget from his waist and pulled out loop after loop of gold chain.

The chain ended with a bright gold watch that ticked loudly and chimed when he pressed a button. He swung it back and forth at eye level.

Richard was hypnotized by the first gold nugget he had seen. The rest of them swarmed around the ring and one man bit it, "I saw a merchant in Algiers do that, but I don't know why." The other hand kept swinging the watch.

"Your gold is waiting for you," said the Huckster. "I've seen nuggets big as chicken eggs. He pointed to Richard's gnarled fingers, "Hold out your hands," and laid the watch fob and chain in them. "You don't want to brag but imagine when you say to your friends, 'Mine is bigger than yours'."

The men burst into a raucous laugh and decided the Irishman was a jolly good fellow. They focused their complete attention on the nuggets.

That is, except for Bjorn who was unconvinced, "That's a mighty fine display but how do I get mine?"

The huckster continued, "I'm glad you asked." He held up a crude map. "I have a map to the gold fields. Here's the route. This circle is Sacramento where people are getting rich, and my claim is the X."

He had the entire group in the palm of his soft smooth hand.

"And the best part is this map is absolutely free—but only for my good friends in the present company."

The gathered tars could scud a clipper through the most vicious storm in the world, but only Richard could read the chart. "Let me see that," and he grabbed the map. He said aloud, "I can get there."

The Huckster gestured to the drifter, "You look to be down from the hills old man. Spare a moment?"

The drifter looked up and said, "Who, me?"

"Any luck?"

He held up a little leather bag made from the scrotum of an elk that was filled with gold dust. He poured a little into his weathered hand. "I drop my pan in the water and this here gold swims right in. Easy as catching a fish." He strutted in front of the spectators showing off the gold dust in his hand. The sailors gawked in amazement.

The huckster continued, "My free map is the way my friends. I happen to have an extra copy or two—but only for you." The drifter shook the bag again.

The crowd grew with more boatloads arriving. The swarm squeezed the heavy bag for good luck and stared at the map, even though they could not read.

Not a man jack had seen the beauty of real gold but boasted anyway.

"Yep, mighty fine looking gold there."

"Real pure if you ask me."

"How much gold is this?"

"About twenty-seven dollars."

The sailors gasped and one said, "That's more'n I get for three months of fightin' Ferreri."

The Huckster pointed to the bag in the drifter's hand, "Your bonanza looks like this. How do you get it, you ask? It's easy, and I'm going to show you how." They crowded around like kids in a candy store.

He picked up a cloth bag printed with the words, *Jacob's Famous Gold Panning System* and removed a shiny fourteen-inch steel pan. It rang like a bell when he tapped it with his nugget ring.

"This is the magic pan that comes with your mining kit. The free map and everything you need is right here.

The men passed the pan around, tapped it, rubbed it, and wondered at it.

"I want to put this complete kit in your hands for the low, low price of only forty-nine dollars. What a bargain," as he held up the bag.

Richard asked, "What is a pan for?"

The Huckster pointed to the drifter. "Show these good folks how this pan works."

"Huh, me," as he looked around.

"You, my good man."

"You starts with gravel and water." The drifter scooped dirt into the pan from the X in the road and dipped water from a horse trough. The miner's practiced hands swirled the debris out and left a bed of fine sand in the bottom.

"There's the gold," he said as he pointed to bright specs of yellow.

Richard and his companions crowded around for a closer look at the native placer gold.

"I'll be damned," Richard said, "the streets in California really are paved with gold."

The Huckster continued, "But wait, there's more." He read the title of a book *How to Find and Retrieve Gold,* a field guide by Charles Garrett and Roy Lagal.

My friends, you get the pan, and the book, and a sieve, and the tweezers all together in this convenient bag. It is sewn by Jacob Davis, the famous Latvian tailor, right here in San Francisco. And don't forget your free map," as he waved it high.

This amazing kit is yours for only forty-nine dollars. I have but a few left as they are most popular. Get yours before they're gone."

Richard said, "Why aren't you panning yourself if this kit is so good? And how do I know this gentleman is a real miner?"

The drifter took a swing at Richard. "I've been mining since you were howling in diapers, sonny, and I ain't no gentleman." Richard returned the swing and missed as the huckster push them apart to prevent actual blows.

"Excellent question. My bank account is filled to overflowing. Your humble servant seeks to pass this good news on while he is able. The kit costs less than the parts. You can recover your investment in one good day. There is no risk."

Richard, Bjorn, and Kawai conferred. Richard said, "I came to California to get a gold mine and this is it. What say we share a kit?"

Bjorn joined with enthusiasm. "Count me in. My father taught me gemstones in Norway and I can find them in California too."

Kawai had a different take. "Mr. Porter, Richard, you my friend, I go too. I never leave ocean before. This new exciting."

They pooled their money and bought a kit. The other sailors crowded around and clamored for theirs too.

When the kits were gone, the huckster changed his spiel without missing a beat.

"The best way to Sacramento is on the Schooner Swiftness. I happen to have a few tickets. Only thirty-five dollars, but you must hurry because she leaves in three hours."

He pointed to the *Swiftness* moored nearby, where boisterous gold seekers congested the gangplank dragging satchels, bags, suitcases, loose stuff, and Jacob's kits aboard.

Richard, Bjorn, and Kawai bought tickets to Sacramento on the *Swiftness*.

Richard grinned and got a glint in his eye. "We need a name for our gold mining gang. How about the Paladíns?"

"What is Paladíns?" said Bjorn.

"Champions in Spanish and we're champions." said Richard.

Kawai said, "What is champions?"

"Champions are winners like a rowing champion."

They made high fives and cheered, "We are the Paladíns."

The eyes of Steward Jackson narrowed to slits at the Paladíns' fervor as he stood off to one side. He never missed a thing, day or night, but almost never said anything either.

The Paladíns made their way up the gangplank with their ditty boxes and kit. They were greeted by a fierce-looking compact little man with a revolver hung low on his hip, standing guard over a mountain of boxes and luggage. The Paladíns added theirs and said, "Defend these with your life or we'll get you."

The guard said, "I ain't never lost nothing yet. That's three dollars." Richard paid him.

The carefree Paladíns, with two hours to kill, left the *Swiftness* to explore the sights in the village of San Francisco.

They were swept into a frenzied celebration. People rushed hither and yon with a gleam in their eyes. Grubby miners in dusty overalls jostled bankers in fine suits. Platoons of soldiers dropped their animosity toward sailors and greeted them with gusto. Diverse Indians walked around groups of chattering Chinese. An occasional forlorn policeman surveyed the passersby with a lazy eye.

Richard's eyes popped at a Spanish Patrón in a saddle bedecked with gold and silver astride a fine horse. He towered over the men in the street and a pair of woman on foot.

Somebody called out to a teamster riding a wagon stacked high with goods, "I'll be damned if it isn't Charley Parkhurst blasting his way through the crowd again." The teamster responded with a stream of profanity as he threaded his supply wagon through the throng. His cussing was as original as the maritime version but with land-based oaths and curses.

The pair of ladies picked their path over dirt, debris, and sundry walking hazards. Every person except the Paladíns had a place to go and something to do.

Certain soiled doves of both the female and male persuasion discretely offered their pleasures with a wink at a fellow or another in the crowd. A few winked back, and occasionally stroked a butt or two.

It was a thrilling day. This was the San Francisco that greeted the Paladíns on the Fourth of July, 1849.

Chapter 6—Gun Loaded

Muddy kachunks on the wooden sidewalks drew attention to men wearing holsters on their hips. Richard noticed that some were tied high for defense while most were hung low for offense. Offense and defense were equal in a gunfight when either side or a bystander, might get plugged by the same gun.

Richard got a good look at an engraved revolver when he slammed into the five-foot-seven gunslinger as they eyed the same lady of the night. "Begging your pardon." He swerved in haste and said, "You're the waiter from the restaurant yesterday."

"Got to make a living somehow."

Richard liked the look of the waiter's revolver low on his hip, so with two hours to kill, he crossed the street to a gun shop. The sign hanging over the entrance displayed a young colt standing over a pistol:

Gun Shop
God made men
I make them equal
Sam Colt

A brace of shiny revolvers in the window called out, "Look at me." Other weapons in the display had long barrels and short barrels.

Richard thought, I need one of those for protection, and entered the small store. A bell on the front door rang his presence.

His nostrils filled with a manly blend of aromas from metal, leather, neatsfoot oil, wood, black powder, and bay rum aftershave. A wall of handguns on the right caught his eye—he ignored the long guns on the left wall and completely overlooked the shelves across the back. They were only stocked with supplies of lead for bullets, bullet molds, and kegs of Orange Express gunpowder labeled Laflin & Rand Powder Company.

The proprietor extended his hand, "Welcome. How can I help you?"

Richard puffed out his chest to look worldly as he strode to the right wall, making the redwood floor creak all the way.

"Mighty fine-looking guns you have. I need something for protection in the gold fields."

The proprietor humored him to make a sale since most of his customers acted the same way, and he gave his standard pitch:

"I see you're a man of distinctive tastes. You're in luck since a new shipment of Colt revolvers came in last week from Hartford, Connecticut.

Richard picked up an engraved model to compare with the one on the gunslinger's hip.

The proprietor said, "You sailors will be interested to know that Sam Colt got the idea for his design at sea. The action of the capstan and ratchet went straight into his patent of 1836 and now actuates his revolvers. You are holding a baby Dragoon which is pretty, but inadequate. Samuel Colt sells this larger model in a 44-caliber that he calls the 1848 Dragoon. He held it out to Richard.

Richard hefted the larger weapon that exuded power. He felt the grip and curves with rapt attention.

"Colt designed this model specifically for the army's regiment of mounted dragoons. The name has stuck to the revolver."

Richard examined it with lust in his eyes. This was the first serious firearm he had held and relished curling its four-and-a-half-pounds with his biceps. Otis's peashooter didn't count. The grip fit his palm as if it was born there.

"This will bring down a man or a horse, but not a grizzly. Lieutenant Sherman wears one most of the time."

Richard twirled the gun around his finger and the proprietor exploded.

"Don't do that. You will blow your balls off, or hurt somebody."

The last statement stopped Richard. "So it don't hurt if I blow my balls off?"

"There are rumors these are popular with cowpokes to rob stagecoaches. They're carried by the bandit, Joaquin Murrieta, and the teamster, Charlie Parkhurst. I can't say how they're used, but the Sierras are real bear country that calls for real firepower.

Richard looked down the muzzle, but the proprietor stopped him again,

"Don't do that either. You'll blow your head off."

Richard sighted along the barrel from the grip end and pointed the gun around the shop.

"Dammit man, don't point at anything you don't intend to shoot."

"Yes, sir."

Richard fingered the blue steel frame, the oiled walnut grip, the brass finger guard, and the cylinder. He spun the cylinder several times and noted the smooth action. He had to own this revolver at any price.

"We have a target in the back. Would you like to try this weapon?" asked the proprietor.

"Lead the way."

The proprietor lubricated the six chambers of the dragoon and loaded black powder, bullets, wadding, and percussion caps. He led Richard to the target about twenty yards behind the store, handed the loaded revolver to Richard, and ducked.

Richard raised the front sight in the general direction of the target and slammed the trigger. The report deafened him and a prodigious plume of smoke and flame shot out eight feet. The smoke smelled acrid and sour like steam with sulfur and a hint of urine. The recoil yanked the barrel into the air and almost out of his hands.

The bullet missed the target, ricocheted off the metal support, and disappeared. A crash of breaking glass came from the direction of the saloon next door. Richard stared at the aftermath and said. "Holy shit."

The gun shop proprietor exploded. "Have you fired a one of these before?"

"No sir, I have not."

They rushed next door through the swinging doors to see the damage. The bullet had lodged in the wall over the bar and they saw Bjorn slowly set his glass of whiskey down with shards of the window in it.

"That was special whiskey."

The bartender yelled out, "This is the third window this year. I'm going to send Josh after you" He ran up to Richard, who held the smoking Colt in his hand. He was followed by a gun fighter holding a drawn weapon and ready for action.

Richard yelled at top volume over the ringing in his ears, "My fault. Are you all right? I'll pay for the window." He scanned the group and saw no serious personal damage beyond an interrupted drinking match.

The bartender said, "Damn right, you will. You can't hit the broadside of a barn and don't yell—I hear you."

The gun store proprietor held up his hands. "Hold your horses. This young fellow needs a lesson in gun handling. Josh, you're the best shot here. Learn this man how to handle a revolver."

Josh confronted Richard with a flinty stare. He was compact at a hundred and thirty-five pounds, and aware of every move in the room. He looked like, and was, a gunslinger for hire but select in his choice of clients. The gunslinger kept order in the saloon and was only needed once or twice a day. He knew his firearms.

"If he aims that son of a bitch elsewhere."

Richard said, "You again. I'll be damned. Don't you ever sleep?"

The gun store proprietor was anxious to change the subject and said, "Follow me."

Bjorn and Kawai followed Richard and the proprietor to the target yard. "We all want to learn," said Richard. Josh followed well behind with his eyes never leaving the dragoon.

Josh said, "First, this gun is always loaded. You shoot where you point. We'll start at the very beginning.

"This long part is the barrel where the bullet comes out. It'll kill ya. Pick it up with the other end. You put your finger in here to pull the trigger when the barrel looks at the target."

Richard and Bjorn rolled their eyes in disgust.

Josh's hair-trigger temper exploded at their attitude. "Damn it, I heard you already caught a cannonball and missed a four-foot target at twenty yards. I don't want no more blood."

He started to draw his gun and plug Richard but turned away at the last moment.

"Load the gun to start." He opened the cylinder and counted the five live loads and one empty under the hammer.

"Never pull the trigger on an empty chamber. Hold the grip with both hands, gun hand high, but keep your trigger finger out of the guard. Feet and hips are shoulder width apart, and knees bent."

He demonstrated proper firing position.

"Face the target—not the saloon. Press the trigger and surprise yourself when it fires."

Richard said, "It surprised me all right."

They worked through a series of smaller weapons up to the mighty dragoons. Josh stood well behind the shooters and was coiled to jump behind a post for protection at any moment.

The bell on the *Swiftness* signaled all aboard, so Richard paid twenty-five dollars for a pair of Colt's 1848 Dragoons. Kawai declined.

As they were leaving, the proprietor said, "Gentlemen, you need a holster and loading materials to go with your new weapon. Here is a package of everything you'll need." He handed them gun kits.

"Practice several times a week to build your skill. It's a pleasure doing business with you." They shook hands.

They almost missed the *Swiftness* by taking time to strap on their new holsters, low and flapping on their hips. The fierce-looking guard bellowed to the Captain, "We got 'em let's go."

The Paladíns joined the stream of forty-niners upriver. Their combined excitement circled overhead like a whirlwind.

Haggard passengers on the *Swiftness* moved over for the Paladíns, their gold kit, ditty boxes, and pistol loading supplies. Identical gold kits decorated many other heaps of luggages, all under the watchful eyes of the armed guard, but there were no other pistol kits. The guard carried his own Dragoon in a holster low and ready for action, coming or going.

Everyone ignored a group of Chinese men in long pigtails and coolie hats who clustered around their own guard. They were as excited as the others were, but chattered in their singsong dialects that other passengers could not understand.

A guide in the bow regaled the passengers with stories funny or bawdy as they glided across San Pablo Bay toward the mouth of the Sacramento River.

> The Spanish explorer, Gabriel Moraga, named this river the 'Rio de Los Sacramentos back in 1808. We call it the Sacramento today.
>
> Have you heard the story of the lumberjack and the ax? He tripped over a rock by the lake and his ax flipped and sank. He sat on the rock frustrated.
>
> A gold fish came out of the lake and asked him, 'What's wrong?'
>
> The lumberjack said, 'I lost my ax in your lake.'
>
> 'I will get it,' said the fish. He returned with a gold ax,
>
> 'Is this it?'

'No, mine was plain and rusty, not gold.'

'Sorry,' said the goldfish and went back down.

'Maybe this is yours?' asked the fish as he returned with a silver ax.

'Nope, ain't mine.'

The gold fish plunged into the lake a third time and came up with his rusty ax and a wooden handle.

'Betsy, you're back. Thank you so much,' he said to the goldfish.

The gold fish said, 'You're an honest man,' and gave him the three axes.

Later, he came back to the lake with his wife. She tripped on the same rock and drowned. That goldfish came out and said,

'What's wrong, lose your ax again?'

'My wife. She drowned in the lake'

"That's not good. I get her out of the lake" said the gold fish and plunged into the water. It came out with a beautiful 20-year-old girl.

'Is this your wife?'

'Yes, she is my wife,' said the lumberjack.

'You surprise me. Last time I gave you with 3 axes for honesty but this time you're dishonest. This girl is not your wife. No more help from me.'

The lumberjack said, 'Last time you gave me three axes, right? And now, if I turn down the first woman you'll give me all three. I don't need three wives! One is plenty. Please stop at the first one."

The passengers chuckled at the story. "Let me tell you about the robber.

'The suspect was lined up with four other men to see if the victim could identify him. The sheriff asked each man to repeat the words, 'Give me all your money or I'll shoot'.

The man shouted, 'That's not what I said.' "

The men on the deck laughed while the women looked away irritated.

"Ladies, how do you turn soup into gold?

You add twenty-four carrots."

Nobody laughed.

Richard turned to his cloth sack emblazoned with "Jacob's Famous Gold Panning System." Did he find gold? I'll bet he makes more money mining the prospectors than he ever did mining the mountains."

He rummaged around in the kit and pulled out a book that he extended to Bjorn and Kawai. "Want to read up on it?" They both shook their heads and said, "I can't read."

Richard looked through the pages and read aloud, "Look at this chapter,"How to Find and Retrieve Gold.:

Here's what we do."

He sketched a diagram in the grime underfoot. "We want a trap in the stream bed that collects the gold. The water should run about six inches deep. We fill the pan with gravel, sling the rocks out, and scoop up the gold. Hell, that old drifter got gold from the street. We can get it from the river."

Bjorn said, "I'm glad to be back on the water."

Richard and Kawai agreed, and Richard said, "It is great to be a passenger instead of a sailor for a change."

Richard sat on a bench and brought his journal up to date.

> The Golden Gate Strait has submerged hazards and the bay is choked with abandoned craft of every description. What a mess.
>
> We Paladíns are on the Schooner Swiftness screaming at 4 knots up the Sacramento river. That trotting horse on shore is getting way ahead of us."

The Paladíns watched the shore slowly slide by—very slowly. They were impatient and Richard said, "I can trim those sails for speed. Let's go." The three adjusted the halyards and doubled their speed.

Said Paladíns were shocked when the *Swiftness* crew rejected their expert seamanship and attacked them. "Hands off my halyards, you stupid swabbies. What the hell are you doing?" yelled the captain.

Porter continued hauling the aft sail, pant, pant. "Any idiot can brace this canvas better than this." Without a word, the *Swiftness* mate threw Richard to the deck and pounded on him. Bjorn and Kawai each seized an arm of the mate and the heap of four husky men tumbled over the luggage in a wild brawl. They mixed twenty-three gold kits into one assorted mess.

"CRACK!"

The concussion deadened everybody's hearing and stopped the fighters cold. Gun smoke drifted from the guard's dragoon. A redheaded man pushed through the cloud and confronted the Paladíns.

"Stop this foolishness immediately," He was a thirty-year-old man who moved and spoke with authority. "What is the meaning of this?"

Hands on the *Swiftness* quickly restored the sails to their previous deliberate and safe trim, and threw the Paladíns a defiant frown. The *Swiftness* slowed down to her previous progress.

The captain pointed at Richard and said to the redheaded man, "This scum upset my sails. My rule is passengers keep your sweaty hands off my lines."

Richard said, "This ignorant crew can't sail a shrimp boat."

The captain was insulted. "It's a ship, not a boat, you jackass."

Richard said, "We just set a record in a vessel twice the size of this piss-ant-boat."

"There's new snags in this crooked river every day. Keep your hands to yourself or I'll jettison the bunch of you overboard."

The redheaded passenger laid down the law as the captain, mate, and Paladíns puffed at each other. "Keep your hands away from the sails, and you, captain, treat your passengers with respect. As you were."

Calm returned but not in time. The *Swiftness* ran aground and stuck in the mud. She listed to one side in the ebbing tide and filled with water. Sailors and a few passengers clung to the upper railing, while the captain rowed the others to shore. The Paladíns stayed because a sloping deck was normal for them. It was about midnight when the flood tide began to flow.

"All aboard," said the captain. He collected the passengers just before the tide lifted her clear of the sandbar. They glided into the channel several hours behind schedule.

At the bow, the leadsman measured the depth of the channel with a line and called out "Mark number two," two fathoms—safe draft for the *Swiftness*."

The mate was a salty old Mississippi river pilot who yelled out, "Say it right—the depth is Mark Twain."

Nature's abundance filled the dawn the next morning on the river. A large tributary joined the Sacramento from starboard and flocks of birds raised a cacophony in the cool air drifting downriver. The redheaded passenger stood at the railing with a sketchpad. He noted observations of the wildlife, described the river entering from starboard, and drew the currents with a clear hand.

Richard took careful notice of the man he remembered from the wager dinner. He had missed the introductions, since he and Chernov were in a visual confrontation, and did not know his name.

The man was about 30 years old and humming to himself. He wasn't tall at five feet eight, but had an intelligent face and bore himself with an erect military posture.

Richard walked over, "Begging pardon, sir that is an interesting sketch."

The military man extended his hand, "Thank you. I find it valuable to record an area that I oversee. That broad valley yesterday was from Sonoma. You should visit the hot springs up there."

Richard shook his hand.

"Look at these marshes," said the man as he waved to starboard. "That's the San Joaquin river that feeds all these striped bass and crappie. Wish I had my shotgun for that pheasant running along the ground."

Richard studied the schools of fish under the *Swiftness*. He itched for a fishing pole too.

The man at the railing said, "I envy those Pomo Indians who have time to fish, even with that raccoon stealing their catch behind their backs."

He looked directly at Richard and said, "What are you up to, besides re-rigging the Swiftness? The Captain is correct about the river, you know, but this ship runs aground frequently. Where are you headed?"

Richard answered, "We've heard about the gold finds at Sutter's Mill and plan to try our luck on land. I am Richard Porter and these are Bjorn Amundson and Kawai. We have this kit guaranteed to find gold."

Bjorn stretched out his hand, "Glad to meet you, sir."

Kawai followed, "Aloha Awakea."

Richard continued. "What is your name, if I may ask?"

"I am Lieutenant William Tecumseh Sherman of the United States Army. I am the AG (adjutant-general) to Colonel Richard Mason, governor of California. We are trying to maintain a little order between American Laws, Mexican laws, and no laws.

Bjorn said, "I'd say no laws for the most part."

"I commanded thousands of men to take Mexico City, but I am reluctant to manage a house lot in San Francisco. Good luck to you all."

The Lieutenant thought as he turned back to his notes, I like that young man even though he's a far cry from a disciplined West Pointer. The other two will never make soldiers.

Richard made a final entry in his journal.

> We met Lieutenant William Sherman today.
> He's my age and speaks well. I'll follow his good manners.

He stood ramrod straight as he bought a cup of hot coffee and fry bread for breakfast.

The *Swiftness* moored late at the quay, and Richard got the last copy of the morning's *Sacramento Transcript*. The front page proclaimed:

> In the previous month there arrived at this city 27 sailing vessels and four steamers. In total, they brought to our city about 1850 souls, essentially all headed upriver to search for their fortune in the gold fields. In the same month, there were opened four new mercantile stores, five bars, and one church.

Inside was a letter to the editor.

> There is a good deal of sin & wickedness going on here, Stealing, lying, swearing, drinking, gambling & murdering. There is a great deal of gambling carried on here. Almost every public house is a place for gambling, & this appears to be the greatest evil that prevails here. Men make & lose thousands in a night, & frequently small boys will go up and bet $5 or $10 — And if they lose all, go the next day and dig more. We are trying to get laws here to

regulate things but it will be very difficult to get
them executed.

The Paladíns looked at each other as they stood in the blazing sun, surrounded by their kits and boxes.

"Where do we go from here?"

An assortment of unsure men milled around a map on the corner of Seventh and J Streets in Sacramento. The Paladíns pushed into the crowd saying, "Maybe they know something."

Richard understood the diagram and said, "It's the local land grant of this area with the rivers and mining claims on it." He read a sheet with instructions on how to file a mining claim nailed alongside the map.

"But the map is in Spanish," said Bjorn.

"This area was owned by Mexico until Colonel Frémont took it over three years ago. They kept their maps in Spanish, of course, but the document filings are in English."

Bjorn studied the map for a long time. He understood the rivers and hills without reading the Spanish. "These mountains are like the Evje-Iveland district of Norway. My Viking ancestors searched the Otra river that runs through it for gemstones, and I worked that same river with my father."

He traced the American River upstream with his finger. "My gut says this is a gold trap where the creek comes in." Richard and Kawai went along since they had no mining experience at all.

The Paladíns overloaded a poor horse with their ditty boxes, gold kit, lead bullets, a little barrel of black powder, and a bag of provisions. They headed upriver along a trampled path that passed little pits of hope filled with miners.

Richard said of one pit, "Drunken mining like that is bound to fail if they don't drown first. Hope they don't have firearms around."

They trudged on through the dusty heat and Bjorn said of another pit, "Those two fellows are organized and digging gravel, but there ain't no gold in that stretch."

Bjorn as lead trudger said, "We're down to a game trail and on our own. Watch for dangerous animals and desperados. They jumped at every rustle, crack, and breeze whether a wren, a rabbit, a snake, a bug.

Richard halted them at the spot Bjorn picked; a creek tumbled into their pristine meadow. The Paladíns unloaded their horse and swatted his rump. The horse trotted back to Sacramento on his own.

Bjorn took charge of the mine set up. "That's a gold trap if I ever saw one. Here's a level spot for our workings, and I'll stake our claim over there. We'll pitch our tent above high water and hoist our food out of a bear's reach."

Richard stacked five stones into a cairn at each corner and shook his hands overhead in triumph. "Yes!"

Richard scooped a pan of wet gravel from the river bottom. He swirled it and the contents sloshed out. "That didn't work very well. I'll go a little slower." He swirled a second pan and the contents still sloshed out. The third time was no charm and Richard grew frustrated.

"Hell, you try it," and handed the pan to Bjorn. He scooped a pan and sloshed the gravel out leaving a little sand in the bottom. He scooped more water and rotated the sand again. They gathered round to examine the results.

Richard exclaimed, "Hot damn, there's little specks of gold. Congratulations, Bjorn, you're a miner." He slapped Bjorn hard on the back causing him to cough.

"I try, I try," Kawai said as he took the pan and stepped into the river. He stopped dead and his eyes got as round as the pan. "Kawai no like cold water," as he scooped a pan of gravel. He swirled and the gravel poured over the edge. He tried again with the same result. "I no like mine." He threw the pan down and stomped out of the river. "I make food, you make mine."

The Paladíns spent the afternoon learning to pan with modest results. Richard hustled to town and returned with a shovel the next day. "That Brannan General store demanded twenty-five dollars, but I had to pay it. I can see why he has to hide his store in Sutter's compound. Guard this with your life."

Bjorn was ecstatic. "Now we're mining."

The shovel sped up the operation as they traded duties from loading to panning to sifting. Their success was better than nine out of ten of the other miners, although they did not know it.

After a day, Richard took stock. "We have a show. I'll register a claim down in Sacramento.

He said, "Pound a stake at each corner by the cairns. Get as many gold traps as you can reach and some dry land. I'll write our names on the stakes when I get back."

Chapter 7—Becky

Richard wiggled his tired body into a bed of warm sand and leaned against a tree. The dancing flames of the fire hypnotized him as the smoke trails drove away the clouds of mosquitoes that appeared at dusk. Richard reminisced in a quiet voice to no one in particular.

"So we've got a nest egg of pay dirt for our efforts. That's good"

He breathed deeply and said, "This dome of stars at night makes up for the day of work. I love the fragrance of the native bushes and wildflowers in the breeze that comes from Devil's Peak."

Richard took his pipe from his mouth and made a quick out-in-out puff. All three Paladíns smiled at the rising smoke ring.

"California sure isn't Boston. I'll never follow a stinking horse through the mud and manure again. Had to grab that iron plow to keep the horseflies from carrying me off."

Kawai looked at Richard, "What is plow?"

"A wide knife that digs the dirt." He drew a diagram in the sand.

"I was an orphan in the house of a sea captain, my uncle. He indentured me out to a landowner that saw to my letters, but God did he work me . . . ."

Kawai wrinkled his face and said, "What is letters?"

"Letters is school. You had school didn't you?"

"I try read and write in missionary school—I forget at sea."

Bjorn stared into the embers of the fire and smoked his pipe in silence.

"Sunday after church we'd visit the Podwinkle farm next to ours. My master rode a fine horse as a man of distinction. I traipsed behind him on foot, but I was running to see Becky."

Bjorn looked up, "Aha! I knew there was a woman somewhere. I want to hear all about her."

"Becky Revere was indentured as a maid for seven years like me. I worked all week for a Sunday afternoon with Becky. My master would test a bottle of whiskey with that old Podwinkle in their rocking chairs on the porch. I can still hear the creak, creak, creak, as they confirmed the quality with another sip, and made double sure by the time they reached the bottom of the jug.

Bjorn and Kawai both said, "A sip of whiskey sounds good right now, but go on."

"The farmers forgot about Becky and me and the womenfolk gossiped and shared recipes. We explored the woods and meadows for hours . . . and hours."

His voice faded as he puffed clouds of smoke into the branches overhead and relived that fateful day.

"The farmer's sissy son left the garden gate open and the pigs got in. Those porkers threw dirt clods in the air, ate the onions, rooted out the carrots, and rolled in the dirt," like this. He tossed several rocks in the air for emphasis.

"Those pigs were in hog heaven, but the garden was history for the growing season of 1844."

Richard pantomimed the landowner. " 'You let the hogs eat my garden. Get over here and take your punishment like a man.' He snatched his whip off his fancy carriage and whoosh-crack, whipped my back. 'I'll show you a thing or two.' "

Bjorn said, "Sounds like my father in Norway."

"I said, 'Like hell you are' and ran off. I didn't mean to leave but I was fast from chasing his damnable horse, and running felt so good I couldn't stop. I was a strong nineteen years old and he was a fat sixty-four.

"I streaked out the gate and through the woods like a fox. The manure dropped from my boots with every stride. That is, until a fur ball between my legs tripped me head over my muddy heels. My head hit a rock and the world disappeared."

Kawai said, "I flip canoe in surf and lose head. It very short."

"I came to with a black cat purring on my chest. It was Morgan, whose broken leg I had mended months ago. I picked him up and we ran through the briers where a weasel couldn't go. That old farmer was slow but smart, and I could hear the thuds of his horse's hooves coming hard after me.

Bjorn said, "Did he get you?"

"There was no help for it . . . I ducked in the kitchen door at Podwinkle's farm. I ran up to Becky and hugged her, even covered in flour. 'One last kiss, I've got to leave.'"

"Only a kiss?" said Bjorn.

"Becky said, 'You can't leave. You're indentured like me.' We held each other like clams."

Richard looked at Bjorn and Kawai, "Haven't you two got someone special?" They shook their heads.

Bjorn said, "I wish I did. I gets real lonesome."

Kawai said, "I have lady friends in Hawaii. No here."

"I said a poem for Becky that I'd worked on for days,

My heart is full of tears at this farewell. You are beautiful, and I will miss you more than words can say.

"Becky pressed her warm body next to mine and sobbed on my shoulder. 'I can't stand five more years of mistress Rachael without you.'

"I dried her tears and watched her hustle around the kitchen to make a vagabond bag. She filled a flour sack with a loaf of bread, sugar-cured sausage, a kitchen knife for protection, and a tidbit for Morgan who pushed between us. We embraced as a horse skidded to a stop at the front door."

He demonstrated on Bjorn who said, "Keep the hell away from me, and tell your damn story."

"Morgan went in the sack too and out we fled. That flour sack bounced around and poor Morgan dug his claws in my back to hang on. I cut through the woods, hit a deer path, and we never looked back."

Richard puffed thoughtfully on his pipe and watched the campfire burn down. A cloud of mosquitoes stormed the Paladíns. Bjorn threw on another log while they swatted at the hungry mosquitoes.

"I swam across the Charles River with Morgan mostly high and dry. Search parties scoured the woods, but Becky taught me how to sneak. We made the outskirts of Boston in a day and half.

Kawai drifted off to sleep and Bjorn nodded.

"We crossed paths with a pair of fine ladies walking down the street. I heard one speak loudly to the other, 'Emily, don't look now but there is a hick from the sticks. We better turn back'. I tipped my hat and worked my way to the forest of masts at the waterfront."

Kawai woke up at the word 'waterfront' and said, "I like mast and ship. I know sail."

"I walked up to a schooner swarming with activity. 'Ahoy, need a hand?'"

"Come aboard, we're a man short. You look like a stout young chap who can handle the rigging. We sail tomorrow for Charleston."

"I've never been to sea."

"All men go to sea ignorant. They learn fast and you will too."

"Away to Charleston I went. My experience got me signed on *Agilis* for a run to Gibraltar. Here I am, still on the *Agilis*—or was."

Richard stood up with a flourish and said, 'Someday I'll ride a fine horse as a man of distinction in the parade,' like that old Podwinkle farmer."

Richard fixed on the image of him riding a fine horse as the dusk matured into night. Morgan curled up in their midst. The moon drifted through the trees and the fragrance of the chaparral blended with the pine and lulled the miners to sleep.

MacIntyre reread his instructions from Boston in the comfort of the cabin he had reclaimed from Otis.

> The firm of William F. Weld & Co., owners of *Agilis*, has made the decision to renounce all connections with the transport of human beings for sale, known as chattel slavery. This impacts the ownership of *Agilis* that was designed and operated as a slave ship.

> Notwithstanding the conversion to a merchantman in 1845, after proper disposal of the cargo, you are hereby directed to sell *Agilis* for the highest possible price in San Francisco. You shall remit all proceeds to the East Boston

Savings Bank for the account of William F. Weld, & Co.

We thank you for your loyal service.

He sighed and replaced the instructions in their envelope. Sitting alone in the cabin, some words slipped out of his mouth. "I have commanded *Agilis* well for four years and she has loved me back. This is not fair. At least I have met Thaddeus Leavenworth who set up that wager."

He thought to himself, Maybe I have a future after all since Leavenworth owns many commercial interests. We could purchase *Agilis* as joint owners. He was impressed with her looks, and a quick run to the Islands would pay her price, even without the wager.

MacIntyre returned the instructions to his desk and prepared to wrap up the voyage. He called through the open door, "Ferreri, please call the officers to my cabin."

He said, "Gentlemen, I recommend we stay at the Niantic Hotel. It is a whaling ship, Niantic of Nantucket, converted to a seafarers lodging. Her ex-captain related in Valparaiso that he sold her for salvage when her crew deserted. An entrepreneur grounded the hull over there and is constructing rooms above the deck as we speak."

They could clearly hear the scrape of the carpenter's saws and bang of the hammers as they echoed across the water from the beached ship.

Steward Jackson said, "I checked it out this morning. Two sleeping rooms rise above deck every a day when they can get lumber. Several layers of paint below cannot mask the smell of whaling and rooms are half price. The captain's cabin is a restaurant."

The group of *Agilis's* officers strode to the corner of Sansome street and mounted the gangplank toward the doors to the new lobby.

They pulled their rank and pushed inside through the throngs of men waiting. The proprietor inside looked up and said, "Shiver me tops'ls if my eyes ain't seein' that old seadog, Alex MacIntyre . . . a master since Noah was a boy." He shook MacIntyre's hand and welcomed the other seafarers as the first guests.

Macintyre said, "I last saw you fighting off a pirate attack in the South China sea. You're here now?"

"Where there is sea there is pirates. Had to hang up my anchor for good this spring. How the hell are you?"

"Needing a place to stay."

"I have rooms done yesterday. Care to see them?" The proprietor led the officers to the brand new quarters that smelled of fresh varnish like the lobby.

MacIntyre said, "Those beds look inviting. We will take them, even though they do not rock back and forth."

The proprietor said, "I've got more rooms below deck for half-price but you don't want them.

MacIntyre said, "We do not expect luxury yet, but someday . . . .",

Jackson said, "Wooden sidewalks are going down as fast as the establishments will pay for them. The *Niantic* is our best choice for rooms. Everything else in town is jammed with two or more men per bed.

"They hurt me inside and out," Richard said the next night. "Our dinghy was tied alongside. I was checking the lashings on a belaying pin when a deck boy dropped his marlinspike overboard. It punched a hole in the bottom of the dinghy and they sank together."

Bjorn said, "Accidents will happen. I've made plenty of mine."

"That first mate turned red in the face, 'You're a country hick from the sticks and a hellion to boot,' and other names I've forgotten. His stream of profanity gave me the idea he disliked me.

"You're a disgrace to every sailor on the deep blue sea, and those under it."

Kawai said, "They call me bad every time, too."

Richard said, "I told him, 'The boards in that boat are rotten and I didn't drop the spike. That boat is older than you.' it was the wrong thing to say. He screamed that,

You showed conduct prejudicial to good order and discipline,

Whatever that means,

And failures to look after the ship's equipment for which you were responsible.

That mate initiated me to the essentials of flogging.

Bjorn said, "Probably served you right."

"Did not."

"Probably did too."

"You know what they made me do? They beat me with a three-foot piece of rope and then said, 'Make this a cat o' nine tails, scumbag,' and posted a guard to tell me how."

Bjorn said, "I made one too, once . . . hated that thing."

"I unraveled two feet into three strands and unraveled each strand into three more for nine tails. I tied three knots in each tail for twenty-seven attack claws."

Bjorn said, "Just like mine."

"Still have it?"

"It went overboard first chance I got."

Richard said, "I kept mine with my dried blood on it. They tied me to the main mast and mustered the ship's company to witness my initiation."

Kawai's eyes opened big at the idea. Hawaiians rarely whipped anyone—they killed them.

"That big bosun went to town. Hell, that old farmer beat me harder just for fun"

Richard stood up and swung a branch to demonstrate the bosun's skill with the cat o' nine tails.

But the bosun warmed up good. "Whoop! . . . pow . . . , pow. Crack . . . bite, wuh-psssh-sting, whooot . . . sting, woosh . . . thud-missed, . . . count to fifteen; whop! . . . wait. That got old after twelve lashes for the conduct and twelve more for the boat part."

He whisked his imaginary cat in rhythm with his story.

"The crew scrambled up the rigging for a better view. When they were done counting and missing a couple, the mate poured seawater over the twenty-six stripes on my back. Damn, that hurt worse but they claim it rinses the wounds and helps them heal. Seemed to work."

Bjorn said, "You still have a big mouth."

"My mouth stayed shut all the way down to Rio. I spent my time carving Becky's face into my ditty box. Garang Wek, a black sailor carver, taught me."

Kawai said, "I see face beautiful. You lucky."

"I look at her every morning inside my ditty box. "She's the only good thing left out of that landowner. We indentured servants were treated worse than the slaves carried in this ship. Apprentices are temporary and disposable but slaves are expensive and permanent."

His lonesome mind pictured Becky's round twinkling eyes and his thoughts returned to Boston, I hope you are well.

The smoke from his pipe drifted through the trees and formed a big smile.

Kawai asked, "Where you get cat?"

Richard began, "Morgan has a story too, and picked up his cat."

Old Dobbin the plow horse stepped on a sleeping cat. The screech spooked him and he kicked that cat to kingdom come." He swung Morgan gently in an arc.

Morgan said, "Meow," and went back to purring.

"The cat limped away on three legs. I fixed his broken leg with a splint and he's followed me ever since. This is Morgan, the seafaring cat. We've been to Charleston, merry old England and the Rock of Gibraltar."

Richard kissed Morgan and stroked his fur. "He has better sea legs than I do. We are here to make our fortune on land that we missed at sea."

They lay back in the dark and Morgan curled up by Richard's feet with a paw over his ankle and purred.

Evening harmony wound up the day's work. Richard watched a chipmunk scurry home to its burrow and Kawai marveled at a raccoon emerging to dig through their trash. The Paladíns receded into their private reveries.

Richard skipped through the woods hand in hand with Becky. Kawai won the Wa'a championship paddling a fast canoe.

Bjorn blew a cloud of smoke through the latticework of branches that glowed in flames of the fire. His rising puff imagined a Viking longship departing a Norwegian fjord. He shook his head and drew a halting breath.

The night was mellow, rabbit meat on a stick sizzled at the fire, the chaparral was pungent, and the coffee was hot. A coyote howled at the the moon, "Whoop . . . aooo, whooo, yip, yip, yip."

Bjorn started in a low voice, " . . . I . . . was born in Drammen, Norway . . . down the fjord from Oslo. My father was a miner man and not rich . . . between a karl and a thrall slave in Viking times. He told stories of our ancestors while we splashed the rivers together."

Richard said, "You're right at home here, huh?"

"I'm not used to the sun yet . . . . My ancestors collected gems for the Viking leaders. The high Jarls were quite vain, you know, and flaunted their jewelry every chance they got, especially their amber."

Kawai said, "What is gems?"

"Pretty rocks that make people crazy, especially women. My father told me the story of our ancestor, Bjorn the Brave. He led the berserker formation in the attack on the fortress of Chartres in the year 911. That was in Frankia, across the ocean. It was the first battle the Vikings lost.

"Hrolf the Walker known as Rollo, the leader of the Vikings, blamed my ancestor. They outlawed Bjorn the Brave and banished him to the remote Otra river valley in Norway. He was lucky to escape the blood eagle."

Richard said, "Bad happens, and it ain't fair." He shook his head.

"My ancestor Bjorn's eyes spotted gemstones in the river like our nuggets. He smuggled them over to Frankia, where the market was better. Our family is haunted by his punishment even today.

"What is haunted?" said Kawai.

"Haunted is when a spirit visits you from your past."

Kawai said, "My father come last night. He say, 'Kawai, you no miner man'."

Bjorn continued, "My father sent me to Hawaii on a whale ship. It was my first time out of Norway and the heat almost killed me. I've circled the world, drunk good rum, met nice ladies, and seen more than you knew was there. My parents died while I was gone."

Richard said, "I lost mine before I left Boston."

"Some Viking I am. I favor rocks over the waves. This gold claim suits me and I'll make a big strike before long. The gods have said so."

The Paladíns drifted into their fantasies of what could be and might have been. They slept as the campfire burned to ashes and the raccoon stole the last piece of meat off the stick by the fire.

Kawai burrowed into his bed of warm sand without a sound and was too self-conscious to share his Hawaiian story in English.

Chapter 8—Boudica

Richard roused the sore and groggy Paladíns out of bed. "Time to get going."

The day promised to be another in a stream of hot workdays. Unproductive, discouraging, workdays. The sun breaking over the mountains blazed more fiercely and the river ran higher than yesterday.

Richard's lanky arms ached under his sunburned neck. His forehead showed white under his sweaty leather hat. The rest of his face was red and chapped, and his eyes stung from the dripping sweat and reflected sunshine. The sparkle was gone from his eyes.

Bjorn's fair Norwegian skin, that was not adapted to the California heat, was blistered. His flowing blond hair hung down in grimy snarls.

Kawai was comfortable in the sun, but he hated the cold water.

Morgan with his black fur was asleep under a bush on the cool ground.

Richard's frustration erupted like the Clear Lake Volcanic Field a hundred miles to the west when he saw Bjorn standing motionless in the river and Kawai sitting on the bank, "Get to work," and he threw a rock at Bjorn.

Bjorn said, "Work yourself!" and threw the pan at Richard. It bounced off his naked shinbone and left a gash.

Richard said, "That hurts like hell, you bastard."

He charged into the river and stabbed his head into Bjorn's gut. They plunged into the flowing water. Bjorn arched to throw Richard off but he clutched him with a new hold.

They wrestled in the river like the amateur scufflers they were, and neither could gain an advantage. They rolled over and over like brawling alligators.

Kawai laughed wildly watching the wrestlers thrash into deeper water and drift downstream. Richard was disgusted when Bjorn screamed as he pissed on himself in panic, "I can't swim".

Richard screamed in his face, "Stand up, the water's only ten inches deep."

Bjorn stumbled to his feet on the rocky bottom and he was upright. He jumped onto Richard's back and tumbled them back down onto the wet rocks.

Kawai had enough. He splashed into the fray like the trained wrestler he was. "No fight, no good, nobody hurt."

Richard, dripping, clenched his long arms around both Kawai and Bjorn, and all three toppled into the river in a three-way match on the rocks. Kawai twisted over the top of the other two. The Paladíns brawled to exhaustion.

By unanimous agreement, they sprawled their panting wet bodies on the bank, mostly out of the water. Morgan came to Richard's side and licked his face in concern.

Bjorn looked at Richard and said, "You're wrinkled like a grandpa."

Kawai said, "No, make like dead fish."

Their muscles ached ankle to shoulder from the rocks and their stomachs growled from hunger.

Richard thought, God, I'm tired. I guess this is my fault too . . . ."

He hung his head a moment but his anger flared up again. "You sons of bitches are the laziest things I ever saw. You're out to get me."

He snatched his revolver from its holster hanging within easy access on a stump. "I hate you." He waved the gun overhead and fired at the blazing sun. The other two dove for cover behind the bushes and flattened themselves against the ground.

Richard's glare fell on the gold pan. "It's your fault," and he shot a hole in the pan. It flipped in the air and his next shot dented the bloody rim and ricocheted into the trees. "I never want to see you again." His third shot missed the pan in the cloud of smoke, and almost creased the heads of Bjorn and Kawai, even though he neglected to aim.

Bjorn seized Richard's gun arm and Kawai the other. They slammed him to the ground and sat on him.

"I'm done with this," said Richard pounding the dirt with his head. "I spin circles day and night, our yield is piss poor, and we can't buy a dead chicken at Brannan's store. I'm tired and cold and hot and hungry. My arms hurt." He lay defeated.

Kawai said, "Me too."

Bjorn responded, "This ain't cold for Norway but you bet I'm hungry. Can we let you up now?"

Their wet bodies shivered as drops of water evaporated in the dry heat. Their wet clothes shrank where they were tossed over the bushes—they hadn't been so clean in weeks. The trousers would no longer stand up on their own with the sweaty salt washed out.

Bjorn chuckled. "You got me a good one."

Kawai smiled with a little laugh, "I like."

Richard raised a grin, broke a smile, and erupted in laughter. "Damn, we're getting a little teched in the head and I feel better already."

"Speak for yourself," said Bjorn.

They playfully punched each other, friends again.

Out came their pipes and they bonded over satisfying puffs.

The sun sank oh so slowly to the western horizon. A cool evening breeze from the mother Sierra Nevada's slopes carried the scent of sage and pine through the camp. The cool moon replaced the sun and sent the daytime critter's home to their nests and burrows. Crickets serenaded the night and wakened the nocturnal critters.

The man in the moon silhouetted a coyote who called to him. "Yip, yip whoop-poo, Yip, yip, whooo-ooo." A chorus from the pack on the hill howled the refrain and a lone dog barked in the distance. The smoke from their pipes drove away the mosquitoes and life was mellow again.

Richard opened their money bag and studied the list of their expenses. "Our bank account is not long for this world without a big strike. But I haven't heard of a big strike. Have you?"

"There's bragging in the bars, but a drifter under a dirty hat looks the same as a man with a mine. A wise man keeps his mouth shut," said Bjorn.

Richard said out loud, "What now for us?"

Bjorn turned philosophical the next afternoon after they quit for the day. "Sunburned though we are, we've got a sweet spot on the river."

He drew an X in the sand. "Here's our claim, there's our gold pan with a hole, and that book that guarantees gold, even if I can't read it 'cause Richard said so. I'm at home and that stick plugs the hole. My pan works."

Richard was not philosophical. "My back burns under my shirt. This cold water hurts my feet, the pan weighs a ton by the end of the day, and my biceps are cramped up. We slave all day to eat beans for supper."

Kawai sighed. So did Bjorn.

"I thought following a horse was hard, but it's nothing like swinging a pan all day."

Kawai faced Richard and Bjorn, "Kawai no like cold water. I want warm waves and no flies." He slapped a big horsefly on his arm where a red welt itched. "Kawai be sad and tired and cold."

Richard added, "These flies are as thick as in Boston but smaller and meaner." He hit a gnat on his face, "Take that, you bastard." It left a streak of blood.

"I miss the cool blue ocean too. Bjorn?"

"I saw you buy that old sextant and manual in San Francisco. Seems to me your heart is down there too."

"Your heart is in rocks man. You like it here."

"I guess so."

Richard came to a decision. "I give my share to Bjorn so he keeps going. I quit."

"Kawai quit too."

"Follow your miner's heart, Bjorn, and you'll make it. We'll head downstream and beg, steal, or borrow a meal on the way." Richard handed a bag of coins to Bjorn from his ditty box.

"Maybe *Agilis* has a couple of open berths since the whole crew is panning the rivers up here."

Kawai gave his tobacco and another bag of coins to Bjorn.

Bjorn sat in silence while he gathered his thoughts. "Mates . . . I've come to value our friendship. I'm sorry you're going, but Godspeed. I will pay you back someday . . . when I can."

Richard and Kawai gave Bjorn a quick hug and headed out with discouraged hearts toting their ditty boxes on their shoulders. Morgan, the cat, followed with his tail dragging on the ground.

Bjorn sat alone on the bank with his head between his legs for a long time. The night shrank around his huddled figure as the campfire burned through the last of its firewood. He let the mosquitoes attack his skin unmolested and their buzz drowned out the crickets.

Bjorn surrendered to waves of weariness and fell asleep in a trance.

Floating in a drowsy world between sleep and wake, Bjorn's eyes jerked open in terror to a thunderous roar. He faced a vision of a bear warrior, eight feet tall. The ancient Viking shouted at him, "Bjorn Amundson, you are a Viking. Watch me."

Bjorn shuddered in terror and sat up.

The vision howled like a wild beast that echoed the length of the fjord five times. He gnawed the iron rim of his shield; he foamed at the mouth; he was a berserker ready for battle. The berserker held high a shield, a spear, a bearskin, boundless courage.

"I am your ancestor for nine hundred years. My name is the same Bjorn that you venerate in our history. We Bjorn's are immune to steel and fire. Know the spirit of the mountain and the river, and they will protect you."

With a mighty war cry, he engaged the battle. An enemy attacked from his right and Bjorn the warrior took him down with a single blow. Two jumped from the left and the warrior twisted the one into the other, and penetrated both with one mighty sword thrust. He fought the entire day with boundless energy. The enemy fled and he mounted a rock victorious. He chanted for the world to know,

"Til Valhalla, Odin owns you all."

He turned to the modern day miner and ordered, "

"A Bjorn never gives up. You win the battle."

The fjord became a flowing river in the moonlight and the vision faded into the trees. The miner remembered the stories from his father when they hunted gems in the river Otra. He awoke a new man, swatted away the mosquitoes, stirred the fire, and prepared for the dawn.

"I will make it," he shouted to the woods.

That same night and miles downstream, Richard wrote a different story in his journal.

I have failed again. The farm ended in a vegetable stew. The sea brought me skills and poverty. I've added a failure at gold panning. Take me back, Neptune, and I'll try to avoid 'conduct prejudicial to good order and discipline'. On to Sacramento with Kawai."

He stopped at the claims office in Sacramento to transfer their ownership, and arranged for the clerk to send a copy upstream to Bjorn. They bought tickets and waited on a street bench for the schooner, *Swiftness*.

Bjorn worked his claim with renewed enthusiasm after his vision, but his luck turned bad with the loss of Richard and Kawai. Alone during his long evenings he argued with himself about anything that came to mind.

"Bjorn, you've had bad luck since they left."

"I know . . . and the work is more."

"What are you going to do about it?"

"I'll find the bodacious outcrop that spawned our, . . . err my, . . . claim."

"Do it."

"But there might be dangerous wildlife."

"Be careful."

"I'm all alone."

"Be twice as careful."

"I'll leave tomorrow."

The next morning, he wrapped his bandanna around a sandwich of elderberry jam on sourdough bread along with a can of beans, slung it over his back, and headed upstream. He scrutinized every naked rock and explored every side draw.

"What are you looking for?"

"The mother lode."

"What in the hell is the 'mother lode'?"

"A vein of oxidized quartz with gold."

"Okay, but where is this thing?"

"Gold is where you find it."

"You make me tired."

"Shut up."

"Fine."

His sweat from the heat of the day sent a powerful warning odor through the woods that a human was coming.

The scattered footprints he followed dissolved into a game trail used by animals shorter than Bjorn's six feet. He scraped away piles of brush and fought his way through tangled branches that scratched his blistered skin to expose likely rock outcrops. He burst through two manzanita bushes into a meadow and sat down to rest.

Since the deer bed in the spot of shade was still warm, Bjorn lay down in the trampled grass. He succumbed to the drowsiness of the hot day and fell into a deep negligent sleep.

In Bjorn's head, the Viking vision resumed where it left off.

The ancient berserker bear warrior shouted his arrival on the battlefield with a loud thunderous cry, 'Away man . . . .' He gnawed the edge of his shield, and raised his seax fighting knife to attack his nearest opponent when . . .,

But the vision was only about berserkers, and never mentioned living breathing bears. Bjorn opened his groggy eyes, but did not see the furry snout emerge from the chaparral bushes and sniff the air. If he had been awake, he would have seen the snout rise seven feet high when a grizzly bear stood on her hind legs for a better sniff of his jam and him. Bjorn was only collateral food.

He missed those black eyes staring impassively and the dark nostrils flaring at the end of the muzzle. He only woke up when the hungry bear exploded and threw clods of earth into the air with her paws. He did not have time to react when, with a muffled snort, she charged across the meadow and pinned him to the ground with her front paws. He remembered grizzlies ate their victims alive, and didn't kill them first.

The bear flipped Bjorn onto his stomach by wrenching his arm high with her jaws. She slashed his scalp with her claws to grab the bandanna where the forbidden treats were. Bjorn instinctively curled into a fetal position and played dead with his hands locked behind his neck.

The sow shredded the bandanna to get the elderberry jam. She nipped a bite of buttock for a meat appetizer that felt like a sledgehammer blow. She stopped for a few seconds to lick the jam off her chops and bit again.

The second attack was worse. He felt himself pulled up by teeth hooked through his butt. The dirt slammed into his face as she squashed and pinned him. Bjorn was in the worst pain he could remember, and the stench was as bad as the bite.

He locked eyes with the bear over his shoulder. "Get off," he screamed into the face not a foot away. The bear released his butt and clamped her jaws through his back muscles. He yelled "Yaaaahooooh . . . ," and tried to stand, but she forced him into the dirt to get a better grip. Without letting open her mouth or paws she shook him sideways.

"Lee. . .tttt. . .me gggg. . gggo."

His blood spattered everywhere and even blinded the animal's face for a second. The bear only growled and shook him again.

Unseen by either, a wizened old prospector burst from the same chaparral. He held a double-barreled 12-gauge shotgun. With a quick aim, he fired a slug into the bear's left front shoulder. The bear dropped Bjorn and charged the skinny prospector instead.

He was ready with the other barrel. By great luck, it entered the grizzly's open mouth, knocked a tooth out, and lodged in her spine. The bear crumpled on the prospector's boot snarling and snapping, but unable to walk. The prospector backed up a safe distance and waited . . ., and waited . . ., some more . . . .

He drew his Colt Dragoon and watched her. She seemed down for good but he wanted to make sure. He fired three well-placed shots into vulnerable points and she lay still. "It was you or me, honey, and it's you today. I'm sorry but that's life in the mountains."

He turned his attention to the bleeding miner who was struggling to sit up. "Lucky I come along, young fellow. You're dumb to be alone and dumber to tote food into bear country. That's how you is food yourself.

Bjorn moaned and felt his heart beating like a racehorse. Between panting and sweating, he said, "Where did that animal come from? I was taking a nap."

"Let's look at you. Hold still and keep your face down."

The prospector turned Bjorn over. He groaned and said, "I'm all numb . . . can't feel a thing."

"Hmmm. Your backside is gonna be sore but it'll heal. Ain't no broken bones. Got to wash off that scratch 'cause the rotten carcass she was eating will corrupt your ass if'n we don't."

Bjorn said, "I'm thirsty. Got a drink of water?"

The prospector scooped a cup of water from the river.

"Much obliged . . . she called me dinner."

"Ain't wrong, pard. Take a nip of whiskey while I sews up them gashes." He pulled a flask from his pocket and cradled the bloody head. With a cough and a shiver, Bjorn took a long welcome swallow.

The prospector retrieved a needle and thread from the pack on his mule, Jasper, who was trembling with terror in the trees. He washed out the wound and sewed up the gashes like a sailor mending a torn sail. He was a runaway sailor from long ago and sewed sails and skin the same way.

Bjorn was stoic through gritted teeth during his repair. When his back was finished, he said, "There's the front part too." The prospector sewed up the front bites.

"Good as new, I reckon. Lucky thing I stumbled across that bear eating the dead elk. I was loading my shotgun when you yelled through the bushes. I watched the two of you put on quite a show." He laughed.

With Bjorn fixed up, the old prospector skinned the hide off the carcass. He kept the head minus a tooth and the claws with their foot pads. He'd seen vaqueros stretch cow hides on the ground to dry so staked the bearskin the same way. The grizzled old mountain man laid strips of bear fat on Bjorn's stitches for healing.

"Bear meat's rank tast'ng in the fall but it keeps you alive." He cut strips of bear meat all afternoon and dried them to jerky over a campfire. "We'll eat this old bear and have us a grand time. Turnabout is fair play.

Bjorn passed out cold instead.

"After you gets around a bit, we'll git you a dog for protection. They is running loose in these hills and you need a good one."

Groggy from whiskey and lack of sleep, the prospector and Bjorn lit their pipes and puffed clouds of smoke. The prospector daydreamed of past times while Bjorn throbbed. The nicotine dulled his pain a little.

The prospector stirred, "So you was walking along the stream? You wouldn't be looking for a gold trap, by any chance?"

"How'd you know? My claim is worked out. I thought up in the mountains I might flush out a strike. The river has to come from a mother lode sooner or later."

"Let's jawbone about that over some grub."

"It's the least I can do, my friend."

Bjorn painfully scavenged his shredded pack for leftovers. The elderberry jam sandwiches were gone. He wiped slobber from the little loaf of bread and handed it and the can of beans to the prospector.

Bjorn said, "My ancestors back in Norway hunted gemstones in the river. Gold is the same but it's more and harder work."

The old prospector said, "You ain't wrong son. I've rambled these hills for neigh onto thirty-four odd years. I've had good finds and no finds. The good ones played out and the years is creeping up on me."

He turned his head to the side and muttered, "—but they's a find upstream."

Bjorn's ears caught the mumble, "Show me where it is?"

"Well now . . . that is a big thing you're asking. You want my wife, too?" He leaned back and blew smoke rings into the still night air for a long time. "Haven't endured a wife since a long time. Did once, but she was nothing but trouble. Had to leave like I jumped that ship. Been me, myself, and I ever since."

Bjorn felt he had insulted the prospector by a mistake he did not understand. His body throbbed under the stitches. He puffed on his pipe to let the nicotine dull the pain and took another swig of whiskey. The columns of rising smoke drifted through the trees and drove away most of the hungry mosquitoes.

The prospector cleared his throat and stood up. "I have to talk to Jasper."

He strolled to his ancient mule and rubbed her ears. "Jasper, you and me been together a long time."

"Ehyonk, ehyonk," hollered Jasper and wiggled her ears.

"Up and down the mountains, cold and hot, wet and dry we been. We is gettin' old together." He hugged her neck.

"What say we ask this whippersnapper to hitch up with us? He'll do the digging and we'll separate the gold. I reckon we can work together."

Jasper twisted her ears and nodded her head up and down. "Hee haw, ehyonk."

"You sure?"

"Ehyonk." Jasper nodded again.

The prospector walked back to Bjorn. "I reckon you heard Jasper. She says me and her and you heads upstream tomorrow."

They slept the night, with Bjorn taking a nip of whiskey now and then.

Breakfast was the last crumbs of bread to scrape out the residue in the bean can. They washed it down with dense black coffee. The little caravan headed upstream, making warning noises against bears. The country got wilder and rougher by their midday stop. The river changed from flowing to rapids as they ascended the foothills of the Sierras toward Chief Granite Peak.

The prospector pointed at the stream, "Grab a handful of that and tell me what you see"

Bjorn reached into the cold water and scooped a handful of gravel. He swirled it in the pan. "Look at that! . . . full of gold. Never seen anything like it."

The prospector looked around to be sure there were no eavesdropping ears attached to man or beast. "We follows that cut to them bare rocks."

Bjorn hobbled in the direction of the prospector's hand, twisted with arthritis, to a small rocky outcrop.

"Whoa! There are two nuggets right there in the rock. And more, and here's another."

"Yup. More'n I can dig out. We stakes our claim on this outcrop and down to the riverbank for water and the placer."

Bjorn hobbled to the prospector and shook his gnarled hands, pain forgotten. The Prospector hugged Jasper's long ears. "Hee haw, hee haw".

"Mighty obliged partner . . . guess we are partners aren't we," Bjorn said.

The Prospector changed the subject. "Coming back to what I said, methinks you need a dog for protection. A good dog warns you of nefarious critters of the two-legged variety and four-legged variety. They is both thick in these parts, but so is stray dogs wanting an owner."

They, meaning a painful Bjorn, pounded stakes at the corners of their claim. Bjorn was pounding the final agonizing stake when he heard a soft whimper under a leafy branch.

He lifted the branch to reveal a trembling clump of fur hoping for a friendly voice. Buried in the leaves was a badly mauled dog. She had a beautiful tan, red, and black coat that was soaked with dried brown blood. Two little puppies about four weeks old lay dead with their tiny mouths on her dry teats. A bright-eyed third puppy suckled a dribble of milk from the final teat.

The mother dog whined and raised her head and pointed ears. She bestowed her final ember of life on Bjorn to plead with her loving eyes, "Will you care for my puppy? She is my last one and I can do no more."

She licked the puppy's face with a supreme effort, folded a bushy tail over the little one, and laid her weary head down with a long sigh. Her faithful brown eyes closed for the last time. The woods were silent.

Bjorn picked the little girl up, and she suckled his finger with a tiny squeal. He rubbed her back and slipped her in his shirt to keep warm. The prospector and he walked to town and bought tins of dried milk, a modern alternative to a cow.

Back in camp, he made a portable pen with a tin water cup and a plate for food. He added an old shirt to lie on and made a shelter from the sun. The prospector nodded approval at every step.

Boudica

The puppy looked at Bjorn and licked his hand. Bjorn said, "What is your name pretty one? You are a little Boudica like that Celtic Queen that fought off the whole Roman army. She gave 'em hell just like you." The puppy wagged her little tail.

Bjorn buried Boudica's faithful family in a simple grave under a shield of stones to ward off coyotes. He marked the spot with a cairn.

Boudica grew rapidly on the mother's lode of milk and love and developed a strong instinct for dangers around the workings. She licked Bjorn to sleep every night as they shared each other's warmth.

Chapter 9—Pomo Indians

The Paladíns, less one, heard a familiar voice from across Sacramento Street as they sat on the bench watching the newcomers pile off *Swiftness*.

"Hello friends. Good to see you again," William Sherman beamed as he strode up. "Where are you headed?"

"Down river to our ship. How have you been?" said Richard.

"Where is your companion? Three of you came upriver with me."

"Bjorn is making a mine. He has a knack for it and we don't. How are you, Lieutenant Sherman?"

"William, not Sherman, since I'm here as a civilian. I am surveying new streets for Sacramento and picking up a little extra money on the side. My lieutenant's pay does not cover my expenses.

Richard said, "Understand that."

"Sacramento is growing by leaps and bounds, but my rod man and chain man deserted last night. I would be much obliged if you would help me finish laying out these streets. It will take only a few days and I can pay you each five dollars a day."

"We've never surveyed but we learn fast and will try, if that is acceptable," said Richard.

"Gentlemen, I have spent my life training men since West Point. I can train you if you can learn."

They shook hands. William taught them the basics of surveying, which is to say the grunt work. "You two are the fastest learners I've trained. Will you stay on?"

"Afraid not, but thanks for the offer. We headed to *Agilis* when we finish your streets."

William looked disappointed for a moment before he regained his military composure.

As they wrapped up the third day, Richard watched William operate the transit and wondered how it worked. "Can I see your surveying instrument?".

"It is called a transit. Stand here and look through this telescope. Keep both eyes open and line up on the stake Kawai just hammered in the ground. Turn the top a quarter turn on this index and motion Kawai to line up again. Place a stake and you have a square corner."

"Very interesting," thought Richard, as he filed the information away for future reference.

At the end of their five-day's work, Richard and Kawai shook Williams's hands in a friendly exit.

Kawai said to Richard, "Now we go ship. Yes?"

"We join the *Agilis*—I hope."

They boarded *Swiftness* with their gear.

William Sherman finished his survey maps and filled in the name of a new street—*Porter Way*.

Richard Porter and Kawai journeyed down the Sacramento River without the enthusiasm they journeyed up with, but kept their hands far away from the rigging. The guard remembered their interference that ran the *Swiftness* aground on the way up and eyeballed their every move like a hawk.

Richard and Kawai stood at the gunwale watching the riverbanks and an occasional shoal arise at the bow and flow past the stern. "You've been quiet today. Tell me about yourself," Richard said.

Kawai was uncomfortable in English but could get by. He was silent for a while and Richard thought he was misunderstood, but Kawai started, "Ko`u ka makuahine, my mother, is Hawaii for forty year. Today, I have twenty year. Ko`u ka Makua kāne, my father, has forty-four year. I swim with two year and row with many year. I best in Oahu and many women like me. Good, yes?"

Richard looked at him with interest. He had never thought about Kawai even having parents. "Very good indeed, my friend."

"I row many faster than this boat. I good canoe row man. You come with me." Kawai puffed out his chest and thumped it several times. He thumped Richard too. You make good row man."

Kawai shivered in the cool morning air and chattered to Richard, "Kawai be cold. No warm no more."

Richard looked at him and said, "We'll leave Swiftness in Vallejo, and you'll like where we go."

At a stopover in Vallejo, Richard and Kawai bought stagecoach tickets to the Boyes Hot Springs. The stage company stored their ditty boxes in a back room since the coach was full of passengers and baggage.

A red-skinned man exuding an air of natural authority waited with them for the stage. His clothes were ordinary but he wore a beautiful headband and walked with a distinctive limp.

Richard struck up a conversation. "Hello there. Looks like we're all going to Boyes Hot Springs."

The gregarious Pomo Indian opened up in fluent English. "I'm returning home from selling a load of baskets in San Francisco. We Pomo are famous basket makers, and people always need them for picnics or storage. Our baskets are so tight they can carry water.

Richard said, "Baskets interest me. We made lightship baskets on Nantucket Island where I'm from too. Couldn't meet the demand."

The Indian continued, "My men make baskets for fish, bird traps, and babies. Women weave others to cook food, store acorns, and the great Kuksu.

Richard held out his hand, "Glad to meet you."

"I am Anthony Kinter. Let me show you around Boyes when we get there."

He turned to Kawai with interest, noting his Hawaiian complexion. "I am happy to meet you. Are you a Kanaka?" as he shook his hand.

Kawai beamed at being recognized and said, "Kawai of Hawaii. You good man I think."

Anthony was outgoing and they soon made jokes and shared tall stories back and forth like long time companions.

They looked up to the rumble of the stagecoach from Sonoma announcing its arrival with squeaks, creaks, clanking chains, hoof beats, and horses blowing. It rattled to a stop and disgorged nine stiff grumpy passengers.

Richard, Kawai, and Anthony boarded first and wedged their three stout hips into the narrow back seat. Three other travelers packed the front seat that was even narrower. Their interlocked knees filled the leg space, and a security bar on either side kept them in.

Somehow three more passengers climbed by hook and crook onto a mid-bench across the security bars and sat on their legs. The three friends and six strangers took turns breathing the hot air as the four horses heaved in the traces and pulled away for Boyes.

Their mental discomfort overtook their physical discomfort when they read a sign at the edge of town.

YOU WILL BE TRAVELING THROUGH
INDIAN COUNTRY AND THE SAFETY
OF YOUR PERSON CANNOT BE
VOUCHSAFED BY ANYONE BUT GOD.
Passengers are recommended to carry
their personal rifles, shot-guns, or
revolvers, heavily charged."

Richard looked at Anthony with a scowl, "Are you a safe Indian to ride with?" The passengers gasped and looked away, down, or out.

The Pomo glared back and let out a shrieking undulating war cry by clapping his mouth, "Wahoo waoo". The lone lady passenger fainted, and the men unsuccessfully reached for their revolvers under their close-packed bodies. Richard and the Pomo glared in each other's faces, nose to nose, and growled as they punched their shoulders. The passengers were tense on high alert.

Richard's mouth began to turn up at the edges, then Anthony's followed. Their four eyes melted from sparks to sparkles and they burst into howls of laughter. They slapped the tops of their thighs in delight and wiggled their shoulders.

Anthony said, "That sign is a joke to sell guns. We Indians haven't attacked a soul in years. The real danger is to us Pomo Indians from those weapons they sell to the newcomers." He beamed at his prank.

The other riders chuckled at the joke and joined the merriment. The woman regained consciousness and snorted, "That was not funny and you look dangerous to me. Humph." She stared out the window and sulked.

They jostled the twenty-six hot miles to Boyes Hot Springs, where the sound of laughter and splashing water signaled they had arrived.

What a scene. Entire Pomo Indian families, naked as jaybirds, leaped in the hot water. Children of every color and nationality made clouds of spray and noise. An army soldier in shorts doused another, while vaqueros squirted children and practically drowned a swimming dog.

Richard and Kawai stacked their clothes in a pile and dove into the natural hot spring pool with a rebel yell, "Yee-aay-eee wa-woo-woohoo!"

Kawai played a fish. He swam deep, made a porpoise leap, and pounded his feet on the water like a beaver. He watched Richard streak through the water like a shark and bump only half the bathers. They bumped back and laughed. The swimmers wore out the warm water with their high spirits.

Kawai grinned, "I be get warm. I like." He loved Richard's response, "Warm is the word of the day. Thank you, God."

A warmed-up Kawai spied a Pomo Indian family and said to Richard, "They look like Hawaii like me with no clothes." He swam over to be friendly.

"Aloha. I like you, you like me. I be Honolulu."

The father of the family paddled to his group and looked at Kawai with a puzzled look. "¿Qué dice Amigo." (What do you say friend?).

Kawai was confused, "What you say?"

The mother tried, "Digmame otro ves más dispacio, por favor." (Please tell me again more slowly).

Kawai turned to Richard. "Help me."

Richard laughed and said, "They think you speak Spanish because you look like them.

"You talk English?" Kawai asked the family. The children jumped up and down to show they did. "We talk English good, we learn in mission school. You talk English?"

Kawai said, "I know English by sailors and mission school. I be Hawaii. Where you be?"

Richard pulled Kawai aside to caution in a low voice, "Only some sailor words are good on land. Be careful what you say."

"I careful, Mr. Richard. I no talk to child like sailor."

The Pomo children beamed, "We're from Boyes Springs." They looked at their parents and asked, "Papa, Mama can we take these men home with us? We practice our English.

Can we?

Can we?

You make supper for them." They jumped up and down.

The baffled parents stared at their children and then the sailors in confusion since they did not understand English well. The children repeated in their Pomo language, and the parents smiled and opened their arms. The children translated to English.

"You are welcome to our food. Come, please."

That afternoon the Pomo family invited Richard and Kawai to sit on the ground in front of their dome-shaped house, constructed of thin willow poles that were covered with bundles of tule reeds and grass.

Richard looked at the boy and said, "Thank your parents for inviting us."

The boy thanked his parents in the Pomo language, and they smiled broadly. The father showed them how to eat by dipping two fingers into a bowl of ground acorn mush. He and Kawai copied them.

Richard was startled at the bitter and astringent taste, but puckered up and said, " . . . Good. Kind of different." He feasted on other dishes the father offered of dried salmon, clams, duck, mushrooms, berries, and unknown foods in fine baskets.

When the eaters could hold no more, the adults enjoyed a delicious smoke of tobacco.

"What's you name?" said Richard looking down with a sparkle in his eyes as the two children rested on his knees.

The children giggled at each other, proud of their importance. The boy of nine cracked a mischievous grin and said with importance, "My name is goat butt." Richard looked at him, "Really? . . . you look like fish tails to me."

The boy spoke to his parents in Pomo and the Indians exploded in goodhearted laughter at the little joke. The girl pointed to Kawai, "Who are you?"

Kawai stood tall and engaged her with a serious look, "My name is Stinks in the River". The girl translated for her family, and they stared among themselves with a puzzled look until Kawai snickered. They giggled and pounded the earth like a cattle stampede.

The men smoked their tobacco and the women played at weaving baskets. Tears of delight ran down their faces.

Richard recovered and said, "I am Richard and this is Kawai."

The boy said, "My school calls me Bob and my sister is Rachel. This is Papa and Mama. Our dog is Beaucoup. You cannot say my Pomo name."

The Father made an announcement through Bob. "We welcome you to our family and make sacred fire Kuksu dance in sweat-lodge for you."

Richard watched the Pomo father carry a full load of wood into the entrance of the central sweat house near the stream bank. Through the door, he could see him build a fire on a bed of dry stones and hear his guttural call to the village elders to prepare the ceremony.

The elders gathered outside in the grassy common area among the scattered lute-domed huts to express the spirits of Pomo life to the rhythmic beats of many drums. Richard was amazed at their ancient costumes of flicker bird feathers, beads, fur, and body paint.

Kawai said, "My family dance too."

Richard did not understand the words and asked Kawai, "What is the story they dance?"

Kawai interpreted their body language and said, "The dancers ask spirits for health, give bountiful harvests, for successful hunts, many babies, and good weather."

Richard tapped his foot to the pulse of the talking drums and imagined a spiritual tunnel leading to the realm of power animals, spirit guides and ancestral spirits. A shaman appeared and invited the listeners to journey through the tunnel to unite with the heartbeat of mother earth.

Kawai whispered the deeper meaning. "The eagle carry message to Creator."

Richard listened, " . . . hummm . . .," and was astonished at the red-beaked supernatural being that stood in the sweat house door. Richard whispered to Kawai, "That is the Anthony Kinter we know."

The shaman spread his giant wings and climaxed the ceremony with a dramatic pantomime dance in a crescendo of drums.

Little Bob whispered, "Red Beak is the great Kuksu spirit who leads us. He purifies the Pomo."

The Kuksu spirit reentered the lodge for the ceremony. The elders removed their costumes and followed the great Kuksu inside. The father carried a large basket that was so finely woven it held water. He motioned Richard and Kawai through the low door last of all.

He ladled water onto the hot stones and raised great vapors of steam. They and the Pomo Indians were brothers in the dark companionship of the lodge. Elders placed white sage leaves on the fire to make incense smoke that washed away lingering body odor and cured colds.

The medicine man, Kuksu Red Beak, opened with a pipe raised to grandfather sky, grandmother earth, and the four directions. He passed the pipe around the circle, shook rattles and chanted songs and incantations while he as the medicine man summoned the force of his power animal. They ended the first part by shaking rattles four times.

On came a second set of heated rocks and basket of water. They offered prayers for the universe, the animals, the birds, the plants, the water spirits, and all of mankind using the ritual of the pipes. They chanted prayers for the participants with the pipe and rattle and became all of one clan. The clan emerged from the sweat lodge and flowed through the commons area purified.

Richard Porter and Kawai were Pomo Indians.

The Father moved next to Richard with Bob, the son. The son translated a quiet moment of sadness for them. "I have a son, Peter, but he is gone. We live without him." Bob and the Father stoically looked at the fire back inside the sweat lodge and were silent.

The Father earnestly looked Richard in the face and pulled him aside. He said, with Bob translating, "Soldiers came to our Mission San Francisco Solano. A bad man robbed a gold candlestick from the chapel. My son tried to stop him but he called Peter a savage Indian thief. They carried him away to jail and we have lost him. Maybe you can find Peter, Mr. Richard. You know the Alcalde, yes?"

Richard said, "I don't know Governor Mason, but I know Lieutenant Sherman who does. I'll see what I can do."

The family gathered around Richard and Kawai and the group hugged. The Father said in halting English, "We happy as new family. Our village build hut for you."

The previous *Agilis* sailors relished their new family, especially Richard, who finally had the family he had never known.

"We're honored to join the Pomo Walden Tribe. I cannot use my new hut because we go to San Francisco, but you are here," said Richard as he touched his heart. He hung his head to sobs as they pulled tight around them.

"We will see you again, but we go for now."

Richard and Kawai as Pomo brothers returned to the stage terminal in a warm glow for a happy good day. Richard turned to Kawai, "Are you warm now?"

"Kawai big warm, big good, in and out. No cold no more."

Richard and Kawai endured the stagecoach ride and schooner trip back to San Francisco. The next day they walked the streets searching for public buildings. They passed Indian labor crews framing new structures as fast as they could but saw nothing that looked governmental.

As a last resort, Richard stepped up to a well-dressed man who looked like a lawyer and asked, "Begging your pardon, my good sir, I'm looking for the court of law and records."

The man replied, "They are just now moving the records and some legal proceedings here to San Francisco from Vallejo. I believe they are housed temporarily in that white building over there," and pointed to a nearby gate in a wall. A small sign read,

Tribunal de Justicia

Archivos

Richard followed by Kawai walked over the new wooden sidewalk to the gate in front of the adobe building. They had bypassed it earlier as a warehouse.

A guard blocked the door. "Pare e identifíquese. Indique su nombre y negocio." (Stop and identify yourself. State your name and business).

Richard asked, "Who is in charge of the records?"

The guard said, "Records? ¿Te refieres a los registros judiciales." (Do you mean court records?)

"I guess so. Are they here?"

"Por allá, señor." (Over there, Sir) The armed man pointed down a short hallway to a massive wooden door. The carvings of the saints on the closed door demanded respect.

Richard knocked and heard a muffled voice from within, "Entra y establece tu negocio." (Come in and state your business.)

A severe, humorless man hunched at his work behind a carved desk covered with stacks of ledger books. An elaborately gilded crest of the previous Mexican government hung on the wall and a musty odor rose from the libros de contabilidad. (ledgers.)

Richard and Kawai stood in front of the clerk for many minutes until he finally looked up in a haughty manner.

"¿*Qué quieres?*" (What do you want?)

Richard said, "My Spanish is not good, sir. May I use English? I am looking for someone."

The clerk sighed with resignation. "This town has fallen apart since you Americans attacked us three years ago. How should I know where someone is? I hardly know where I am.

Richard continued in English, "Honorable sir, the man I seek is jailed unjustly. Soldiers ransacked the Mission at Boyes Springs and looted a golden candlestick from the altar. It was a gift from the Russian Church at Fort Ross and their most prized possession."

The clerk's face clouded with concern at the mention of the mission.

"A young Pomo accosted the thief but the soldier was stronger and seized him instead. They arrested Peter and took him to jail. Will you help me find him . . . please?"

Richard thought the clerk softened and thought about his own family. "Do you have a teenage son by any chance?"

"I have two hijos. We spend Sunday afternoons at the plaza. I suppose even a miserable Pomo Indian might miss a son."

Richard and Kawai nodded.

"There is a chance if his name appears in the court papers. My Mexican administration kept accurate records that have been moved to this office. We work with Governor Mason to maintain order—which is almost impossible. What is this boy's name?"

Richard said, "He is Peter Walden, a Pomo Indian about seventeen years old. He was arrested near Boyes Springs and encarcelado (jailed) about nineteen months ago."

The clerk consulted a large volume covering records from that period. "Perhaps this is he. On December 22, 1847, one P. Walden was arrested for theft of a candlestick from the Church of our Lord. He was jailed in Vallejo, where his case will be heard when the authorities are able to do so."

Richard said, "Would it be possible to gain an audience with that authority?"

The clerk grew irritable. "You must understand señor Rubio is a busy man. You would not imagine the criminals and gamblers and lowlifes who flood California. The worst are those Chinese pirates from Hawaii that infest my state. Señor Rubio is struggling to maintain control with the assistance of Governor Mason."

Richard said, "I've seen my share too."

"Spies are everywhere. They attack vulnerable shipments of gold when they can and sell it in El Pueblo de Nuestra Señora la Reina de los Ángeles de Porciúncula. You crudely call that town Los Angeles."

He spit on the floor.

"There is a reward of five thousand dollars from the Honolulu banks for the capture of the ringleader, Poison Dragon."

Kawai doubted the benefits of a bureaucracy to control pirates, but Richard said, "Esteemed Sir, you have our word we will watch for the pirates and spies. We're from the merchant ship, *Agilis*, and want to stop this piracy as much as you do."

The clerk relaxed, "Your assistance is appreciated. About Mr. Walden, I cannot release him, but I can ask the authorities in

Vallejo to accept his jail time as sufficient and release him. Do you know his family?"

"Their Christian name is Walden of Boyes Springs and Peter is our spiritual brother. Their Father oversees the vineyards for the Mission San Francisco Solano and faithfully supports the same. My deepest appreciation for your help."

Richard and Kawai shook hands with the clerk and returned to the new sidewalk.

Peter walked into the family tule in Boyes Springs later that month. He never knew why he was released.

Kawai walked over to the William Whippy Kanaka Boarding House while Richard explored the byways of San Francisco. They were waiting for Steward Jackson to open his crew sign up station later that morning.

Richard sat on a bench and reflected about the strange turns in his life. He recalled some painful memories. My parents were not there when my crying Aunt Matilda hugged me into her soft bosom and said, 'You're all mine.' My uncle patted me on the head and said, 'You'll live with us now.' My Aunt went away and a man whispered a word I did not understand, something like cholera. They took her away in a white blanket.

Richard watched a pair of mourning doves sleeping on a branch with their heads on their shoulders. He noted they did not tuck their heads under their wings like the birds he knew in Concord.

I loved those towering masts and sculpted figureheads on the ships in Boston Harbor. My uncle and I walked the deck of a square rigger when he said, 'I am Captain of this ship and embark for Canton tomorrow. You are indentured to the MacDonald farm west of Boston for seven years to learn land.

The mourning doves flew away.

I learned the land but also learned about bad men. I followed my uncle to sea and sought my fortune in California. I lost both and am back where I started. I hope Steward Jackson will sign me as an ordinary sailor.

He crossed the street to a display of new firearms in the window of the gun shop. The proprietor remembered him and said, "Hello young man. I am glad to see you, but you look a bit worse for the wear."

"I've breathed clear air and stood in cold water with good friends, but I still got poor. Maybe I can ship out on the *Agilis*."

The proprietor shook his hand and said, "Fare thee well. Where are you headed?

"The Master made a wager to race the *Zebra* to the Hawaiian Islands. I embark tomorrow if he'll have me."

The proprietor frowned at Richard in concern and said, "The *Zebra* you say? A man, Hornigold I think he said, claimed he was the Master and dragged a group of unsavory characters in yesterday. What he was doing with so many little men with pigtails, I don't know. He bought every one of them a pistol, lead, and powder.

I warn you they had a Chinese man named Poison Dragon with them who demanded my strongest firearms. He bought five Colts. I asked him who wanted them and he said, "My men, for protection."

Richard paid apt attention.

Those men are Chinese pirates and they refused any kind of training because they are so arrogant. You are a big stout man and look at how you did with your target practice. Those Chinks are half your size. The real danger is when their shots scatter all over hell and back. You're safer in front of the muzzle.

Richard looked at the shelves on the back wall, "Warning noted . . . what's that stuff on the top shelf?"

"I'm a pawnbroker on the side. I see a stream of down and out miners every day. They pawn what's left for a ticket home. I resell the stuff to newcomers for a good profit."

Richard spied a gold candlestick covered with dust hidden in the back. "What about that little candlestick?"

"These are crazy times, my friend. Gold in this town is so common its worth less than food to eat. Nobody has looked at that candlestick for months. Take a gander."

The proprietor rubbed the dust off before he handed it to Richard.

Richard hefted it in his hands and said, "How did this come in?"

"About a year and a half ago, a soldier in Colonel Frémont's army brought it in. He claimed he found it up north and had to pawn it to cover a gambling debt. He never returned and I've been stuck with it. Why? Do you want to pray on board?"

"An open candle fire on a wooden ship is a bad idea, but a family friend might be interested. What do you want for it?"

"That candlestick has collected dust for a long time. You're the first person with any interest. What say about twenty-five dollars?"

"Would you take half now and the other half when I return from the Islands? I know you don't give credit but Master MacIntyre will vouch for me." He thought, I hope he will.

The proprietor hesitated for a few moments and said, "With half now and a promise to pay, I'll let you have it. This is not a popular item."

Richard emptied his remaining money onto the counter and departed the shop polishing the candlestick with his hand.

He walked around the corner to a little church and approached the Padre bent over in a niche at the back. Richard stood in front of him with his head bowed.

"¿Cómo puedo ayudarle a mi hijo?" (How may I help you, my son?)," said the Padre.

Richard said in English, "There is a mission church at Boyes Hot Springs. I would like to make a donation but expect to leave in the morning. Can you take my small gift to that church?"

"I am leaving this afternoon to visit that very parish. What is your donation?" Richard handed the candlestick to the Padre.

The churchman gasped. "Dios Madre (Mother of God), I thought it was gone forever. Where did you get it?"

"From an old soldier around the corner."

"I stood at the altar a year and a half ago with my altar boy, Peter. He was a young Pomo Indian. This heathen soldier crashed in and blasphemed against God most obscene. He snatched the candlestick from the alter—it was the only valuable item we had. Bless you, my son. There will be joy in the Mission when it returns. What is your name?"

"I'm a lowly sailor and my name is not important."

The Padre said a short prayer of thanksgiving and sent Richard on his way in a state of grace.

It was his first time in a long time.

Agilis strutted her masts at anchor amid the forest of other masts. Hers stood the tallest. Down below on deck, a torrent of harsh words drove the indifferent efforts of lazy hands hired for the day.

Missing Porter in the extreme, bosun Babbitt raged at the unloading crew, "Get a move on! You're the laziest bunch of worthless degenerates that ever fouled the Pacific Ocean. Get those crates out of here. I don't have all day."

Master MacIntyre and Ferreri as first mate inspected the masts, rigging, and hull. MacIntyre said, "I want a report on our damage around the Horn. This gold fever has sucked repairmen from every port between Valparaiso and Monterey."

Ferreri summarized his observations. "We lost our fore-topmast overboard and sprung our mainmast. That obnoxious banker, Otis, that we picked up in Panama made everything worse by his hell bent rush to San Francisco. I can repair the mainmast with a sister spar alongside—adequate if we evade heavy weather."

MacIntyre had an idea. "Inquire of the harbormaster about his abandoned ships. Tell him we plan to cannibalize the owner-less vessels for spars. Of course, we will cannibalize anything else useful, but that goes without saying. We will make permanent repairs in Honolulu."

Ferreri knocked on the door of the harbormaster. "Good day sir. Might I have a moment of your time?"

The harbormaster finished examining records and looked up with irritation. "What now?"

"I am from *Agilis* and we suffered considerable damage rounding Cape Horn. I request permission to borrow replacements from an abandoned ship in your harbor."

The harbormaster said, "We're chock-full of abandoned vessels. Eight or ten more come every day and I can't find enough bar pilots to escort them in safe. The captains run the treacherous Golden Gate Strait on their own and collide or founder on those hidden shoals. I'm doing my best with what I've got.

Ferreri said, "We saw the wreck of the Stag Hound on the way in."

"That was the latest. Those two-bit vessels never leave after the crews desert. We're awash with the flotsam and jetsam of the Pacific." He sighed and looked at Ferreri and Jackson. "You can strip the whole damn fleet for all I care."

Ferreri said, "We displace a hundred and thirty-five tons. We need a top-foremast, two yardarms, and a sister for the mainmast,"

The harbormaster pointed them to a large book. "There's the record of every vessel we've inspected, and here's a map of their location. Where are you moored?"

Ferreri made an X at the foot of Clay Street and rowed *Agilis* next to it. He noted the names of several abandoned ships and turned to leave.

The harbormaster held up his hand to detain them with a strange face. He cleared his throat and hesitated a moment. "Don't under any circumstances board *Xenophonia*. There is 'quarantine' written on her side and the skull and crossbones on the map.

Here's her story.

The harbormaster said, "My inspector visits every vessel for a clean bill of health as soon as it arrives. It's hard with ten more coming in every day and his visit is sometimes delayed. He missed the Xenophonia for three weeks."

Ferreri said, "You do a good job in spite of that."

"That good man puked one day from the foulest odor he had ever smelled. It came out of that vessel. He reported that he climbed over the gunwale and saw a mangy dog slink away. His nose led him to a scene in the hold that petrified him. It was the remains of a man chained to the bulkhead."

Ferreri said, "Oh my God."

"The shredded coat was that of the Captain, a hated Captain I should think."

Jackson said, "Why the Captain? He should have been in command."

The harbormaster explained, "The rats and the abandoned dog had chewed on his body for some time to all appearances. His arm and part of his thigh were eaten down to the bone. Mere ligaments attached his putrefied hand to his arm."

Ferreri said, "Sounds like a mutiny."

Jackson said, "That's a lack of discipline for you."

"His neck was encircled with a hangman's noose. Both a dried-out bowl of water and a plate of food under a glass cover against the rats were just out of reach on the floor. Any movement on his part would tighten the noose.

Ferreri shuddered at the memory of a thief he had hanged who had choked and twitched for a long time.

The harbormaster finished his story, "He was marooned there and died in agony. His rotted body effused that putrid stink. My inspector rushed back to the office and quit on the spot."

Ferreri said, "Can you blame him?"

"Our search crew found no records. The ship's log was missing, there was no crew list, and no manifest. I found a tiny corner of a leather-bound volume in the galley stove. My men rescued the dog and no one has been on Xenophonia since."

A dog came up and licked the officers of *Agilis*.

That dog made a good companion after we washed the maggots out of his mouth and cleaned him up. We named him

Bones McKinsey or Bones for short. He is licking your hand right now."

Ferreri jerked his hand up and kicked Bones away knowing he had eaten human flesh. He wiped his hand on his pants. The dog yelped and lay down.

"The *Xenophonia* is a complete mystery. We've no idea where she came from, where she was headed, or who was aboard. The Captain was unrecognizable. The rats had eaten his hair and he was stuck down in a pool of dried blood and urine.

"Skip the details, I can imagine it," said Ferreri.

"Many claim to see the Captain's ghost when the fog rolls in. They say he climbs high and low searching for his crew to exact his revenge. Others see him in the crow's nest, his outline at the bow, or hear mournful cries below deck."

Bones always knew who didn't like him and was determined to make friends at any cost, even if he got a kick to the ribs. He licked Ferreri and Ferreri kicked him away a second time. The dog moved to a corner and locked an eagle eye on his attacker. Ferreri wiped his hands on his pants, on the chair, on the tablecloth. He shivered.

"The superstitious call this the ghost ship and won't go near it, and I strongly advise you to avoid her. I don't personally believe in ghosts, but it never hurts to be safe. I'll burn her to the waterline and scuttle the keel when I get time. These myths addle our workmen and drive away the few we've got left."

Ferreri said, "Thank you for your time. I'll keep you informed of my progress."

He roamed the streets with Jackson to muster a crew of drunken derelicts and penniless broken forty-niners for the cannibalism. The motley collection to a man demanded an outrageous three dollars an hour per man, which was several times the going rate and would work for only a day.

The officers prepared to strip a nearby brig, but steered around the *Xenophonia* without a glance. The crew removed the fore-topmast and main-topmast and spars from a brig. They floated them to *Agilis* and hauled them onto the deck, amid the usual naval language and under the expert eye of Babbitt. The second band of derelicts strengthened the mainmast with a parallel sister mast the next day.

Agilis was as fit as she was going to be.

Feverish activity in the harbor and the flotilla of vendors all gave *Xenophonia* a wide berth.

Chapter 10—Abducted

Alex MacIntyre sat back and relaxed with Thaddeus Leavenworth in the elegant-by-California-standards conference room of the City Hotel. With giant quill pens, the two men added elaborate signatures to the bottom of a fancy sheet of paper that was covered with legal language, embosssed seals, and flowery signatures. A waiter poured each of them a brandy and presented a humidor of fine cigars on a silver platter. They each selected one.

MacIntyre demonstrated the proper etiquette to smoke a cigar. He smelled the wrapper to make sure it was fresh and felt the body to assure it was firm and supple. The waiter handed him a guillotine cutter and he sliced through the cap on the head for a good draw. MacIntyre ignited a thin cedar stick over a small whale oil lamp on the table and lit the cigar by rotating it through the flame. He got an even burn by drawing slow gentle puffs.

MacIntyre luxuriated and said, "A fine cigar is like a fine wine. I appreciate the flavors of chestnut and spicy sweet aroma in this fine parejo, my friend." He held up the smoking creation.

Leavenworth lit his cigar and said, "This is a fitting celebration of our partnership. Yours is the swiftest vessel of her size afloat. My restaurants and markets are the most hungary on land. I foresee a prosperous future between us."

MacIntyre leaned back in his chair with an air of satisfaction and studied a dramatic painting on the wall, *The Battle of Quiberon Bay, 20th of November 1759.*

Leavenworth said, "I always conduct my business here in William Leidesdorff's conference room, and the outcome is uniformly successful."

MacIntyre said, "He certainly provides fine accommodations."

Leavenworth continued babbling, "Six thousand dollars to buy the *Agilis*. Why, she cost sixty thousand, if a penny, to build but her owners are fortunate to get anything. Believe me when I tell you, Alex, every damn seaman is digging for gold in the river at Sutter's Mill. You will be hard put to engage a crew."

MacIntyre said, "My officers, cook, and carpenter are loyal. Steward Jackson came around the Horn with me and he can pull a crew together if anybody can."

"You expressed a desire to cap your career with one more voyage. *Agilis* is the right vessel, this is the right time, and you are the right master. I have a commission for Hawaii and a return of foodstuffs."

MacIntyre said, "I believe the opportunities here are outstanding."

Leavenworth said, "I agree. Captain Cook changed the name from Hawaii to Sandwich Islands back in seventy-eight. I don't know the Earl of Sandwich, and I don't like his name. I will use Hawai'i from now on. Stick it to the Brits, I say."

MacIntyre picked up the thought, Um . . . What trade goods do we have in the commission?

Leavenworth lowered his voice to a whisper and cupped his hand over Macintyre's ear. "I have a secret shipment aboard of one million dollars of gold for the Bank of Honolulu. Every bandit, thief, ladrone, and pirate in the region is hungry for it, but I am using secrecy instead of a heavy corps of guards. Guards have loose lips and Chinese spies have big ears."

MacIntyre whispered back, "Those Chinese again. Are they getting worse?"

Leavenworth continued in a normal voice, "Outbound is tallow, leather hides, and quicksilver, all in demand. For the return, this community is desperate to eat and the local farms cannot keep up. I have a contract *Agilis* can handle superbly, but with a catch. Dirk Hornigold of the *Zebra* has a long-term agreement on the same contract if he can outrace us."

MacIntyre said, "Anything else?"

"The yellow commodity is packed in crates ten by sixteen inches that weigh two hundred and fifty pounds. I erased the U. S. Govt. Assay Office stamp, but kept the crate number. Time is of the essence and you need a crew. Better get going."

MacIntyre beamed as he said, "I last visited the islands seven years ago and enjoyed them immensely. I anticipate a calm voyage over pleasant waters."

He left humming *Bonnie Dundee*, a Scottish Highlands song, to search for Steward Jackson.

MacIntyre raged up and down the waterfront at Steward Jackson. "My ship lies rigged and ready in the harbor and the hold is stuffed with trade goods, but where the hell is the crew? They're off on a wild goose chase in the bloody damn mountains, three sheets to the wind drunk and chasing the Jezebels of San Rafael."

"Aye, sir."

"With luck, the sea will lure Porter back. I can train neophytes if need be, but it takes time. Do your best to sign the officers and procure a crew of twelve hands straight away."

Jackson jumped to the task. "I'll start with the Kanakas from Hawaii, I mean the Sandwich Islands. They idle away their days in the William Whippy House, but are good able-bodied seamen."

Jackson schemed how to get a crew. "Madam Belle Cora's girls or her make-believe girls will plant salty ideas in their client's lusty ears for forty dollars. I can grab them from the barrooms . . . it's not kidnapping when they're unconscious out back."

He made the rounds throughout San Francisco all morning and reported back to MacIntyre, "Even a miserable vagrant demands two hundred dollars to set foot on deck. Ought to be thirty, but this gold disease has poisoned their mind."

MacIntyre sighed. "Damn two hundred dollars all to hell, but so be it. Promise one fifty if you can. We will embark when you take on the damn seamen." He left for other business.

Jackson prowled by the Blue Crane Bar on his way to the Kanaka boarding house, glancing everywhere for oblivious drunks. It was too early in the afternoon and the occupants were yet upright.

Jackson walked between a pair of Tiki gods holding torches that guarded the *William Whippy Kanaka Boarding House.* He entered into a cacophony of chants, stories, and clouds of smoke. The Polynesian weapons that covered the walls portended dark purposes.

Jackson was intimidated as a non-Hawaiian and shuddered at the thought of the weapons in the hands of robust angry men.

He looked at the sling stones and spears, shark-toothed war clubs, strangulation cords, throwing axes, and daggers. He could hear cheers from gamblers in the back hidden by the smoke.

Five Kanakas lounging around the front of the room in complete idleness greeted Jackson. "Aloha, man. Come on." He'd heard they cared for nobody and enjoyed a grand time drinking, smoking, playing cards, and carousing in every way, but they welcomed him with open arms and smiles.

Their friendliness overwhelmed his natural reserve, but he couldn't shake the image of the shark-tooth club flying in a melee. Those rumors of heathen behavior and the stories of death and mutiny in foreign ports, capped by cannibalism, unnerved him.

Jackson shouted, "Uh . . . who . . . wants . . . to go home to Oahu?"

A young native Hawaiian, who spoke English with a Boston accent he had learned in a school in Nantucket stepped forward, "I be Ikaika and no have money. I no have money, we no money. You need sailor, we sailor," pointing his thumb at his chest.

Jackson gestured toward Ikaika, "You come."

Ikaika stood by Jackson with a huge grin.

What is your name?" said Jackson as he pointed to another man.

"I Kalani. I talk English good, no?"

A huge third man rumbled, "Koa. Very strong." He flexed his gigantic bicep covered with tattoos. "I warrior, and Koa tree make hardwood for club." He showed off animal designs, circles and lines, and even a tattoo on his tongue. "I break many bone in enemy."

They crowded around Jackson to his sweaty discomfort.

"I, Makani, make music. My name is 'from the heavens'".

"I Surfer. I know water and ocean good. Good sailor for you."

"Come to *Agilis* in two days," as he pointed to each Kanaka around him, "One, two, three, four, and five."

"We go Oahu for you," they cheered.

These honorable men never signed the crew book because they always kept their word.

To himself, Jackson muttered,

"Five good men but I need six more. Let's see what the scum from the alley has to offer."

Steward Jackson, with high hopes but low expectations, sat behind a small table facing down the hall to the door opening on the waterfront. The rough floorboards were bare of any finish or rug and the place echoed.

He checked his roster and said aloud, "MacIntyre wants sixteen hands signed today and I have five Kanaka. What more can I do?"

MacIntyre strode in and said, "How goes it? Any luck?"

Jackson said, "Five Kanaka are coming. I slipped Madame Cora a little money and she will help. Maybe she will send some drunken sailors our way. I posted notices around town and passed word to barbers, bartenders, boardinghouses, and brothels for the rest."

"You visited Madam Cora?" said MacIntyre.

"I assure you it was totally professional, mine that is, not hers."

"I have sent for bosun, Benjamin Babbitt, and first mate, Alfonso Ferreri, at the Niantic and left messages for the carpenter, John Alden, and cook, Marco José Tavares Silva."

He looked out the door. "Where the hell are they?"

"Carry on. That sounds like the best you can do."

Jackson waited. A tall-case clock in another room chimed nine dignified times. He drank a cup of coffee and waited. He reviewed the ship's stores and waited. Ten distant chimes marked another hour. He lit his meerschaum pipe and puffed clouds to the ceiling. Would he never get a crew?

His anticipation rose with the jangle of the front door bell. A vigorous man forty years old, taller than average with a lean build strode confidently down the hallway. His gray hair framed a no-nonsense face and his years at sea had chiseled his body into a ball of fire. The muffled clock rang half past ten.

"Anyone here?" he called in a voice clearly able to command a hand anywhere on deck.

"Down here. Please come in," said Jackson.

"Good morning, Mr. Ferreri, and thank you for coming. Your good reputation precedes you as the ship's mate. This interview is a legal formality but please tell me about yourself."

Alfonso Ferreri shook hands.

"I ran away to sea at sixteen and have been there ever since. My eyes have taken thousands of sextant readings. I can handle men and do not hesitate to apply severe discipline when necessary."

Ferreri paused a moment because the interview was a complete surprise. "My maps are filled with notes from the seven seas and I can navigate any weather. On a personal note, my lady friend put me out calling me demanding and stubborn. I do better at sea."

Jackson said, "You will rejoin *Agilis* as the first mate. Sign here. We weigh anchor in two days."

Jackson said to himself, Six down, eight to go.

"I'm in here," called the Jackson as the front door quietly opened and tinkled the hanging bells. A good-looking man thirty-seven years old entered. He had dark brown hair over his ruddy complexion that confirmed he was a dyed-in-the-wool sailor. His manners bespoke the gentleman's family he was from. Babbitt was smaller than Ferreri but more refined. His quick eyes took in the room.

"Benjamin Babbitt, is it not? Glad to see you again."

"The pleasure is mine."

Jackson said, "You did a good job around the horn and this chat is a mere formality, but why are you here?"

"I love that beautiful ship, the *Agilis*, and desire to serve as bosun. There is damage to repair and paint to renew. I stow cargo faster than any other and keep the crew disciplined.

Jackson held up his hand, "I know all that, but I hear you do not get along with the men."

Babbitt said, "I am careful but not punctilious. It is important that the deck be first-class when we weigh anchor. The Baltimore Clipper is the most gorgeous creation designed by man and I intend to keep her that way."

"I look forward to you as bosun, Mr. Babbitt, but you are behind in your work. We have an account to pay for repairs and you have two days to prepare."

Babbitt eagerly said, "The main mast is sprung but I can sister and brace it by tomorrow. I will address minor issues today and defer permanent repairs to Honolulu. That hired crew did a sloppy job."

Jackson ignored his enthusiasm and said, "Sign the book. We weigh anchor in two days."

As he left the building into the sunshine, Babbitt's lonesome mind wandered back to his wife, Priscilla, in beautiful Charleston.

I so miss you and my two daughters. I pray you are well by the grace of our Lord. I hate this song by a forlorn sailor's wife.

> Then I'll haste to wed a sailor,
> And send him off to sea
> For a life of independence
> Is the pleasant life for me

> But when he says 'Goodbye my love,
> I'm off across the sea'
> First, I cry for his departure,
> Then laugh because I'm free

"I will be home as soon as I can." He retrieved his ditty box from the *Niantic* and boarded the *Agilis*.

"Sailors here," shouted a group of rowdies who slammed the front door open and rattled the glass. They were two-thirds drunk and roared down the hall to the steward's table. Thumping marked their way.

One of them said, "Hey steward, we're here. Madam Cora says you need a crew. You got one right here. *Agilis* has a nice hull and we like nice hulls, don't we mates?"

They all laughed.

Jackson cleared his throat and spoke in an authoritative voice, "How do I know you're sailors? The truth, no sea stories."

The sailors talked all at once and the gist of their story was that they were in from Hong Kong. They had survived a typhoon, a pirate attack, a small fire aboard, and still made a fast run.

"We're ready to muster, sir." The group neglected to mention that four of their number had jumped ship and three of the present company had never been to sea. They forgot to say they were broke but Jackson knew they were.

He held up his hand. "You with the wooden leg and scrawny parrot on your shoulder, what good are you in the rigging?"

The seaman thumped the floor with his peg leg. "I am Levi Pembroke and I'll have you know I stand the watch with any tar alive day or night. I climb the rigging like a monkey with this hook on my leg." He held up his peg leg to show it off.

Pembroke's companions bolstered his case, "Got to have Levi, oops, I mean Broken Pen. He saws the best fiddle on the water for chanties and hornpipes. Can't work without Levi. We got to have Rudy the parrot to start our stories."

Pembroke and Rudy strutted around in a display as if they were leading a parade. His cohorts clapped in a chantey's rhythm to the thumps of his peg leg on the floor.

The steward asked the group a small question. "What was your pay to cross the Pacific?"

The assembled sailors changed to stony from rowdy. A young man of twenty-six stepped out. "William O'Sullivan at your service, sir. San Francisco ain't Canton with unemployed sailors a plenty. Ain't none except for us here. A mate gets two hundred and ten dollars and we're the same, only fair."

Jackson exploded "No! The cargo will rot in hell first. We can go one hundred and eighty dollars."

The sailors made a tight huddle among themselves. O'Sullivan folded his arms across his chest and the others followed. "We'll sail on your broken-down *Agilis* for two hundred dollars."

Jackson tapped his pencil in frustration. He thought and mumbled and pounded the desk in frustration. The sailors glanced at one another with sly grins.

133

He decided he had to yield under the circumstances. "Two hundred dollars for the round trip then. Shore leave in Honolulu but no wages until you are back in San Francisco."

"Agreed."

"Sign here. We sail in two days.

"Well enough sir." Each made his mark, except for Pembroke who signed with his real name.

Rudiger, the green parrot, opened his beak, "Squawk. Rudy like *Agilis*," and pooped on the page for his mark.

They whooped out to continue their entertainment such as available with no money in a boom town. Proprietors lined the street and offered every inducement to take any remaining coins.

The crew clapped the landlubbers in their group on the back, "We'll make sailors of you when you get some tattoos."

Jackson muttered as he wiped off the ship's crew list, "Damn bandits."

A dusty-looking miner stumbled in the front door the sailors had left open. He yelled, "Gi'me a drink. I needs a drink quick. I gets gold from the dirt on the ground and learned them sailor boys to use their gold pan. They says you need a hand, I am a hand, and I need a drink now." He pounded the desk and upset the ink well.

Jackson jumped up and swung a fist at the drifter. "Get out of here you stinking old sot." The drifter was quicker than he appeared from lots of street fights, sober or drunk, and jumped back to safety.

"I saw you trick my crew the other day. Gold from the street indeed. You dumped that dust in the street just before the boat came. Get out. I don't tolerate frauds."

The drifter shuffled out to his next victim. "It was worth a try. You can't win them all, and they ain't no whiskey on a ship nohow."

Jackson scanned the partial crew list with mixed feelings and prepared to wait out until noon. I have signed some decent sailors, or not, but where are the idlers?

A pair of men wandered in. One was lean, about forty-five years old and appeared crusty. The other was smallish with a Spanish complexion. He was well fed and carried a jovial smile.

They interrupted Jackson's paperwork and he looked up irritated. "What do you want? I need a carpenter and cook but neither of you looks qualified."

The lean man said, "We request to join your crew. He is a cook and I'm a carpenter. We came from Boston on the *Agilis*."

Jackson said, "I want a carpenter and cook but not you two."

On the other hand, the ship will disintegrate with no carpenter and they'll mutiny with bad food.

Jackson said to Alden, "Those hands might be skilled at woodworking but tell me how you can help the *Agilis*?"

The lean man said, "I am the wizard of wood, John Alden. I can turn a tree into anything you need on board. My blades are so sharp they can shave a chip thin as newspaper."

Jackson said, "So can other carpenters. How are you any better?"

Alden said, "For three months I carved the figurehead that leads the *Agilis*. That devil *Zebra* ship shot my lady in her eyes and I need to restore her vision. I am a good carpenter, but the only thing is, I hope Babbitt is not bosun. That man irritates me."

"How is that?"

"He's so particular about every detail but misses the big damage that can sink us. He painted the broken mainmast but would not help to strengthen it."

Jackson was indifferent.

"Confirm your name, please?"

"I am John Alden, they call me Chips. The company says I complain a lot but I get my work done."

"You're our carpenter, Mr. Alden. Get your supplies because we sail in two days."

Jackson's eyes drilled into the Spanish-looking man. "Who are you?"

"Si señor. My name is Marco José Tavares Silva. I cook good and make food for you. You make crew for *Agilis*?"

Jackson said, "I've heard your name around town and people say you're a keeper. What is your name again?"

"Marco José Tavares Silva. I am from Jamaica and make comeda muy savoroso (cook food very tasty) with spices from my island. I learned from my wife, the witch doctor, to heal sickness."

"You are famous in the sailing community for food afloat, and the men you saved with your fever treatment swear by your skills. Get your supplies before we weigh anchor.

"Gracias señor Sir. Muy bien (Thank you sir, very good)."

The Steward turned to business. "Both of you, there is an account for provisions. Make sure you load enough. We sail in two days."

"Well enough sir."

The two C's exited in soaring spirits with their arms on each other's shoulders.

Jackson closed his book and was leaving when he heard the front door creak open one more time and the bells ring clearly. He sighed and sat back down. A six foot tall young man accompanied by a Hawaiian Kanaka walked down the hall and stood facing him. The clock chimed noon.

"Can I help you?" Jackson said.

"Sir, my name is Richard Porter. I was the second mate on the *Agilis*."

Jackson looked at a man who stood taller than average, had a work-hardened build, and was about twenty-four years old. A sparkle in his eyes radiated good humor and an outgoing nature.

Jackson said, "I remember you. You deserted *Agilis* and left in the company of those common sailors. That's a poor recommendation to bring you back, don't you think?

"Yes, sir."

"And further, young man, you haven't seen an ocean-going vessel for some time."

"No sir."

"What have you been doing?"

"Working here and there."

"From the looks of those wrinkled hands, sunburned arms, and stooped posture you've been in the goldfields. Am I wrong?"

Porter blushed from his lanky arms to his sunburned neck and wrinkled fingers. "Jacob's Famous Gold Mining Kit guaranteed me to catch gold, but Jacob lied. I want to return to the *Agilis* . . . if you will have me."

"What do you know about navigation?"

"I can plot courses and take celestial readings. I can handle the deck when tying up. I keep a good watch and have secured many tons of freight. I want to go back.

You abandoned ship."

"Yes sir That was a big mistake. My companions at sea are true, not like those greedy gold diggers."

"What will you do if I do not sign you?"

"Buy a farm up north in the Sonoma Valley. I've wanted a piece of land since I was enslaved, er . . . I mean indentured.

"Why were you put out to work?"

"I'm an orphan, and my uncle left Boston on his voyage to Canton. He wanted to lose me."

"I have heard that story other times too. Go on."

"Some day, I will ride a fine horse as a man of distinction and raise food for the good people here. Brannan's General Store is making way more money than the gold miners."

Jackson thought to himself about Richard's aspirations, Good ambition but I wonder about his motivation.

"I will sign you as the second mate, but if you ever desert you will be severely punished and never sail again if I can help it. Understood?"

"Understood."

"We sail in two days." They shook hands.

"And who are you, may I ask?" he said turning to the Kanaka.

The man was a rich brown with a splendid physique. He was six feet tall with expressive features and lively dark eyes. His carriage was easy, firm, and graceful. His limbs were fine and muscular and he looked like a burnished bronze statue.

"I be good sailor. Me Kawai. I know wind, waves, storms, and I very strong," as he flexed his biceps and danced his tattoos, especially a lovely hula girl. I row canoe good. I big man in Ohau."

Jackson stopped Kawai with his hand. "Five of your countrymen are signed. Do you know them? Let's see, there is Ikaika, Koa, and three more."

"Koa big man and friend. Very big like this, no?" Kawai spread his arms six feet wide to show Koa's size."

"Very well. What is your name again?"

With tranquil poise he said, "I Kawai."

"We sail in two days."

Jackson entered Kawai's name into the crew list, closed his book, and left the hall in high spirits. He had a crew, even if some of the men had never seen the sea.

Richard Porter and Kawai were jubilant. "I see the sea ahead of me," said Richard. Kawai whooped.

A rowdy boatload of newfound companions, including Richard Porter of course, swaggered up Pine Street on their awkward sea legs, hooting and hollering. They stopped to ogle a display of knives, revolvers, and specialized tools that only a mariner could understand.

Richard studied a map to the Hawaiian Islands that showed the prevailing winds, currents, hazards, and navigation advice. This was in preparation for the race and atonement for his desertion.

The group rounded the corner without him.

Colorful details of the Honolulu harbor exploded in Richard's head and the map rolled sideways. His vision of the islands erupted in a galaxy of bright stars and his right leg collapsed in a painful instant. The world went dark under a thick blindfold, a gag stifled his cry for help, and the ground slammed his head.

Many hands flipped him over and his face jammed into the dust. A pain shot through his shoulders when his arms were wrenched behind his back and his wrists tied. In an instant, he was dumped in a cart and buried under a pile of straw. He passed out.

The companions around the corner missed him.

"Where's Richard?"

"He doesn't like our company eh?"

"Ain't no skin off my back."

They pressed on to the Blue Crane Bar.

Richard's world came back into focus from the knock on the head and he wondered,

Why me? No money and no enemies outside Ferreri.

Richard knew from the squeaks of the wheels that he was being hauled off. He could follow his route from inside the blindfold.

There's the anvil in Hanley's Blacksmith shop . . . hey, I smell sourdough bread from Boudin's bakery. We're going north on Stockton Street.

He counted off about ten or twelve streets from the sounds of horse tackle and chattering passersby. " . . . can't hear anything. We're out of town now."

Richard felt the cart stop and the pain in his shoulder ease without the jostling. He heard a strange foreign accent that shifted from singsong to thick English that sounded Slavic or maybe Russian.

"Vhat have you brought me?"

Peeking from under his blindfold, Richard saw the crest of the Romanov family on the ring that the immense hand wore when it flipped the straw away. He saw it again when the hand grabbed the cart in front of his face and hurled him out onto his sore hip. The hand pulled the blindfold off.

Richard's blue eyes met two black eyes that drilled into his trussed-up body. The Russian spit on the ground, "A common sailor. You vaste my time." He kicked the wheel of the cart. "Nobody in town gives ten dollars to get him back."

Richard was highly offended by this valuation and yelled from under his gag, "I'm ... ah ... worth..twenty-five dollars at least ... you Russki scum."

The Russki scum re-wrapped his blindfold and tightened it.

Richard felt like he was being stoned as sharp punches rained on his body from voices crying in a mix of words from English, Russian, and Chinese, "Worthless ... trash ... common seaman ... why alive ... what you do here?"

Suddenly. Everything stopped dead. Richard heard an authoritative voice order, "Lock up, tap head, dump in bay. Problem gone."

The Russian said, "Honorable Poison Dragon. I did not hear you arrive. So sorry. Vise words as usual."

The gag intercepted Richard's blind responses, much to his benefit under the circumstances.

He heard a rickety door creak open and became disoriented when he was rolled off the cart onto the ground. His butt picked up splinters from the threshold, his hip hurt on the hard dirt floor, and he tried to cough when a shower of itchy straw buried him. He didn't hear the click of the lock on the door.

They could have dumped the straw first and me on top. Bastards. Where the hell am I? Solitary, splinters up my ass, shoulder hurts, hip killing me, knee aches, a knot on my head, and can't see shit.

Richard was back to full alert in spite of the shooting pain in his hip from the Kung Fu kidnap attack. He was tough and ignored the pain.

Now what, he thought as he rotated his jaw in a circle. The creaking jawbone was enough to moisten the rag stuffed in his mouth, and with several bites, he spit the gag out. "I can talk."

Richard was a sailor and sailors know more about knots, lines, and ropes than any derelict on land, especially a Chinese derelict.

He muttered to himself, "Those ignorant little Asian bastards can't even tie my hands right," as he located some play in the bulky hemp rope around his wrists. He gave a quick flex of his strong hands and loosened the knot. His left hand slipped the rough ropes off the right and did the same thing for the blindfold and feet. He was free.

As he struggled to stand up, a murmur of agitated voices through the back wall caused him to freeze just short of the roof. The wall felt like a bulkhead on *Agilis* with action on the other side. He grasped his knife and dug into the soft redwood boards with the same enthusiasm he had used to attack the bowsprit on the *Zebra*. He quickly made a good-sized peephole. The knife broke through into open air.

He did not know his hole poked through the eye of a carved dragon on the inside. The glint from moving twisting tip of his knife appeared to be an actual eye to the superstitious coolies within. He heard the rabble make a terrified rush to the opposite wall and away from the Dragon. Richard was elated to see the entire room through his peephole.

The interior displayed more elegance than the dining room of the City Hotel. A gilt and red lacquered table with an exquisite game of jade chess pieces on top took his breath away. A mirror on the far wall reflected a dragon back at Richard. He moved his head and the eye of the dragon moved. He was the eye of a gold dragon against a midnight blue background with four writhing claws and a mouth that belched fire.

Richard put his mouth to the peephole and gave a loud, "Haaaa . . . huh . . . ." Five coolies bowed to a statue of Buddha at the door and one rubbed his belly for protection. Richard said again, "Huhhh . . . oooouuu . . . ."

The fragrance of sandalwood, spice, and camphor filled his lungs when he caught his breath and he coughed. The little puffs of smoke terrorized the group even more and they packed into the back corner. He could see the fragrant wisp of smoke rose from a time-stick burning in an ancient incense clock.

Richard looked at the reflection of a doorway in a side wall and said, "I'll be damned. What's Hornigold doing here? . . . Chernov's enough."

The master of the *Zebra* towered above the lopsided room of tough-looking Chinese. He was as incongruous at six feet tall as the flamboyant Russian standing next to him but was not as well dressed. The Russian was forty-seven years old with a beard and piercing black eyes. His fine clothes and ushanka fur hat contrasted with the baggy pants and shirts draped on the skinny frames of the orientals wearing their conical coolie hats.

Hornigold said, "I give you Gurii Chernov, my guard." Chernov walked to the back in greeted them in their own language. He and Hornigold spoke the Taishanese dialect of Canton, which was the Chinese pirates' homeland.

Richard listened as Hornigold and Chernov approached the deserted area in front of his carved dragon wall for a private conversation.

"What happened to your ship in Sitka?"

"Those damn pirates working the China strait hijacked so many of my furs I went bankrupt."

"You were tough enough to escape slaughter but not bankruptcy, eh."

"You got it." Chernov spit on the floor.

Richard's skin crawled at Hornigold's next words since he had seen his attitude toward safety in the Golden Gate. "I and you don't let details stop us. I like your style, Chernov."

"There's work to be done for sure," Chernov said, but what he thought was, I need a post and Hornigold's a winner. I'll join forces and keep my band of rogues busy.

New arrivals streamed in the front door and blocked Richard's peephole. He listened to them deeply inhale the sandalwood incense to warm their souls and relax their bodies. Some of the newcomers squatted, their pigtails coiling on the floor.

A well-dressed servant said, "Silence." When raised his hand to silence the chatter everyone squatted and Richard could see again. It was clear from their body language that they were tense. The servant slid open a silk panel decorated with an imperial dragon carved from teak.

Dramatic and haughty, an oriental man in an embroidered full-length Changshan robe that radiated authority stepped into the room. His demeanor dominated the group and the flash of his dark eyes demanded obedience.

Richard thought to himself, He looks dangerous. I'd hate to go against him.

Richard could see the Chinese pirates were intimidated by the mark of the Mandarin square and lion on his chest and the hat knob on his black velvet cap. Even he could appreciate the beautiful silk slippers peering from under the embroidered robe.

The servant announced, "Poison Dragon, master above all things."

The assembly bowed lower yet as the man in the robe stabbed them with his eyes. Hornigold made a slight bow for appearances sake. Chernov stood ramrod straight and did not bow.

Speaking in a formal Cantonese dialect the embroidered man proclaimed, "I, Poison Dragon, am grand leader always." Richard could see the handle of a dagger lurking in his sleeve, but it was hidden from everyone else.

"Welcome to my humble presence. Disgusting peasant design on house outside trick visitor and disguise power inside."

He spoke to Chernov in English, "Inform me of your activities."

"Honorable Poison Dragon, we have problems from Los Angeles to Sitka. Russians harvested one boat of five when we defeated the Tlingit Indians, but the Americans have many guards . . . ugh. It's harder and harder for us honest pirates to work."

Hornigold said, "Esteemed Dragon, I beg to interrupt. You know the most ruthless piraticals are in the China Strait they are now my men." He paused for effect.

Richard looked at individual Chinese thugs squatted on the floor and realized he had seen the combined forces of Hornigold and Chernov leaning over the gunwales of the *Zebra*.

"Go on," said Poison Dragon.

"They board a ship without mercy and exterminate all fighters," Chernov said.

"Well done. I approve," said Poison Dragon.

He clapped twice and a man entered from behind him. The servant announced, "Kongsi Master is Snakehead."

Poison Dragon said, "Know your Kongsi leader, Snakehead, who bring report to Poison Dragon. Poison Dragon correct wrong behavior." He glared ferociously around the room.

Snakehead stood at Poison Dragon's side and bowed to him. His formal Changshan robe was simpler than Poison Dragon's but still compelling.

"He take report for movement of gold."

Richard was interested to learn about the challenge facing him, but his neck ached from straining to see through the peephole. He rotated his head a few times to loosen up and returned to the peephole just in time to hear Poison Dragon say, "You are Ghost Shadows. Watch with eye, listen with ear." He pointed to his eye and ear. "Silent like moon on lake surface."

The men chanted in unison, "Ghost Shadow report all to Snakehead. Ghost Shadow report all to Snakehead."

Poison Dragon said, "Report minerman by night and follow shipment by day. Harvest small boat to feed cause, pass big boat many guard."

He turned to his right, "Snakehead have further good duty. Explain."

Snakehead stood tall and said, "Ghost Shadow steal rich man off street, get money. Most important. Follow man day, night, work, all time."

Richard thought, That's why they kidnapped me. But I'm not rich . . . yet.

"Ghost Shadow take hostage. Hide in Xenophonia. Good luck rub Buddha."

Richard watched the Ghost Shadows file past the little ivory statue and rub the smooth belly. He suspected that some wanted good luck and others simply followed the leader.

"We make strong plans," said Poison Dragon to Hornigold and Chernov after they were gone.

Richard sat down and massaged his stiff neck.

Poison Dragon explained his plans in English to Hornigold. A servant translated to the Chinese who squatted in a circle around Snakehead with their a long pig-tails brushing the floor.

"I operate from my house at the edge of town. Few come this way and none leave. My base on the water is the Xenophonia. Her name looks like this".

He wrote X E N O P H O N I A in big letters on a piece of paper and pointed out the window.

"See red vessel and no important is sign on side, Quarantine."

The men crowded around the window to see the ship, and understood that Poison Dragon considered her important, even without understanding the English words.

Hornigold and Chernov noted the ship moored near *Agilis*. Hornigold said, "I've never about quarantine but that skull and crossed bones on the notice keeps trespassers away.

Poison Dragon switched to the common Yue dialect to emphasize his directions to the Ghost Shadows in the room.

"Heaven and Earth Society promise you job when leave mud and pig shit of Canton. The Kongsi organization bring you miserable immigrants over big water. Ugh . . . . You pay me for joy to come here."

Several people shuddered as he described their situation perfectly.

"My lookout on Point Fort Rock see ship enter Golden Gate. Trusted Ghost Shadow greet immigrant. Explain with force that

Heaven and Earth Kongsi Society know their family in China. Each immigrant follow orders for sake of ancestors."

Two coolies bowed their heads in humiliation.

"You are Ghost Shadows and report to Kongsi contact, Snakehead. That is all to know. Report to Snakehead what see with eye and hear with ear. Make wrong action you die," from five thunderbolts on your head.

"Family get three kinship extermination," said Poison Dragon. "That mild punishment kill only father, son, and grandson. We reserve nine kindred extermination for serious error."

"Each Ghost Shadow make three payments to his Kongsi for his passage and keep one. You lucky to be here and must pay. Russian friend, Chernov, is Tall Volcano."

He turned toward Chernov who pointed to his chest.

"Tall Volcano enter where Chinese man cannot." Poison Dragon burned his words into the eyes of each man.

Chernov understood the body language, if not the words. He stood straight with a menace. Each member present bowed solemnly to Poison Dragon. Chernov did not bow.

Tall Volcano and Snakehead left to strong-arm new arrivals in Chinatown to join the Ghost Shadows. They confronted any Chinaman anywhere on the streets with the gentle three-extermination policy of Poison Dragon.

Richard hit his head on a low beam when he stood up in the darkness. He was stiff from staring through the peephole for so long and everything hurt, but his self-control stifled his torrent of profanity.

He stumbled over a metal bar and fell flat anyway, but he grabbed it and said, "Might come in handy."

The Ghost Shadows inside started gambling to release their tension.

Richard felt around the inside of his prison and determined it was a lean-to framed of rotten boards nailed to posts from the outside. It huddled under a sloping roof that was attached to the headquarters shack, and was just high enough for the short Asians who built it.

Richard put his hands on a gray weathered board and froze, listening to the murmurs over the clicks of pieces that sounded like ivory. He took his chance when he heard a great shout, and pushed the board outward. Several nails clinked to the ground.

He used the metal bar during the next cheer to pry two more boards off. He pushed his shoulders through, but unfortunately, several more loose boards crashed into the dirt and the gambling stopped cold.

Richard dove through the hole and rolled a forward somersault. His body hit the ground running. He was barely ahead of his captors pouring from the shack like screaming army ants. He streaked along Stockton Street past the bakery and headed straight toward Hanley's blacksmith shop.

His long-running legs outpaced the short legs chasing him, and the metal bar in one hand balanced the opposite sore hip until he slipped in a puddle of water. He hung on to the bar but tumbled in a heap.

The short legs caught up and Richard swung the bar at the nearest attacker, connected, and heard a yell. He saw the little thug hold up a broken arm with a hand flopping at the end.

Richard sprinted through the open door of the blacksmith shop. "They're after me!" Blacksmith Hanley ran around the anvil carrying a sledgehammer in one hand and a red-hot poker in the other. He waved them at the mob to show he had the skill to use them. They turned tail.

"Many thanks. They were on me."

"Any time. I'll chase every chink I can get my hands on. We ought to send them back to China if you ask me. There's all those empty ships and I'd start with that hoard behind you," waving the red-hot poker at the vanishing pigtails.

Richard quit panting and looked around the blacksmith shop. It was lined with tools and works in progress. A stack of steel bands caught his eye.

"Those are trusses to mount a spar to a mast. My ship needs some hardware. Can you make us some?"

Hanley said, "I'll forge anything you want, but I'm busy so tell me right away."

"I'll send Babbitt over when I find him. Thanks again."

Richard limped off to find Babbitt.

Richard's stomach growled when he walked by the Coffee Stand tent on the wharf and read the sign that hung in front to entice the customers. The aroma advertised charcoal-grilled fish.

> Gude bad and
> indiferent spirits
> sold here at
> twenty-five cents each

Richard heard his companions inside washing down fish with spirits. He scanned the modest smoke-filled room. There was a stove and grill at the back where the cook roasted fresh fish to a customer's order. The far wall was occupied with a bar under a dirty painting of a Clipper in full sail dangling from a post. Patrons stood round five small tables that filled the place.

Richard charged up to a group. "There you are, you sons of bitches. I'm kidnapped while you're drunk and stuffing your face. What the hell kind of friends are you?" They exchanged words but shortly calmed down with another drink.

"Listen up mates. Several chinks jumped me. This is the worst port I've been in, and we best stay together. Watch for shady people in the alleys. That's where they got me."

The sailors paid no attention and returned to their boozing. Richard later told his shipmates about the abduction. The others neglected to tell anyone.

Richard never found Babbitt.

The Ghost Shadows did not neglect anything when they returned to their shack. When they gave an excuse for the dilapidated condition of the storage shack, Chernov chastised them with a vengeance for losing his hostage.

"Watch me make a knot that holds," as he demonstrated on the splint he strapped to the broken arm. "If you let a hostage loose again, Poison Dragon will use the three kindred exterminations on your family."

Poison Dragon gave the next lesson on how to select a kidnapping target. "We want a man who is prosperous, physically soft, and with access to money like a fat merchant. Search with eyes and ears but silent like ghost."

The following night was especially foggy. The kidnap squad lurked in a deep shadow outside the dining emporium at the *Niantic Hotel*. The second merchant who had joined the wager, Julian Skinner, emerged more than a little tipsy and alone. His huge belly had not seen physical activity in many a year and his person was surrounded by a cloud of spicy perfume.

The Ghost Shadows blindfolded, gagged, and tripped him backward in a swift coordinated assault. He became an awkward deadweight when they lost control of his flabby torso and his head whacked the stone carving that flanked the entrance.

The confused Skinner came to in the dark. "What is that God-awful smell? I'm going to throw up." He tried to move his hands and legs. "I'm in chains. Help! Help anybody. Help. These chains are killing me."

The wooden deck under his butt creaked as it rocked back and forth and stunk of death. The odor in his stuffy wooden prison was a choking blend of a sickly-sweet odor, cadaverine (the odor of decomposed bodies), oakum pine tar, and stale sweat.

Skinner could not imagine where he was until he heard a voice with a Russian accent through the bulkhead.

He will not escape the chains this time. I don't know how you wrestled his carcass on board the Xenophonia, but that pile of blubber is worth ten thousand dollars when his associates get our ransom note in the morning. Good job.

Chapter 11—Hides, Horns, and Quicksilver

Back on the *Agilis*, Babbitt was tense as his degenerate gang of laborers loaded the hold. "You worthless louts can't lash anything. Tighten those hold downs."

He turned to Richard Porter the second mate, "Do something."

Porter barked commands at the laborers who did not want them. "You there, easy with those barrels. Lash 'em down, boys. Hides to port . . . botas to starboard . . . move smart now."

Most of the men didn't know port from starboard or left from right. Their efforts were chaotic, and the sweating men grumbled, "We know old woman, leave us alone." They were harried as they tried to speed the storage process and get back to the gambling halls.

Porter didn't care and hollered, "This old woman says, 'Move it'." To Babbitt, he said, "They ignore my every command."

Porter looked at Ferreri overseeing the chaos, "What are we loading?"

"It's hides, horns, tallow, wheat, and quicksilver." Ferreri cupped his hand over Porter's ear and whispered, "We have a confidential shipment of a million dollars in gold for the Bank of Honolulu. It's twenty-two hundred pounds in unmarked crates. Stow it forward.

Porter had deduced the contents and guarded the heavy little boxes like a hawk. "We'll handle these ourselves," he said, as he directed two *Agilis* crewmen to stow them down the forward hatch.

Ferreri was concerned about the cargo shifting and asked both Porter and Babbitt, "How goes it below?" Porter responded in frustration. "I've never seen dumber hands than these landlubbers. You say aft and they come back at you,

'My ass is fine, how's yours?'

"You say starboard and they say,

'Ain't no stars, it's daytime'.

"You say a lash the cargo, and they use a granny knot. I'll have the crew check them before we weigh anchor, if they ever finish."

In the mayhem, Porter overlooked a lone dory floating near the stern of the *Xenophonia*. The fisherman wore a conical reed hat. He rowed close to the quarters (the blind area off the stern) of *Agilis* and shimmied up a padded grappling hook.

Peeking around the corner of the deckhouse, he noted the crewmen hoisting small heavy crates aboard with a block and tackle hung from the main yardarm. Their weight was a dead giveaway of the contents. He memorized the serial numbers, which were the same numerals as used back home, and silently returned to the dory. With a fishing line trailing in the water, he rowed around the stern of *Xenophonia*.

Porter was too busy to hear the Russian's questions from the deck of the *Xenophonia*, "Where is the gold?"

The spy reported his information, "See ten boxes labeled A46 to A56. Very heavy down forward hold. Laborer no can touch."

"And seamen?"

"Four Kanaka and five seamen, two mate, carpenter."

"What took so long?"

Porter and Babbitt were still too busy to see more rough-looking undesirables board the *Xenophonia* on the side away from the *Agilis*.

Porter did note that a crew of stevedores loaded *Zebra* in record time to the screamed commands of Hornigold. He wondered how they engaged such a quick team of immigrant laborers.

"We're embarking tomorrow, are we ready?" Porter said to Babbitt.

"Believe so, sir. Here comes Pembroke with his parrot, and you've got your cat."

Porter said, "I'm always excited to start a new journey."

Agilis pulsated with activity as the new hands mounted the rope ladder by ones and twos, each shouldering his ditty box.

Rudy the green parrot squawked at the world from atop Pembroke's box. "Squawk, Rudy like boat, squawk."

"Dammit Rudiger, I've told you it's a ship, not a boat," said Pembroke. "Squawk, dammit, boat, boat, boat. Squawk." Pembroke grunted, "Stupid bird," and climbed aboard using the hook in his peg leg on the rungs of the ladder.

Porter, dropping his name of Richard that he used ashore, held Morgan his black cat who watched through wide yellow eyes. The ship's cat purred to think of the young rats on board as he watched a tail disappear under a tarpaulin. He loved the big ones, the little ones, but hated the parrot. Morgan hissed and the bird screeched "Gawk," flapped its wings, and flew up to safety on the yardarm.

Porter could see that some of the seamen were old salts and others were on saltwater for the first time. He said to Babbitt, "Their ditty boxes, or sea chests as you call them, are more interesting than the men.

Babbitt said, "They're a perfect size at a foot square by thirty inches, but don't mess with those locks. That's private."

Porter said, "Some, like mine, have a memory inside the lid of a beautiful woman from a distant port or a vessel they know. I don't expect many journals since they don't read or write for the most part.

Sea dogs and newcomer's headed down to the forecastle. "Stinks same as when I left," said an old sailor to a neophyte.

"I'd say so," he said. "Worse'n the boarding house I slept in."

The forecastle was cramped, dark and dank. It smelled of pine tar from the oakum in the cracks that mingled with the reek of men living and smoking too close together.

"Be like home in a day or two," said the old salt. "Glad to be back."

The forecastle was twenty-two feet long. It tapered from sixteen feet wide aft to four feet wide forward where they stacked their ditty boxes. The low overhead beams just cleared the men at five and a half feet. Each tar got twenty-one inches to sling his hammock, one above another, from cleats in the ceiling above their heads.

Pembroke and Kawai boarded together. Pembroke mocked his riches. "Here's what I got to show for thirty-one years on the water. There's clothes, my knife, a flute, and stuff. I'd trade it all to get my leg back. Let's mark our berths."

They pulled hammocks from a pile and he printed "Pembroke" and "Kawai" on them with a piece of charcoal. He marked the cleats overhead where they would hang.

Porter checking the rigging watched Jackson enter the Master's cabin at the stern, and lay his book on the desk in front of MacIntyre. He overheard him say, "Sir, I have gathered twelve hands. They are the least bad but they need training to make reliable sailors."

MacIntyre replied, "You did a yeoman's job to sign a crew under the circumstances, Jackson. I look forward to casting off tomorrow. Babbitt is instructing the men how to manage a clipper as we speak."

Babbitt dropped down the forecastle ladder with a thud, followed by Porter. Babbitt said, "Listen up men. In the morning when you hear 'Lash up and stow,' you'll clear the area for the day. Roll your hammocks and stow 'em in these nets."

He pointed to nets overhead with canvas covers to keep them dry.

"Eat on your ditty boxes or standing, I don't care which. The cook will bring your mess down in a pot to share. Most of you have shipped before and know the rules, but Master MacIntyre will refresh your memories shortly."

Ferreri's voice interrupted the instructions with a command that echoed over the bay, "All hands on deck."

The crew poured from the forecastle and blinked in the bright sunlight as they clustered on the foredeck. The planks underfoot had lots of splinters which needed the holystone, but the heavily callused feet ignored them.

The crew milled around and nursed their handovers.

MacIntyre emerged from his cabin, cleared his throat and said, "We are about to embark on a round trip to the Sandwich Islands that the natives call the Hawaiian islands."

The Kanaka's nodded their approval at the customary name of their home land.

"There are two parts to the ship—fore and aft. The officers live aft . . .,"

He pointed toward the stern,

"And the crew lives forward . . .,"

He pointed to the bow.

"I distinctly want it understood that we both live in our respective places."

He emphasized his point with a severe look.

"*Agilis* Is not a hell ship by any means, but I expect an order from myself or an officer to be executed promptly and quickly. Sailors are known to fight now and then, and you are sailors. God gave you fists to fight like men. Use them. If any man pulls his knife against another, he will be severely punished."

Two hands put up their fists and playfully punched toward each other. Others eyed one another and measured their skills in a fist fight. Porter did the same.

"Pay attention. I have made a wager that the *Agilis*, on whose deck we are standing, will race the *Zebra* over there to the Islands and back. Our race will commence tomorrow and there is an extra thirty dollars plus a pint of rum to every tar if we prevail. Are you winners?"

"Aye, sir," cheered the crew.

"God Speed. Dismissed."

Alex MacIntyre was nobody's fool with many decades as a master. He knew that part of his crew were not mariners and was determined to give them a quick lesson in seamanship. "Mr. Ferreri, please instruct the crew on sails and seamanship."

Ferreri began. "Many of you are old salts but some are not. Listen up. On the *Agilis*, as on any wind-powered vessel, there is the foremast toward the bow and the mainmast toward the stern."

He pointed to the two masts and the sails starting with the lowest.

"Each mast has four sails. The lowest sheet just above your heads is the main course. Above it is the topgallant. Next, is a topsail and on top the royal sail. Their name is the mast and the sail together, fore-topgallant sail for example."

The old salts were bored and the newcomers were confused so Ferreri gave them a final admonition.

"You will learn the canvas by my instruction or at the end of a lash. But make no mistake you will, by God, learn them."

Porter looked into the face of each man to weigh their competence and character and thought, There's the usual range from the man you'd sail into hell with to somebody barely there. At the same time, they are my men and I am their mate.

Chapter 12—Escape from Alcatraz

Porter arose early on the day of departure to review the navigation charts of the bay. The warning from a harbor pilot about Blossom Rock echoed through his head.

You face a perilous channel, my lad, but you'll be safe if you line up Yerba Buena Island with the guide trees on the west side of Palos Colorados hill.

Porter repeated his instructions, "The first hazard is Blossom Rock that's five feet deep at low or ebb tide. We weigh anchor on the ebb tide, wouldn't you know. The tidal currents roar past Alcatraz island and foam up against Shag Rock and Arch Rock on our way out to sea. And, we're not even to the Golden Gate yet."

With his finger, he traced the channel west from Arch Rock. "Here's the Golden Gate between Point Diablo and Fort Point Rock where we saw the remains of Stag Hound."

He punched the chart with his finger, "And the Mile Rock beyond the gate has claimed more bottoms than the rest of the bay combined. I understand what the man meant when he said, 'Miss the Mile Rocks by a mile.'"

Porter mounted the deck from the cabin in anticipation of the race. The sunrise was brilliant and he sneezed. He said to the officers, "It's a grand sight to see *Agilis* and *Zebra* rigged and ready in the harbor." He waved to the hands in the yards aloft and they waved back. The company waited anxiously for the command to unfurl the sails.

"Helmsman, mark ready."

The helmsmen gripped their tillers while the Masters paced the decks.

Word of the race energized every corner of San Francisco as far as the eye could see.

Hundreds of spectators streamed to the wharf making raucous chatter the whole way. Onlookers sipped a cup of lemonade or whiskey as they entertained their companions with jokes.

Porter looked at his favorite Irish bookmaker charlatan taking bets from all comers at a small table near the wharf. The table legs were planted firmly in the mud against being upset.

The bookmaker entered each bettor's name into a little notebook and added his wager to the heap of money on the top. He kept a balance scale handy for bets made with gold dust. The dust was added to a small chest.

Porter's keen eyes also noticed a small man standing back with his revolver ready for instant use. He recognized the waiter, Josh, from the *Niantic Hotel,* who had trained him to shoot his new Colt dragoon.

Rowdy gamblers besieged the Irishman with sacks of gold dust. He adjusted the odds on a small tablet from time to time, but nobody paid any attention, and most didn't know what odds were anyway.

Porter turned at a shout from Thaddeus Leavenworth in his best suit. The man worked the crowd with a megaphone. Leavenworth planned to run for Mayor in the fall election and wanted all the exposure he could get.

"We need food for our growing community. I am happy to report these friendly rivals, Masters Hornigold and MacIntyre, are wagering their own money. Each asserts they command the fastest vessel to the Hawaiian Islands and back. Regardless of the victor, both will bring supplies to you hungry citizens."

A cheer went up from the crowd.

"Both Masters assure me they know the bay and have refused the services of a pilot. Please give a round of applause as I prepare to send these gentlemen on their way."

The crowd applauded, the baker sold pastries hand over fist, a tobacco vendor offered exotic tobaccos, and a lively man in a hat peddled bottles of beer from a street cart. The spigot on the barrel of whiskey never interrupted its stream of golden courage to the line of thirsty men.

Porter thought, The real contest is between the gamblers, drinks, and food to see which hawker can snatch the money first.

He glanced down Stockton Street through the buildings where horses pulled floats in a parade to entertain the throng. The brand new Community Brass Band struck up a march and followed with an ignored concert. Mr. J. C. Greene cut his cornet solo short in disgust, and the Grand Wedding March by Mendelssohn brought hoots of derision. "There ain't a women to marry in a hundred miles."

Leavenworth interrupted the good times with his megaphone. "Your attention, please."

The crowd became silent.

"Gentlemen, are you ready?" Both masters gestured yes. He looked around to be sure all was in order.

"The winner will be the first person to return their silverware to this circle with a cargo of food to fill your empty bellies. Here is the design on the silver so make no mistake."

He held up a spoon from the *Niantic* dining room to the crowd.

"Good luck to you both."

He painted a circle on the wharf.

"At the sound of the cannon, the race will commence."

"Lieutenant Sherman, the signal if you would."

Sherman, splendid in his full uniform and astride his magnificent horse, raised his sword and galloped through the crowd to the cannon at the shoreline. It was carefully pointed at open water and manned by well-trained soldiers—very well trained.

"Ready!"

"Aim!"

"Fire!"

He dropped his sword and the cannon spit a tongue of flame eleven feet over the water. It sent a rolling boom to the distant hills and back.

The race was on!

The crowd cheered with their participation in the excitement of San Francisco.

Porter was awed by the sight of Sherman on his fine horse carrying a shiny sword. "That will be me someday."

The chef in the *Niantic Hotel* restaurant grumbled, "Very well and good but who is going to pay for that silver knife and fork? It cost me a pretty penny to have my crest engraved by Bernard and Sons in London.

The Irish huckster commented to his companion as they watched the departure, "You can see a clipper ship is not like a racehorse. It takes them forever to get under weigh. I'm amazed they go at all."

The boom of the cannon faded as the near and opposite shores traded echos. It was noon and a steady breeze blew from the northwest. The tide flowed out past Blossom Rock and Alcatraz Island.

Porter ordered, "Lay aloft. Loose topgallants and royals. Move smart now."

From across the water, they could hear a similar command from the *Zebra*. "Lay aloft. Loose all sails. Jump to it!"

Both clippers began to move out—kind of.

Half of *Agilis* crew lay aloft poised on the rigging. The other half held the halyard lines for the fore and main topsails hanging down at the masts. Ferreri was the officer of the deck. "Prepare to set sail. Porter at the helm."

Porter relieved the helmsman and clutched the tiller.

Ferreri said, "Brace three points to starboard." The object was to rotate the yards horizontally to catch the wind. This required teamwork where none existed to shorten the starboard braces and lengthen the port side.

Ferreri went wild. "Look at the damn yard. Port forward with a long line and starboard aft with a short line. Use the lines in your hands. Lift the topsails."

Two hands hauled the halyards and raised the topsail yards to the sailing position. He watched the topsails rotate to catch the wind.

Porter thought, . . . arghhhhh, what a slapdash mess, Ferreri.

Ferreri screamed, "Weigh anchor!" Before the crew could execute this command, Ferreri ordered, "Loose the topsails." The riggers released the gaskets which held the sailcloth rolled up on top of the yard. "Unfurl topsails."

The crew pushed the sails over the front of the yard and let them fall free into their gear, or at least the sailors at the foremast did. The topsail on the main mast got tangled and did not fall. *Agilis* pivoted out of control with the rudder being useless without forward motion.

Ferreri exploded, "Loosen the main topsail, you ignorant landlubbers" and threw a belaying pin at the confused recruit. The pin missed when the ship lurched.

Ferreri, Porter, and Babbitt screamed competing commands to the seamen in chaotic naval profanity and added to the confusion.

Porter glanced at the splendid *Zebra* as she made full and by north with every canvas catching the wind. *Agilis* sails also caught the wind, but because the anchor still gripped the sea floor, she twisted and headed downwind and astern toward *Xenophonia*.

Porter cried at the top of his lungs, "Prepare for contact." The anchor chain was so long in the reverse direction that *Agilis* crunched stern-wise into the side of the *Xenophonia*. The rudder flipped from the impact and threw Porter over the tiller. He jumped up to resume his grip and made a quick check of the part of the stern he could see. He said, "No significant damage."

Ferreri yelled again, "Weigh anchor!" and this time the hands got the anchor fully raised and freed the *Agilis*. By now, the main topgallant sail had unfurled and the crew accidentally set the topsails right.

Ferreri struck the errant *Agilis* sailor across his back as MacIntyre roared, "Listen to the mates."

Porter let out a long, "Whew," now that *Agilis* was under way and headed in the right direction.

MacIntyre and Ferreri stood at the starboard and port gunwales and passed observations to Porter at the tiller.

Porter corrected her course northwest toward the North Point, but his attention was riveted aft on the damage to the *Xenophonia*.

Looking back at the *Xenophonia*, he did not see much external damage apart from a cracked railing and scratched planks. He couldn't see the Chinese pirates below decks who felt the jolt of the *Agilis,* but anticipated their noon meal more.

Zebra was far ahead of them.

From down inside *Xenophonia*, Chernov reviewed the lessons learned from the abduction of Julian Skinner. He pointed to the splint on the arm of the man and said, "The hostage is as secure as the knots on your arm, like I showed you. He won't get loose this time. I don't know how you got that fat hulk aboard."

Chernov looked down the hall to the galley where the cook stoked a raging fire beneath his steel wok pan on the galley stove. He needed blistering hot oil for his stir fry and the flames blazed around the edges higher than any ship's cook would ever allow, but that was how he stir fried chicken. The hungry pirates squatted with their chopsticks in one hand and bowl of rice in the other.

Strollers along the waterfront, if they looked askance at dreaded *Xenophonia* at all, assumed the column of smoke was an early wisp of afternoon fog and looked away.

The shock from the collision had knocked the *Xenophonia* into a starboard list and toppled the pirates onto the floor. They watched in panic as the round-bottom wok tipped on the galley stove and spilled the oil into the fire. The boiling, burning oil poured onto the grease-stained deck and set the galley on fire.

The flames poured across the floor toward Chernov and the pirates. Rolling away from them they charged out the smoke-filled hatch to the boat and set a speed record back to the shack. Chernov and Poison Dragon fumed over the loss of their second hostage and their hostage ship with its cargo of stolen gold and goods.

Red fire consumed *Xenophonia* from the inside out. The rising smoke was obvious to horrified observers but their superstitions blamed the fires of hell, not the summer fog that came every afternoon.

Dread gripped the mob of spectators but turned to terror at Julian Skinner's howls and banging on the hull from below deck. The muffled screams soon ceased as the flames intensified, and only then did cooler heads move nearby vessels away from the conflagration.

Flames enveloped the *Xenophonia* and raced up the tar-filled shrouds to the mast head tops. The blazing planks of the deck created a black column of smoke that twisted like seamen writhing in agony from the gusty changing winds.

The crowd on shore watched in awe, while the ever-ready huckster added a choice of bets on how long the hull would float.

The spellbound onlookers gave a collective moan when the burned timbers of the *Xenophonia* sputtered in the water and sank out of sight. The masts continued burning like two torches standing in the water. *Xenophonia* was no more, but the legend of the Ghost of the Xenophonia sprang from the hissing waves.

One man said to another, "Did you hear Satan howl from the hull?" The other said, "I heard lost souls of hell hammering to escape their flames." A third said, "I saw the ghosts of dead sailors climbing the rising smoke."

Seventeen versions of that new legend circulated in the saloons that night. The guitar player wrote a ballad in a corner of the Blue Crane Bar while he strummed his guitar. He titled it, *The Legend of the Ghost Ship Xenophonia.*

> Ghost ships are sailing on empty seas
> So wait until tomorrow and then we'll see
> I don't know about tomorrow
>
> It's just the captain and crew jumping off of the
> mast
> All aboard on the ghost ship of cannibal rats
> All aboard on the ghost ship of cannibal rats

The drinkers of the Blue Crane bar sang the ballad the rest of the night.

Porter was stunned by the rising column astern of black smoke from the *Xenophonia.* He suspected he was responsible somehow, but nonetheless, steadied the helm as he navigated *Agilis* to the northwest.

Ferreri said, "That is Russian Hill with a cemetery on top and we are coming up on Telegraph Hill with its cemetery for non-Catholic seamen at the base. Thought you should know."

Porter looked up but kept his hands on the tiller as Master MacIntyre approached. "Steady as she goes. Line up Yerba Buena Island with those two redwood navigation trees on Colinas Palos Colorados (Redwood Hills) across the bay."

He pointed out the hill and the indistinct redwood trees in the haze.

"With that alignment, you will avoid the submerged Blossom Rock in the channel. Keep Alcatraz Island to port and head for the center of the Golden Gate Strait. Devote your absolute attention to this dangerous channel."

Porter was determined to redeem himself in the eyes of MacIntyre. He studied the distant grove of redwood trees through the developing afternoon haze but unfortunately mistook redwoods on the eastern slope for the taller navigation trees on the western slope. He lined up on the eastern trees.

He compounded his mistake against Macintyre's direct orders by switching his gaze between the spectacular fire astern and the vanishing *Zebra* to starboard. He tried to read the water between gazes, but the variable winds obscured the contrary tide and the cursing on deck distracted his attention.

Total commitment to his navigation went overboard. He forgot to line up the northern tip of Yerba Buena Island with even the two eastern redwood trees sixteen miles distant on Redwood Hill. The *Agilis'* hull jerked Porter to port with a crash.

Porter shouted, "Oh no. What did I hit?" The sister repairs on the overhead mast cracked.

"What the hell is that?" said MacIntyre. He spied the Blossom Rock that was submerged less than a fathom under the starboard bow. He well knew *Agilis* had a deep draft as loaded and there was no way they could clear the rock.

The stern collided a second time, even as Porter trimmed the rudder hard to port. He saw MacIntyre trip and fall against the pinrail. Porter broke out in a cold sweat and gripped the tiller with a death hold.

MacIntyre and Ferreri both spotted the marker buoy forty-five yards away in the ebbing tide. It had been dragged off position by an out-of-control vessel the day before. Master MacIntyre roared to Ferreri, "What damages have we sustained?"

Ferreri passed the command on down and said, "Babbitt, make an inspection."

"We appear to have breached the hold," said Babbitt after a quick check.

The officers made a more thorough examination but could find no huge damage, since the cargo was stacked in front of the hull. "A leak is evidenced in the area of impact but we can handle it with the bilge pump," said Babbitt.

The green crew members didn't think anything about the accident. They were accustomed to harder impacts stumbling from bar to bar.

Master MacIntyre exploded, "Where the bloody hell are you going, Porter? Pay damn attention. Watch the water and follow the outgoing tide around that rock. That is an order."

Porter offered a comment "Sir, with respect, the tiller is behind the deckhouse with no view forward. I did see the swirl around the rock from a distance and followed the buoy over there. A spotter at the bow would be a tremendous help in these congested waters. You, sir, left your position at the bow."

"No excuses, Porter. I will direct my own ship, thank you, and you will focus on the tiller. I will not tolerate insubordination in my command."

Chatting in the stern of the *Zebra*, Hornigold said to Chernov as they stared back at the *Agilis*, "They're headed straight toward Blossom Rock . . . likely snap a mast or breach her hull for sure." Chernov swelled with pride as he admired the full spread of gray sails aloft that soared to impossible heights. The belly of each canvas bulged in the wind and sped the vessel through the Golden

Gate. Chernov directed his helmsman around the Mile Rocks off Land's End, as he contemplated a fresh shipwreck stranded there and they entered the Pacific ocean.

By contrast, the hands on *Agilis* were clumsy and unsure of themselves. They clambered up and down the ratlines in response to conflicting orders from Ferreri and Babbitt. Porter got in a few shouted orders from the helm as well. It was by chance the riggers re-braced the sails to cope with the wind from a different quarter as they rounded North Point and headed west toward Alcatraz.

The race was on.

"Ahhh . . . back to the briny deep. I am more elated to be leaving the Golden Gate than I was to enter," MacIntyre said to Porter as he repeated his navigational directions.

Porter paid especially close attention to Macintyre's next words, "We are passing Alcatraz now. Avoid the wreck of the Stag Hound on Fort Point Rock to port, but give the spray from Point Diablo to starboard a wide berth as well. Get past Point Bonita, evade Mile Rocks, and bear south. This San Francisco Bay is a ship-eating demon as it breathes tides in and out. Eyes alert, Mr. Porter."

He listened intently as MacIntyre continued.

"These winds are notoriously fickle and will drop to a dead calm in a heartbeat. We would be helpless in the currents and could drift to our demise."

MacIntyre went forward and said to Ferreri and Babbitt, "Mount all the sail you can stand until we clear the strait."

Porter guided *Agilis* in a big loop around the new shipwreck on Mile Rocks and entered the Pacific Ocean, grateful to be out of the San Francisco Bay.

A line of choppy waves from a distant tropical storm combined with a rare south wind to slow the *Zebra* and allow *Agilis* to approach, until she too was slowed by the same conditions. The racing brigs headed south by southwest by keeping the shaft of smoke over the Santa Cruz mountains dead astern.

They made it five miles before the winds subsided and forward momentum slowed to a walk, to a crawl. The watch called out eight bells as the last breath of wind died and *Agilis* stopped dead in the water. She was adrift halfway to Monterrey with the waning column of smoke from the Xenophonia still visible astern.

The competing crews shouted crude insults across the water although they could barely hear each other.

"May your hammer be brittle"

"Away, you three-inch fool!"

"I desire we be better strangers"

"May the cat eat you and the devil eat the cat"

"May the devil make a ladder of your back bones while picking apples in the garden of hell"

"Your face would drive rats from a barn"

Porter was conflicted. He had let his men down but did not know how to redeem himself. He went over the charts of the inlet again and again and asked himself,

What did I miss? I am not sure, but never again.

Porter felt the calm sea air and tried overcame his depression, but Macintyre's next admonition brought it all back.

"Ferreri, come with me to the helm. I want a private word with my mates."

He forgot a sailor in the rigging who could hear clearly.

"I expect my commands to be obeyed exactly and promptly. When I say, 'Watch for a hazard', that is what I mean. Porter failed at Blossom Rock. Do not repeat that mistake again."

The mates said, "Yes, sir."

MacIntyre said, "Carry on."

Porter fumed in frustration, "I can still see Pillar Point and Half Moon Bay from the damn deck. No need to climb a single ratline. There's a clan of Ohlone Indians laughing at us from the shore, sir."

"I can see them," as MacIntyre stomped into his cabin and slammed the door.

Porter located the *Zebra* who was becalmed a mile farther southwest.

Ferreri said to the crew, "We are becalmed."

Someone said, "No shit."

Two hands crawled out the bowsprit and paddled furiously. *Agilis* laughed at their feeble efforts. The *Agilis's* only forward progress came from the ocean current that flowed at a blistering rate of four knots a day, and south not southwest like they needed.

An orca circled around them jumping into the air and laughing at their clumsy water skills. It hurled itself out of the water and drenched the men with a big wave when it splashed back. Two sailors held their hands to its skin and one said to the other, "That fish is longer than us and a hell of a lot faster." The other said, "It's a whale, not a fish and let's throw a harness on it. Think it knows the way to Hawaii?" They laughed half seriously.

Porter did some mental figuring.

We will enter Honolulu in only 656 days. At this rate, we'll be manned by a crew of white bones. Tiny rat skeletons will decorate the timbers and the only thing left alive will be one fat rat.

"I demand wind."

Babbitt gave his morning report to Porter who relayed it to Ferreri and he to MacIntyre in the cabin.

Porter summarized the ominous news, "The bilge water is rising seven inches a day. It takes four hours of pumping during a watch to limit the level. We traveled six nautical miles since yesterday. At this rate, we'll be dead when our bones reach Honolulu. Otherwise, all's well.

MacIntyre said, "Go on."

"Every sheet of canvas is unfurled in its gear. This is the light-air plan of sails I was taught to use when you are becalmed as we are. The rigging is taut and the decks are in order. If a solitary bird flies by we'll move.

MacIntyre grunted, "Thank you, Porter. Notify me if the bilge turns for the worse. Keep the men occupied until we are underway again."

One of the hands, O'Sullivan, whistled an idle Irish tune on deck as he carved a scrimshaw design into a whale tooth. His design was of *Agilis* winning the race to the cheers of the crowd.

Ferreri was on edge and jumped down his throat, "Stop that whistling. You'll call up a storm."

O'sullivan stopped his whistling but soon started humming, *My Bonnie Lies Over the Ocean*. Pretty soon, Palmieri's operatic voice took up the song and the company exploded in unison,

> *My Bonnie lies over the ocean*
> *My Bonnie lies over the sea*

My Bonnie lies over the ocean
Oh, bring back my Bonnie to me . . .

The crew finished in a mighty crescendo.

MY BONNIE LIES OVER THE OCEAN!
OH, BLOW BACK MY BONNIE TO ME!

. . . ON A WIND! ! !

MacIntyre took up the tune with tears in his eyes. "Aye there, O'Sullivan. My Bonnie true awaits far away in me Scotland. How I wish she were here beside me."

O'sullivan muttered,

I'm from Ireland, not Scotland, but I still love Bonnie.

After two more days under a hot sun, Porter decided to test the whistling superstition with O'sullivan. "Whistle a tune, but not too hard, since we want a breeze not a gale."

Porter sometimes joined O'sullivan in inflicting two days of raspy whistles on the *Agilis*. They knew a whistle brought wind, but not when nor how much. The two whistlers brought out their raunchiest efforts.

Porter called out, "Time for the big guns, mates. You drink to it, let's make wind with it. Everybody now, *Friggin' in the Riggin'*. The deck became a glee club.

It was on the good ship Venus
By Christ, you should've seen us
The figurehead was a whore in bed
And the mast was a mammoth penis

Friggin' in the riggin'
Friggin' in the riggin'
There was fuck all else to do

The superstition failed to deliver any wind, but they enjoyed the chantey and the fond memories it brought of one kind and another.

The superstition generated another kind of storm. Babbitt shouted and ran through the musicians waving his hands, "The song is 'The Good Ship Venus', and she was lost off Van Diemen's Land in 1806. Show some respect, sing Dixie."

Porter called out, "*Dixie* it is.

Oh, I wish I was in the land of cotton . . .

Dixie it was but no wind blew.

Penbroke said, "I know something that never fails." He reached into his bag of lore and pulled out a spell for wind and rain. Out of practice and sitting on the capstan, energy flooded him from the clear atmosphere. He only hurt a little and cast the spell.

Tempestatis procella magna voco

He used a lot of energy and expected the spell to last many hours, but the sailors Kalani and O'sullivan scanned the vacant horizon in disappointment.

Hot and irritable, O'Sullivan bumped into Kalani who swung back. They grappled and knocked boxes around on the deck and into other tars from the forecastle. Kalani pulled his knife and attacked O'Sullivan. O'Sullivan was good at knife fighting and responded in kind. They circled about the deck and Kalani nicked O' Sullivan's defensive arm.

Babbitt roared out, "No knives. Macintyre's rule is fists only."

The commotion brought MacIntyre from his cabin in a rage. "I told you not a week ago, 'if a man fights with his knife he will be severely punished.' "

To Porter he said, "Seven lashes tomorrow at noon for those men fighting with knives."

Porter confiscated their knives and ordered two sailors who were watching the fight, "Chain these two below and keep 'em apart."

O'sullivan and Kalani spit at each other as the tars hauled them down the hatch. Kalani kicked at O'sullivan who swung a backhand. Both missed.

Chains clanked when they were clamped around the feet of the two fighters. They were just out of reach of each other in the hold, the same area where Porter had been confined. It was stifling from the sun pouring onto the overhead deck and without a breath of wind.

O'sullivan complained, "Beyond fierce weather hot 'tis. I'm arseways now."

Tar from oakum oozed up from joints in the planks and gripped the feet. *Agilis* floated in a ring of jettisoned trash that even the sharks rejected.

Porter wracked his brain how to occupy his men of action and keep them from fighting. "We'll instruct in the morning and compete in the afternoon."

He asked Babbitt. "How do sails make us go?" Several seamen listened in and one commented, "Looks like witchcraft to me."

Babbitt could not ignore the witchcraft reference since it outraged his religious background. "It's not witchcraft, you ignorant jack-tar. Watch my hand."

He pointed at seabirds flying through the rigging. "Those are *Sooty Shearwater* birds like we see everywhere. Their wings are curved on the top and flat on the bottom. As they glide, the air goes faster over the top and pulls the bird up.

A sail works the same but flat ways. The wind billows the sail and makes the air flow faster over the bulge. It is the round side of the bulge that pulls us along. We brace sails sideways to catch the wind."

Porter said, "Now I know, maybe," and the others nodded. He waved to the ship's carpenter, "Chips Alden, get over here and tell us about wood."

Alden showed how to sister a mast. "We temporarily rig a sprung mast to get us home. Make a flat side on the sister and hold that against the damaged mast." He picked the end of a cannibalized foremast and flattened one side with his knife. Alden liked to show off his wicked-sharp edges by slicing paper-thin chips. "Hold this up, you two."

Porter and a sailor climbed to the main top and hauled up the flattened sister spar. They held it against the sprung mast and Alden showed them how to tie a jury mast knot above and below the break. "Let go now." He followed up with several intermediate knots for safety.

"This jury mast knot will get us home if we don't hit heavy weather." He showed off another skill by throwing a hammer with his eyes closed to a mark that was ten feet away.

The mustered tars on deck were tense with dread as they watched the officers prepare for the flogging. Chips Alden inserted hooks into the foremast and the mainmast eight feet high. After sailors cleared the deck around the masts, the preparations were complete.

Porter listened as MacIntyre discussed the punishment with Ferreri. "I am making this public for its utmost impact. We must have discipline for our safety and the launch of a voyage is a good time to start."

Ferreri nodded, but Porter was silent, thinking about his own experience under the cat.

"Administer the flogging boldly for these are tough men, but not so vigorously as to draw blood, although we may see an occasional cut. The men will return to their stations afterward. Call me when you're ready."

Ferreri asked, "Is there a cat o' nine tails available?" Porter said, "I'll get mine. I knotted it myself and it tickled my back on my first voyage." He snatched the cat from his ditty box and handed it to Babbitt.

Babbitt held the cat high to show off the handle stained with sweat and the tails caked in dried blood. He placed it on the polished capstan where Kalani and O'Sullivan. could see it. They stared at the cat with horror.

Ferreri directed hands to seize Kalani and O'Sullivan. to the hooks on the masts. The mates pulled their shirts down to expose both bare backs. They stretched their wrists so high that their toes barely touched the deck. Kalani was stoic and resigned, as he had experienced the cat before. O'Sullivan. was a virgin, and terrified. It didn't matter as they were both strung up the same way.

"Do your duty when you are ready, Mr. Babbitt, or you'll be there yourself," said Ferreri.

Babbitt stood four feet back and whizzed the cat overhead three times for suspense. A new recruit retched in empathy while the officers and crew strained for a glimpse. Babbitt coiled his body to full force and whipped the cat o' nine tails across Kalani's naked back; swish, crack, contact.

Porter counted, "That's one."

Babbitt waited twenty seconds for effect; a swish, a crack, contact.

"That's two."

Through all seven lashes, Kalani made no sound beyond a grunt.

Porter twisted Kalani's face to his and roared, "Will you draw your knife on a fellow sailor again?" The man gritted his teeth and managed a low, "No, sir."

"I'll return your knife, but use it properly."

Babbitt faced O' Sullivan's unprotected back hanging on the other mast. He was terrified from seeing Kalani's treatment. Warm-up, swish, crack, pain, wait twenty seconds.

"That's one,"

"That's two,"

"That's three."

The first three strokes knocked the wind out of O'sullivan. He was rigid and could utter no sound. At stroke four, he caught his breath and blurted out, "Oh, Jesus Christ, oh, help me." These words so offended Babbitt with his Christian upbringing that he redoubled his swing for the last three lashes. He added a gratuitous eighth for good measure which was not counted and stepped back panting.

Porter faced O'Sullivan. "Will you draw your knife on a fellow sailor again?" The man writhed in pain but muttered, "No sir." Porter screamed in his ear, "I can't hear you." O'Sullivan belted out a loud, "No, sir, never again, sir."

"Here is your knife back. Use it properly."

MacIntyre ordered, "Wash them down and put them to work." Babbitt splashed a bucket of cold seawater over the blistered back of each man to disinfect the cuts and heighten the pain. The salt heightened the pain for sure.

Kalani was expecting this, clenched his teeth, shook the water off his head, and took it. O'Sullivan. was not expecting the salt-water drench and bit his tongue from the stab of pain. He howled without words and shuddered. He would have taken the infection instead.

MacIntyre summarized the reason for the punishment in a loud voice. "I want it clearly understood that my commands will be obeyed. Orders from the officers will be followed as though they are mine. Dismissed."

O'sullivan and Kalani trudged to their stations. Their numbness wore off by mid-afternoon and they agonized through the last half of their watch.

That night, they lay their hammocks on the floor as a thin mattress to sleep on their stomachs. They kept their shirts off to let their backs heal.

Before bed, they strutted around the forecastle proudly showing off their reddened battle scars.

Ferreri pulled Porter aside. "To maintain your license as the second mate, you must pass my navigational test. You will not have time to run up and down the mast like a common sailor."

Ferreri took out his sextant and waved it in front of the crew before handing it to Porter. "Show us how to take a reading."

Porter moved the sextant to his left hand, sighted, and adjusted the mechanism with his right. He measured the angle from the sun to the horizon as he explained the procedure. "You measure the angle of the sun at noon and convert it to your position with this table in this book." He relied on his experience with the transit in Sacramento and the directions from his book of the sextant.

In his journal, he wrote down their latitude as thirty-seven degrees twenty-three minutes and fourteen seconds north of the equator without saying anything. He handed the sextant to Ferreri, "Your turn."

Ferreri demonstrated the same technique and called out his reading. Porter said, pointing to his reading, "There's my reading; we are not six seconds apart. That's less than a nautical mile on the ocean."

"Way to go, sir," said Amundson. "You got our back."

Ferreri grunted and said, "I'll record in the log that you passed the test."

Porter and Ferreri disliked each other but had to cooperate as mates. Ferreri was impressed with Porter's accuracy, but refused to admit it.

Porter put his sextant away and gathered the sailors. "We live close together and you're used to our smell, but the good people ashore are not. You want to entice the ladies of leisure, don't you? But their cost goes up when you stink doesn't it? Cook Silva has a remedy for you."

A voice came from the group, "They're all fun. Besides, some are sweet on us as we are."

"Yeah," said someone else.

Porter said, "If we ever get to Honolulu, wash up and splash yourself with Silva's bay rum to stink good before you get off. Ladies will chase you down the street."

"They'll do that?" The men laughed in hopeful disbelief.

"If you got money, they will."

Porter continued, "Cook Silva soaks leaves of the bay tree in rum to make a natural smell good. He calls it bay rum. The buccaneers of the Caribbean stole the idea from the Caribe Indians. It works and Silva has a batch in the galley."

"I'll hide my stink from the inside out," piped up O'sullivan. to a pantomime of drinking from a bottle.

Silva slapped him on the back. "Stay away from me, apestoso (stinky). I made bay rum. You do what you want, but wait 'til we get there."

The jack-tars of the forecastle tired of teaching old sea chanteys to new recruits. They had plenty of tobacco but the flow of verses slowed to a dribble.

Blown out was,

Blow the Man Down

They'd solved the riddle of,

What do you do with a Drunken Sailor?

Worn out were,

The Ladies of Spain.

However, the restless crew couldn't stay quiet for long. They started picking on their favorite target, Pembroke, who took it but returned better than he got.

Porter listened down the forecastle hatch but didn't want to break into their free time.

Levi Pembroke, nicknamed Broken Pen, liked to sling stories from his thirty-three years at sea when he got bored, but

Amundson triggered the storytelling this time when he said, "What about your green-arse parrot there?"

Broken Pen shot back, "Were you drunk when the press-gang got you?"

"Of course and what about the bird?"

"He's my friend. I played poker for a day and a half in Bremerhaven, Germany. Me and this other tar cleaned out the room."

"Yeah, and . . . ,"

"It was down to us two and we showed our cards. He had a jack-high flush, a strong hand. I had a queen-high flush and took the pot. He got mad and said, 'Deal, you son of a bitch'. I put up everything I was wearing, like this shirt off an Indian sultan." His two pair of jacks, kicker two, lost against my two pair of jacks, kicker three. God was he mad."

"I'd a been mad too," said Amundson.

"He squirmed on his slippery butt and declared, 'I bet my parrot, Rudiger. This hand is mine.' He was naked and there weren't anywhere to hide a card to cheat. His hand was two pair, kings and queens. I laid down three pair of twos and Rudiger was mine. I gave him back his greasy clothes and left."

"Like these?", Amundson held up a pair of trousers filled with tar.

"This little bird has roosted on my shoulder for twenty-seven years. His name is Rudiger. He curses in three languages and starts stories. Say something."

"Squawk, luridi branco di cani bastardi (filthy bunch of sons-of-bitches)."

Pembroke explained, "He learned that in Naples, Italy."

"Squawk, Du Fickfehler (You are a fuck error)".

"Hamburg, Germany."

"Squawk. Cachu bant ti cachu mes (Fuck off you sheep-shagger)."

Pembroke turned a little red and said, "Rudy soaks up words like a sponge. We were in the Cardiff Docks in Wales."

"Squawk. Tu gato es feo (Your cat is ugly)."

Pembroke shouted, "Shut up! You go too far when you insult an animal."

Rudiger flapped his wings for attention, "Squawk! Rudy want a story."

His owner screamed, "I said, shut up." Rudy pouted and hid his head under his wing.

"Watch your language or he'll throw it right back at you, and he never forgets."

Amundson was skeptical, "That's nothing, I can curse in three languages too but is he quiet at night?"

"He talks all the time. You put this hood over his head to make him go to sleep. Watch sharp he doesn't trick you 'cause he talks like anybody. He surprises me after twenty-seven years. Waugh . . . ." he said to Rudiger.

The crew sat on their ditty boxes and talked, while Rudiger flew to a cross member and stared at the cat.

The forecastle had that rank smell that would be normal in a day or two. Each man blamed the others for his fragrance until he figured out it was him.

Rudiger startled the crew with an outburst, "Squawk! Rudy want a story." He hated being ignored for long.

He wasn't.

Morgan the black cat leaped out of the shadows onto his back with a mighty howl. Rudiger clamped his powerful beak onto Morgan's tail and the two fell squawking and screaming to the floor. Rudiger pecked Morgan on the head and Morgan opened his teeth for a better grip.

In a cloud of green feathers, Rudiger back flew up to the cross timber while Morgan jumped as high as he could but missed.

Porter jumped down the hatch and grabbed Morgan as the two glared at each other. "Bad cat. Leave that bird alone, you hear? He can fight back."

Porter shook his fist in Morgan's face, but Morgan just purred. Porter sat down on an unused ditty box and restrained Morgan, "Sorry about that. I'd a thought rats are enough to chase. Apparently not." He leaned against the ladder holding Morgan.

Pembroke, a.k.a. Broken Pen, began a story. "Some of you tars haven't sailed before." He got no response but the three novice hands stood out because their naked skin had never seen a tattooist's needle. Porter noted the difference because his skin was blank as well.

"Tattoos is good luck. Like . . . where we've been . . . what we've done . . . ladies we've met. Very lucky when everybody has a tattoo." He gestured to reveal one of each type as he spoke.

"What d'you mean protect us? I think they look good," a well-tattooed ordinary sailor said.

Pembroke held up his good foot showing a rooster. "This cock-a-doodle-do shows the way to shore if I fall in the water, an' don't let me drown. A pig is the same, but he is gone. Anchors are steady as she goes when you cross the Atlantic," he said when he flexed his left arm.

O'sullivan wiggled his anchor around his belly button.

"Porter's black cat, Morgan, is lucky, too. They says Morgan, but I calls him Fore 'n Aft with a white spot on his chest and white feet aft. Why is he lucky? Rats. Cats eat rats."

He lowered his voice and the crew strained to hear, "I am here to tell you cats has magic powers. If Fore 'n Aft comes to you, it's good luck 'til dusk. Halfway and retreats, you is unlucky until dusk. Overboard in a storm, we're lost. Rescued we're cursed for nine years 'cause cats don't like water. And this ain't no tall tale of the sea neither."

Fore 'n Aft knew he had a friend and climbed into Pembroke's lap. Rudiger was jealous and screamed from overhead. "Kraal, Rudy hate black cat. Rudy hate all cats. Rudy hate Morgan. screech, wrack, aaaawk, squawk." He flapped his wings in anger at sharing his owner with a feline.

Rats didn't bother Rudiger because he perched where rats couldn't. But Fore 'n Aft stalked Rudiger everywhere to ambush him.

Cook Marco José Tavares Silva spread the grandest dinner he could muster with his Caribbean galley skills. Around the dining table in the cabin were seated the officers, mates, bosun, and carpenter. Silva entered with a gigantic bowl of Jamaican barbacoa and placed it as the centerpiece. He had barbecued a pig seasoned with Jamaican spice and herb rubs over a makeshift charcoal grill for two nights and a day.

Wafting aromas had teased the crew's appetites all afternoon. Stomachs growled. Silva added a few simple side dishes of rabbit braised in butter, mango chicken, pan-fried red snapper on a platter, plantains sautéed in ghee, and callaloo made with amaranth leaves for the token vegetable. He trimmed the rim of the table with bottles of wine, brandy, and fine rums.

The officers relaxed around the groaning table in high spirits and raised a forest of glasses in frequent toasts. Ferreri was flying high and saluted the hanging lantern with a brandy.

"I'll bet nobody knows the story of Drake's drum." He looked around and saw the hollow stares confirm his remark.

> A drum once owned by Sir Francis Drake has magic powers. When dying off of Panama in 1596, Drake ordered his drum returned home to Plymouth, England, and it hangs there to this very day. Drake vowed that if England was in danger he would beat on the drum and would return.

Porter said, "I've seen the drum. This is a true story."

> That drum rolled out ghostly moans when Napoleon was brought to Plymouth as a prisoner after the battle at Waterloo. England is safe with Sir Drake to the rescue."

"Amazing."

MacIntyre cleared his throat. "Ahem, gentlemen, did you know we have pirates of the Pacific like in the Caribbean? There is a buried treasure south of us."

The company's attention halted at the word treasure, buried or not. They scrutinized the face of the Master with bated breath and every mind asked, 'How far south?'.

"I heard this from a man who, himself, had deceived the Spaniards.

> The Spanish moved their stolen gold from mountain mines down to Acapulco under a

uniformed guard. Their galleons took it to Spain from there, unless Señor Benito "Bloody Sword" Bonito hijacked them first.

Porter said, "That's like bringing gold to San Francisco from Sacramento. Maybe we need uniformed guards to hold off the pirates."

Could be. In any case, Bonito's crew captured the guards and donned their uniforms. They stole a year's production without firing a shot. Bonito buried it on Cocos Island. He was later betrayed by two Englishmen and hanged. Those bars are still buried on the island but nobody knows where. Many have searched.

Somebody asked for all, "Where is Cocos Island?"

"Only about four thousand nautical miles due south, off the province of Costa Rica. Do you want to go?"

"Let's go."

"We can't go anywhere without we get some wind. We are becalmed if you notice."

Porter took the floor with sparkling eyes. He loved to tell jokes when Pembroke was not around.

It was a stormy night and Eugene stood his first guard duty. Captain Murdoch strolled by with his dog, and the nervous young seaman snapped to attention with a salute. 'Good evening, sir.'

The Captain said, 'Good evening seaman, nice night isn't it?' Eugene would not disagree and replied, 'Yes sir.'

Murdoch continued, 'There's something soothing about a stormy night, don't you agree?' Eugene didn't but was only a seaman, and responded, 'Yes, sir.'

The Captain pointed at the dog and said, 'This is a highland terrier, the best to train. I got him for my wife.' Eugene, with a glint in his eye, responded, 'Excellent trade, sir.'

The company laughed and quaffed another glass to wash down the spicy barbacoa.

MacIntyre said, "Silva, you have outdone yourself tonight. This is the best feast we on *Agilis* have ever enjoyed."

They all nodded enthusiastically and Porter said, "A toast to the chef." He held up his glass and lead a round of drinks to thank Silva.

But MacIntyre grew irritated. "Why is that lantern getting dim? Somebody turn it up. And this ship is rocking, but why isn't that lantern swaying?"

He grasped the edge of the table and swayed back and forth in his chair. "I can hardly sit in my chair. Are we in a storm? And yet that lantern doesn't move."

MacIntyre knocked over his wine glass. He tried to pick it up but the glass fell to the floor, followed by a full bottle of wine. His head cocked sideways motionless and he couldn't speak. The party stared at him in alarm.

Porter was the first to understand how badly off MacIntyre was because he had seen it once before. He moved to his side and held his head. "MacIntyre, talk to me. What's wrong?" Porter slapped his face to keep him awake.

MacIntyre tried to speak but could only babble from the right side of his mouth. The left side was rigid. "I ca'hant heer syou. Vought parish?" He grasped his head with both hands and moaned, "Oh, oh, ooh." He rocked side to side between the arms of his captain's chair.

Porter knew another test. "Smile and raise your arms." He grimaced and his upraised left arm drifted downward, although he was not conscious of it. Silva understood, too, and jumped to the other side of MacIntyre. He had seen his father suffer this attack in Jamaica and recalled the treatment which his curandera (witch doctor) wife had applied.

Porter and Silva said at the same time, "The Master has an attack of apoplexy." Silva said, "This is bad but I have medicine for him." He fetched a large box from his galley and opened it to reveal rows of herbs, extracts, various salves, and elixirs, each marked with the malady it was effective to treat. He pulled out a jar of wild lettuce extract and a box of powdered willow bark. "Rub this extract on his face to ease his pain."

Porter poured some black extract into his palm and massaged it into Macintyre's temples. The ship's master sank back in his chair with a sigh.

Silva continued, "Master MacIntyre must drink this willow bark powder to protect his blood. Mix it with wine and pour it down his throat. Be sure he swallows."

Silva made the mixture and held the glass to Macintyre's mouth as Porter tipped a portion onto his tongue. Most spilled out, but Porter tilted Macintyre's head back a little more and Silva repeated the treatment. MacIntyre finally swallowed an effective dose.

Ferreri butted in with an overbearing attitude. "Stand back. I can treat apoplexy. Heat a metal cup on the fire to cup him. I'll bleed half a wine bottle of bad blood while it heats." He pulled out his knife to slice Macintyre's arm, but Porter knocked it out of his hands. Silva froze.

Porter exclaimed, "Your old wife's tales will kill him. He doesn't need to be bled."

Silva said, "Willow bark heals his blood."

Porter said, "You are not putting that hot cup anywhere near MacIntyre."

Silva said, " . . . and no spices on his feet. I know better."

Ferreri backed down in the face of the united opposition.

They laid MacIntyre in his bed. Silva's medicine slowly took effect and his moaning faded to murmurs. He fell into a deep slumber.

Cook Silva said, "El está en la mano de Dios. (He is in the hand of God). We can but wait."

Ferreri asked in a panic, "What is the problem? Oh, this is terrible, terrible." He paced up and down the cabin.

Porter solemnly informed the group, "Master MacIntyre will be indisposed for some time. I saw apoplexy like this in a farmer, and he recovered after some weeks. MacIntyre is thinking clearly, even if he cannot speak. We must help him communicate and follow his commands."

Ferreri astonished all present. "I now take charge of the *Agilis*. Mr. Porter will assume the duties of the first mate in addition to those of the second mate. I will notify the crew immediately."

No one said anything.

Porter led Ferreri and Babbitt to the deck where Ferreri called the crew in a rattled but loud voice, "All hands on deck. Master MacIntyre is ill and I have assumed the duties of Master. Porter is both first and second mate. Babbitt assists the second mate and continues as bosun. You will support the officers in their new roles as you do now. Dismissed."

A crew member spoke up, "Sir, how ill is Master MacIntyre? Will he still be our Master?"

"I am your Master and you will obey my orders. Master MacIntyre is temporarily ill and that's all I know. I'm Master Ferreri now, to repeat myself. Man your posts."

Porter stepped up to his officer of the deck duties. "Clean up that mess at the bow. Holystone the decks, because they are full of splinters and slippery. Tighten those the halyards. Split up your work. Get it done!"

Babbitt was overcome with agitation as he approached the mates. "Sirs, I heard your discussion against Master MacIntyre. I don't know how he is ill, but you are wrong to make a mutiny and take over the ship. I stand by him while he recovers. I must enter your action in the ship's log."

Ferreri flared up, "You will do no such thing. I said temporary and temporary it is. I am Master and find it unnecessary to make a log entry at this time. You're unqualified to determine the medical condition of MacIntyre."

Babbitt replied, "I may not be a doctor but I know you should surrender *Agilis* to a superior officer until MacIntyre recovers."

Ferreri attacked back, "What the hell do you know? You're a lowly bosun, and an old one at that. Shut your mouth and get to work. I will not tolerate insubordination."

Babbitt dropped his head, walked forward, and bellowed at the distressed sailors. "You there, clean up that damn mess and holystone these decks like Mr. Porter ordered. Snap to it, dammit."

The crew was distraught and clumsy at everything they did.

Porter looked on and thought, What has happened? This is bad.

Chapter 13—My Men

Temporary master, Ferreri, cornered Porter and said, "Mr. Porter, you are young and inexperienced. As second mate, you must maintain the proper distance between yourself and the crew. You fraternize with the hands in the forecastle and make a problem for yourself."

Porter knew what was coming but said with a bland face, "How is that, sir?"

"There is no time to spare from your heavy duties. The tars in the forecastle must instantly execute your commands, or it will endanger the ship. Command with authority. You shall you shall plot courses, take star fixes, handle the after deck, and stand the twelve to four watch. Any questions Mr. Porter?"

"This is good advice and I thank you for it. I am guided by the example of Lieutenant William Sherman, whom I met in Sacramento. He graduated from the Military Academy at West Point. I may be few in years but I am many in experience. I am loyal to the forecastle because they follow me from respect."

Ferreri said, "I do not allow argument, especially yours. You obviously lack experience to command. I admonish you to act with authority because those rude jack tars react only to strict discipline. That is your control over them."

"Aye sir," said Porter, as he hung his head and thought to himself, These are my men and I will lead them as I see fit in spite of what you say.

The blistering sun smothered the placid ocean surface. Tempers rose with the temperature and agitated the crew.

Amundson put on a new shirt he sewed for his coming shore leave in Honolulu. "What do you think?"

Pembroke said, "Maybe a hussy over fifty."

Amundson towel snapped him over the head.

"Yahoo . . . ."

O'sullivan danced the can-can kicking his legs high with a piece of canvas wrapped around his waist like a short skirt. Kawai wrapped a sheet around him like a white ghost and snuck up on a fellow reading a picture book titled Frankenstein. "Whooooo, moan . . . , groan, and achhh . . . ," and a sweaty hug. The reader screamed and ran across the deck to peals of laughter that rocked the *Agilis*.

Porter said to Babbitt, "Those jack-tars make good use of old sails."

"It's the best they have."

Scattered hands puffed on pipes, talked, and two went back to their picture books. Others mended torn clothes.

Pembroke resumed carving a whaling ship into a tooth he bought from a whaler somewhere along the line. He added an inscription from the man who sold it.

Amundson could not read and said, "What does that say?"

> This is the tooth of a sperm whale taken
> near Cocos Island by the crew of the ship Essex
> and made 100 barrels of oil, 1817.

"You know about the buried treasure on Cocos Island too?" said Amundson.

Pembroke smiled and kept on scraping.

"What treasure?"

He rubbed tobacco juice into the grooves to make them stand out and called his masterpiece done.

The heat intensified under the midday sun and the Kanakas dove into the ocean to cool off.

Pembroke and Rudiger panted and watched each other from opposite gunwales. Rudiger flapped his green wings and started in, "Squawk. Rudy want a story."

"Shut up, you damn parrot," said a sailor.

Rudy turned and said, "Squawk, squawk, squawk—story, story," and flew to Pembroke's shoulder.

Pembroke liked to talk to whoever would listen and whoever would not too. "Did I ever tell you how I lost my leg?"

"About a hundred times," said a groaning voice from the bow.

"Here it comes again."

> We was chasing a whale off the Azores back in '33. That was a beautiful right whale and we needed the oil. We rowed like crazy and managed to get a harpoon in his side. That beast took off and pulled our boat through the water like a hurricane. But the thing got tired and says to hisself, 'Time to break loose.'

O'Sullivan said, "Them whales are smart like I said." Pembroke kept on.

> He raised those flukes and sliced my boat in half like Silva cuts a pig. I flipped out and whacked the water astride the fin of a requiem shark. That shark was pissed and grabbed me.

"I can't imagine," came a voice from the listeners.

His blue-gray snout broke the surface with rows of white teeth across his mouth. My leg was between his teeth and jaws and there weren't no pulling out. I beat on his snout but that fish twisted my leg off and swam away with it in his mouth. He left a red trail through the water, my red, damn his hide. My pig tattoo was on that leg.

Kalani stuck out a leg with a pig on it. "Like this?"
"Go to hell."
"Grandmother say 'no feed the sharks.'"

I splashed hard but sank lower and lower 'cause I couldn't swim even with two legs. Mr. Davy Jones was coming for me when the water below my leg got firm and I could push up a little. The water drained off and here was this dolphin looking up at me. My mates pulled me into the other boat.

"Good to have two boats."
"Yeah. The Captain sewed me up and Chips made me this." Pembroke held up his wooden leg. "There's a hook so's I can climb the rigging. I'm good as ever, and this story is the gen-u-ine truth."
Rudiger agreed, "Squawk. Gen-u-ine truth."

That bastard requiem shark came back with
an empty mouth and chased my ship for days to
get the rest of me 'cause I taste so good.

He smiled and took a bow.
"Shark!" he pointed to a fin in the water.
"Shark!" The Kanakas leaped aboard and
watched a dark gray fin.
The disappointed shark circled and circled and left hungry.

More bored than ever, the Kanaka sailors challenged the
ordinary sailors to sing their loudest.

Porter agreed and hollered, "Give me a song and make it
loud," He jokingly put his hands over his ears as a bellowed
chantey arose where each verse was louder and raunchier than the
last.

Down the way where the nights are gay
And the sun shines daily on the mountain top
I took a trip on a sailing ship
And when I reached Jamaica
I made a stop

"What did you do?"

But I'm sad to say, I'm on my way
Won't be back for many a day
My heart is down my head is turning around
I had to leave a little girl in Kingston town

They bellowed out the final chorus. You could hear them for miles, even on the *Zebra*. The sailors over there had no morale to sing, and only grumbled.

Not to be outdone, the Kanaka's began singing their guttural ancestors' songs of blended chants and dances. They launched into the mix of a *mele* dance with a loud song and a *hula* dance that flowed to the swells of the ocean.

Their diverse hedonism escalated to bellowed rhythms, screaming instruments, jumps, and voices, all from a simple melody. They brought out a musical instrument made from an *ipu heke* (a double gourd) fashioned into a pahu (sharkskin-covered drum) for their mele. A drummer shook the deck with devastating rhythms as though he was attacking an enemy, which he had done in the past.

Babbitt said to Porter, "I'd hate to face that, wouldn't you."

"Sure would."

The port and starboard teams competed for hours. Sometimes the Kanaka's won and sometimes the sailors.

A few tone-deaf members wrestled since they couldn't sing a note. The men were stout and rough and relished good physical sport. In the end, the Kanaka won because they grew up play fighting each other from toddlers to old men. The ordinary sailors were rough and tumble in a brawl, but were poor wrestlers.

They sang and wrestled the sunny afternoon away until the boredom wore out Porter's patience. He had a better idea. "Attention all hands. Who dances better, Kanaka or sailors?"

The Kanaka yelled, "We do," as the drummer redoubled his complex rhythms on his gourd drum. The Islanders broke into a full-fledged hula story. They told by their flowing arms and swiveling hips of their immigration from Bora-Bora and the raging battles across the islands of Polynesia. They won every conflict, of course.

Not to be outdone, the ordinary sailors cheered, "Our hornpipe beats that any day—like this." Pembroke started a fast drumbeat on an overturned barrel head lashed to the gunwale. Six sailors stood erect, folded their arms, and tapped their right foot eight times. They kicked their right legs to the right, followed by their left legs to the left. Up into the air they jumped.

"That's how we do it," they said, while they stomped the deck boards to make noise.

Porter saw he was on to something. "Good start. Team sailors to port and team Kanaka to starboard. Musicians, start your music."

Pembroke took out his fiddle from the forecastle. Kalani had his gourd drum ready. Each musician faced off against each other in volume and speed, and the dancers freelanced it.

Kawai explained to Porter, "Hula is hide a Lua fight. Lua man is old as island and strong like Koa. Koa use dance to scare enemy before battle. Missionary say he pagan."

Porter said, "Glad to have Koa on my side. You too."

Kalani shouted "Hula kahiko. We travel across ocean". Each of the Kanaka made ocean waves with their arms that evolved into a far more evocative dance. Each dancer proudly displayed his *Mele ma' i*, which is to say his procreative talent. Six Kanaka each danced his personal burlesque that showed off what he offered to the girls of the islands.

Babbitt knew that at birth a Hawaiian child received a pet name for his private parts and a regular name for daily use. Hawaiians believed that through the piko come descendants, and composed a private chant for every new baby as their mark of distinction. The Kanakas prized their private parts for perpetuation of the family line.

The *Mele ma'i* was popular and colorful but offended Babbitt's genteel upraising. One look at the *Mele ma' i* movements and he yelled in a loud voice, "Stop! Not on my ship, hula only. No filthy, obscene pagan dances."

The dancers grinned and shifted to a modest hula dance. They switched to their native Hawaiian words without missing a beat of rhythm, "No love, no babies, no babies no more."

Babbitt was none the wiser as he couldn't understand their words nor see the humping movements behind his back.

Pembroke's fiddle sang an Irish ditty. He didn't know he was playing ancient folk songs that his ancestors enjoyed for hundreds of years. The sailors leaped into their hornpipe with gusto, but kicked each other and got in each other's way. The activity degenerated to swings of their fists that were not included in the usual hornpipe steps. The classic hornpipe dance kept the arms stiffly at the sides—these sailors were far from classic.

The fiddle died and Pembroke yelled, "Stop! Fists are not hornpipe. Go on three and keep your hands to yourself. One, two, three." The hornpipers jumped in a grand spectacle of pride.

One of the Kanakas turned a somersault in the air and his companions launched the Hawaiian sword dance. The Kanaka's were great mimes and made fun of the mates, Babbitt, the hornepipers, and everyone else behind their backs and sometimes in front. All had a good-natured time.

The sailors danced higher and broke into pantomimes of hand-to-hand combat and rig climbing.

The Kanakas joined in the play war. In one particularly exuberant swing, Kawai's war club slipped out of his hand and bounced off the main mast, leaving a giant gash. The dancers ducked as it spun back onto deck like a boomerang.

A good time was had by all and the excess energy was dissipated.

The men lay panting on the decks as Porter judged the dance off. "The ordinary sailors are cruder at singing but the Kanaka are better at dancing. The Master sends these two bottles of liquor forward for you to splice the main brace." He held up two bottles of spirits that he had borrowed from Macintyre's cabinet.

The men cheered as one voice, "Three cheers for Porter." They were free to celebrate on their own time for the rest of the day.

The dance-off ended with a loud cheer. The sailors opened their two bottles of spirits and knew what to do to the contents.

Porter slipped around the deckhouse to try some dance steps for himself.

He wildly threw his arms overhead in a somersault. He turned halfway and dropped flat on his back with the wind knocked out of him. To himself he thought, I'm not as young as I used to be, but then I never was. We won't try that again, but how about this?

He wiggled through a stolen *Mele ma' i* with the rhythm of a tree trunk.

Two Kanakas peeked around the corner, "You dance with your grandmother to the moon on her pet lizard. You never have son with that Mele ma' i. No woman want you." They laughed and chest bumped each other at full speed.

The Kanakas embarrassed Porter and he exploded, "Back to the forecastle you two." He shifted to the hornpipe whistling the melody as he kicked.

Babbitt walked around the other corner to see Porter's clumsiness. "Man, you got that all wrong. Watch me."

At that moment, an Irish jig floated from Ferreri's violin in the cabin as he played to soothe Macintyre's foggy mind. Ferreri told him, "This hornpipe comes from an Irish dance I've enjoyed since my childhood."

Porter and Babbitt pranced around the binnacle to the welcome accompaniment. They jumped through many hornpipes. They kicked each other from time to time, and Porter grinned, "That's harder than it ever looks". Babbitt agreed. "It took a voyage to learn that."

They fell laughing at each other and walked away humming a hornpipe.

Drowsy with their bellies of spirits and supper chased down with grog, the sailors smoked their strong tobacco and lolled around the forecastle. A surreptitious third bottle of liquor passed from hand to hand.

A raspy screech, "Squawk! Rudy want a story," shattered the tranquility.

"Squawk to you too, dumb ass green beak," said a lounging tar. Groans swept the forecastle. "Stifle that parrot. One of your stories a day is all I can take."

Levi replied in a low and ominous voice, "This . . . mate . . . is a story you want to hear. Bizarre accidents of nature happen when you're becalmed like we are."

"What the hell is 'bizarre?"

"Strange. Now listen up."

Porter was working on the deck and heard Levi start. He knew Levi usually had some sense in his stories, and stuck his head down the hatch to hear better.

Levi said, "A shipmate told me, who heard it from an old salt, who got it from the ancient mariner, who was there.

They was in the Grand Harbor of Malta. That's ten days east of Gibraltar. It was hot and still, and blokes like us rowed the galleys in the bay."

Pembroke lowered his voice to a whisper, A green malocchio (evil eye) appeared on the water.

He drew a six-foot circle on the floor in front of the men.

It gave a predatory stare out of a dark band . . . like the black eye when you fight.

His listeners stared back and were afraid to blink.

That eye rose out of the water and attacked the ships.

Pembroke raised his arms overhead and dramatically waved them.

They screamed and ran if they had a place to go. The ships was helpless at their anchors.

The tars in the forecastle trusted any superstition, especially an evil one. Porter was not superstitious but was still interested.

Them people watched a monster with arms arise from that eye. They was light and dark and moved like tentacles on an octopus. The sea breathed mists to protect those arms.

Some sailors knew what an octopus was and some did not, but they all could imagine a grasping monster wallowing in the sea.

That hairy arm seized the clouds and rocked the galleys to their anchors, but you could see through it. They was fish whirling inside and I don't mean no flying fish. Seaweed mashed with debris was twisted around a small child.

Pembroke's voice rose in dramatic fervor as he described the destruction with sweeping gestures. He added thunder with his wooden leg pounding the deck boards. Rudy flapped his wings overhead to show storm clouds.

That monster wrecked the harbor. It capsized the galley, Santa Fé, and dumped her slaves in the water.

He demonstrated by throwing Morgan upside down. Morgan meowed and ran off.

The San Michele and San Filippo was next and then San Claudio. That evil monster killed six hundred people 'fore it roared and died. Them poor devils chained to the oars never had a chance. Rain poured out of the sky with fish, turtles, frogs, rocks, seaweed, and the child.

The crew watched the performance with wide eyes and bated breath.

Somebody heard a knocking in a keeled-over hull. They punched a hole and rescued the grand commander, Mathurin Romegas, and his pet monkey.

He ended with a whisper, "Note well this evil monster of the doldrums. That old sailor spoke God's own truth."

Rudy said, "Squawk. Truth. Squawk."

The crew stared at each other in terrified wonder. "We're dead for sure if one of these monsters comes."

Porter thought, I've heard of storms called tornadoes. This sounds like one of them over the bay.

The sailors settled into a routine about the forecastle and tried to forget the image of the malocchio evil eye. Porter often joined them, as his custom from earlier voyages, even though he was now a second mate and officially their superior.

An ordinary sailor, Guido Palmieri, more than anybody else loved to sing. He said to no one in particular, "I used to sing opera at the Teatro di San Carlo in Naples until the conductor threw me out. He claimed I was in bed with his mistress."

"Were you?"

"Well . . . yes, but you keep me anyway."

He traded verses in a tenor voice with Porter in a rich baritone singing an ancient chantey famous on the foam, and the land as well.

> As I was a-walking down Paradise Street,
> To me way-aye, blow the man down.
> A pretty young damsel
> I chanced for to meet.
>
> Oh, blow the man down, bullies, blow the man down!
> To me way-aye, blow the man down.
> She was round in the counter and bluff in the bow,"
> To me way-aye, blow the man down.

They sang deep into the night as the accumulated smoke erased the universal hangovers.

Porter loved singing along and added verses of his own. The upshot was you have to beware of damsels who will get you into trouble.

Chapter 13—Stronger, Younger, Older, Ruthless

The first and second mates resumed their argument about fraternizing with the tars. "Porter, I have told you time and time again officers must distance themselves from the crew. Pull your rank at every opportunity and discipline freely. I heard you arguing with a sailor the other day. That is unacceptable."

Porter said, "They're loyal mates who watch my back."

"The safety of the ship is at stake," said Ferreri.

"They're the best sailors in the world."

"You, sir, are insubordinate."

"You, sir, are arrogant."

Ferreri swung at Porter who deflected his oncoming fist. Ferreri clutched him and they twisted, clinched, and crashed to the deck. Porter was stronger and younger, but Ferreri was older and treacherous.

He flipped the second mate face down and jammed his forearms under each shoulder. He locked his hands behind Porter's neck and twisted his head down in a neck crank with the intention to cripple him for life. Porter was dazed but his strength saved him.

Porter didn't have a good defense but Ferreri didn't have a good follow-up either. They clenched in a tense standoff between strangling and submitting.

Babbitt reacted to the situation with alarm. He pounded his fists on the head and back of Ferreri, who released his hold.

Babbitt helped Porter to their feet and said, "Sir and sir, take this below decks, the men are watching. I don't know why you're fighting, but *Agilis* can't have you at each other's throats."

Even though they outranked Babbitt, their sense of duty reluctantly conceded that he was right, and they voluntarily entered their bunks glaring at each other from four feet apart. Babbitt took over as officer of the deck to finish the watch.

Still panting, Ferreri said, "Babbitt . . . is . . . right. We . . . have . . . different . . . points of view, but our obligation is *Agilis*."

"If . . . you . . . say so."

"Consider my words, Porter. I grant a happy crew makes for a smooth operation, but . . . ,"

Porter interrupted, "I'll suspend my argument for this voyage, and we will go out separate ways."

Ferreri said, "Well enough, I never want to see you again."

"Me neither."

They turned to opposite walls and waited for the end of the watch.

Babbitt was lonesome with only himself for company. Being officer of the deck with the mates holed up in their bunks and MacIntyre indisposed was an isolated situation. He looked at his arms and said to himself,

These hands learned from the blacksmith how to fashion whatever you desire in wood or iron, but not to lead others.

He looked up at the limp hanging sails and slack lines by the maintop platform.

"Ahoy, any action?"

The lookout scanned the horizon for any movement of air but there was none in sight. "None, sir."

Babbitt kept talking to himself,

I want *Agilis* top-notch at all times. She is man's most beautiful work of art afloat. I can make naval knots but not friends. The seamen won't have me, not that I want them. I'm too shy to befriend the officers and MacIntyre is off limits. I am alone.

After walking the deck for the ninth time, he lowered himself into the hold to check the provisions.

"What is that?" He almost jumped out of his skin to feel something furry rub his leg. An image of a giant rat came to mind and he kicked it. Instead of a squeak, all he heard was a soft "Meow, meow, purrrr."

Babbitt said, "Little kitty, you are the best friend I have. You welcome me to your side and we make a good team." Hi picked up Morgan Fore 'n Aft and petted him.

The cat of the ship sensed the bosun was in distress and adopted him. Morgan followed him around all day every day after capturing his ration of rats, and slept curled up with him every night.

Dead but uneasy air smothered the brig for yet another tropical day. Shimmering heat waves from the glistening surface rose through the humid air. The smell of abandoned trash, which floated around *Agilis* like a collar, overwhelmed the nose blindness from the forecastle. It stank.

Porter said looking through a telescope borrowed from MacIntyre, "The line of the *Zebra*'s masts sway like the Arabic belly dancer I saw in Gibraltar. 'Take it off lady!' " He followed the heat waves that rippled up toward a cumulus cloud blocking the burning sun. An invisible funnel twisted down from the cloud to the stagnant ocean.

The surface wasn't stagnant for long.

Kawai drew on his experience in these waters and pointed over the gunwale. "Wind change funny. Big eye in water look like dark circle. He have black eye from lose fight."

Porter was awed by the twisting funnel that jutted out of the eye and danced as it looked at Kawai and him. He said, "Kawai sees right. There's a ring around the colored eye with arms reaching up. Look at that."

The crew rushed to the gunwale to see. They watched the bands of mist rise and roll out of the ring and close like tentacles circling the shaft of water and the bed of trash from the *Agilis*. The shaft climbed to the cloud in a vertical display of fish and marine life.

Porter remembered the tale of Malta and studied the phenomenon with dread. He whooped, "Blow me away mates. That's the first water spout I ever saw, and it's in a foul mood. Batten down the hatches. MacIntyre! You've got to see this."

"Holy mackerel, that is a genuine waterspout," said Ferreri.

MacIntyre limped to the deck and instantly recognized the phenomenon, even in his debilitated condition. "I've seen seven in my time at sea. Watch inside the shaft. It picks up fish, sand, and seaweed."

Porter said, "No sand here in the middle of the ocean."

The column howled and danced like a raging, twisting, jumping sea serpent. It turned on the *Agilis*. Porter was dismayed when it tore loose the fourth topsail yard, pulled three lines away, and disordered all the braces.

With it's evil done, the waterspout collapsed over the deck. Fish, seaweed, jettisoned garbage, and debris plunged onto *Agilis*. The flood drained away through the scuppers and left a clutter on deck.

"Hot damn," said Porter when he slipped on a flopping fish and sprained the ankle on his bad leg. He tossed the fish to Cook Silva, who wrapped it with a strip of sailcloth. These are good eating so give me a hand." The crew recovered sixty-five fish for their mess.

The *Zebra* escaped the waterspout by a mile and a half and celebrated the misfortune of her rival with a cheer.

"Take that, you scummy tub," they hollered across the water.

Agilis was too far away to hear.

MacIntyre said, "Enter into the log, 'Waterspout of diameter ten feet and height of thousand feet today. *Agilis* attacked. Damage incurred.'"

Later that famous night, the moon dropped below the glassy ocean and all was quiet while the crew slumbered in their hammocks.

Only Rudiger was awake—and bored. He shook off the hood covering his head and flew up to a high perch. Imitating Ferreri's foghorn voice, Rudy barked a command "Squawk. All hands on deck. Emergency. All hands on deck. Emergency! All hands on deck now! Squawk."

The sleeping men aroused in a panic since they knew Ferreri demanded instant action and missed the squawk part of the command. They rolled out of their hammocks and knocked heads with each other in the dark. Like a swarm of hornets, they gushed out of the forecastle and lined up in front of the nonexistent Ferreri. "Aye, Aye, sir, Ready for duty."

The silent deck was empty apart from the night watch, who was not Ferreri of course. He was equally confused. "What's going on? All's quiet and you pile up on deck."

Porter said, "I heard a commotion. You should move so fast during the day," as he and Ferreri emerged from below.

A sailor said, "You ordered all hands on deck, Mr. Ferreri. Reporting for duty, sir." Ferreri responded angrily, "I did no such thing."

Rudy shrieked again, "Squawk. All hands on deck." He looked around with his beak high in the air.

Ferreri lunged for him. "I'll fix you, stupid bird," but tripped on a hook in the deck.

Rudy flew up to the mainsail yardarm where the full moon silhouetted him like a Halloween raven and mocked the first mate, "Squawk, screech . . . chop, chirp, kiss . . . scream, wwwiiiiiiiisssssttlle, squawk," as he flapped his wings like a flying witch in the night. Ferreri, from flat on his back, shook his fist at Rudy. "I'll get you."

False alarm or not, the crew was worked up and Porter said, "Stifle your damn bird or he's rat food. I won't have him wake the crew."

"Shut up," said the hands as they threw stuff at Rudy that he dodged in the moonlight. "Squawk, squeak, cheep, squawk."

Porter said, "Back to sleep, and quiet that mess of flapping green feathers or I will. Silva, can you make parrot stew?"

"Si señor, like a tough old chicken."

Rudy flew down to Pembroke's shoulder for protection and his peg leg owner tied the shroud over his head just short of asphyxiation. He slammed Rudy on a perch and scolded him. "How do you make parrot stew?"

"I boil a parrot and an old boot in water and when the boot is tender eat it and throw away the parrot."

Porter said, "Those green feathers would look good on a hat, and I've got an old boot right here."

213

Rudy croaked in his hood, tucked his head under his wing, and chuckled as he went to sleep.

Chapter 14—Chinese Pirates

Kawai watched distant clouds build in the clear sky to the west. "Mr. Porter, bad sky come."

Porter was worried as well. He reached into his knowledge of seagoing folklore and said to the crew, "I see a bad storm coming and any tar knows an indebted man worsens the storm. Anybody have a debt?"

There is a long pause as the men looked sheepishly at their compatriots.

Ferreri said in irritation, "Does anyone owe a debt to another?"

More minutes passed before O'sullivan spoke up. "I owe a debt to Chips Alden. I didn't pay him for my ditty box."

"But you are using the box, O'sullivan."

"I had to install the hinge and lock myself so it wasn't finished."

Ferreri ignored this last comment. "Settle up your account."

O'sullivan removed some coins from his ditty box and passed them to Alden.

Porter jumped in with bright eyes. "I hear lots of dice games rattling in the forecastle. Somebody loses, you can't all be square."

He stared at the crew but received no response. "Any tar holding a debt endangers your fellow seamen, so settle up. I'll write an IOU as good as money if you're broke. The storm

215

considers an IOU as settled—right storm?" as he gazed at the roiling clouds.

Porter said to Kawai, "You're right. The air smells different after that waterspout. Something's stirring."

Drowsy men shook off their lethargy and stirred too.

"How hard have you seen it blow?" someone asked Pembroke. "I saw a wind so hard it blew the feathers off the chickens and tore the clothes off the backs of the men. You should see a naked sailor chase a nude chicken on a wet deck." Men chuckled at the idea.

Kawai wore a nervous face as he walked up to Porter, "Big wind come. We get ready, maybe now?" Ferreri overheard him and agreed.

"Porter, prepare for a gale."

Orders rolled downhill from Ferreri to Porter to Babbitt to the deck hands, "Secure loose items on deck and batten down the hatches. Reef all sails except the topsail. Rig the lifelines along the deck."

Ferreri checked the barometer in the cabin and saw it had dropped over several hours. There was little for him to do, but he did that well.

They waited for the gale to arrive.

Porter's said, "What was that puff of air? It feels strange, bizarre even, but we're becalmed." He grinned at Pembroke who used the word in his waterspout story.

Amundson said, "I don't know what it means."

Porter looked around and saw nothing for a pregnant moment; then the storm slammed the rigging. He was deafened by the protests from the lines as they heeled *Agilis* hard to starboard. A mighty clap of thunder announced the storm, and rain pelted the deck. Instant swells pounded the hull and fought for direction.

The new sailors were terrified by the raw force of the wind shrieking through the masts. Palmieri was the most challenged and wanted to set more sail to outrun the wind. The experienced sailors restrained him since too much canvas would lose control, but they couldn't restrain Ferreri.

Ferreri's navigational mistake lay in what he did next. He hove to on port tack, which was proper south of the Equator and when not in the path of a storm. Unfortunately, *Agilis* was in the direct path of a storm and north of the equator. Navigation was opposite from the southern hemisphere because the storm rotated counterclockwise instead of clockwise—if you had a clock, or even if you didn't.

Porter could see by the steady fall of the barometer that the storm was on them. "We run with the wind on our starboard quarter until the barometer stabilizes, and then heave to . . . ," he said to Ferreri.

Ferreri said, "No, damn it . . . heave to on port tack. I'm the Master and want no back talk."

Neither Porter nor Kawai could convince the other officers, since Porter was a green second mate paired with an ignorant Kanaka. No way were they smarter than a certified first mate and properly (previously) qualified Master.

Porter said, "Koa, we need you on the tiller. You're the strongest mariner we've got."

Kawai said, "Mr. Porter, wind come straight on us.

Those who were there bragged for years afterward that these were the highest swells they ever saw. *Agilis* fell off due to Ferreri's direction as a ship always does when hove to. The first wave breached the hull sideways across the wind.

Agilis rolled to starboard and submerged her lee side gunwales below the surface. Before she was fully upright, a contrary wave rolled over the bow and flushed the deck of seamen and contents like a scythe.

The next wave poured over the stern. The stern sank and pitched the bowsprit up. Loose deck equipment mixed with men reaching for the lifelines tumbled aft. One or another of them might have caught a grip on a stanchion, but the oncoming bedlam tore their hands away.

Kawai saw the disaster coming and sprang to the mainsail from atop the cabin. He missed and the flood swept him over the stern taffrail like a piece of flotsam. The strapping Koa was able to keep one huge arm on the tiller and reached out to seize Kawai's hair. Koa pulled him back over the gunwale but scraped his body

The third wave threw the mass of bodies to port and Kawai into the binnacle.

Wind? No one had ever seen such a wind. Loud? It whistled through the rigging like a flock of banshees. The surging waves drowned the gunwales from port to starboard and careened her almost to capsizing. Only the mighty Koa with all his strength could control the tiller.

McIntyre, supported by Ferreri, gripped his cabin doorjamb. Between the wind and the Master's apoplexy, the mates could barely understand his words of experience.

"We . . . must have . . . a . . . sea . . . .anchor."

Ferreri said, "Get to it now, Alden. Make a canvas bag with an open mouth. We'll drag it behind and keep our stern to the wind.

Alden strained to hear but could read Ferreri's lips.

"It is our only chance to survive."

Chips Alden pulled himself along the lifeline to the hatch over the shop. He cracked it enough to slip in.

Since he had been working on a sea anchor of old torn sails already, it should have been easy to finish, but he ran the needle through his hand when the ship rolled. An overhead lantern gashed his scalp when it rolled back. His dripping blood made the stitching slippery, and he finished with a red sea anchor.

During a lull, he tossed the bloody sea anchor onto the deck and scrambled after it. Before he could grab the lifeline a wave tangled him in the sea anchor and threw him hard against the gunwale. Only a jutting hook saved him from pitching overboard.

Chips passed the anchor to other hands. They kept one grip on the safety line when the waves came, and managed to hitch the sea anchor to the boat davits astern. "There you go," they said over the howl of the wind as they pitched the sea anchor behind the stern.

The bag floated under the surface at the end of a long line and turned the bow of *Agilis* downwind and stable.

Howling winds tore the canvas off the yardarms, jerked on the repair off the fore-topmast, and shredded the running gear.

Even so, Kawai said to Porter, "Storm weak. No typhoon, change come now."

In spite of Kawai's optimism, the messy storm center moved over *Agilis* and the wind fell to quiet whiffs. Porter noted the roars from all around and braced against the waves that rose to thirty-five feet. He said to Ferreri and MacIntyre, "We're unstable because our sea anchor has no effect without wind. I can't do anything."

Ferreri said, "Watch anyway."

The bold wooden world of the brig hung in midair bridging two waves with her bow and stern. Gravity took over and dropped her into the trough with a mighty shudder. The remaining rigging jerked and creaked. Several waves merged into a rogue wave sixty-three feet tall and raised *Agilis* on a knife edge by her mid-point. The little brig groaned and shook and slammed and crashed, but held together.

Porter said to Babbitt during a lull, "You can see our *Agilis* is constructed of white oak timbers. They were the best her German shipwrights could smuggle from the New World through the British blockade to Bremerhaven in 1841."

Babbitt said, "I know. They say our white oak timbers are a third stronger than European oak. Thank God for them, they are saving our life in this storm."

A whoosh of wind roared out of the opposite direction. Porter watched the repair of the fore-topmast waver and fail with a crash, bringing the skysail with it. The heavy spar swung around in a tangle of lines and flying canvas and threatened to take out more rigging.

Babbitt said to Porter, "I did the best I could but it wasn't enough."

"The mast is too weak," Ferreri said. "Furl sails, skysail first".

The riggers loosed the main-skysail and lowered it down the careening mast to the deck. The last sail flying resisted from the force of the wind and the riggers shouted, " . . . can't move it."

It didn't matter as the next gust shredded the canvas to tatters. The sailors aloft on the foot ropes locked their arms around the spars to keep from blowing away like the tattered canvas.

Porter yelled over the wind, "Down on deck, hang on and get down."

Ferrari said, "Torn sails won't sink us but a falling spar will kill you. Look sharp."

The crew cut away the damaged masts and fished the swinging broken spars together with temporary bindings. They waited to ride out the storm.

At midnight the wind slackened, then bore from a new direction.

Ferreri ordered, "Tack three points to starboard."

Despite the careful turn taken by Koa, the winds changed again and fractured the other temporary bindings. The lower rigging wrapped around the flailing sections of the yardarm while the topsail yard swung and cut the braces.

Porter said to Kawai, "Follow me. We'll check the damage." He and Kawai climbed aloft to survey the losses. They had just reached the top platform when an unexpected gust rocked the ship, tore the broken yard loose and wrapped Porter and Kawai together like a pair of trussed up Christmas geese.

The tangled mess sideswiped the gunwale as it dragged them overboard. The enraged seas banged them senseless against hull. Porter and Kawai were in real danger as the wooden spar wanted to float but the blocks and tarred lines wanted to sink. Churning waves slammed them again and again against the hull.

The water revived Porter first, the only sailor beside the Kanakas who could swim. He untangled himself, circled his legs around the spar, and held Kawai's head out of the water. Porter held on to the wreckage until the rescue boat and strong hands pulled them in.

Kawai's consciousness returned to a healthy normal and he shook his head, "You save my life . . . be family forever, Mr. Porter."

Porter assessed the situation. "The replacement masts lashed to the deck survived the gale, but we can't fit them at sea, especially in this gale."

As the gale gradually faded, MacIntyre reviewed said, "That was as bad as I have seen, but thanks to the Almighty we came through. We lost no one and our newbies are now seasoned sailors. On to Honolulu."

Even Palmieri held his head up in pride.

Hornigold laughed at *Agilis* through his eyeglass. "That's the sorriest spectacle I ever saw. Those clumsy sailors in a breeze. Sea rats & rover pirates ye be . . . get off my ocean."

And it was true. *Zebra* smartly recovered from the gale because her crew was expert. The crews of *Zebra* and *Agilis* impugned the other's integrity, although they couldn't hear the shouts from the other ship.

"Your vile face sours beer and curdles milk."

"Away, you starveling, bull's-pizzle, you stock-fish!"

"Come over unable worms!"

"Would thou wert clean enough to spit upon"

The run settled down to a rivalry of endurance. *Zebra* mocked her opponent by zigzagging her elegant stern as she sped over the horizon towards Oahu.

Agilis ended the day plowing through the Pacific at three knots.

After several more days, they picked up the trade winds and their progress increased to nearly five knots. The days actually became pleasant.

Zebra anchored in Honolulu harbor on Oahu a full day ahead of *Agilis*. Hornigold moored far offshore, as was his custom. A great crowd of canoes got to the anchorage before *Zebra* stopped moving. Dancing beauties, wearing little but their beautiful tan skin and flowers in their hair stood in every one. Many held up fruit and trinkets and all chattered in many languages with occasional English words thrown in. They waved to the ship-worn sailors who waved wildly back.

One sailor spread his arms wide and said, "I'm yours." Three whines elbowed each other and tried to climb aboard to get him, but Hornigold bellowed, "Away. No one aboard." He always prohibited visits by the local maidens of any age, which this time brought the men closer than ever to a mutiny.

As the anchor chain clattered down, Hornigold sent a scrawny little man wearing black to shore, where his shifty eyes locked onto a waiting contact.

The contact rushed up, "What did you see in California?" The shifty person replied, "I spied like a stevedore. I crammed hides and tallow down *Agilis*. Much work—too hard."

The contact on shore said, "I don't give a damn about your work. The gold, remember?"

"A special crew stowed ten crates in the forward hatch. They were heavy because they needed two men on each. I counted four hands on deck, two in the rigging, and the boss man. Five Ghost Shadows can manage the crew, but the hands are tough, watch out."

The shifty little man relaxed his knotted guts and said, "Is our pilot Franklin ready for the *Agilis*?"

"Shake hands with Mr. Franklin now," as a hard-looking man about forty-five years old walked up and offered his limp sweaty hand.

Shifty continued, "*Agilis* is crippled by a lost fore-topmast, the spars are wrong and in sloppy trim. You can expect to lay eyes on the wreck tomorrow. I bring five Colt revolvers to the Ghost Shadows in Hawaii. These command respect in California and Mexico. Are our Ghost Shadows ready?"

The contact said, "We're hot to go."

Back offshore, Hornigold secured his vessel against the tides and rowed to the wharf, where he collected a gang of loose dockhands to unload her. *Zebra's* main cargo was a plot to seize the gold on *Agilis*, and she carried only a modest load of trade goods as a decoy. It was the reason she loaded so quickly in San Francisco. It was going to be so easy.

The stranded sailors with no shore leave grumbled mightily.

"We haven't been off this stinking hulk since Sitka. That ice for the rich people in California was a mess. Hornigold imprisoned us in 'Frisco and now Honolulu. When our feet hit dirt, we're making tracks in it."

The next day, a sad crippled brig limped past the beach at Waimānalo on the eastern edge of Oahu. It glided passed the rock, Lēʻahi, that the British called Diamond Head.

The remnants of *Agilis* rounded the point and hove to, waiting for a harbor pilot. A small boat approached from which the man in the bow called out, "Ahoy, do you need a pilot?"

Ferreri replied, "Welcome to *Agilis*, sir. I am Alfonso Ferreri as first mate and temporary master. Master MacIntyre is indisposed but gives you his regards. He may join us shortly."

The pilot said, "Franklin here. I'll pilot you in." They shook hands and watched as Porter emerged from the cabin discretely supporting MacIntyre. They came to the pilot, "MacIntyre here. Welcome aboard." They shook shaky hands.

The pilot said, "Time to get going."

MacIntyre muttered as he leaned on Ferreri,

I don't know this fellow or trust him, but we lack a choice. Watch close.

Franklin directed *Agilis* toward a mooring site away from the cluster of vessels near town. He pointed to a remote spot hidden by a huge four-masted whaler. The pilot demanded, "Drop anchor here."

MacIntyre disagreed, "This is way . . . to hell and gone . . . from the wharf. I demand . . . to be moved."

Porter protested, "Why here? It's a hell of a long way to the wharf."

The pilot insisted, and after a lengthy argument, *Agilis* crew doused her sails and dropped anchor.

Porter said, "This stinks."

Before the men on *Agilis* could drop the anchor, a grappling hook clunked the gunwale amidships and scratched off a patch of dried blood. Babbitt cried, "You're ruining my paint. Nobody boards like that."

Porter grabbed the man climbing the hook but his companion below boosted him onto the deck before Porter could stop him. Four more followed and overwhelmed Porter. He recognized the Ghost Shadows from their clothes during his kidnapping and exclaimed, "You're thieving pirates."

The leader said in broken English as they pulled their dragoon revolvers from their clothes, "We are honest pirates, mate, and we'll take your excess gold, if you please." He fired a shot into the air without aiming that narrowly missed Kawai in the rigging overhead.

Porter glanced up and saw Kawai motion to Ikaika on an adjacent foot rope for silence. Porter made a slight nod and turned to face the black muzzle of another Dragoon revolver. It spit red and he felt a bullet crease his scalp. Groggy or not, he charged through the cloud at the shooter and knocked the gunman flat. The big shiny revolver skidded across the deck.

The leader of the Ghost Shadows pulled the pirate up by his pigtail as he counted the seven men on deck and retrieved the pistol. He waved *Agilis* company into a tight group included MacIntyre leaning on Ferreri.

MacIntyre said, "Get off my ship." He did not notice Franklin, the pilot, who discretely sneaked behind the deckhouse.

The leader screamed, "The gold and nobody gets hurt. You loaded ten crates in San Francisco. Haul them up." He fired another round overhead that nicked Ikaika's foot.

MacIntyre said, "We are a . . . simple merchant ship . . . loaded with hides and tallow. What you're talking about."

But he thought, Those damn Chinese spies again. I was warned about them and here they are.

He nodded to Porter who said, "Bring up the crates starting with A53."

O'sullivan and Palmieri clambered into the hold and boosted crate A53 overhead out the hatch. It was obviously heavy and took all their strength to put it onto the deck without the capstan. The shifty leader screamed, "Get the other nine—now!" He fired another shot that grazed Kawai's arm. The pirates never looked up.

The Ghost Shadow ordered, "To our boat." O'Sullivan and Palmieri lugged the crate to the gunwale and balanced it on the edge. They looked at the hostages with helpless faces and back at Porter.

He nodded his head strongly down. They tipped the crate over the gunwale into the pirates' boat. The heavy crate slipped through the Shadow's upraised hands and plunged through the boat's wooden hull to the harbor floor. The boat took on water and followed the crate.

The pirates leaped to the gunwale as the boat went down and the Ghost Shadow leader exclaimed, "You clumsy idiot. You sink boat, we take yours." He and an accomplice dropped the stern boat from its davits and watched it splash into the water.

The third Ghost Shadow ordered, "Load new boat, and dammit be careful."

Porter and Ferreri exchanged looks and Porter waved at the Kanaka.

Instead of bringing up crates, they broke into a deafening ear-splitting sword dance that completely unnerved the pirates. "Quiet," they screamed in panic. The dancers moved in blurs and the pirates couldn't aim their pistols—not that they could aim in silence either. The Kanaka swarmed and deafened the deck.

Kawai and Ikaika, unseen overhead, slid down the forestay to the deck at the bow. Incensed by their gunshot injuries, they pulled two belaying pins from their sockets. The loosed lines released the fore-topgallant yardarm and it crashed down.

The pirates looked up at the unexpected crash overhead. Porter and Palmieri jumped the backs of two and wrenched their pistols out of their hands. Being larger and stronger, they restrained both Shadows.

Flying random bullets from the remaining pirates assaulted every exposed man on deck. The Ghost Shadows were quite untrained with their powerful new pistols and in no way were gunslingers. Kawai and Ikaika tapped two more on the head with the belaying pins and that pair crumpled into unconscious heaps.

Ferreri clamped his powerful wrestling hold on the remaining Ghost Shadow while other staunch crew members seized the revolvers. They didn't know much about revolvers either, but knew how to use the handles.

The sailors semi-suffocated the five Ghost Shadows that lay restrained on the deck by sitting on their heads. The rest of the crew tied them up.

Porter pulled his knife and stood facing them until they regained consciousness. Their eyes stared at the knife glinting in his hand and squirmed to get away. Their wild chattering rose to agonized screeches when he cut the first pig tail off and threw it overboard. Porter knew that losing their pigtails grown over a lifetime was their ultimate humiliation.

Two nodded to their crotch and pleaded. "Cut here, not hair." Porter cut their hair instead.

Porter yanked the pilot from behind the deckhouse and thrust him in front of MacIntyre. The pilot stood with his mouth open and a look of dread on his face. This was not the way it was supposed to go.

MacIntyre said, "You are in . . . cahoots and . . . I am going to . . . teach you a lesson."

Porter said, "This pilot betrayed us. Tie him too," as he threw the pilot to the crew. Eager hands trussed the pilot like a barbacoa roast. He was fortunate cook Silva did not have his rotisserie going.

MacIntyre said, "Deliver these . . . trussed-up desperadoes . . . to the authorities in Honolulu. There is a reward . . . and you will receive your share."

Porter said, "We're the fearless shipmates of the sea."

"Aye, aye, sir." the crew shouted.

"I'm sorry I lost the crate. I hate for those ruffians to get anything from us," Porter said to the officers.

MacIntyre chuckled. "Not to worry. I planned for this eventuality and numbered the crates in sequence. Crate A53 contained quicksilver. It was a nice decoy even though it was not as heavy the others.

Porter shook his head and laughed from his gut. "Yes!"

"That was beautiful when you sank their boat. The water is only three fathoms deep and Kanaka divers will recover that crate tomorrow. Drop a buoy to mark the spot and let us *Agilis* to a more suitable berth."

MacIntyre muttered to Ferreri as they passed the isolated *Zebra,*

I hate those Chinese spies, and they are everywhere. There are more along the deck. Go to hell, Hornigold and Chernov.

The port authorities prepared enough charges against the captured Chinese immigrants to lock them up for a long time.

Excited hands from *Agilis* disembarked through the throng of floating temptations and made straight toward the onshore delights.

Chapter 15—Kawai's Luau

Kawai posed under the billowing white sails of *Agilis* like a natural figurehead at the very tip of the bowsprit as it reached the Nu'uanu Avenue wharf. He proclaimed his homecoming to Hawaii at the top of his lungs, "Kawai be glad to see you."

Children screamed, teenage girls shrieked, young athletes cheered, and adults shouted, "Kawai is Home! Yeaah, yeaah, Kawai." A little girl ran to the home of Kawai's mother calling, "Kawai is come. I show you."

Kawai's parents raced to the wharf shouting "Come see my son," They met the proud *Agilis* moored alongside the wharf. Her masts stood the tallest in the harbor. They pushed aside the spectators to wave to their son. His father pointed to Kawai and said, "My son be champion hei hei wa'a rower," as Kawai leaped into the arms of the crowd on the wharf. "Yeaah . . . "

A young girl arrayed five fragrant leis over Kawai's head, two over Richard Porter's head, and singles over the rest of the crew. The enthusiastic throng of mingled Hawaiians, Chinese, Polynesians, English, French, Americans, bewildered whalers, and travelers from across the vast Pacific surrounded them.

Some withdrawn missionaries at the back, the self-appointed guardians of the public morals, were interested, reserved, and concerned.

This was the Hawai'i of Kawai.

Kawai's uncle hollered to the crowd, "Music make a parade."

"You lead," he said to a musician holding a large conch shell made into a trumpet. The holder blew a long note that carried two miles across the town and called the musicians together. A cart lumbered into view with a selection of drummers beating the folk rhythms of Polynesia on their sharkskin drums.

"Need you too," he motioned to a several men with bamboo pipes of varying lengths. They waved to others carrying stringed ukeke's. Volunteers carried their bamboo nose flutes, rattles, coconut shell rattles, and even tapping sticks. The musicians assembled anything to make noise and led a festive procession along Nu'uanu Avenue to Kawai's childhood home.

The family planned to dedicate a sea-going canoe that afternoon named *Ka Manu o Honolua* (The Bird of Honolua). They simply expanded the ceremony to include Kawai's homecoming and dedicated the canoe to him instead.

The celebrations started with a grand *WA' a* (canoe) procession. Six stout young men hoisted a canoe onto their shoulders and boosted Kawai into the seat of honor. Kawai had won the *Wa'a* championship paddling that very canoe. Fifteen young men competed in the ancient Hawaiian sport of spear throwing to start the procession. There was an 'awa ceremony, a *hula kahiko*, and musical stories.

Kawai roused the crowd by waving his arms overhead, "I be real Hawaii man." He stood up and danced his provocative *Mele ma'i* as his wa'a canoe passed in front of a group of young girls who squealed in ecstasy.

The local Baptist missionary folded his arms over his chest in disgust, and stared ahead with a face of stone like a statue from Easter Island.

231

A beautiful woman threw a flower into Kawai's arms. "Aloha, thank you." He kissed the flower and slipped it into his lei. Another woman threw a flower that Kawai sniffed, "How good it smell," and placed it by the first one.

He threw the crowd a kiss. The shower of flowers from the bystanders filled his canoe and framed his grin. A wave of songs followed the parade route.

Kawai was their national hero and his mother the beloved matriarch. She rode on a wide float in a sea of flowers and was escorted by a throng of hula dancers. She radiated a mother's pride that out shined the flowers.

The crew of *Agilis* cheered from the sidelines. Levi Pembroke—Levi on land- told anybody who would listen and one who wouldn't, "That's our mate we sail with."

Even Rudiger spoke up "Squawk. Rudy like a parade." Rudy's bright green eyes took in everything. Bystanders gawked at the parrot and turned back to the parade.

People stood elbow to elbow to see, except for a little girl about three years old at Porter's feet. She jumped up and down and said," I no see, you too big," and she kicked him in the shins.

"Hey, little lady, let's get you on top of things," Porter chuckled as he hoisted the girl onto his shoulder.

She waved madly, "Uncle Kawai! Uncle Kawai. I Lani." Kawai flashed a wide smile and waved back from the parade. The little girl said to those within earshot, "See Uncle Kawai. He big man, no? Whoopeeeee."

Her eyes spied Rudiger perched on Levi's shoulder. "Oh, you a beautiful green bird. What is your name?" Rudy squawked, "I Rudy. I Rudy," and flapped his wings. The little girl caught a loose green feather and giggled with delight. "I never see green bird like you. Polly want a cracker?"

Rudy cocked his head sideways. He didn't know Polly and had never seen a cracker. "Squawk. Rudy like a parade." Lani and Rudy had a good conversation before they turned back to the parade.

The entire island of Oahu celebrated Kawai's return.

The parade poured into a grassy commons amid a massive Ho' molecular celebration of gratitude with impromptu hula dancing, music, food, and games of wrestling, spear throwing, and other competitions.

Kawai's mother had watched many celebrations like this one, and they blurred into the memory of a sunny day twenty years ago.

She was large in the belly and felt her time coming so she retreated to the fern forest under the koa trees. She prepared a shelter over the birthing stone and covered it with mats and leaves. The baby that squirmed inside her was anxious to meet the world.

She stood, and kneeled, and sat, and hung from a tree branch to move the baby down. When the urge to push came, she eased herself into the chair-shaped hollow of the birthing stone. She knew the rocks were known as *pohaku* and contained *mana*, the power to ease the labor pains of childbirth. She also knew a baby born there in the piko (navel) of the island was destined to be an important leader of the people.

She delivered a rollicking baby boy whose first touch was the leaves spread on the stone. He was a lusty fellow who bellowed at the top of his lungs, "Waah . . . waah."

She lifted him up with love and said, "Hello Kawai, my son. Your name is the 'living force of the water' ". She cleaned him off as he let out another holler that echoed through the woods and scared a flock of birds. Kawai was ready to take on the world and the world awaited Kawai.

A beautiful Nene bird with her distinctive striped neck settled onto the birthing stone and placed her beak on Kawai's chest. She delivered a message in a powerful, but soft, voice. "I represent the god, Kanaloa, who rules the waves, and the god, Lono, who rules the air. I represent the god, Pele, who rules the lightning and winds, and the greatest of all, Kane, who rules living creatures."

Kawai stopped howling for a moment.

"We bestow on Kawai the power of our forces. You are in harmony with the great mother of the natural world. You will be famous on and under the water, and the great volcano, Maunaloa, will honor you."

The mother spoke the language of the birds but these words surpassed even her understanding. She said in gratitude *Mahalo Nui Loa* (thank you very much)."

Kawai's mother carried Kawai to the village where a group of anxious midwives surrounded her and prepared to present him to his beaming father. Kawai's father hugged his son. More importantly, he buried the placenta under the family home to connect Kawai with his ancestors, to dream, and to die when his time came.

The father's voice called to the village, "Come see my new son." The people crowded around and congratulated the new parents. The men laid back to smoke large pipes and the women planned a luau feast for that night. They sent runners to villages throughout Oahu to invite their performers, dancers, and musicians.

Back in the present, Kawai's mother joined the women organizing the luau and prepared to welcome Kawai home in style.

High in a mansion overlooking Pearl Harbor, the Chinese Ambassador stomped around the room in a foul mood. "I have many sources of information from Sitka to Hawaii. I pay many hands and for what? My five Ghost Shadows and pilot sit in jail, my gold rots in the Bank of Honolulu, and I have nothing. Nothing!"

He raged from room to room through his quarters. His staff angrily smashed a priceless Ming vase and clubbed to bits an ancient jade incense burner.

"Where is that master of the *Zebra*? He's late and I do not tolerate late."

He stopped at a timid knock and watched a panel slide open. A richly dressed Chinese man entered with a very deep bow. "By your pleasure, a visitor requests to enter your presence." The servant extended a gold plate that held a fancy calling card with the printing engraved, "Dirk Hornigold, Master of *Zebra*".

"Bring him in".

Hornigold entered wearing an elegant suit and carrying a black gentleman's cane. He bowed slightly and said, "Mr. Ambassador, we meet again. I trust you are well."

"Welcome. I am well", he said with a smile.

"But then again I am not well," he said with a ferocious scowl.

"How did you lose the gold shipment from *Agilis*?"

"Uh . . . ."

The Ambassador cut him short with a wave of his arm. "I do not accept excuses. This will never happen again."

Hornigold said, "Upon my honor it will not. The master of *Agilis* is weak and my men will overcome him."

"See that they do."

The anger in the ambassador dissipated as he stormed around the room for several moments and settled into a gilded chair. "Please sit down. We must plan for the next time."

He rang a bell for the servant to bring hot wine and teacakes for their deliberations.

A cadre of organizers, led by Kawai's aunt, left the parade to prepare the luau for the guests of honor, Kawai, his parents, shipmates, and friends from near and far. His mother ran up, "I will help too."

They laid out space for a mob of guests. The elders followed their ancient Polynesian traditions and the ensemble of the performers composed rousing new hula dances and songs. Everyone wanted the best luau ever to mark the return of their national hero.

Koa and Ikaika saw Kawai every day on the *Agilis*. Nothing about the parade impressed them and Koa said, "Why Kawai get big feast 'aha'aina (gathering meal). I stronger, you faster." as he pointed to Ikaika. They shook their heads. "We no launch new canoe and make no war. He safe, we safe, all same."

Kawai's aunt heard them and exclaimed, "Quiet. 'Aha'aina luau is for you too."

She directed the servants to cover the ground with lauhala leaf mats. Lani, Kawai's niece, gathered flowers for the leis during the afternoon. Her helper chanted prayers to *Laka* and the forest gods to bless each flower that they picked from its liana vine.

Kawai's father approached the man who was guarding three whole pigs he had salted inside and out. He had filled the insides with hot stones, wrapped them in kapa and mats, and cooked them in a fire-lined *imu* pit since the night before. "Bring to luau for Kawai, yes?"

"Yes, ready to eat tonight. I make blessing and aloha first."

Musicians and hula dancers rehearsed their stories of adventure and love to end the evening. Most important of all was the hot water an honored servant was making ready to pour over the sacred kava roots in the huge communal kava bowl.

Like a culinary magnet, the meandering aromas of cooking meats and sweet flowers lured the guests to the celebration with whoops and greetings. A beautiful young girl presented a fragrant lei and a pot of poi to each guest. Everybody wanted to talk to everyone else and the chatter was deafening. Long-lost friends who hadn't seen each other since yesterday yelled regards over the heads of the jabbering revelers. The lead drummer silenced it all with a reverberating roll on a gigantic pahu drum. All eyes turned to the entrance.

Kawai burst into the gathering holding out his arms, "Aloha." The guests cheered, "Aloha Kawai! aloha Kawai! Kawai!" They applauded and threw petals from their leis over him. He hugged those he could reach and waved to those beyond.

Kawai tugged on Richard and said, "Richard be my friend. Him happy, me happy." People made a path for the pair to sit on the mat of honor. Kawai's family pushed to his side, and wiggled down giggling. Others of the female persuasion crowded next to Richard. Kawai's cousin of astonishing beauty elbowed her way through and pushed the others away.

Richard, surrounded by a swirl of seduction, leaned to the gorgeous angel on his right and stuttered, "A . . . a . . . loha. Thou be wicked beautiful. Uh . . . aloha." He blushed under his deep tan.

She rubbed noses with him in the traditional Hawaiian greeting as she replied, "Aloha to thee." She caressed his back at the last ripple of muscle free from other massaging female fingers.

Richard was embarrassed. "How could I say such a thing to a girl I've never met?" She smiled and laughed and smiled again, looked at Richard coquettishly and glanced down with fluttering eyelids. He didn't know what to do and hesitated. Another nose rubbed his and he looked into the lively dark eyes of the most gorgeous face he had ever seen on a woman. He hugged her and felt the luscious curves of her body. He patted a little tush.

Richard was entranced but self-conscious and unsure what to do next. So, watching the other guests, he dipped his fingers into the pot of poi and licked them off. His female companion licked a dip of poi from her fingers as she teased Richard with a grin, but demure eyes.

She took his gnarled hand in hers, dipped it into the poi and licked his fingers clean—and then licked his palm with no poi. Her dark eyes gazed into his and she kissed him lightly. She turned her eyes down seductively. Richard's passion triumphed over his inhibitions and he lost all control.

After all, Richard was a stranger to softness for these endless months past and his nostrils were innocent of any sweet fragrance. She rubbed her rich olive-brown skin against his sunburned arms and laughed at the contrast. He hugged her and then hugged a cluster of three. With a long arm, he patted a silky-smooth tush with outstretched fingertips. The laughing good-natured whines jostled for a chance to lick poi from Richard's fingers and he from theirs. Ardor filled the air with its natural perfume.

It was when they licked his big toes that he exclaimed, "Hey that tickles," and pulled his feet up.

Richard decided then and there that he liked lu'aus.

Another mighty roll from the hula pa'u drum was joined by sensuous rattles from the uli gourds to announce the kava ceremony. By ancient custom, the village chief approached the great communal bowl and drank the first cup of kava with a great smile.

Kawai instructed Richard in the etiquette of kava. "We clap hands, drink, clap hands three times." They watched important guests dip an ipu coconut cup of kava from the communal bowl, splash a sip on the floor for the gods, and announce, "Life." Those within earshot said, "Blessed Be," and the guests emptied the ipu.

Kawai motioned a server to dip tan-colored ipu cups into the kava for Richard and him.

Richard asked, "What is this?"

" 'Awa or some say kava, our Hawaii drink. You like, yes?" They clapped together and Kawai drank. He clapped three times.

Richard looked at his coconut cup with a wry face but felt obligated to honor his friend. "Do I want to drink this?" He emptied the cup in one swallow. "Not too bad, not too good."

In a few moments, he began to feel happy and optimistic— and then fearless. His emotions soared into harmony with the universe, but his mouth turned numb to speech. Visions of the world exploded in his head and formed into grass hula skirts adorning rich brown hips and swaying to the waves on the voyage from Bora ages ago. The soreness vanished from his hip and his muscles relaxed. No longer tired, he extended his cup for a refill.

People ate with their fingers while seated on the lauhala mats. They told elaborate stories over ti leaf-covered tables set with extravagant centerpieces. Each guest kept their bowl of poi within convenient reach. Servers refilled kava cups as soon as they were drained, and a dip of poi from taro root refreshed their palates between dishes.

Kawai took Richard around to meet his extended family, "My friend always." They adopted him from this luau on. Kawai's endless deluge of family names merged into an exaltation of love and the Hawaiian family was almost as proud of Richard as of Kawai. Richard was now their newest member, and Kawai had a twenty-four-year-old big brother.

Richard and Kawai returned to their seats of honor within the bevy of girls who smothered them with attention. Kawai slipped his hands around the hips of the gorgeous woman standing over him in a grass skirt and waved them back and forth. "Aloha you."

Her eyes twinkled as she chanted,

> The day of revealing shall see what it sees:
> A seeing of facts, a sifting of rumors,
> An insight won by the black sacred 'awa,
> A vision like that of a sacred god!

> Accessible is the day whereby knowledge is gained,
> Knowledge from the source, knowledge by hearing,

Like the flourishing `awa plant is the knowledge of the gods,
O hear me.

Kawai was transfixed, "You beautiful and swing hula fine, yes?" She smiled mysteriously and said, "You have to open your eyes to see," as she took a kava root she had been chewing and slipped it between Kawai's lips.

"Kava drinker be happy," Kawai said to Richard with a smile between chomps of the root. "No angry no fight," as she bent down to rub noses.

Richard's spread his long-armed embrace over as many girls as he could reach and tickled those beyond. Words slid off his tongue in flowing, muffled tones, "I'm in . . . paradise. Ahh . . . , ahh . . . , good . . . ." He leaned back and shivered from the tickles of the young girls when they searched in vain for tattoos anywhere on his body.

One said, "You no have tattoos, who you be? We make picture here," as she slid her hands down the back of his trousers. He snuggled his face into the grass skirt, smiled, dipped her hand into poi and licked it from her fingers. She twittered with glee.

Kawai broke in to introduce Richard to the main drink, okolehao. "Big drink of Hawaii make you more good." Kawai motioned at a server to fill their cups with a brown liquid. Richard said with gusto after the first taste, "This tastes like brandy. Very beyond kava."

Richard picked up on Macintyre's comment to Alfonso Ferreri since they sat in the same group. "It was seventy-five years ago that Captain Cook's sailors taught these Hawaiians how to distill Kava. I am not sure this improved these islands. They do not handle it well."

Richard thought, We handle it very well indeed. I've never felt better.

He ate with camaraderie and listened to good-natured ribald jokes told by his new family. When the time for dancing and entertainment arrived, Richard felt no pain, or his fingers or toes, either. He could hardly say, "Gi'me another one," which he didn't need as he waved for more *okolehao*.

Richard's last memory of the evening was Kawai's introduction to the hula dance. "We make love and life to hula. Men and women hula to live our history. I give you special hula hapa haole hapa for a white foreign man. You now Hawaiian."

Richard was profoundly touched and wobbled to his feet. "Thank you, broth'r. I never had a family b'fore," as he stretched his arms wide with sparkling bleary eyes and a gargantuan smile.

"To hula is to dance. Hula hula hue is fast hips to end celebration and see who dance longest. Hula 'auana good."

Richard turned to the girl at his side, "Hula 'auana? Yes?" She giggled. "Yes," and earthquakes rippled through his drunken body.

The company of musicians in a chorus of drums, gourds, and flutes started the entertainment, and a dancer leaped into the open area with a wild hula hapa haole hapa.

Kawai chanted, "Richard, Richard, Aloha for you." Richard motioned to a server for another okolehao. He didn't know what it was anymore but knew he was happy drinking it. "More!"

The combined effects of the kava and okolehao seriously affected Richard. Kawai was engrossed with his flock of whines and ignored Richard's growing inebriation.

Richard barely noticed as his cluster of ravishing women drifted away from his obnoxiousness.

The hula entertained the party with gusto. Richard insisted he had to join in, although he had never been able to dance a step in his entire life. It didn't matter that he was three sheets to the wind drunk.

He grabbed one of the dancers during the slow *hula hue* phase. When the fast hips began, he swayed, stumbled, and fell on his back laughing hysterically, "Ha, ha . . . ,I like . . . hula."

Richard reverted to his days of a hick from the sticks and a hellion to boot. After he passed out several men rolled him to the edge of the mats and left him under a tropical bush to sleep it off.

The luau continued throughout the night better without him. The remaining guests ebbed away from the luau to private spots as couples, families, and a few singles.

Richard snored under the leaves of the banana tree, alone.

The sun rose high the next morning, as it did every morning in tropical Hawaii. The sunbeams peeking through the banana tree leaves illuminated a puffy face on a nearly dead body unconscious on the ground.

Richard's eyes struggled to open in the bright sunlight. He sneezed to pain as he had never experienced. He crawled out of the edge of the jungle and felt sick, really sick. "Oh my God. Somebody ate cat shit with my mouth. My head falls off. My stomach won't eat ever again. My hair hurts. Oh, oh, oh . . . let me die . . . evil kava."

The tempest in Richard's belly surpassed the gale of a few days before. His waves surged higher and higher until he threw up the corruption from the night before.

Kawai wandered out of the jungle with a grin. "How be you?" Richard groaned and pulled a banana leaf over his head, "Go away and let me die."

Kawai chuckled and said, "You hurt? You be good Hawaiian now. I think you alone last night, no woman. You never have son like that. You like our okolehao? Yes."

Richard groaned. "Go away. I die."

Kawai said, "No die. We drink coffee and be good again. We go you see."

He dragged a groaning Richard to his feet. "You eyes all red. You no see good, I think." Richard leaned against a tree, vomited, and groaned again. "I will never drink again".

Kawai said, "Until next time."

They shuffled to a local coffee shop with Kawai humming and Richard groaning in all kinds of pain.

"Never again," he vowed.

Richard and Kawai felt revived after the ritual of strong coffee and enjoyed the sights along Nu'uanu Avenue. Richard vaguely remembered a hand sliding down his back searching for a spot to make a picture. The idea of a tattoo down there intrigued him.

They approached a busy tattoo shop with tempting flash sheets plastered on its windows. He and Kawai joined a queue of bare sailors waiting to enter. Streams of inked cocky men come out the other door.

"I want a tattoo like you," Richard said looking at Kawai, who still had some unmarked skin that he wanted to fill.

Richard stared at a hula girl on his side. Kawai wiggled a muscle and the girl danced the hula. Showman Kawai entertained the entire queue by animating each tattoo separately. Dancing from an early age, he could flex every muscle independently and make the image over it jump. Richard was blank and envious as he watched Kawai's show. Every man in the queue turned to watch, and the front man missed his turn to enter the shop.

Kawai joked, "You no sailor, Mr. Richard. It time we make you a man."

The walls of the crowded shop awed crowded clients with hundreds of exotic designs. The tattoo artist explained their meanings. "Here is a rooster and a pig. They show your feet the way to shore and you will not drown. Those designs of anchors are steady as she goes. If you crossed the Atlantic and returned, you get a nice anchor. That hula girl means you came to Hawaii."

The artist asked Richard, "Where's your swallow when you left home?"

"I left home in a hurry."

"Add a sparrow every five thousand miles. That little bird carries your soul home if you die at sea. I have a design for a man of distinction. Where should I start?"

Kawai exclaimed, "You ready for sparrow in San Francisco. You need this one and this, and that," as he picked out design on top of design.

Richard held up his hand in protest. "Ain't enough skin on my little six-foot body for these tattoos," as he studied the offerings of tattoo art plastering the walls.

Kawai said, "You my family now. We get same tattoo, yes?" The artist sketched designs on their limbs and torsos.

Richard sprinted out of the shop to retrieve his ditty box. He opened the lid to the image of Becky he had carved. I want her over my heart and her name below." He pointed at several tattoos on Kawai. He said, "Show him your anchor so I can get one. Then we are a good team and I am a sailor.

Kawai paraded his anchor tattoo that was hanging by the chain from his belly button. They selected the same flowing hula dancer to honor their luau.

Richard had the sister of his hula dancer, also named Becky, but she was down on his left buttock where he could not see it. He didn't know about the name. This might cause a headache in the future, but not now. He showed off his sparrows and anchor.

Beaming but sore they strutted down Nu'uanu Avenue. Kawai danced his new hula girl and Richard displayed a woman named Becky. With their arms on each other's shoulders, they belted out a sea chantey to inform passersby they were the saltiest sailors on the block.

Chapter 16—Sabotage

A serene night caressed the harbor and the volcanoes puffed a little steam in the background to celebrate the tattoos. A solitary rat on *Agilis* quietly munched a piece of hardtack, his senses on the alert for Fore 'n Aft. His ears pricked up at a quiet rustling outside the hull. Dripping water ran down the side and his instincts bred into his intelligent rat brain turned to high.

This is most unusual—what is going on?

A fisherman on a catamaran in the water had a better view.

A small man in black pulled himself over the gunwale with a padded grappling hook. His shifty eyes surveyed the binnacle, tiller, and decks. They noted the guard snoring softly in a coil of rope, as he tiptoed around the deckhouse cabin to the stern.

Zodiacal light from the night sky illuminated the waist-high binnacle and reflected the compass on top. Two large iron balls on arms protruded from either side to correct the needle for the magnetism of the hull.

Drops of water marked his path to the binnacle. He felt around the binnacle support and attached a magnetized piece of black iron to a bolt. The compass needle rotated four degrees to the north-northwest where it had pointed to true north.

He chuckled to himself,

That ignorant helmsman won't notice until he's stranded in the northern Pacific doldrums. Serves you right for running such a sorry operation.

Done with the sabotage, he tiptoed past the sleeping watch to his boat with no one the wiser except the little rat and the fisherman who was landing a catch. He paddled back to shore where a mean-looking man with a scar across his face met him.

"Did you watch the compass needle move with the magnet?"

"It stayed crooked. *Agilis* will be lost in the doldrums before you can shake a belaying pin. I guarantee you will win the twenty-five thousand dollars".

A brief rainstorm washed away the drops on the deck. *Agilis* creaked and rocked at anchor, while the stars shown from the night sky. No one was aware of the sabotage except the binnacle, and it could not speak.

Bent on hell raising, a gang of drunk hands from *Agilis* and *Zebra* stumbled into the Red Lion Grog Shop. They could see through the smoke as thick as the San Francisco fog that it was a small place with a bar along one wall and three sturdy tables circled by stools.

O'sullivan said, "Butts on the stools and elbows on the bar. We stand, mates."

They barely noticed the old seaman, Levi, in the corner with his peg leg propped on a stool. He and his green parrot were spinning a yarn to oblivious listeners.

"Squawk! Rudy like a fight."

" . . . as I was saying, I'm here to tell you that . . . "

Just in front of him, a sailor from *Agilis* faced off against a rival who hurled an insult,

"You're thick as horse shit and half as useful."

O'sullivan punched his shoulder with a comment,

"May the cat eat your ass and the devil eat the cat."

The *Zebra-ite* swung a fist but in his drunken aim hit Kawai instead. Kawai knocked him flat on the floor with one backhand.

The peg-leg wonder, Levi, pulled off his wooden leg and broke it over the *Zebra* sailor's thick skull. He crawled back to his stool and tossed down a drink of liquid courage. "Ya got me a good one, mate," he said rubbing his head.

This was their recreation and not a serious altercation yet.

Levi hopped back to his corner and resumed sweet talk with a sinewy woman of the night. "You're a fine lady, Jersey. We must get to know each other better." He wrapped an arm around her only to have a pasty heavy-set tar stagger out of the haze.

"What's a crippled lout like you doing with a fine lady like Jersey?"

Jersey's soft brown eyes turned to cold steel gray. A scowl descended across her face and her long eyelashes snapped in rage. "Mr. Levi is a better man than you any day, and any night too. Be gone."

Levi was a little drunk and the pasty man a lot drunk. Levi came back, "Jersey and me are friends, you three-inch fool."

In spite of his missing leg, Levi was the toughest man in the bar, but the intoxicated attacker didn't know it. He aimed a left hook at Levi's chin that missed and grazed Kawai again.

"You will do," he said as he slugged Kawai to the floor. The pasty sailor banged Kawai's head into the wooden boards with both hands.

Kawai heaved up and faced his attacker. They grappled and fell back to the floor. Levi still held the broken end of his wooden leg and raised his arm to stab the attacker with the sharp end.

But before Levi could crawl to a good stabbing position, a face appeared in the grill over the window. It was Richard.

Richard saw Kawai was in a fight and dove feet first through the grill. He skidded across the floor riding on the shattered grill and tossed the pasty man off Kawai. The man stumbled up and Richard decked him with a roundhouse punch to the jaw.

Richard looked around, "Next?" He was the second toughest man in the grog shop.

The patrons returned to their cards and drinks. The excitement was over.

Kawai said, "You fighter, Mr. Porter."

"That's what friends do, but hey, I am Richard onshore, remember?.

"Yes Mr. Richard sir, I remember."

"Richard will do."

"We family, yes?"

"Yes."

They left the bar roaring a sea shanty with Levi leaning on another drunken mariner.

Richard turned to Kawai and said, "Your six feet hide the heart of a Polynesian lion."

In the ensuing days, Kawai would run risks that no one could dream of.

Chapter 17—Load *Zebra*

Whalers, merchant craft, frigates, men of war—all needed longshoremen to load and unload their cargo. Hornigold, himself, engaged a group of nondescript hangers-on for double the normal rate of pay. He said to Chernov, "All the decent workers are over in California scrounging for gold."

Unskilled dockworkers meant trouble later because they couldn't arrange the cargo properly. Worse, the *Zebra's* crew bribed two sweating Hawaiians to smuggle bananas aboard, wrapped in old tarpaulins made to look like normal freight. They had eaten through their food stores from Sitka and were desperate for fresh food. *Zebra's* crew members took turns distracting Chernov while the Hawaiians concealed the bundles underneath legitimate cargo in the tightly sealed hold.

Loading proceeded apace. Chernov was in a hurry and abused the workers, "Bust a nut, you lazy gutter whores."

Chernov noticed the diagonal stays from the deck to the main mast were slack. He commanded a nearby tar, "Yo, adjust the mainstay." The hand undid the seizing where the deck end passed around a deck eye, tightened the stayline to remove the slack, and re-seized the end around the eye.

It was slack again the next morning, and Chernov was worried because the masts were in sections and the stays were critical for support. To his misfortune the same hand happened by and Chernov jumped on him, "Dammit, I said adjust the mainstay."

He tightened the stay a second time and went aloft to find the problem. He called down to Chernov, "Sir, the tension has bent the metal cradle where the stayline holds the mast. It's a piece of trash from China, but I'll try to fix it." He patched up the bent ironwork as best he could, but he couldn't do much.

Hornigold stormed up, "What is the problem? I have to embark now to win that wager. Take a shortcut if you have to."

Chernov sighed to himself.

Over on the *Agilis*, Porter and Babbitt supervised their smoothly functioning team of dockworkers. These honest men were the only dockhands the Port authority trusted to take the gold to the bank. In gratitude for the shipment from San Francisco, the Bank of Honolulu paid their wages to load the *Agilis*.

Porter kept the group on to install the replacement spars. Alden supervised the repairs and the shipboard crew provided the muscle.

Agilis was fit and strong on the eve of her return to North America.

"Squawk. Rudy like a story," said the parrot. Pembroke cleared his throat and spoke in a scratchy voice held over from last night. "Did you see what I just saw?"

"No, and we ain't gonna listen," said the tars in unison, as five scrambled up the forecastle ladder to escape.

Pembroke ignored the customary objection and continued, "I'm here to say I like bananas. I can eat a bunch but not on board. Why is that you ask?"

A sailor said, "I didn't ask." The men peeped down the hatch because they liked his stories, but didn't want him to know it. He usually passed along good information.

"Them there sailors on the *Zebra* is wrapping canvas around bunches of bananas and smuggling them aboard."

A bunch of naked bananas dangling from the block and tackle that hoisted cargo into the *Agilis* appeared over the gunwale. Babbitt stopped him cold, "No bananas. I've told you twice."

The disgusted dockhand threw the bunch overboard and left in a huff.

Pembroke resumed. "We was on a trip from Dominica to Rio de Janeiro and left the island with bananas, rum, and bay leaves."

"Bay leaves?"

"Tell you later."

His narration dropped to a rumbling whisper. "We headed to Rio. It was summer and them clusters ripened all at once. The tars gobbled them and tossed the peels on the deck. We slid to hell and back, let me tell you. Had to bang a few heads over that."

Several tars laughed and slid into each other's chests. "Here comes a banana peel." Crash!

Pembroke ignored the interruption and said, "It got worse. Old Johnson went down the hold for food and got corrupted without the benefit of rum. Wilson went to get him and plumb passed out. We barely rescued them two from the poison gas those bananas made.

O'sullivan said, "What in the hell caused that?"

"They makes poison gas when they ripen. Don't know how but damn we got hungry. Bananas is bad luck on a ship."

"Still don't know why."

"And they brings spiders. One bite and you is gone."

Two tars began snoring.

"My own two eyes saw this spider bite old Johnson. Poor guy was dead afore he got to the gunwale. I clobbered that spider into a grease spot with a belaying pin. No bananas since.

This story is the gen-u-ine truth as I am sitting in front of you."

Agilis crew was asleep and snoring.

The *Zebra* crew was smuggling bananas.

Richard strolled through the open-air marketplace in downtown Honolulu. He recalled his astonishment that Brannan's market in Sacramento could sell eggs for a dollar each to the miners. He got an idea.

Eggs come from chickens and chickens are running all over this place. They're tough. I'll take five back to California.

The idea of selling eggs for a dollar, or discounted to eighty-five cents on sale, excited Richard more than digging yellow metal from a cold river ever had. He said too himself,

I'll show you, Brannan, yuck, yuck, yuck, you greedy old grocer.

Richard followed the throngs through the bustling market and down mysterious tunnels lined by booths from exotic worlds.

One flat area held Muslims kneeling to Mecca on their little prayer rugs. Wondrous fragrances of spices and incense floated down the aisles. Breads, snacks, fruits, drinks, trinkets, and crafts of all types tempted the shoppers. A moneychanger converted coins from one country into coins from another, always with a cut and always with an argument. Loud haggling filled the marketplace.

Underfoot everywhere were beaks and, "Cluck, cheep, cluck, waaaaay..," and, "Ruku-kuku-do," from a rooster. Effusions from the other end were spread around too.

Richard eyed chickens in colors of white, brown, and speckles. They came in small, medium, large, and loud. Hens and roosters mingled. In the chaos, he came to a stall displaying live chickens with their legs tied together and hanging from hooks.

"Like me when I was kidnapped," he said to the proprietor, "except I got loose."

Richard said, "Give me five hens and that rooster." The shop owner proudly picked out five and added the rooster, who made a furious ruckus.

"With my compliments," as he handed the flapping mess to Richard. "Only twenty-four dollars, please."

"No way. They're not worth a penny over a dollar each." The owner hung his head and looked highly insulted.

"Esteemed sir, you see how fat they are. They lay many eggs for you. Only three dollars and half—but just for you."

"Too much. That skinny one can't walk and her feathers are gone from her back." Richard walked away.

"Mr. sailorman, very good chickens and you like. I make mistake, I mean three dollars."

He kept walking.

"Most excellent fine birds, sir. Fifteen dollars and bag of food," he called down the aisle as he hung a chicken by her legs. The hen flapped her wings in protest.

Richard slowly returned, gazing at the wares inside other shops on the way. "Fourteen dollars for six. That is more money than around the corner, but I like you."

The vendor writhed as if in pain, "You are hard but the day is late so I give you six chickens for fifteen dollars." The sun was high overhead.

They made the exchange and Richard tied twelve legs together. He carried the flapping, shrieking cloud from the stall. Feathers flew in all directions in a bedlam of brown and white. Richard stuffed the birds in a basket from a nearby stall to calm them down.

He spotted Chips Alden across the street admiring a display of Polynesian carvings.

"Look at that detail and the expression on that face. And that fertile fellow looks to excite the ladies. I favor that fertility bowl in the form of a turtle."

Richard interrupted his erotic fantasy. "I need a cage for these chickens before we embark."

"So I have nothing to do but make a cage for you and a new leg for Levi? He could fight with a belaying pin or a bottle, couldn't he? But no, he busts his leg instead. I hear he won the fight."

Richard said, "If you made stronger legs, they wouldn't break."

Alden said, "I'll break you too with that kind of attitude."

Richard said "Thank you, sir. That's about right and we appreciate what you do."

"I have to fix up you tars every time we go ashore. I suppose you want a door and holder for food and straw in the bottom of your cages too. Is there no end to your demands?"

"No."

"Humph."

Hornigold of the *Zebra,* the steward and bosun inspected the packed hold as they prepared to leave.

He said, "We need this space to carry another three hundred dollars worth of goods. Those barrels of rations are surplus—get rid of them."

The steward marked three barrels with an X.

"Sell these somewhere. Try the *Agilis.* They'll buy anything."

The hands objected to selling the barrels. "With respect, sir, we need that food for the return trip."

The bosun jumped down their throat, "Do it! My cat 'o nine tails hasn't tasted blood in a long time."

"But sir, we're hungry."

"No, by God, and no grog tonight. Off with those barrels."

Grumbling, the sailors removed the barrels.

The loaders filled the empty space with produce from the islands and buried the smuggled bananas even deeper under the cargo.

Hornigold followed the barrels of surplus food to shore. After the sale, he joined the Chinese Ambassador in the Captain's Dining Room in the best hotel in Honolulu. He ordered the Commodore Special Dinner and added a bottle of 1846 *Meursault-Charmes* wine.

The waiter bowed and said, "Excellent choice, sir. "This vintage presents to your refined palate subtle aromas of lime, grapefruit, chalk, and earth, with the slightest aftertaste of caramel.

Hornigold held up his glass in a toast, "Mr. Ambassador, it is a pleasure to see you again. You are looking well."

"Indeed I am well, and my network of Ghost Shadows is gathering information coming and going in California, Hawaii, and Canton. We have gathered profitable harvests from California, although there is room for improvement."

Hornigold said, "All it takes is a little discipline."

"We can do better, especially in California. We have to be nimble to keep up with the gold rush. Our take from Canton to Singapore is shrinking because of increased resistance. Those merchant's vessels have replaced their cargo with armaments, and it is unsafe for a simple pirate to board."

Hornigold said, "What visions does your fertile Chinese mind see on the horizon? I'll have twenty-five thousand dollars for new ventures after this race."

"Back here in Honolulu, those vessels are like sitting ducks in the Golden Pond. Rub the belly of Buddha to bring abundance and contentment, even to ship's masters." They rubbed the belly of the little golden Buddha on the table, laughed, and returned to their glasses of wine.

The Ambassador puffed his after-dinner cigar in deep thought. I am still distressed over the loss of our gold from *Agilis*. Worse, my six men and pilot lie in jail not producing anything. I cannot let this stand.

While the pirate members awaited sentencing, he as the Chinese Ambassador was free under diplomatic immunity. He seethed with rage as he glared out the window at the gorgeous view of the harbor.

"You're mine next time," he said, looking at *Agilis* and *Zebra* floating in the congested harbor among the whalers, merchant ships, frigates, and floating vessels of all descriptions. The joyful king with ten of his many wives surfed the waves in the royal Kamehameha canoe.

He turned to Hornigold, "Here is my idea. I have greased the palms of the guards at the jail. The Ghost Shadows will be free by nightfall. You will return them to the crew of the *Zebra*. Use their skills to board targets and take control. Do not fail as you did on *Agilis*."

In spite of their best efforts, the racing brigs left the Honolulu harbor bowsprit to bowsprit. The disorganized passage was strewn with ships from around the world and it was difficult to maneuver.

The *Zebra* managed to discharge her pilot first. *Agilis* was behind but in a better position in the channel. The crews were too busy to trade more than a couple of insults.

"You look like eel-skin"

"You are bull's-pizzle"

Porter talked to the crew as they reached the blue water beyond the harbor. "Our return passage will be difficult. We'll cruise north to catch the trade winds from Russia that blow down the Alaska coast. The winds that pushed us from California won't let us return that way."

He drew an imaginary chart in the air. "Babbitt wants to say something."

Babbitt spoke up, "There is an ancient custom that says 'Touch the collar of a sailor for good luck before a difficult task.' Some say this is bupkis but sailors swear by it."

Palmieri held up his hand, "Sir, what is bupkis?"

Babbitt forgot his southern gentleman's upbringing and said, "'Shivering shit balls' is what bupkis means. Goat droppings, worthless. Don't you know anything? I'm going to touch Mr. Palmieri's collar."

He walked over, swiped the grimy collar, and thought to himself, I hope this works, because I need that prize money.

There are violent storms in the Pacific and we need all the help we can get.

Porter also touched the collar, but Ferreri looked the other way.

Palmieri didn't know what to do and did nothing. He shuddered at their touch, even for the safety of *Agilis*.

Ferreri, as a practical man, was concerned about the immediate condition of *Agilis* and said to Babbitt, "Update me on the status of our bilge. You report we are shipping more water every day?"

"The bilge has increased to fifteen inches a day from six. I have a hand manning the pump most of the day. We should careen the hull for an inspection when we next raise port—if we make port."

Over on the *Zebra*, Hornigold queried his bosun as well, even though it was a little late, "Are you certain our cargo is well secured?"

"As well as possible, sir, with those incompetent stevedores. We can make sail with good progress if we avoid heavy weather. Those spaces from the excess barrels of supplies are filled with paying cargo."

MacIntyre and the mates, Ferreri and Porter, studied the chart as *Agilis* sailed into the North Pacific. The team sensed something was wrong. Their plotted position compared to the sun was off. They closely examined the binnacle and discovered the magnet placed by the saboteur. Porter pried it off and the compass rotated 4 degrees clockwise.

"Blast me timbers, we have been hornswaggled," said MacIntyre to the mates.

Ferreri immediately understood what had happened. "Damn my eyes, we have been sailing four degrees off our plotted heading. We are headed straight into the northern Pacific doldrums.

MacIntyre said, "Pray we can raise sufficient wind to get back on course. Porter, check the deck, rigging, and hull for other sabotage. We are losing time with every passing hourglass. I expected that scummy *Zebra* to pull something and sure enough, they did."

Porter said, "About what you'd expect from Hornigold."

MacIntyre swore and continued, "This sabotage is lower than dog shit. It puts us in danger and has no place at sea. We shall take multiple readings at noon to correct our actual location."

He held up his sextant from it's elegant silver case. Damn my eyes, I wish I could see like I used to."

"I want readings from Ferreri, kid Porter, and Babbitt. We'll compare results and get back on course."

MacIntyre said, "When your eyes get cloudy from the years at sea like mine it is difficult to take a reading."

Still, MacIntyre and Ferreri each read the angle of the sun with their sextants.

Ferreri said, "I believe my reading of 29.8 degrees north latitude is accurate, sir."

MacIntyre exploded, "Mr. Ferreri, I suggest you learn to navigate. The correct position is 28.5 degrees. You are over a degree off and one hundred and twenty-seven miles too far north. We will miss the westerly winds. I can't believe after all these years you are unable to take a proper reading."

"I believe my sextant is well adjusted, sir."

"Clearly you are in error. The correct reading is 28.5 degrees. Enter that into the log. I shall give you a sextant lesson as soon as I am able." He tried to stomp to his cabin, but careened into the doorway and stumbled to his desk.

Ignored and unseen, Porter read his sextant and agreed with Ferreri using the skill he picked up from Sherman's transit in Sacramento.

Ferreri turned to Porter, "And what does an inexperienced hand, such as yourself, find? I saw you sneak behind my back with your old beat up sextant."

Porter thought a moment before speaking. "My sextant gives a reading of twenty-nine point eight degrees."

"Humph, a lucky guess—you overheard me. Give me that thing." He examined it closely. "Hmmm, used but well-made. Let us see what it reads in the hands of an expert."

Even though it was slightly past midday, Ferreri confirmed his reading of twenty-nine point eight degrees. "Same as before. I'll enter twenty-nine point eight degrees in the log and re-plot our position accordingly. You agree, do you not?"

"I agree, sir."

He passed the sextant to Babbitt. "Might as well confirm once more, even by a mere petty officer."

In truth, Babbitt had more experience in navigation than either of the mates and reported his reading as twenty-nine point eight degrees. MacIntyre overheard from his cabin and stormed out, grasping the doorway.

"You ignorant pressed escapee, I do not trust your reading as far as I can throw this ship. You are conspiring against me, but I am the Master and any action against my authority is mutiny."

Babbitt hung his head and said nothing.

"Mr. Ferreri will enter our position in the log as twenty-eight point five degrees north latitude. I know where the hell we are and will correct our chart accordingly," he said as he slammed the door.

Ferreri said to Porter. "I know my reading is accurate because I adjusted my instrument and took the readings in a clear sky. Even you agreed, as did Babbitt. It's three to one."

"Here is the dilemma. If we accept Macintyre's reading, we over-correct our bearing and enter the doldrums. On the other hand, if we stand against him it is deemed a mutiny."

Porter said, "Our safety demands an accurate position. MacIntyre is befuddled since that mind attack, and I am willing to accept our readings regardless of the consequences. Our first duty is to protect the *Agilis*.

Ferreri muttered to himself,

MacIntyre knows the sun by instinct. His instinct says we are in trouble, but I'll stand by my result. Plotting the wrong position in these waters is dangerous.

He paced the deck and made up his mind. "Mr. Porter, if you will, enter the reading of 29.8 degrees north latitude in the log."

Porter corrected Macintyre's' reading.

Ferreri checked his personal sextant and found there were no errors, as he had adjusted it that morning. He handed it to Porter who found none either. He passed it to Babbitt saying, "We mates see no errors." Babbitt agreed and laid it back in the leather case.

The next instrument was Porter's. Ferreri minutely examined it and said, "I find a small error in the index mirror and the others are sloppy but adequate."

Babbitt made the minor correction and confirmed the other adjustments were spot on. The bosun returned it to its beat-up carrying case.

Ferreri took the elegant sextant belonging to MacIntyre from its case on the table. "This is dirty and completely out of whack." He handed it to Babbitt. "Clean this, I refuse to touch it in this condition."

Babbitt examined MacIntyre's sextant. "Look at this gentleman. The sight is filthy and the mirrors are awry. I see four errors." He wiped clean the metal arms and optical parts of the neglected instrument. "I'll make preliminary corrections to start, so please watch me."

Babbitt adjusted the navigational instrument under the intense eyes of the mates. The sextant passed three times around the hands of the officers.

"Accurate, gentleman?"

"Yes."

"Yes."

Babbitt returned the corrected sextant to its elegant, silver trimmed carrying case. Ferreri slipped it back onto the desk with the sleeping MacIntyre none the wiser.

Porter elaborated in his private journal that night.

> I have committed a significant act that can send me before a Court of Inquiry. Can I say, 'Others were with me?' The Court would charge me with mutiny on the high seas, regardless. I made this decision and will accept the consequences alone.

Chapter 18—Used Rum

Cook Silva knocked and entered the cabin to check on MacIntyre, who sat up in bed.

"How do you feel today, sir?"

"I am floating on a bilious sea. I'm surrounded by shoals and blinded by fog-never felt worse. I hate this and I'm hungry to boot." He groaned as he closed his eyes and leaned back on the pillow.

Cook Silva searched his healing experience. "I have willow bark and wild lettuce extract to ease the pain, but there is something better. You, Master MacIntyre, need a bowl of chicken soup to heal the body."

He hummed as he returned to the galley,

> The skipper's in the wardroom drinkin' gin,
> Hi, ho, chicken on a raft!
> I don't mind a-knockin', but I ain't a-goin' in!
> Hi, ho, chicken on a raft!

"For chicken soup you need a chicken—but where is one?"

"Cluck, cluck," came from cages on the deck, and a rooster crowed, "Ruku-kuku-do." A muffled, "Squawk. Ruku-kuku-do, do," came from the forecastle.

The Cook muttered, Damn parrot. I'll throw him in the pot too.

Back to the medicinal chicken, he thought, Porter will never miss one. He's got so many.

In the twinkling of an eye, Cook Silva twisted a fat chicken's head off, cleaned the body, and dropped it into a big pot of vegetables. He burned the guts, feathers, and feet in the galley stove. The parrot was safe until the next time.

Porter smelled the tantalizing chicken stew wafting across the deck and was instantly suspicious. He counted his chickens and came up one short. He counted them again and was still short. He walked to the stove stack and choked on the fumes from the burning feathers and chicken feet. It was clear what was going on.

Porter's vision of eggs at one dollar each that the chicken would never lay shot through his head. He dropped to the galley stove and seized the cook. "You stole my chicken . . . I can smell it . . . ."

Cook Silva had been under the weather for several days and was irritable. "Out of my galley. I got to make mess for the crew."

This was too much for Porter and he punched Silva. Silva grabbed a butcher knife and attacked the mate. The mate caught the cook's uplifted knife hand and both men fell against the hot stove, with Porter on the stove side. His skin sizzled. He scrambled up the hatch ladder one rung ahead of the raging Cook swinging the knife like a saber.

There was murder in Silva's eye and Porter knew it. The mate deflected the Cook's knife between his knees and clamped his legs in a vice. The knife slashed a gash through Porter's pants and is calf bled like the chicken with its head twisted off.

Babbitt and Ferreri rushed in to stop the fight. Babbitt wrapped his arms around Silva and grabbed the fist holding the knife. He bent the hand back until the knife clattered to the deck. Ferreri clinched Porter in a bear hug. The fighters blew like porpoises and cursed each other in highly creative terms.

Porter was seething so hard he didn't notice his cut until Ferreri a pulled away. His first step was awkward because his foot went sideways. He looked down at the blood on his leg and cried, "I'm murdered."

The rescuers rolled up Parker's trouser leg to expose the gash.

Ferreri examined the cut in detail. "No telling what Silva cut with that knife, but for sure he cut up that filthy chicken, feathers, and guts. You have to clean that wound but our water is bad and the ocean no better from all that trash. Rum it has to be. Your choice, new or used?"

"Used, of course. New rum is for drinking."

Ferreri said to himself, Porter thinks like a common sailor. Used rum indeed. Huh.

Babbitt had the opposite reaction which he wisely kept to himself. Porter knows the ways of the world.

Ferreri motioned to Kawai, "Make water on this cut."

Kawai looked confused, "Sir, what you mean make water?"

Ferreri thought to himself, Ignorant Kanaka. Why can't you learn English? I did.

What he said out loud was, "Piss on the cut to wash it out."

Kawai peed over Porter's blood-soaked leg. "Mr. Porter be my brother forever, you and me."

As Ferreri wrapped a piece of used sailcloth around the cut he said, "This will stick together in a day and heal in a week. The knife missed anything important."

Porter thought to himself, Easy enough for you to say 'anything important'. It's my leg, you son of a bitch.

He was learning a little self-control, but only a little. At least he did not take a swing at Ferreri.

Their attention turned to the mouth-watering aroma of chicken stew from the galley. With a glaring eye on Porter, Cook Silva carried a steaming pot to MacIntyre. "For you, sir. Magic chicken soup to cure you."

MacIntyre slurped the soup. "Well done, Silva." His condition improved as he talked. "Aah . . . , this heals my stomach and returns the strength to my bones. Yum Yum Yum."

A wave of regret subdued Cook Silva as he left the cabin.

I cut Mr. Porter. What is wrong with me?

He walked over to a suspicious Porter who was tensed for defense. The Cook removed the wrap to examine the cut while Porter guarded him with a wary eye. "Back to finish the job are you?"

"Please, I treat your leg with good medicine." He applied a poultice of herbs designed to heal a wound, and re-wrapped the cut. Porter noticed his leg felt better, or at least did not hurt as much, and he could almost walk with a normal stride. Silva also compounded a salve from grease and other herbs to soothe the burn on his arm.

Ferreri approached Cook Silva, "The rule against fighting with knives on *Agilis* is iron clad, and you disobeyed. I sentence you to be locked in irons for a week when you're not cooking. No grog and keep your knives in your food."

Rudiger piped up. "Squawk! Rudy like a story. Squawk!"

Pembroke turned on his storytelling voice. "Have you heard about the Eyes of the Ship? An old sailor told me when we were chained in the brig together."

"Not again. Is that all you know—old sailors, you old fart? Can't you shut up and leave us alone." Several walked away with their fingers in the ears. Two dropped their pants and mooned Pembroke.

Pembroke continued like a lava flow from a Hawaiian volcano. "Early ships had mythological heads carved in the bow."

"There you go again. What is mythological?" said Palmieri."

Levi said, "From old times, you ignorant tar." He cleared his throat.

"We call 'em 'eyes of the ship' and some call 'em 'figureheads'. I am here to tell you every Chinese junk in Canton has big eyes on the bow. A Chinaman knows better'n you."

O'sullivan said, "Go to China."

"Them eyes know the way through a storm. Here is a story."

The men in the forecastle groaned aloud but listened anyway.

An old Captain was sailing the next day. He bought his wife two green emeralds, but she didn't like 'em. He was heartbroken and put them in the eyes of his figurehead. His wife changed her mind that night and unbeknownst to her husband, picked out the emeralds and planned a surprise on his return from the voyage.

But he never returned. His ship went down a typhoon because the figurehead was blind without her eyes. When the wife heard the news, she cried and cried and fell into a deep sleep. She was blind when she awoke. . . . and the two beautiful emeralds vanished forever.'

Several men said, "Ohhhhh damn. Where was this again?" They believed in every superstition and tall tale, even Pembroke's.

"Chips Alden was mad when *Zebra* shot out our figurehead's eyes. But not to worry 'cause he's carved new ones.

Our lady guides us again. Chips Alden is a real treasure."

All joined in, "Yeah, Alden."

Silva paced the deck after his week's confinement. "I can't forgive myself for cutting my friend Porter."

He climbed past the head at the bow and out to the end of the bowsprit to be alone with his thoughts. Watching the flow of the sea take him away from his home in Jamaica and looking at the figurehead underneath, he said, "She protects us on the way home to Jamaica."

On a double-take, the figurehead looked familiar,

—very familiar,

—very, very familiar.

Silva leaned lower to examine the details in the carved face and almost fell off the bowsprit in surprise. He reached down and felt the face under the new paint.

"Madre de Dios. (Mother of God), It's Juanita, my very own daughter." He rubbed the face all over until waves of indignation overwhelmed him. Cook Silva screamed as he dropped like a rock into the carpenter's shop.

"You filthy bastard. You're the tar who stole my Juanita's heart."

"What the hell are you talking about, you greasy ratbag," said Chips Alden thoroughly confused.

"You put stars in her eyes, a baby in her belly, and deserted like a gutless milksop. My Juanita leads *Agilis* with fins. You stole her legs."

He grabbed the nearest tool which happened to be a hammer. Chips Alden was dumbfounded and seized a defensive wrench.

Silva went after Alden. "You stole Juanita's face. Eres el bastardo que abandonó a mi hija sola. (You are the bastard who abandoned my daughter alone)."

He lunged at Alden who jumped back. "Just a damn a minute you greasy hugger-mugger. I carved her from memory and she's a mermaid—she has fins. Juanita is the only woman I've known, and I took three months to carve her perfect."

Silva growled at him.

Porter stuck his head down the hatch, "What is going on? Put those weapons down and use your fists. Silva, you just finished one term for cutting people. Don't do it again."

Alden said, "I was pressed onto a frigate and locked in irons. We left Kingston the next morning for the Falkland Islands. I fought Argentina, chased a slaver to Africa, and raised the Indian Ocean. I couldn't send a message."

Cook Silva lowered the hammer, "You speak straight? I lost friends to the British Navy, too."

He sighed. "My Juanita has a daughter, Maria, who is the light of my life in Jamaica.

Chips Alden's jaw dropped open, "I have a daughter? I'm a father? I've got to get to Jamaica. Is Maria all right?"

Silva continued, "Juanita pines for your presence and turns away all suitors. It's hard to raise Maria alone. You can be proud of them.

Alden said, "My figurehead, the family. So we're related. I'll be damned."

They hugged each other.

Babbitt pulled up the stick that measured the level of the bilge water, and called over to show Porter, "Sir, the level rises faster every day. It takes hours to pump it out and the men are almost ready to mutiny over the extra duty."

Porter said, "Has the crew inspected the hull for leaks?"

"Yes, but they could never find anything visible. The bilge fills with a mind of its own. I'm worried and gauge the depth several times a day."

Porter passed Babbitt's concern up the chain of command to Ferreri who passed it to MacIntyre. "Sir, the bilge is rising eighteen inches a day. We're pumping nine hours and are shorthanded for other duties. That enormous sail area is responsible."

MacIntyre considered this information without comment. "Carry on, Ferreri, but keep me up-to-date. We will make port in about two or three weeks."

Macintyre's comments rippled back down the chain of command to Babbitt who muttered to himself, I cannot find the damage, but this sail over-stresses my masts and the ship itself. I hear wood cracking all the time.

"Squawk! Rudy like a story!" Pembroke stretched his sore muscles and aching peg leg. "Not today, I'm tired."

Rudy squawked and screeched and flapped his wings. He wouldn't shut up, so Pembroke started a long story about the lurking shark. The men were too beat up to argue.

"A shark follows a ship of death. This is a gen-u-wine tale of the sea, and I was there at the center of things, you might say.

"There was this West African missionary, the Rev. Bryan Roe. His diary said,

> Two or three sharks, it may be, followed our vessel's wake, attracted, it would seem, by a sick man lying on board. The old, weather-beaten, quarter-Master, kind of like me, confidentially informed the clerical passenger (Mr. Roe) that he would soon have a burial job on hand.
>
> The quarter-Master was an authority on sharks. 'Them there sharks,' he explained, 'haves more sense in them than most Christchuns. They knows wot's wot, I can tell yer; doctors ain't in it with sharks. I've heard sharks larf when the doctor has told a sick man he was convalescent— larf, sir, outright, 'cos they knew what a blessed mistake he was making. They are following the scent of a man that's going to die, and they'll not leave us until such times be as they get him.'

Pembroke said, "A vicious hungry shark followed my ship same way. A mate was obeying the call of nature when he leaned too far and fell overboard. We hauled him into the dinghy licketly-split, but that gray brown shark considered hisself cheated and fastened those beady eyes on me. His big head rose over my oar and yanked me out. The bastard clamped them rows of teeth on my leg and twisted it right off."

A sailor said, "Oh my God."

O'sullivan asked, "Why didn't you swim away?"

"Well son, I was short a flipper and the shark had his two plus mine.

I was beating the water and goin' down. But I seen three gray dolphins racing toward me. They rammed that shark and he belched, but kept my leg. He flashed his white belly and swam away leaving a red trail of my blood behind.

But I'm still a kicking, can climb the rigging, play my fiddle, and I'll tell you a story now and then."

A couple of sailors snored as they leaned back on their ditty boxes.

One slept with his mouth open and somebody stuffed a belaying pin in it to wake him up.

Another said, "You told it different last time. A whale broke your boat you said."

"Don't matter. That shark ate my good luck tattoo of a rooster. I hope he choked on it. But them dolphins is good folks."

Ferreri gave Porter a lesson in Pacific ocean geography and history. "You see, Captain Cook explored the Pacific Ocean seventy-seven years ago. The mapmaker on board drew the Pacific rim and wrote Ring of Fire for the volcanoes around the coastlines."

Porter was always interested in history, even from Ferreri, and listened intently.

"They knew about earthquakes, but never imagined the bottom of the sea could move—but it could."

Porter said, "Really? I didn't know that."

Unseen underneath *Agilis*, a nine-mile rupture opened in the sea floor north of Moloka'i. The southern half sprang upward six feet in seven seconds. The mighty shock wave raced nine thousand feet to the surface and untold miles outward. *Agilis* had the misfortune to be directly over the rupture.

Porter was standing by Ferreri when the massive jolt that lasted eighty-five seconds stopped them dead in the water. He could hear Silva's cooking items cascade from the shelves in the galley and add their noise to the clang of wicked-sharp falling chisels that gouged the floor of the carpenter's shop.

The timbers of the skeleton groaned, and the rigging lines convulsed side to side almost jerking the masts down. The keel sounded like it was grinding over a reef of rocks, yet the closest rocks were two miles down.

Porter said, "What the hell? We jerked but I don't see any waves."

Porter surveyed the ocean surface but saw no material danger or the submerged rocks that he was so familiar with. To those below, it sounded like empty barrels rolling across the deck, while to Porter above it was thunder in the air. The vibration underfoot died away but the thunder to southwest faded to a low roar over the horizon.

Ferreri and Porter looked at each other, "That was an earthquake under the sea," Ferreri said, "Check for damage."

A panicked voice shouted from the hold, "Water everywhere. Our hull is breached where we hit Blossom Rock." A roar of water deafened the men.

Porter knew who was at the tiller when they collided with Blossom Rock in San Francisco—him. He dreaded to see the damage, but ordered, "Move that cargo and brace the leak. You're in charge, Mr. Alden. Our life depends on you."

Alden took over. "Need bracing material—push the timbers back and seal with oakum."

Unfortunately, the rupture was below the water line and hidden behind the stowed cargo that was beginning to float loose.

The crew could hear the water gushing but couldn't see from where.

Porter dropped into the hold to help shift barrels and boxes. "Move these crates." Several hands dove into the stacked cargo and opened a path to the breach.

Porter had seen a breach before and called up to Kawai, "Stanch the leak with a sail." To others, "Man the bilge pump."

Kawai grabbed a folded sail from the top of the pile and dove over the gunwale as smooth as the shark with Levi's leg. He reached out to stuff the canvas into the leak when the concussion from an aftershock stunned him.

The hands inside pounded wooden wedges into the breach but the water pressure blew them out again. One flying wedge broke a man's little finger but he kept fighting. They attempted to place shoring, but it blew out too. The amassed crew was simply not strong enough to staunch the incoming flood.

Porter cried, "We need stronger backup. Cover a board with material and hold forth over the hole. Brace a timber bulkhead against a hull member."

This was easier to say than to do because of the blasting water pressure.

"We're headed under if we can't stop that leak," said Porter.

The Master climbed to the gunwale wand was dismayed to see the folded canvas slip from Kawai's hands and sink. "Kawai! You all right?" He watched the in-rushing flow slam his limp torso against the fractured hull. Hands in the hold were relieved to see the gushing water stop, but knew the tattoo on the skin stretched outside the breach meant their mate was the stopper.

Koa cried, "Kawai! . . . Kawai!" and pounded his fist on the dripping planks.

Kawai regained consciousness and pushed away from the hull, letting the water pour in again. The men fighting the leak groaned, "Here she comes," and pushed more barriers against the water.

Their efforts were undone by a severe aftershock that shook the barriers loose and pushed Kawai back into the breach.

Kawai instinctively held his breath but there wasn't any air left to hold. In his mind, he entered a black tunnel with a white light at the end. Darkness closed in from all sides and he thought, No like, not ready, not die.

An involuntary reflex demanded, "breathe," and his chest filled with pure sea water. It was so easy . . . visions of his victory in the *Hawaiki Nui Va'a* canoe race came to mind as the weight of the water crushed against the hull.

"This is much big wave I ever see. I paddle but sun is dim . . . it rises . . . more dim. My family wave—I wave. My canoe. . .top. . .wave, . . .fast, fast. . .I paddle. . .slide down. My. . .family ride canoe, whale on canoe. . .hard paddle . . . . . . .with me . . . . . . .aloha. . . . . . a l   .   .   .   . oo . . . . .hhh . . . . .aaaa."

Kawai departed this world in peace. His tattooed body staunched the ruptured timbers and let his shipmates pound wedges that held from the inside. They braced a bulkhead behind the wedges, and finally took a breath of air while standing in water up to their waist.

Agilis was secure and all that remained was to pump out the bilge.

Kawai saved the *Agilis*—but at what cost?

The Kanakas in the hold were wise in the power of water and recognized what the tattoos pushing through the breach had meant. "That is Kawai."

All five Kanakas dove overboard to retrieve Kawai who was drifting down toward the depths. They fought off ravenous sharks and raised him above the surface to outstretched hands.

Porter laid Kawai face down over a barrel and rolled him back and forth. Water poured from his lungs, sputtered out in waves, dribbled out, and stopped but it was too late. Kawai was gone, they could tell. Each one looked down alone with his thoughts.

Porter stumbled to a far corner in despair, "What have I done?"

The Kanaka's began a low kanikau, or death chant, that recorded Kawai's family history he celebrated in his Mele. It had been composed by Kawai's family to preserve his lineage. This kanikau was impromptu and immediate.

> *Ua pau, ua hala lakou*
> *Koe no na hana no' eau*
> (Their days are over
> They have all departed
> Their artistic handiwork lives on.)

The shipboard complement of Kanaka's chanted the stories and accomplishments of Kawai's life with sobbing laments. Their tears flowed without shame.

The Hawaiian brothers held an ancient memorial through the night, but the crew only listened in silence.

Chapter 19—Funeral at Sea

Early the next morning, Porter prepared *Agilis* for Kawai's burial at sea, and to show respect. "Cockbill (place at a slant) the four-topgallant yards and the main-topgallant yards. Lower the ensign to half-mast. Cockup the other sails to the weather so that some catch wind and some fall back to stop us dead in the water. We will square them after dark."

To the sail maker, he said, "Chips Alden, if you would, wrap a length of chain around Kawai's middle and sew him in an old sail."

As was customary, Porter himself inserted the final stitch through Kawai's nose as assurance that he was really dead. "I am sorry, my friend. Hope you can't feel this."

He hung his head for a moment and turned to Alden, "How much weight did you use?"

"I made sure he sinks to the sea floor and evades the sharks. There aren't any cannonballs so I wrapped twenty feet of chain, which is all I can spare."

While the ship prepared for burial, the Kanakas drew Kawai's chest tattoo on his shroud with a piece of charcoal from the galley stove.

Porter murmured to Babbitt. "Death is always solemn, but at sea with Kawai it's especially hard. We pack a dozen good men together in a little brig. They live with each other's voices and presence, and one is taken away. They'll miss Kawai at every turn."

Respect is all we can offer but we offer it generously. The crew assembled amidships in silence.

Koa spoke to Porter with better English than the other Kanakas. "In our culture, we wear white to funerals. We celebrate a life, not grieve for their death. We carry ti leaf and put salt on our bodies to chase away evil spirits so nothing comes back from the gravesite."

Porter hung his head in private shame.

"We believe a dead person returns as a shark that is the family's 'aumakua, a guardian spirit. Nine of our gods are from sharks: Kamohoali'i, Kua, Kuhaimoana, Kawelomahamahai'a, Kane'apua, Kaholia-Kane, Ka'ahupahau, Keali'ikau o Ka'u and Kaehuikimano o Pu'uloa."

Ikaika and Makani hurled their mouths against the mainmast. They followed their ancient Hawaiian ritual to knock out teeth at the death of a revered one. The others watched in silence.

Koa murmured, "Many things are secret behind new ways. We do hula, talk our words, and more. We cannot draw on our jungle beauty to heal sadness in our hearts. No lei to float on water.

Porter whispered, "Not even a flower for Kawai."

Koa said, "I say poem of Hawaii. I no say God like Christian prayer. Our poem maybe not for you."

> *Ha'aheo e ka ua i nā pali*
> Proudly swept the rain by the cliffs
>
> *Ke nihi a'ela i ka nahele*
> As it glided through the trees

E hahai uhai ana paha i ka liko
Still following ever the bud

Pua 'āhihi lehua o uka
The 'āhihi lehua of the vale

Hui:
Chorus:

Aloha 'oe,
Farewell to thee,

Aloha 'oe
Farewell to thee

The crew bowed their heads. Master MacIntyre listened with reverence and motioned Ferreri to the cabin to leave the deck private.

The crew meditated on the uncertain nature of life at sea.

Powerful drone bass sounds joined a nasal screaming melody from the open door of the cabin. The sailors were dumb with wonder as an unknown man stepped forth holding an astonishing musical instrument. He wore a kilt woven of MacIntyre tartan. None on board had marched into battle following a band of bagpipes or seen a kilt.

MacIntyre, clad in magnificent Highland Regimental Piper attire, mounted the deck with his bagpipes singing to their lost comrade. He pushed Ferreri aside, who was trying to support his elbow, and stood proud.

Clifford Farris

Master MacIntyre marched to Kawai's shroud and paused in silence. The great voice of the bagpipes resumed with the ancient Scottish hymn, *Abide With Me*

Undisguised tears wetted more than one rough face as the bagpipes finished their mournful prayer.

Rudiger flew around the forecastle in terrified circles and Morgan Fore 'n Aft squeezed into the tiniest hole he could find. Two rats jumped into the sea.

Porter remembered the second verse from a recent hymn in Sunday school and offered it to Kawai as his tribute in a clear baritone voice that carried even to *Zebra*.

... nearer to Thee

Though like the wanderer, the sun gone down
Darkness be over me, my rest a stone
Yet in my dreams I'd be
Nearer my God to Thee.

Nearer, my God to thee
Nearer to Thee.

MacIntyre handed the bagpipes to Ferreri and cleared his throat.

"Men of the *Agilis*, 'Greater love hath no man than he lay down his life for his friends.' The prophet John wrote these words two thousand years ago and they are as true today as they were then.

Kawai was your friend and my friend, too. He was always happy and ever willing to do his duty. Kawai was the first to dive and save our ship, and to him we owe our eternal thanks."

Each hearer hung his head in quiet gratitude.

"The Bible records that the Lord was in the fisherman's boat when a great storm came upon them, and the fishermen feared they would drown. Jesus said to them, 'Have faith in me', and it is recorded that in faith they survived. We must have faith as well."

There were those among the crew who would remember this lesson and some who would not.

"No mariner has served without knowing any given day could be his last, and that there can be no marker where he lies at sea. That his ship might not see the sun rise tomorrow.

Porter nodded and thought, How true.

"You, his shipmates, are the family we all must share to survive another day. You served a voyage well, Kawai. May God rest your soul.

The Lord gave and the Lord hath taken away. Blessed be the name of the Lord. Amen."

He bowed his head.

The company saluted, each with his special gesture from a proper military snap to a two-fingered scout salute. Kawai got a good laugh from afar at the diverse but sincere gestures.

Porter placed his lucky gold doubloon into Kawai's shroud to pay for his section of the gold kit. "For you, my faithful companion."

Koa struggled to give a short poem in his best broken English, "I learn this from Alaska Inuit,"

> God grant that I may live to fish
> Until my dying day
> And when it comes to my last cast
> I then most humbly pray

When in the Lord's safe landing net
I'm peacefully asleep
That in his mercy I be judged
As big enough to keep

And yet there is only one great thing, The
only thing
To live to see the great day that dawns
And the light that fills the world.

Porter said, "Company . . . , off hats."

MacIntyre prayed, "Glory be to the Father, and to the Son, and to the Holy Ghost; As it was in the beginning, is now, and ever shall be, World without end. Amen."

All waited in reverent silence as Macintyre's bagpipes sang the ancient Scottish farewell, *Will Ye No Come Back Again?*

"We commit this body to the deep, looking for the resurrection of the body when the sea shall give up her dead and the life in the world to come, through our Lord Jesus Christ."

Before he could raise his arm to slip Kawai to his final resting place, a mighty hum of voices surrounded the ship from the sound of the waves,

"We welcome Kawai to our eternal home."

"I, the god of the waves, Kanaloa,"
"I, the ruler of the air, Lono,"
"I, the god of lightening and winds, Pele,"
"I, the greatest of all, Kane, who rules living creatures."

Piercing the white capped waves from far away, a pod of dolphins whistled at every leap, "Kawai, we are coming for you." Above the dolphins soared a magnificent white albatross with twelve-foot wings.

The albatross soared over Kawai and blended his spirit with infinity. They circled the masts and soared to the heavens.

The sailors murmured among them, "May yon albatross carry Kawai's soul forever."

MacIntyre nodded, and the dolphins stood on their tails to ease Kawai into the water as his shroud slid over the gunwale.

The dolphins escorted his earthly remains as deep as they could to ward off the sharks, and sent him to his final resting place on the ocean floor far, far below.

Porter sounded the bell eight slow peals to signify, "The End of the Watch."

Kawai's life was complete.

The crew returned to the forecastle where they chanted several low choruses. The officers gave them space for the rest of the day and an extra ration of grog that night.

Rudiger flew to his perch. "Squawk. Rudy sad. Rudy love Kawai."

Pembroke opened his shirt. "See this here tattoo-a dagger through a heart for my comrades asleep in the deep. There are many for the sea is harsh. I will add another when we get to port."

"Me too."

"Me too."

Porter stared at the empty ocean for a long time. "Fare thee well, my friend."

Chapter 20—Final Exit

Babbitt interrupted Porter's troubled thoughts and said, "Sun's down, time to right the ship." Porter looked in disbelief at the tone of disrespect, although he knew Babbitt was right.

Porter took charge and called the hands to the deck. "Brace the fore-topgallant yards and main-topgallant yards. Raise the ensign to full. Set the mainsails to the weather and square them up. Catch all the wind we can muster." He gazed into the lonesome sunset.

The ship's company left him alone in the hazy ebbing dusk. They missed Kawai too.

Porter retrieved the old cannon ball from his ditty box and limped on his painful leg to a hidden spot at the stern. He could see that strong hands steadied the tiller to keep *Agilis* straight and true. He thought back to his hands on that same tiller that had maneuvered his *Agilis* into the Blossom Rock.

Macintyre's admonition crashed through his mind like bolts of lightning. Line up on the navigation trees-the Colinas Palos Colorados. We're in your hands.

Porter's head sank to the gunwale,

You watched the *Zebra*, the Xenophonia, and missed the navigation trees. But you did not miss Blossom Rock, did you?

He reviled himself,

I sent my loyal friend down, and now he's gone. Kawai will never teach me to row—my fault, my guilt, my failure.

He cried bitterly at the accusations from the dark spirits and sank into an agonized despair.

You attacked the passenger; led your mates on a wild goose chase for your gold mine; abandoned Becky to the witch; and the luau. You fought Silva trying to save Master MacIntyre. Even Morgan Fore 'n Aft has abandoned you.

A final thought tyrannized him,

. . . why are you even here?

He stumbled on a length of chain forgotten in the walkway. It was three times as long as Alden had wrapped around Kawai and was a tripping hazard in the dark. Porter hoisted the heavy links around his waist and tied them with a strip from his shirt. He pushed the cannon ball down the front.

Richard Porter, mate, hung his head and whispered into the gray haze on the horizon, Will I see the dawn?

He looked at the ocean flowing by. Stars danced on the tips of the waves. The hypnotic surface was seductive and murmured, "Come to Neptune and no more pain." The warm gentle water caressed his spirit and said, "I am waiting for you."

Porter wanted a better look and approached the nearest shroud that supported the mainmast. He hoisted himself onto the gunwale by the lowest ratline. Fresh paint could not hide the gash from the grappling hook. "Babbitt won't like that," he whispered.

O' Sullivan's hook for his flogging was still in the mast.

I made a damn good cat o' nine tails if I do say so myself.

The stars danced on the waves thirteen beautiful feet below, so soft and oh so deep.

The next ratline was only a handhold higher. It was easy to pull up to the third. There in the wood of the mast was the impression of Kawai's war club when it slipped during the dance-off.

Ratline by hesitant ratline, he climbed to the bottom of the tops platform.

Morgan made those claw marks when he chased Rudy up the mast. He hated that bird.

Porter looked down to the deck.

I somersaulted on my ass behind the deckhouse. Should have stayed there.

The oily surface blended into sheets of undulations only sixty-three feet below-not far enough. Porter shifted his gashed unhealed leg up the futtock shrouds over the edge of the platform and stood erect.

The graffiti that he carved with Bjorn Amundson on their first climb was still there if a bit weathered.

He listened to the silvery bow wave, seventy-three feet down, as it waved goodbye to the figurehead. A wake of blue-green phosphorescence stretched far astern. He sensed voices in the void, "We are ready for you."

Above his head, the top crosstree was only thirty-five feet higher.

I'll soar like a bird from there, . . . or not?

He hoisted his aching, exhausted body higher ratline by ratline. His panting showed he hadn't climbed the rigging in a while and his strength was flagging. The crosstree stopped his rise with a knock on his head.

He looked up to the ensign swaying higher yet at one hundred and thirty-nine feet above the waves—a third more than the length of the *Agilis*. Richard Porter was rock bottom at the highest point of his world. His pride to sail was dead.

Porter stared at the beckoning sea a hundred and fifteen feet below, and prepared for the soothing, welcoming swells to end his pain with nature's magnificent relief.

"Now!"

He flexed his knees, tightened his abdomen, tensed his toes, took a deep breath—,

"Mr. Porter, is that you?" A voice from the dark froze him in mid-release.

He gulped and clamped the shroud line. An apparition appeared over the crosstree. "What are you doing up here, sir?"

"What . . . are you . . . doing?" Porter said in fractured confusion.

The apparition said, "I wish it was me, not him."

Porter became a second mate and said, "Don't talk that way. The brotherhood of the forecastle needs you, sailor. Rejoin them."

Porter talked to himself more than to the sailor.

Your comrades need you, Richard Jeremiah Porter, too. Those recruits are green and want for your leadership. MacIntyre is sick. Jettison those chains and get down where you belong.

Porter's words admonished them together, "Slay the past and live for the future to honor Kawai. Get back to duty and make him proud."

Porter faced the apparition directly with new confidence, "Promise me you'll remember: You're braver than you believe, and stronger than you think."

They awkwardly shook a piece of each other's shoulders. Thinning clouds revealed a brilliant planet Venus balanced on the tip of the crescent moon. The symbol of ancient Byzantium foretold youth and growth for them.

Porter raised his chin high and heaved the chains and cannonball far into the night.

"Let's go."

The two mariners climbed down hand over hand to the deck, where the watch said,

"That splash must have been a whale," said the watch when they thumped onto the deck.

Agilis lay dead in the water. She was upwind from *Zebra* who was also dead in the water. The canvas sheets hung flat. Men held up their hands to catch any breath of wind. The seamen unfurled top sails, sky sails, studding sails, main sails, royals, old sails, and new sails. They stacked barrels high on the deck. It would have helped but not a breath of air came their way. Both crews cheered when one lone gust moved the hulls a few feet and stopped.

The tars argued ways to sabotage the *Zebra* in revenge for the magnet on the binnacle.

"We'll pump the stinking bilge water into the ocean and drift it downwind to *Zebra*." said O'Sullivan.

"Too much work and too much ocean.

"How else?" Palmieri asked.

Pembroke cleared his throat.

"Oh my God, not another story," said an anonymous voice.

"You never know, maybe this one is good."

"No it aint."

Pembroke droned on because you couldn't shut him up. "Wonder why I crumble egg shells afore I throw them overboard?"

"I don't give a damn, old-timer."

Pembroke ignored the comments and said, "Inside an eggshell lives a little witch. She will capsize a ship in no wind. Sinbad the sailor told me."

"You're hanging the lantern, mate," called out a listener in the dark.

Pembroke dropped his voice.

> Sinbad's eyes watched tiny witches sink his fleet by sorcery with the loss of all hands. They was off Tortuga to the north of Jamaica in a dead calm like we gots now. Mark my words, and crunch up egg shells 'fore you toss them."

A sailor said, "I know something else. I wrote the name of a badass sailor on a rotten egg and smashed it on his ditty box. That forecastle stunk, but the thieving bastard stole the boat and we never laid eyes on him again.

Write '*Zebra*'' on a rotten egg and cast it to *Zebra*."

Rudy agreed "Squawk. Go away. Squawk"

Palmieri eyeballed the sailor with a tired look and said, "We don't have a rotten egg on the *Agilis*. We eat 'em 'fore they're out of the chicken."

"That's the way you feel, go to hell and see if I care. Sabotage *Zebra* your own damn way," said Pembroke.

Zebra had her problems caused by the inexperienced stevedores in Honolulu who stashed the cargo wrong. The bales and barrels slid heavily to port in the first squall. The *Zebra* listed so heavily she could not brace the sails properly and refused to follow her helm. She zigzagged through the water like a shark in a school of fish as the wind freshened.

Hornigold stomped the deck in a rage. "What the hell is wrong with the masts? Trim the stays right or I'll lock you in the brig, even if you are the bosun."

Though they were under full sail, the crew added new fixing points at the deck level, but could not repair the weak iron attachments on the masts.

When the mate reduced sail to lower the stress on the masts, Chernov screamed, "More sail not less."

"But sir, they can barely stand the canvas as it is," said the bosun.

Chernov said, "It's not my ship and we have to win. That damn *Agilis* is pulling ahead of us." The riggers had to zigzag eastward with a heavy list although the masts groaned and creaked.

The first mate brought up to Chernov the problem of the unproductive Chinese pirates, since they were his men. "They're demanding, filthy, and their food stinks to high heaven. Why do we carry them?"

Chernov said, "The Master approves of them, and I have my good reasons."

He followed Hornigold into the cabin and slammed the door.

Chapter 21—Rescue

The watch on *Agilis* said, "I swear I heard something happening over on *Zebra*.

Porter said, "There it is again—and look! They're tying a man to a broken spar and flogging him. He is screaming and his blood is all over."

The second mate heard the counting, " . . . eight, nine, ten . . . twenty-eight, twenty-nine, thirty. That will do for starters."

Porter repeated Hornigold's words that he heard across the water, "The devil take you to the deep blue sea, Jonah, and your worthless spar with you. I'm tired of fighting the two of you."

Agilis seamen watched in horror.

Babbitt said, "They can't do that, but they are. Three crewmen lashed the sailor to the broken spar and threw him overboard with a cheer."

Agilis watch said, "That's an execution, not a flogging, and they're holding their course.

Porter hollered, "Man overboard! Lower the boat and rescue that man. Reduce sail, brace those yardarms backward to stop our progress."

Several hands rowed to the bleeding sailor tied on the drifting spar. The injured man gave a low groan when the spar rolled him face down and his breath bubbled underwater. A rescuer turned the spar back up and several hands untied his ropes. O'Sullivan said, "Look at his back, man," when he saw the torn body covered with lacerations. He remembered his own flogging and said, "We're mates of the cat, we are."

The rescuers carried the unconscious fellow back to the *Agilis*. Cook Silva applied a sailor's remedy his skin. Porter and Silva draped the unconscious man's head face down over a barrel and rolled his body back and forth. Seawater poured from his lungs. Porter pounded the man's back to expel the water. He coughed violently, came to, took a halting breath, and coughed again.

Porter slapped his face, "Stay with us. You had a close call and we almost lost you."

The rescued sailor was tough and came around in good time. He coughed the remaining water from his lungs, and tried to explain, " . . . *cough* . . . I was a goner . . . *cough* . . . when I went over that gunwale. That salt water . . . *cough* . . . on my back gave me lightning and stars . . . *cough*. Maybe it heals a . . . *cough* . . . flogging but it's not fun."

He grasped the gunwale to take deep breaths. "Big thanks."

Porter said, "Welcome aboard. We live on this ocean together and watch out for our own."

Pembroke said, "Glad to meet you, mate," and shook his hand.

Porter led the rescued seaman to the cabin to show Ferreri and MacIntyre. "We have rescued a man overboard from the *Zebra*."

"Overboard from the *Zebra*, you say? Bring him in and let us look at him," said MacIntyre.

Porter and Ferreri supported each arm of the rescued man as they guided him to MacIntyre. The Master stared at him for several minutes while the man groaned and slumped over.

MacIntyre said, "Who are you?"

"I am Oscar Jones of the *Zebra*, or used to be." He coughed as he looked at Macintyre's feet and slumped again.

"Why were you in the water? Come, come, now, it cannot so bad as to lose your life." He wanted to be sure that the man had not abandoned the *Zebra* voluntarily.

Jones breathed heavily and straightened up as much as he could with his stiff painful back. "They'd doubled that yardarm over and over. Last time in China, they wouldn't pay what the repairman wanted and left it as it was.

Porter said, "Typical of that rat."

"I was unfurling the sail when the yardarm split completely and dragged me to the deck. I was all twisted in the lines. Chernov wrapped me to the splintered section so tight I couldn't breathe. They propped me against the mast and flogged me. I counted sixteen lashes before I passed out. They kept going."

Porter said, "That's right. We could hear it from here."

"When I woke up, Chernov yelled I was an unlucky Jonah son of a bitch and jettisoned me and the spar overboard. Them superstitious swabbies cheered when I hit the water.

Amundson said, "Damn his hide. I'd abandon him, I would like I did."

"I knew I was gone when I sank below the salt water and couldn't move. That iron yoke on the spar turned me face down."

Porter said, " 'twas a good thing our watch saw you. We barely got you out."

Jones said between coughs, "I . . . will join . . . cough . . . your crew and . . . cough, cough, . . . and ask no pay. I am not Jonah . . . cough . . . , I am good luck."

MacIntyre said, "Have Cook Silva patch his back. We need an extra hand on our bilge pump," He was secretly relieved to have another sailor aboard, especially one willing to work for free.

The Master intended to pay Jones a fair share if he proved a competent hand.

"Welcome to the *Agilis*."

Porter said, "Glad to have you in our crew, Mr. Jones."

A relieved Oscar Jones emerged from the cabin into the sun and began to dry off his shredded pants. He didn't have a shirt or shoes, but wore a crisscross of angry red welts on his back.

Jones' despair as he leaned against the gunwale moved Chips Alden deeply. "This boy has nothing and no broken box to store it in."

Chips Alden pulled several boards from storage, sawed those, cut dovetail joints, and glued them into a ditty box complete with hinges and a lock.

"Here is a box for the clothes that you'll make from this old sails," Alden said when he handed the box and used canvas to Jones.

Porter made a short introduction to the occupants of the forecastle.

"Levi Pembroke over there is Broken Pen. We'll call Oscar Jones here Broken Spar. Welcome on board, Mr. Spar."

Jones was overwhelmed. "I'm grateful but my money is on the *Zebra*, not that I'll ever see it."

"Give it no mind, this is yours," said Chips Alden. "A dolphin protects your spar," and he quickly cut a dolphin bearing the broken spar to safety into the lid.

Jones shook Alden's hand. "Much obliged, I am."

The crew cheered to have an extra hand, and looked forward to a new set of sea stories.

Dirk Hornigold and Gurii Chernov gathered the *Zebra's* strike team on deck. The Russian's long coat was impractical for close hand-to-hand fighting and he had exchanged it for a shirt to allow access to the knife in his belt. His dark eyes atop his bushy black beard made a frightening appearance.

Hornigold laid out their plan. "We attack the jury-rigged *Agilis* tonight. The zodiac light from the stars is enough to see by. Your goal is that silver fork—get it. It's in MacIntyre's cabin somewhere."

Shifting to Chinese, he looked at the Asian members of the boarding force. "Do you know what a fork looks like? I know you use chopsticks, but a fork looks like this." He drew a picture of a fork on the deck and added the crest on the handle.

"Control the deck and get that fork. Grab some hard tack from the hold if you can."

The crew was unhappy with the planned attack. They wanted food instead of a fork and grumbled under their breath.

I got nothing against those mates.

I won't take this anymore.

The muttering was low but the first mate picked up enough to realize it could become a full-fledged mutiny. He knew the men were dispirited, and ii was a dangerous situation.

Hornigold continued, "When the moon sets, douse your lanterns, cover anything shiny, and unfurl the black topsails, but not the skull and crossbones. This is a surprise attack."

We're only off this stinking tub to attack another vessel?

They're just like us.

"Take out the helmsman first. Pull our gunwales together with grappling hooks and rush their deck. Watch for that big bastard second mate. He's smart and tough. Take him out permanently."

We should take you out.

Shut your mouth. He'll hear you.

"Batten down the hatch over the forecastle to lock in the crew. Every man for himself. Ten pieces of eight to the man bringing me that silver fork."

The crew waited in the forecastle for night to come. They started a game of Ship Captain and Crew.

"Top two winners take down that big arse hole," said Chernov.

They gambled for an hour.. Chernov was adroit at cheating and got himself declared the first winner.

Ship Captain and Crew continued to the middle of the night. The second winner was a wizened little pirate from southern China.

"Hey there, little shrimp. I've seen bigger leeches on the ass of a whale. What good are you?" said Chernov.

The Chinese man stood up and quietly said, "I fight big man, little man, all you man."

Chernov stood up, "Show me."

The chinaman was a good head and a half shorter and not muscular. The tars cleared space for a fight ring in the center of the forecastle.

In a blazing instant, the oriental took the Russian down with a lightning floor sweep of his foot. He followed up with a jump onto his chest and his hand across the throat. "You dead if hand is knife." Chernov felt a shooting pain in his twisted hip.

That chinaman, like many warriors, honed his fighting skills at the ancient Shaolin Temple in central China where he was a master instructor. His certificate of achievement would later be called ninth degree black belt. The crew backed away in awe and resumed their game.

The two winners schemed to get the fork and the food, although in the reverse order. Others plotted to take down Porter and capture the *Agilis*.

The first mate stuck his head down the hatch. "Quiet. Time for action."

All was quiet aboard the *Agilis*. Three peals on the bell marked the midnight to four watch in the dark of the night. Light came from the binnacle to show the helmsman his tiller from the faint shine of the stars, but the moon was dark.

By contrast, the *Zebra* buzzed with silent activity. Chernov whispered, "Quiet!"

Her crew extinguished every light, covered every shiny surface above and below decks, and wrapped loose items to prevent rattles. All was silent anticipation.

With the helm hard alee and three small black sails carefully trimmed, the black *Zebra* stalked the *Agilis*.

Chernov pointed to the long boat and three crewmen lowered it into the water. Loaded with three attackers, the boat slipped through the starlit water under the stern of the *Agilis*. One sailor leaped at the stern, missed, and fell into the ocean. He splashed violently but did not cry out.

The other two leaped onto the *Agilis*. One slapped his arm around the mouth of the helmsman peering over the gunwale, and the other pinned his arms. The first grabbed a loose belaying pin and rapped the helmsman's head. He crumpled unconscious.

The silent hulk of *Zebra* loomed closer and closer, but the watch was unobservant until *Zebra* collided with unguided *Agilis*.

A scream shattered the night as the closing hulls crushed the man in the water to bloody shark bait.

Zebra's crew threw their five grappling hooks over *Agilis'* gunwales and pulled the brigs together. Faint starlight silhouetted vague forms running on both decks. Friends and foes looked alike except for Porter's distinctive baritone voice. "We're under attack. All hands on deck

A big and a small attacker leaped to *Agilis*. Chernov, the towering volcano, concealed his face behind a black mustache inside a black beard. The little chinaman brought his martial arts fighting skills from a lifetime at the Shaolin temple.

They charged at Porter using his voice as a beacon. Chernov distracted Porter with the glint of a knife and gave an opening for the Chinese fighter to execute a perfect floor sweep with his foot and trip Porter backward. It had worked when they kidnapped Porter and it surprised him again in the dark.

But Porter was ready this time and cocked both legs on the way down. He hit hard on his back but was ready for action. One leg slammed into Chernov's balls, neutralizing him. His knife slid across the deck and out a scupper hole. The mate's other leg flipped a second knife out of the hand of the little attacker. That knife bounced off the foremast and Babbitt grabbed it in the reflected starlight.

Richard's clenched fist erupted from the deck to smash the jaw of the little attacker. He fell unconscious alongside the Russian who was groaning in agony.

Porter shouted again, "All hands on deck. We're under attack."

More crew from *Zebra* poured onto *Agilis*. One headed to batten down the hatch over the forecastle, but Pembroke was alert and blocked it open with his peg leg. The crew swarmed out of the forecastle like a cloud of angry hornets, each with his knife drawn.

From the corner of his eye, Porter spied an attacker headed to the cabin. He yelled at Ferreri, "MacIntyre." The first mate chased the attacker into the cabin where he ran to a sleepy MacIntyre. "I want the silver fork now."

Ferreri flattened the attacker from behind and threw him up the short ladder into the chaos on deck. He was right behind him.

More attackers flooded over, some with knives and all with fists. One attacker recognized Oscar Jones. "Damn my eyes if it ain't the Jonah. We got rid of you once and I'll finish the job now." He charged Jones and they wrestled over and over. Pembroke swung at Jones' ex-shipmate with a belaying pin in the midst of a flop, but he connected the shoulder of Jones.

His second swing was more careful to knock the attacker unconscious with a good one on his head. He rolled flat on the deck as Jones jumped up. "Thanks Mate . . . I think . . . ," rubbed his shoulder, and rejoined the fray.

Koa emerged from the galley to face an attacker who sliced his forearm. Koa stabbed a big butcher knife through the nearby foot and pinned the pirate to the deck. The attacker plunged his knife into Koa's arm, but Koa extracted the knife and pinned the other foot. Koa joined another fight.

O'Sullivan confronted the *Zebra* and said, "We're under attack".

"No kidding," said a disconnected voice.

Ferreri showed off his boxing fists to an attacker, but the opponent surprised him with a push and knocked him backward, collapsing the chicken coop. Alden had designed it to hold chickens, not fighters.

"Weak, weak . . . .rwack . . . ," terrified chickens ran in all directions. A hen flew into the face of Ferreri's attacker blinding him. Ferreri grabbed the pirate's shoulders and twisted him into the capstan where he crumpled into a motionless heap.

Dangerous knife skirmishes broke out over the deck area. Weapons flashed and blood flowed from attackers and defenders alike. Knives slipped from bloodied hands, broke, or soared overboard. The brawlers wrestled on the treacherous decks as amateurs.

The Kanakas wrestled as genuine athletes, with skills practiced since infancy. Porter was stronger with more skills and exchanged fisticuffs with the renegades as they stepped up.

The chaos degenerated into a messy stalemate.

Bam! MacIntyre emerged from his cabin with a pistol in each hand. He fired a second shot into the air, just missing Rudiger.

"Stop! We have you surrounded. Give up or we take down every last man jack." He held up a lantern. The fighters looked at him in stunned silence. This was getting serious.

Chernov climbed on the deckhouse and bellowed, "All hands to the *Zebra*. We're done here."

Hornigold screamed in frustration over the combined gunwales, "You have one of my men. I want him back."

MacIntyre and the mates shouted in unison, "Jones is our man now."

It was obvious to Hornigold that his surprise attack had failed. He stomped into his cabin and locked the door. He completed the night with a glass of scotch whiskey.

Porter could see the carnage by the light of the rising moon. "What a mess. Blood from our sailors, blood from theirs, feathers, and chicken shit all over."

He motioned to the few attackers still standing, "Over there and drag those unconscious louts with you." To his *Agilis* crew he said, "Guard these bastards and if they look sideways have at 'em. Throw water on Babbitt to bring him around and don't forget our helmsman. We need all hands."

Porter faced the attackers and said, "What the hell are you renegades up to? Talk to me."

The first mate from *Zebra* coughed, hung his head, and spoke quietly. "We're not renegades, sir, but desperate. Hornigold sold our rations on the black market. We're out of biscuit what with feeding those worthless Chinese pirates." He turned to one of the Asian attackers, "I mean you. No work, just eat."

The man did not understand English and squatted with a stoic face.

"The men are about to mutiny. We sent a hand down for supplies but the poison banana gas knocked him out. His rescuer too. We tied a rope on a third to pull out the first two. Can't reach our rotten food. None left anyway."

Porter looked at Ferreri and Babbitt, "Bananas are like Pembroke said. What da ya know."

The *Zebra* mate said, "We ask you, as an honorable man, to give us something. Old and moldy, we'll take it. We'll make no trouble."

The members of *Agilis* conferred around MacIntyre's table. Speaking for MacIntyre, Porter said, "As you know, *Zebra* pirates have requested food. They claim short rations since Sitka."

MacIntyre said, "They are weak from hunger and we overcame them easily."

Porter said, "It wasn't that easy, but we did prevail."

MacIntyre said, "Compassion urges assistance, but common sense insists we send this mutinous bunch back. What say you?"

Ferreri pounded the table and shouted "Not a crumb. We manage our stores and they can manage theirs."

Steward Jackson said, "Absolutely correct. Not a crumb."

Babbitt pointed out, "We ride the deep as brothers and support each other in distress."

A huge argument raged around the cabin.

Silva always fed a hungry man, and Chips Alden was neutral.

Porter surveyed the table. "Here is where we stand. Three no's and two yea's. I can vote yea and give this to Master MacIntyre or vote no and end it."

He paused to let his comments sink in. "Are these bad men or seamen merely serving under a bad master?" He paced the cabin. "Will we sail as companions in the future? Would they help us? Some might."

Babbitt and Alden nodded in agreement.

"I say we offer help. We have barrels of hardtack and salt pork already opened. I recommend we cast those and these men off together. Losing the weight might speed our return a tiny bit and perhaps help them make it.

The Jackson and Ferreri looked skeptical.

"The *Zebra* is in a bad way. Her cargo has shifted, her trim is poor, and the men cannot enter the hold to secure the cargo or eat."

Babbitt said, "It is obvious just looking at the *Zebra* that this is true."

Porter said, "The bad banana gas will go in a week and they'll regain control, although they can't repair their damaged masts at sea."

After more discussion, pro and con, the men at the table recommended to release the partly used provisions.

Porter said, "You are honorable mariners. I agree with this course of action."

The subdued tars from the *Zebra* watched *Agilis* crew lift two barrels by the light of the moon. They rolled them over the bloody gunwales to drop onto their deck and jumped after. It took only a moment to loosen the grappling hooks and let the two vessels drift apart.

Sometime later, after the *Zebra* was reorganized, the wounds treated, and the barrels stowed, Hornigold unlocked his cabin door and emerged to yell, "To your stations, you lazy bastards. We're behind."

MacIntyre, much improved, called the mates to his cabin. "We are approaching the channel of the Golden Gate. Would that we were farther ahead of the *Zebra*, but never mind, we are in a good position to make port. I want no mistakes."

The mates nodded.

"Splendid. I want you, Ferreri, on deck because of the condition of our rigging and missing spars. Mount the maximum canvas that we can carry. The crew will perform magnificently, I have no doubt."

Turning to Porter, "I want you to manage the helm. You know well the location of Blossom Rock. Seize the first open space as close to the wharf as you can find. We might be victorious over the *Zebra* yet."

Ferreri called out, "All hands on deck".

Porter cried out on entering the San Francisco Bay, "Fort Point Rock to starboard. I can see the ruined timbers of Stag Hound on the shoals."

Porter spotted a lookout high on Fort Point Rock scanning the horizon with his telescope. Even from afar, Porter saw the lookout was stiff from his long vigil and acted bored. A little boy played at his feet.

Porter's sharp eyes saw the lookout turn with attention when the ships changed from gray spots in the haze to the high tips of sails. As their twin hulls raced past the rock, he could see from the lookout jumping up and down that they were recognized.

By now, *Agilis* was right under the lookout, and close enough that Porter could hear the call, "They're back! Tell Leavenworth." The little boy ran off on his speedy young legs to spread the news.

Porter looked over both vessels to see which one was more decrepit. The *Zebra* listed to port and zigzagged through the water. *Agilis* had missing spars that left huge gaps in the rigging like missing teeth. The racers were neck in neck and carrying more canvas than Porter thought possible in their unseaworthy conditions.

Agilis tracked poorly due to her unbalanced rigging, but she moved eagerly through the waves.

Thaddeus Leavenworth on hearing the news, sent his runner to Lieutenant Sherman, who dispatched his gunners to the cannons emplaced above the town—facing out toward the clear blue water.

The gunners fired their artillery as the vessels passed the Golden Gate and rounded North Point in a dead heat. Three powerful explosions, all blanks, rocked the town.

The booms provided the signal to start a grand celebration, not that any was needed. The gunsmith closed his shop, the blacksmith dropped his hammer, the baker left sourdough bread rising, and the bars disgorged their patrons into the streets.

A barker ran up and down Clay street crying through a megaphone, "They're back! Come one, come all."

Leavenworth, with another megaphone displaying the logo *Thaddeus for Mayor,* hastened to the wharf to greet the arriving vessels.

He renewed the circle on the wharf and addressed the crowd. "As you remember, my good friends, there is a wager between these two vessels. They bring new supplies of foodstuffs to our fair city, and we are the winners in any case."

The crowd cheered lustily for the excitement of the gamble and their bellies anticipated fresh provisions.

"The first Master to place his silver in this circle shall be the winner of the twenty-five-thousand-dollar prize." He held up a spoon from the Niantic Hotel dining room, "This is the crest that we are looking for."

The crowd grew with all eyes facing the bay. They watched the beautiful clippers approaching the wharf at full speed—or as full as they could manage.

They saw *Zebra* shudder and list even more.

Somebody observed, "I do believe she has found Blossom Rock. We really must replace those marker buoys. Maybe some miners with their explosives can blast that rock to smithereens, if they will leave their gold insanity long enough."

"Here they come!"

In spite of *Zebra's* list, Hornigold threw caution to the overhead winds in his frantic haste to enter the harbor. Like Porter on the outgoing passage, the helmsman diverted his attention to the *Agilis*.

The *Zebra* bashed hard into the jagged tops of Blossom Rock. Chernov checked down the mid-hatchway and glimpsed a bundle of rotten bananas floating across the floor in a gush of water. "The *Zebra* collided with a submerged rock. She is foundering," he yelled.

The *Zebra* was overloaded with cargo and her draft was deeper than *Agilis* had been when Porter found the same rock. The *Zebra* hit hard and the damage was severe.

Hornigold heard the water pouring in but said, "It'll make it to the wharf. Repair it later."

Hornigold grabbed a belaying pin and beat the helmsman about his shoulders and back. The helmsman kept his hands on the wheel out of a sense of duty, only letting go when he fell unconscious.

"Get over here," Hornigold said to another crew member. "And pay attention," He kicked the unconscious fellow to the gunwale and stomped to the bow.

The *Zebra* jockeyed with *Agilis* for any opening at the Clay Street wharf to drop anchor.

Chapter 22—Race to the Circle

The crowd swelled around Leavenworth standing on the wharf and included bystanders, spectators, drinkers or drunkards, and a flock of soiled doves. The Irish bookie hustled out a small table where gamblers mobbed him waving money to bet on the winner. One of the doves said, "I know Hornigold. He's a gombeen who would peel an orange in his pocket to not have to share it."

The massive gathering roared a mighty cheer for one or the other ships, or simply for the exuberance of their arrival. No one noticed roaming Chinese pickpockets who enriched themselves from time to time. One slipped a gold pocket watch from the distracted Irishman who was too busy grubbing money to notice.

The vessels rounded North Point and streamed toward the wharf. The froth thrown up by the bow waves looked like two hungry sharks chasing a harbor seal to the finish line. The Irishman said, "Place your bets, my friends. There is time until we have a winner. Step right up."

Several men from the street and two ladies of the night made sizable last-minute bets. The doves based their bets on clients they knew from one ship or on rumors from the other. As the ladies moved to better vantage points, certain of the men discreetly tipped their hats.

The happy harlots of both the female and male persuasion swung their arms madly to the approaching ships. One hollered to a rigger overhead, "Are you as good on the water as you are in bed? Show me your stuff."

Leavenworth whipped up excitement among the crowd using his best campaign voice through his megaphone, "Hasten to anchor my mates. May the best man win, or a good man win. Faster, faster. Who will it be?"

The two magnificent vessels wobbled full speed toward the spectators.

An old sea captain warned, "Mind, you do not stand in front of these vessels. I doubt they can stop in time."

The furious displays of marine skills captured the attention of land-based experts. They stood solidly on shore watching the rival brigs arrive to their left and right. Capricious winds forced the riggers to make constant adjustments to the sails to maintain control.

It was difficult to navigate the harbor under the best of times and this was among the worst of times. Blue profanity drove everything and caution was missing. The vessels aimed for the same empty slot some distance from Clay Street.

The wharf itself was on the verge of collapse from the weight of the excited spectators and Leavenworth ran to the edge, "Some of you get off. The landing is not strong enough to support so much agitated weight." Several spectators moved back to the shore.

Both Masters crunched their ships aground in the first open spots they could see. The *Zebra* scraped bottom farther out because she was sinking. The two crews swarmed overboard in the dinghies to secure the beach.

Agilis and the *Zebra* dropped their boats with their masters in the bows and sprint rowed to shore. Hornigold held his silver knife and MacIntyre his fork.

"Faster, you lubber, faster".

"Is that all you've got?"

"You're going to the brig."

"Ten lashes."

The boats grated on the beach next to each other, but two full blocks away from the winner's circle on the Clay Street wharf. The Masters bounded from their boats into a massive wall of swinging fists wielded by crewmen from the *Zebra* and *Agilis*.

Spectators circled the combat zone and cheered—this was the best action they had seen in a long time.

The melee surged back and forth. *Agilis* contingent prevailed. Now the *Zebra*. Friend to foe, friend to friend, foe to foe. Who could tell? A kick here, sand in the face there.

This fight was on solid land at last for the *Zebra* crew, even though they couldn't walk very well. The fisticuffs were more vicious than usual because the fighters were sober and could feel the blows.

Like a gladiatorial combat in the Roman Coliseum, the Kanakas brought their fearsome weapons to the fight. Kalani destroyed an opponent with a shark-toothed club. Ikaika tripped a sailor's legs with a pikoi, a long cord with a weight in the end. Makani moved in with a stone mace. Spectators cheered each bloodcurdling face off from a safe distance out of range of the splattered blood.

The Masters charged each other. These two men of the sea had never backed down from anything and would not start now.

MacIntyre made a feint with his fork toward Hornigold. Hornigold responded with a lunge. Rings of husky young sailors defended their masters, who howled at one another.

"You attacked my ship."

"You stole my man."

The *Zebra* master handed his silver knife to Chernov and pointed to the wharf. The Russian took off.

MacIntyre was unsteady on his feet and could not run either. He handed his silver fork to Porter saying, "The circle." Porter raced toward the wharf after the big Russian on the same path with the opposing piece of silver glinting in his hand.

Porter attacked him from behind and Chernov went down.

Porter confirmed that a fork is a poor offensive weapon.

Chernov was a trained saber fighter in Moscow but was now stiff. He yelled, "Fore!" and slashed at the fork. The knife was dull and didn't break Porter's skin.

They engaged in a sorry pantomime of a sword fight would have cracked up the Three Musketeers. The cutlery inflicted no wounds but suffered great nicks and gashes. The engraved crests didn't fight well.

The Russian feinted and knocked Porter to the ground. Porter leaped up with a roundhouse punch by his loose arm.

Both fighters wanted for current sword fighting experience. The Russian seized an opening and sped toward Leavenworth standing tall on the wharf. Porter ducked around a pair of fighters and dashed after him.

They aimed at the sound of the megaphone where Leavenworth acted like the mayor he wanted to be, "Hurry, my mates." The crowd cheered to make noise and a group of gamblers converged on the Irish huckster.

The runners stumbled through the sand. Who was leading? It could have been either, or both, or neither.

With a fatalistic roar, Porter lunged at the Russian. The gigantic man toppled face down onto a rock crab that bit him through his beard. Richard flipped the silver knife out of his distracted hand and it sailed into the water.

Porter jumped onto the wharf and dramatically centered his poor battered fork in the white circle. He raised his arms overhead and said with a flourish, "*Agilis* is here. Three cheers for *Agilis*.

Hip hip—Hooray.

Hip hip—Hooray.

Hip hip—Hooray."

A regiment of rifles and amateur assorted pistols blasted into the air. The cloud of smoke blinded the spectators and hid where those bullets came down. Three of them just missed the new windows in the saloon by the gun shop, but the proprietor didn't care.

The warring crews stopped their mayhem at the sound of the pistols and stumbled through the cloud of gun smoke.

"It don't matter who won." said one of the *Zebra's* combatants. "We're on solid ground—no more growling stomachs at sea." He jumped up and down on the shore. "I feel the dirt at last."

Steward Jackson said, "It is a good thing the fight is over because those Hawaiians were making mincemeat of the *Zebra* crew with their melee weapons and their ancient martial art of Lua.

A hand shouted, "To the Blue Crane Bar, mates," which was approved unanimously. Both crews merged onto a happy mob, at least temporarily.

313

Bloody footprints marked the way to the *Blue Crane Bar*.

Some made it but many were waylaid by a familiar voice that called out, "Gold! my friends. Gold in the hills, rivers too." The barker called the crowd to his table without missing a breath. "Line up 'cause I can't handle all of you at once. Your bets are covered."

In the same pitch he said, "I have a limited number of gold kits for those who desire to be rich and not waste their filthy money."

The rest is history.

The crew of the *Zebra* never looked back and never sailed on her again. The *Zebra* sank in place next to the burned-out hulk of the *Xenophonia*, and was never recovered. Landfill soon covered both derelicts to accommodate the growing town of San Francisco.

Dirk Hornigold joined a group of broken-down sea captains who spent every day rehashing lies from their hazy memories of life at sea. He never received another commission.

Babbitt and Morgan Fore 'n Aft, purring with his tail high, walked a little apart from Cook Silva and Chips Alden into the golden sunset on their way to the *Niantic Hotel.*

"Father-in-Law".

"Grandpa."

Richard Porter strutted up Clay Street with his shiny pistol handing high on his hip. His shining eyes checked out every passerby, especially the rare females.

He glanced at a well-dressed man on the porch of the hotel with his chair rocked back against the wall. The man blew a fat cloud of cigar smoke in Richard's face as he walked by and Richard stopped with surprise. "What's that all about?"

The well-dressed man held out his hand with a grin, "Ahoy mate, you look mighty fine today."

"Bjorn Amundson, you old son of a gun. How the hell are you?"

They shook hands and Porter sat down.

"I want to thank you for the gold kit. I fought that claim for weeks but then worked my way upstream. I hit a good outcrop that a grizzly bear claimed was hers."

"I didn't see any grizzlies."

"They come out in the fall. She ate a chunk of my ass and tried for the rest of me."

Bjorn pulled up his shirt and showed off his chest scars that looked like Indian hieroglyphics. He turned around and displayed the hole in his behind. "That beast was eat'n on me when an old prospector stumbled into camp with shotgun. He got the bear before the bear got him."

"Glad you made it, old friend."

"That prospector was lonesome for human company but, damn, he smelled like a stranger to water."

"Ain't that the truth. I've smelled them in town."

"We jawed a while and he says, 'Lookin' for gold are ya?' and I said, 'Reckon so.' We filed a claim on his mother lode outcrop."

"That became the New Viking Gold Mine you've maybe heard about. That prospector gets free tobacco, liquor, and food for life."

"Congratulations. I always knew you had it in you."

"Two men work for me. It's more fun to be the boss than the worker."

Richard said, "Depends. Sometimes it is and sometimes it isn't."

"Hey, I hear you won the race. Let's be partners. We both want a farm and General Vallejo has some land up by Boyes Springs."

Richard said, "Let's share a bottle. I'll buy."

The most remarkable feature in Bjorn's room was the bear rug. It contained a head with teeth showing a gap and a little black tail on the other end. All four legs ended in five formidable claws. Bjorn beamed, "Pretty big, isn't she? I walk on her every day to show who's boss."

They sat back in big comfortable chairs with fragrant cigars and stared at the chandelier.

Richard mulled the idea over, 'We were a team until I shot holes in the mining pan. Fixed those?"

"That blacksmith patched them good as new."

"You've hired workers?"

"Me and the twins from Kentucky run the mine. What about my proposal?"

Richard spoke deliberately, "Governor Figueroa made a land grant to Mariano Vallejo back in 1833. You say Señor Vallejo wants to sell a vineyard? Can we see it?"

"I'm ready. By the way, remember that woman on *Agilis*?"

"The one we dropped off at the City Hotel? Beautiful?"

"Señor Vallejo is her uncle. Her name is Maria Juana Castañeda Rojas. She gave me a note with her name when Otis jettisoned her. We're kind of matched up, you might say."

"You old sea dog. I'd like to see her again. Let's go to Boyes Springs."

After an uneventful trip, Richard dismounted outside the house of the Pomo Indian family who adopted him. Two small children ran out with a shout, "Richard is here! Richard! We see you again."

The Papa and Mama approached with a youth Richard had never seen and hugged him. The little boy said, "Peter is here, my brother." The family introduced Peter. Over a delicious Pomo dinner, Richard told them of their desire to buy land.

Through the son as interpreter, Papa passed on good information. "I am overseer on the Rancho Petaluma. I know a vineyard that makes good wine and I think Señor Vallejo wants to sell this land. You can see him, he is in town for a few days."

Richard spoke to General Vallejo as Maria sat next to Bjorn. "Esteemed Sir, it is a great honor to meet you and your niece again. We would like to explore the purchase of a vineyard from your land grant. What would be your pleasure?"

After a lengthy negotiation, the parties agreed on the parcel of land. They determined a fair price and agreed to finish the transaction in the near future.

Richard and Bjorn ended the day with thanks to the Pomo family, and returned to San Francisco in soaring spirits.

The dining room of the *Niantic Hotel* was softly lit. The elegant tables gleamed and the polished silverware was carefully positioned on soft white napkins. A harpist played relaxing dinner music in a corner.

MacIntyre and Leavenworth sat on opposite sides of the table from Hornigold and Sherman. Porter and Chernov occupied straight chairs behind their respective masters. They hated each other even worse now and personally as well.

Leavenworth made a short announcement. "Gentlemen, it's good to see you again. Sadly, I fear Julian Skinner has mysteriously gone missing without a trace since our last dinner."

Fewer sea stories flowed through the swirling clouds of Cuban cigar smoke this time, although the wine and brandy were still excellent.

Alex MacIntyre started, "May I congratulate the Master Of the *Zebra*, Dirk Hornigold. He ran a hard-fought race and the outcome was doubtful until the end."

Hornigold was silent but thought to himself, Doubtful is not the right word. You stole one of my sailors, locked my wind, and foisted barrels of rotten food on my crew.

MacIntyre continued, "I daresay *Agilis* encountered certain difficulties of her own. I'm proud of my officers and credit my crew." He puffed a big smoke circle toward the ceiling and leaned back in his chair with his fingers in a small tent on the table.

Hornigold grunted, "Harrumph. I admire your confidence in your vessel, MacIntyre. *Agilis* is a good vessel, but the *Zebra* is better. We suffered unforeseen difficulties beyond our control.

Nonetheless, under the rules laid down, I must concede that *Agilis* won this modest contest."

Leavenworth looked around the table. "According to the terms of our wager, the first Master to return his silver cutlery to the wharf is deemed the winner, and that was *Agilis*. Gentlemen, our table setting is back and complete."

Two pieces, a knife and a fork, showed deep gouges and scrapes and looked out of place.

MacIntyre will accompany me to the Bank of San Francisco to receive a credit for twenty-five thousand dollars. Congratulations to Master Alex MacIntyre of *Agilis*. The party clapped with degrees of enthusiasm that ranged from great to none.

The Masters glared at each other over the remains of the gourmet dinner. Hornigold mumbled to himself,

You haven't seen the last of me.

He was a compulsive gambler who hated to lose and doubled down on the wager. He stood and said, "I hereby propose a more significant contest. After the *Zebra* is repaired, we shall race to China and settle this contest once and for all."

Lieutenant Sherman responded, "With the successful return of your ships, the Army is well supplied for the foreseeable future. We are not in a position to place another wager. We are certainly prepared, however, to purchase foodstuffs from the islands.

Leavenworth said, "I am engaged in a campaign for mayor of San Francisco at the moment and am not available. Such a contest could be of interest in the future."

Hornigold looked around and said, "I see. If you will excuse me, gentlemen, I have business elsewhere." He motioned to Gurii Chernov and they left through the kitchen to join his group of broken-down cronies at the City Hotel.

MacIntyre signaled to the best waiter in San Francisco and the best shot if need be with his brandy snifter,

"A round of your oldest brandy and your finest Havana cigars to the three best mariners on the sea."

The best waiter in San Francisco and the best shot if need be invited the *Agilis* mariners to relax after supper in the smoking salon of the City Hotel.

MacIntyre said, "Are you comfortable? You have your cigars and brandy, I see. Thank you, Josh.

He started, "Let me thank you for coming. I have something to say."

Richard's heart sank. What have I done now?

"You both performed magnificently on our run to the islands. We had our difficulties, as every voyage does, and you handled them well."

Richard thought, You really think so?

"The tides and time wait for no one, least of all Alex MacIntyre. His time is running down and the rigors of the sea are burdensome—"

Ferreri protested, "But sir, you are most fit."

"The sea is the same as when men first launched boats. Any fool can carry on, but a wise man knows to shorten sail in time. I would be that wise man."

Porter was surprised, "What do you mean?"

"I have plowed the seven seas. As we cruise through life, we arrive at crossroads. In nautical terms, we call them waypoints where we decide the proper course to continue.

"After forty-one years on the ocean, I have reached a waypoint. It is time for me to stow my anchor one last time,"

"Sam Brannan and I have purchased a second vessel, *Dauntless*. Her officers will stay with the ship, although engaging a crew will be as difficult as before. She is four hundred and twenty-five tons placement.

I am promoting Alfonso to her Master, should he be willing. Your skills with the men can stand a little work, but you have knowledge of the sea, fine navigational skills, and good judgment.

Alfonso Ferreri was overwhelmed. "I accept your offer with gratitude. I despaired of ever rising above a first mate and pledge to serve your interests and Dauntless as my own."

"Congratulations, sir." They shook hands.

Richard squirmed to relieve pressure on his sore leg.

Alex looked at Richard for a long time. "You are an exasperating mix of accidents and judgment, my son, but you have matured since you deserted my command in San Francisco. Have you learned your lesson?"

"Yes, sir."

Alex continued "I applaud your way with the crew. You saved me from my apoplexy, and guided *Agilis* well.

It is unusual for a second mate to become a master in one step, but you have shown the initiative to make this jump."

Richard was confused and silent with anxiety.

"I am promoting you to Master of *Agilis*, should you be willing to accept."

Richard examined himself before answering, as he remembered his despair after Kawai's funeral. "I am humbled, Sir. This honor is more than I hoped for, but it has been my goal from Boston. I accept as Master of *Agilis* and will serve you well."

Alex MacIntyre shook the new masters' hands with tears in his eyes and said, "Welcome to the world of masters and, perhaps someday, captains. You must learn to represent the owners, and place their needs first. A shining future awaits you both on the seas of the world and I want to send you to it."

Richard Porter and Alonso Ferreri were speechless.

"Let us retire to the registrar's office to sign your promotion papers. Welcome Masters Ferreri and Porter. I am pleased that we will be working together."

After the formalities, Alex MacIntyre ended with a look at his future.

"My life with my wife is land-based and will be here in San Francisco. I am not leaving the sea, however."

Porter said, "Thank God for that."

"This town is destined to grow. We are constructing a home in Oakland where you will be always welcome. 'May you new masters have a fair wind and following seas.' "

Porter responded, "To you, sir, a fair wind and following seas, and long may your big jib draw."

Chapter 42—Big Man on a White Horse

Richard Porter bought a fine suit from the tailor, Jacob Davis, who he met over a drink with Levi Strauss. Richard rented a dashing horse for the day and borrowed a sword from Lieutenant Sherman. On the day before, he got a good buy on a magnificent saddle trimmed in gold and silver and made on a Spanish rancho deep in Mexico. His last visit was to the best barber in town for a shave and splash of bay rum aftershave.

Richard rode up and down the hills of San Francisco in high style. "Top of the day to you, sir."

"At your service, Madam."

"I trust you are well, sir."

Bystanders were impressed and said, "Who is that man?"

"I have not seen him before but he cuts a fine figure," said a captain's wife to another. "We must get to know him."

"Certainly, and soon."

Richard hired a photographer. "My good man, would you be so kind as to take a photograph of me on horseback?

"Absolutely. The light is good and this is a fine time for my new French daguerreotype process. I've used it for ten years with great success. You have to hold still for only a few minutes. How many copies did you say?"

"I should like two, if you please."

"Each copy requires a separate exposure. It will double the cost."

The photographer said, "I must say, Master Porter that you are a distinguished looking young man sitting there on your fine horse, and that is some spectacular sword."

Richard Porter felt good but was not quite finished.

"Please mount the daguerreotypes over this inscription." He wrote out the words,

Richard J. Porter, Master of *Agilis*
San Francisco, California
October 15, 1849

While the images were developing, he arranged with a captain leaving for Boston to deliver them. One was addressed to The Owner, MacDonald Farm, Concord, Massachusetts, United States of America.

Richard held the other in his hands for a long time. He said, "Godspeed, Becky, my love." He addressed the envelope.

Becky Revere
c/o Podwinkle Farm
Concord, Massachusetts
United States of America

"I shall return."

###

Acknowledgment

"You have written only a third of a book." was the early encouragement from a salty old mariner in the Rocky Mountain Shipwright's Club.

Later beta readers offered insights that improved this book, as did fellow authors in the group "Men Who Write Books" and "The Writer's Group" at the Tattered Cover bookstore in Aspen Grove.

Don Prowse, who rescued drowning people off Cornwall, England, described the ways of the sea. Kevin Litwack, who piloted a sailboat from San Francisco to the Hawaiian Islands in 2009-2010, encouraged me to use his log as the basis for the race in the narrative.

Historical research into San Francisco in 1849, the gold rush, nautical superstitions, and the Hawaiian Islands (Sandwich Islands for you Britishers), was gleaned from untold Internet pages. Especially important were the experiences of Richard Dana aboard the *Pilgrim* in "*Two Years Before the Mast*" for much of the California history. Mariners from captains to ordinary sailors, as well as passengers, have written their memoirs of life on 19th-century tall ships and from which I drew detailed insights. Especially useful was the "*Memoirs of General William T. Sherman, Written by Himself,*" for insight into California's cultural and economic conditions in 1849.

The library of the Rocky Mountain Shipwright's Club, as well as my personal library, provided descriptions of square-rigged clippers. Hands-on ship handling techniques were taken from the "*Eagle Seamanship, a Manual for Square-Rigger Sailing*," that is issued by the United States Coast Guard to cadets as they head to sea each summer on the USCG Cutter *Eagle*.

My personal gold panning experience (unsuccessful) was the basis for the gold placer mining difficulties.

Writing this book has been a whale of an adventure. Thanks to those whom I have met along the way.

Request for Reviews

Thank you for reading my book. If you enjoyed Richard Porter's adventures, other readers would appreciate your honest review at the bookseller where you bought the book. You can contact me directly or on my website.

CliffordFarris@DesertCoyotePress.com.

DesertCoyotePress.com

About the Author

Drawing on his life as a cowboy, farmer, engineer, and author, Clifford Farris brings gripping stories about real folks to his novels—always with a touch of humor. He has penned and published writings on woodworking, gardening, and meat smokers. Other credits include short stories, a musical melodrama, and a hundred and fifty technical writings. He and his wife, Ann, live in the Denver Metro area of Littleton, Colorado.

About Desert Coyote Press

Homeland of Desert Coyote Press

Your book is a portable piece of magic. Immerse your adventurous and independent spirit in historical fiction from the Desert Coyote Press DCP. Novels are filled with adventure stories of heroes and villains, escape and companionship, lives and travel set in historical times. One reader said it a vacation with interesting people to intriguing places.

Our motto is, Sit down and have a drink, read something.

Invest in the books that you love. Live with complex characters and everyday people facing extraordinary challenges in vivid locations. You will have a thrill, a laugh, shed a tear or two and live moments of sheer terror. Enjoy the ride.

Clifford Farris founded DCP in 2019 on the premise that you should live with passion. Come join our community and journey with us.

"Fair winds and following seas," to you the reader.

www.ingramcontent.com/pod-product-compliance
Lightning Source LLC
Chambersburg PA
CBHW051952240626
47153CB00005B/1724